BLACK BOX

Dennis,
Welcome to the world of the Triad!
Thanks for the support.

[signature]

BLACK BOX

Book I of the Triad Series

D. A. Rally

Copyright © 2009 by D. A. Rally.

ISBN:	Hardcover	978-1-4415-5990-6
	Softcover	978-1-4415-5989-0

All rights reserved. No part of this book may be reproduced or transmitted in any form or by any means, electronic or mechanical, including photocopying, recording, or by any information storage and retrieval system, without permission in writing from the copyright owner.

This is a work of fiction. Names, characters, places and incidents either are the product of the author's imagination or are used fictitiously, and any resemblance to any actual persons, living or dead, events, or locales is entirely coincidental.

This book was printed in the United States of America.

To order additional copies of this book, contact:
Xlibris Corporation
1-888-795-4274
www.Xlibris.com
Orders@Xlibris.com
66751

For Orion. You are my friend, Baby Boy, and hero. I owe you my life, buddy.

For Tom. You have been there for me my entire life in every way.

Mom and Dad. You never gave up and always believed in me.

Thank You.

ACKNOWLEDGEMENT

Editing by Emily (Emma) Burke

Author photograph by Alexander Rally

CHAPTER 1

The sound of the great turbine engines far overhead was blended into the background like bird songs in the suburbs surrounding Pittsburgh International Airport. Eli subconsciously took notice of the jet that flew close by overhead as he reached up to pluck an apple from the nearest tree. He wiped it off with his flannel shirt and began to take an aggressive, yet pleasurable bite from the large green apple. His subtle awareness of the aircraft peaked as the sky suddenly became silent.

With his teeth buried into the skin of the crisp apple, the early teenager turned his gaze toward the clear blue September sky. Eli dropped his hand as he came to a complete halt in the looming silence, allowing the apple to fall from his mouth. The thump of the apple hitting the ground struck Eli's ears as thunderous compared to the silence he witnessed as he stared with wide blue eyes at the 737 that glided through the perfect, still sky above him.

Eli watched as the massive steel construction continued on its destined course through the beautiful bright blue sky. He saw the nose of the jet dip thousands of feet above him, then turn the plane into a vertical position as the power of gravity took hold and pulled the overweight front end toward the Earth. The air was filled with groaning, whining, and whistling sounds as the passenger plane cut through the air and came ever closer to the boy's position on the ground.

As the plane grew larger in Eli's eyes, he knew that he should run, just run.

Get as far away as possible. His mind told him.

Eli was terrified, having no idea where the jet was going to fall to earth or *where* he should run. Beyond anything that he could have ever imagined, the blue eyed boy stared in horror as the large, white, bird shaped apparition dove towards him from the sky above, and only one thought repeated itself in his mind.

Oh Dear God, it's gonna crash! Oh Dear God, it's gonna crash! Oh Dear God, It's gonna-

His thought was cut off and his mind seemed to go blank as he realized that it wasn't just the monstrous steel object cutting through the air that he heard. As he saw the front end of the massive plane rush toward a clear hilltop in the distance, Eli was sure that he could hear voices; screaming voices.

The nose of the 737 slammed into the tender, unmolested earth of Raccoon Township with thunder that shook all of the neighboring townships. The body of the aircraft continued to rush toward the ground after, crumpling itself downward. For only a fraction of a second, the great jet resembled an accordion as the heavy steel that made up its outer shell folded beneath the force of the impact. The ground shook under Eli's feet as the thunderous explosion that followed destroyed almost all of what was left of the plane and its contents. A massive ball of flame and a thick, black cloud of smoke reached up into the sky and far around the point of impact, engulfing many trees and greenery around it.

Eli stood frozen as the 737 blew itself apart in front of his eyes, and he could begin to see parts of the plane moving at a high velocity in all directions. He started to crouch down and duck his head as something thumped him in the right side of his head, hard. Thrown upon the ground and lying on his side, he faced the devastating explosion.

A piece of steel about the size of a car door flew past the stunned and bewildered boy, missing him by a matter of inches. Had he still been crouching, Eli's torso would have been sheared clean off by the blazing hot steel from the rest of his body like a blade of grass cut by a lawnmower. The boy struggled for consciousness with a throbbing head, finding enough inner strength to thank God that he had been knocked over.

Eli watched as the flames continued to blaze and the debris settled. He sat up and rubbed his right cheekbone and ear, where he had been struck. Feeling a thick, warm wetness when he touched the wound, the dazed boy pulled his hand in front of his eyes to see that it was covered in blood.

Oh shit! It cut me!

Eli looked down at himself to find blood splattered all over his flannel, his T-shirt, and jeans, creating a quick, frantic thought.

Well, these are ruined. Mom's gonna kill me.

Eli held a hand to the side of his head again, searching for any type of cut in the skin, only feeling the beginnings of an egg sized knot forming beneath his fingers. Looking around to see just what it was that had hit him, the bewildered boy noticed a blinding reflection of sunlight behind him, causing him to shield his eyes and move his head away from the glare in order to see the object. Eli's stomach churned, and terror filled his mind as the full realization of what had just happened overwhelmed him. The idea that he had just watched hundreds of innocent people die in a horrible plane crash made him dizzy. Eli's head swam with ideas of screams and apples and blue skies and belts and puppy kisses and screams and thunder and screams and smoke and blood and even more screams. Fighting the burning in his eyelids because of the inferno and tragedy before him, Eli clenched his tear filled eyes tight. And the young boy threw up in the grass next to him.

As he glanced to his side after the explosion and vomited all that he had eaten that day, Eli saw what it was that had struck him. A human arm, roughly severed a few inches above the elbow, was what had knocked the boy to the ground and saved him from the blazing hot piece of aircraft debris. It was the gold plated watch that had blinded him with the reflection of bright sunlight, still strapped to the arm that lay charred and bleeding in the grass close to him as he stared at it with disgust and horror.

Pulling himself to his sick, shaky feet and looking at the arm before him, Eli turned and gazed at the burning, smoking wreckage of the airliner that he had watched plummet to the earth. Closing his eyes in denial of what he was currently seeing, and the thirty seconds of tragedy he had already witnessed, Eli ran. He opened his deep blue eyes and ran as fast as he possibly could with tears and the blood of another running down his face.

As Elijah Marshall ran through the woods with terror in his mind, the families and friends of the passengers of Flight 427 sat inside Pittsburgh International Airport awaiting their arrival, which would never come.

*

Eli sat on his bed with his hands clasped between his knees, rocking back and forth, unable to control himself while tears ran down his boyish cheeks as he heard the first sirens begin to wail.

The tears joined Eli's sweat as it dripped from his chin onto his knees and the hands between. His thin chest hitched along with his quiet sobs, and his eyes were narrow as the flow of his tears blurred the vision in his empty gaze. Eli rested his feet upon the wooden rail that ran along the length of his bed frame, squinting through tear-blurred eyes at the closed door of his bedroom as he continued rocking on his bed. The subtle sound of the creaking bedsprings in his otherwise quiet room was interrupted by the distant cry of emergency sirens.

Knowing precisely why the sirens were wailing as soon as the sound reached his ears, Eli ceased his rocking and sat upright with his head cocked to one side, listening. He felt the remote sensation of a drop of mixed sweat and tears form on his chin as the emergency siren lowered intensity before its resurgence. The young boy knew that the sweat-tear would collect itself there until it was heavy enough to break away from his innocent, childish skin with a minute tug on his chin. In the moment it took for the siren to regain strength in its cycle, the sweat-tear fell in what seemed like a timeless descent.

Eli could hear the chorus of other sirens joining the first in that moment. He could almost see the spastically rotating red and blue lights flashing from atop the roofs of the police cars, ambulances, fire engines, and all other emergency vehicles as they sped their way through the streets of Aliquippa, headed for the previously peaceful and remote piece of God's Earth that had now become a disaster area. An area that the boy had occupied not too long ago.

Eli could feel the cool September air brushing against his skin. He could hear the deafening silence, as the airplane above grew quiet and plunged to the earth all over again even as he sat in his room. His ears echoed and his body shook with the tremors that the fallen aircraft drove into the earth. The heat and light of the ball of flame that took hold of every living thing around it threatened to burn and blind Eli's eyes even though he had fled from it. The sight of the steel remnants of the plane sailing through the air in all directions away from the flames was fresh in his mind as the boy once again felt the jolt against the side of his head. Again, he saw the severed arm lying in the grass as fresh, bright red blood flowed from the charred, sleeved arm of what could have been a businessman on his way home to his family.

The sweat-tear struck his clasped hands and Elijah let out a cry that no thirteen year old boy should ever produce. He didn't care if his mother or brother heard him this time. The intensity of his cries seemed to blend with the rise and fall of the sirens he heard outside as he threw his slender body onto the bed and covered his eyes with his hands. Eli cried in horror and revulsion as the sirens blared their way into his mind, tossing and turning in his bed with his hands to his face as he wailed in despair, oblivious to everything except the sirens. Feeling the stickiness of the drying blood left behind by the random, severed arm, as his right hand brushed by the wound near his temple, he only cried harder. The traumatized thirteen year old boy immersed himself entirely into the horrifying images in his mind, wondering if he was on the brink of madness.

Elijah Marshall's life was changed forever within that brief span of time. He lost his innocence that early September evening, never able to regain his childhood. The crash of Flight 427 denied him the life he might have lived, had he not been witness to it. He would never know that life.

Elijah's destiny lay along another path.

*

"My God! 'Lijah, what happened to you? Are you okay?"

The young boy pulled his hands away from his drying eyes and dazedly turned his head toward the panicked voice of his mother. He could see, through his blurred vision, the fear and worry on his mother's face as she rushed across the bedroom toward him. A new bought of tears took hold of him as his heart reached out for any form of comfort or form of salvation from the sound of the sirens, and the horror they inferred.

Eli sat up in his bed as fresh tears flowed from his eyes and his chest began to shudder, holding his arms out to his frantic mother as she came to him and held him close. The traumatized boy buried his soft, adolescent face into his mother's shoulder and cried. He could hear her voice, but it seemed very far away from him, as if she was on the other side of a long, empty hallway. All he could truly hear was the sound. Not of the sirens that continued to wail through the air, or the explosion, or the deafening crash of the airliner against the earth. It was the brief period of apparent silence after the roar of the jet engines stopped and before the drowning explosion of the crash of the jet. The silence that wasn't really silent. The muffled and distant screams of panic, fear, and despair that came to him from the falling plane were all that rang in his ears. The cries of the dying.

Virginia Marshall released her embrace, placing her hands on her son's face and holding him at arm's length. The loving look in his mother's eyes caused Eli to attempt to subdue his cries and explain why he was upset. Before he could stop his chest from hitching with tears, she questioned him again.

"Elijah, what happened to you? Where did this blood come from? Are you okay? Where are you hurt? Did you hit your head?" She moved her hand to the bulging knot on his head where he had been struck by the burnt, bloody arm.

Eli's mind whirled as he searched for one, simple answer to all of his mother's frantic questions. The tears continued to flow from his eyes as he opened his mouth to speak, hitching short breaths between his sobs. His mind could only muster one image, and his adolescent voice escaped his lips in a high pitched squeal.

"They're dead! They're all dead! One of 'em hit me!" He said the last with a childish tone of accusation.

His mother held his cheeks strong in her hands as she moved her face closer. "Who hit you? Eli, were you in a fight?" She asked with disapproval in her voice. Virginia was used to her eldest son getting into trouble.

Eli held his same, high pitched squeal. "Didn't you hear me? They're all dead! And I heard them scream! They all screamed! I can still hear 'em!" Eli looked at his mother with tear filled, pleading eyes. "Make it stop, Mom. Make it stop."

Elijah Marshall buried his face, once again, into his mother's shoulder as he nearly screamed, "I don't want to hear them dying anymore!"

*

The aftermath of the plane crash was nearly unbearable for the citizens of the surrounding area. The main roads leading into Raccoon Township were immediately closed off as members of the local fire department blockaded the area with their vehicles, while police officers were called from supporting townships to assist in the redirecting of traffic. Many sadistic onlookers caused traffic jams, and even residents living near the crash site couldn't get home that night. The sound of sirens rang through the air while television and radio stations spoke continuously of the tragedy throughout the night, repeating the same vague information over and over again.

*

Robert Mikush sat at the desk in his study, entranced by yet another of the books he had dug up at the university. The rest lay spread across the wide expanse of the oak desk, some opened to a specific page, some closed and stacked on top of each other with a bookmark hanging out of the top. Three notebooks lay scattered in front of the aging, divorced professor, each one displaying his scrawling, hurried script. The lamp on the far right hand corner of the desk was the only source of light in Bob's study. The walls were strewn with carven, stained wood, the hardwood floor was polished, and the furniture was made of finely crafted oak. Only the desk lamp stood out as an oddity in this room, its dulling brass casing gleaming as it blared its light onto the oak desk. It had been broad daylight when the professor had entered the study that afternoon, following his history classes, but now only darkness peered in through the large windows that filled two of the walls in the room.

Almost snoring as he lifted his eyes away from *Fabled Myths and Lost Artifacts*, the professor pulled his small-lensed glasses from his face and pinched the bridge of his nose. Billie Holiday crooned from the stereo in the living room as he tossed the reading glasses onto one of the many notebooks lying upon the desk and let out an exhausted groan. Robert's eyes were tired, his back was sore, and his rear end was numb. As he looked around the room, he was shocked to see the darkness in the windows. He gazed at the gaudy brass lamp with wonder, not remembering when he had turned it on. Reaching for his mug of cold coffee, Robert stood up. The aging professor scooted the leather chair back with his legs, letting out another groan as he stretched and flexed his stiff and aching body. Robert reached for the ancient lamp that he had bought at a pawn shop as a student in college, what must have been eons ago, and then stopped. He hadn't turned any other lights on in the house, and he knew that he would surely bash his shins if he attempted to walk through the house in the dark, even though he had lived there for decades. Besides, he might want to do some more reading before he called it a night.

Robert carried his mug of cold coffee into the doorway of the living room, reaching his free hand out to his right and turning on the overhead light. He walked through the spacious living room, where the multi-thousand dollar stereo system now blared lively John Coltrane through the five hundred dollar speakers, and walked into the kitchen. Robert dumped the wasted coffee into the sink, rinsed out the mug, and left it sitting in the sink to wash later. He yawned as he reached for the refrigerator door, meaning to grab a quick snack to last him until dinner, as the digital clock on the microwave caught his eye. It claimed that the time of night was 9:52, and a quick glance at the clock on the wall concurred. He stood shocked in front of his fridge, not believing that he had been reading for as many hours as he had.

Jesus! Six hours? How did that happen? I still have so much to do!

Robert hurried out of the kitchen, rushed up the stairs to the bathroom, and undressed in a hurry, seeing the reflection of his tall, thin frame in the mirror. He looked at his aging face, the sunken eyes, the high cheek bones, the long thin nose, and the tight, thin lipped mouth below his graying mustache. Lifting a hand to the thick mat of brown and gray hair on his head, he smiled, knowing that he was the stereotype of a college professor, that his wealth of knowledge and intelligence made up for the lack of physique. As he showered, Robert's mind wandered toward the approaching day.

He would wake up at 6:00 a.m., an hour earlier than normal, and make the trip to the airport. His first class wasn't until nine-thirty, so that gave Robert plenty of time to make it to the airport receiving terminals, which were about two miles past the airport exit of the highway, where Federal Express, UPS, the U. S. Postal Service, and RPS stored their deliveries after unloading from their cargo planes. This particular cargo had special arrangements made for its delivery, and it was arriving on a passenger plane. The package was marked for pick up only, and Robert Mikush planned on being at the terminal to pick it up as early as possible. Jacob Sherman, an old college buddy and age old good friend, had arranged the delivery before heading off to Miami to speak about his latest book. Excitement and anticipation filled Professor Mikush as he thought of where the package would be now.

It should be on a truck headed for the receiving terminals. Maybe it's already there, in a separate holding area than the rest.

The aging professor smiled at the white tile wall of the shower, knowing that the study he had privately undertaken for the past eight years or more was about to climax. Tomorrow. All the reading, all the searching, all the phone calls and cashed in favors, they were all finally paying off. He would finally have it. *It.* And he would be able to study and examine and experiment with it. The smile of excitement and anticipation felt glued to Bob's face as his heart sped up.

How am I even going to be able to focus on my lectures tomorrow, or the following week for that matter? I've waited so long and worked so hard for this; I'm not gonna want to do anything else.

He figured that the issue of focusing on classroom lectures could be tackled later. At that moment, the aging professor just wanted to go to bed so that he could sleep through the agonizing wait of the final few hours before he was on his way to pick up his special prize.

After he showered and dressed in comfortable clothes, Bob ventured back down the stairs to the living room, dousing the volume of John Coltrane and turning on the television. The news was due to come on, and he figured he could have a pair of cold sandwiches while he listened to the drone of current events.

Robert's mind was distracted by age old mythology and what many of his colleagues saw as fiction, as he made his roast beef and ham sandwiches, thinking again about the big day ahead. He could hear news anchors on the TV, but a quick glance at the clock told him that the news was still ten minutes away. Robert continued to make his late night sandwiches, contemplating what he had read and anticipating the day to come. Holding the refrigerator door open so that he could put the mayonnaise jar away, something from the TV caught his attention.

Holding the mayonnaise jar in his right hand, Robert considered what he thought he had heard, and allowed the door to close, looking at the piece of paper hanging on the refrigerator door. His good old buddy, Jake, had called two days ago giving him the details of the delivery of the package. Robert now looked very closely at the note written in his hurried script:

USAir Flight 427

Thursday, 7:15 p.m.

Pickup Terminal 2

Special Delivery

Friday, 7:30 a.m.

Ask for Bill

Tip Bill

Doctor and Professor Robert Mikush tried to listen to the television, but the first line of his note glared out at him as though it were alive.

Black Box

It's just on my mind, that's all. They didn't actually say it. No way. Why would they? Unless someone found it and . . .

Bob's feet carried him to the archway that divided the living room and kitchen of his immaculate house, his eyes and ears focused on the TV, his right hand still holding the mayonnaise jar, and his mind whirling with the one thing he thought he had heard from the TV.

"427"

He watched closely, using the remote control to turn up the volume.

A well dressed, well groomed anchor-man spoke loudly into the empty living room. "Once again, two hundred fifty passengers and crew members are dead or unaccounted for following the crash of USAir Flight 427 earlier this evening . . ."

The mayonnaise jar exploded as it struck the floor next to Robert's slippered feet, tossing glass and thick white globs of mayonnaise in a four-foot radius. The somewhat aged man moved as though he were twenty years younger towards the television, unaware that he had even been holding the jar, let alone that he had dropped it. He stood in front of the TV with wide eyes, a gaping mouth, and slumped shoulders, watching and listening, but not believing. It couldn't have happened this way, couldn't have. It was so close, he almost had it.

Dear God! Bob thought, raising a trembling hand to his mouth.

"Dear God! All those people! All those innocent people!" Tears stood out in Robert's eyes as he watched the restricted footage of the crash site. Fear began to creep in on him as if he had somehow brought this on himself through his indulgence in his own questions and wonderings. In the midst of the news footage, Bob thought of all that he had been reading.

"It's true. All the stories, the myths, it's all true. Dear God! What if . . ."

He abandoned the television as he began to scurry aimlessly about the house, looking at the ground and running a hand through his freshly washed hair. "I have to get it away from there. I *cannot* allow some fool to come across it. I have to find it! I have to-"

"-find the black box." The news anchor chimed in. Robert's heart stuck in his throat for a brief second. He was horrified to think that they knew about his special prize. "FAA officials will begin searching the wreckage during daylight hours tomorrow morning, hoping to find the black box as soon as possible so as to determine the cause of the accident."

Had he not been so frightened, Robert would have laughed at his foolishness, realizing that the anchor-man was talking about the black box on an aircraft, the computerized device that records all happening during a flight. Robert hurried into his study, where the ancient lamp still burned bright, stood in front of his chair, and flipped through his notes. Not finding what he was looking for and moving to look through his books, Bob became so frantic trying to recall that one bit of information he had read, that he ended up tossing his books onto the floor, losing his page markers and open pages. He grasped one of the several hundred page books and hurled it across the room, letting out a cry of frustration and distress. The professor dropped into his chair listlessly, burying his head in his hands. Tears escaped his eyes as a flurry of emotions ran through him. He sat that way, thinking about all his efforts and studies, his personal mission to uncover long lost secrets, the absolute horror of the crash itself, and the fear of what could still come about if . . .

At 11:03 p.m., the phone rang. Robert knew immediately who it was. The nightly news would have just come on in Miami, headlining with the crash of Flight 427 that fell from the sky only twenty or so miles from his home. He answered the phone without lifting his head.

"What do we do now, Jake?"

*

Throughout a night laden with devastation and sorrow, Elijah Marshall tossed and turned in his sweaty bed, dreaming about the screams as he slept, and waking with screams of his own on his horrified lips. Robert Mikush lay fully awake in his bed, staring at the ceiling, horrified by what his own interests may have caused to two hundred fifty innocent people.

In the still, cool September darkness, the scattered hulks of aircraft steel continued to send drifts of smoke up toward the heavens from their resting place in the hills of Raccoon Township. The cleanup was scheduled to begin the following morning, as soon as the sun broke the horizon. That was still five hours away. Until then, the area had been entirely cordoned off, not a single soul allowed into the area, badge or not, volunteer or not. The bloody, dismembered corpses continued to smolder as well, emitting the stink of burning flesh into the night air. The dead were allowed to rest in peace that night, as prayers and tears went out to them from loved ones and strangers alike.

In the dark stillness that seemed to encompass the area of death and destruction, one shadowy figure shuffled through the wreckage of man and machine searching.

CHAPTER 2

Splish! Splish! Splish! Bloop.
Splish! Splish! Bloop.
Splish! Splish! Splish! Splish! Bloop.
The thin, rounded stones twisted and whirled on their way to the soft, muddy bed of the creek through the chilled, flowing rush of water. The young, thin teenage boy sat cross-legged upon the bank of the creek, mindlessly plucking stones from the ground next to him. He would grip each flat, smooth stone in his right hand, placing it into the crook of his hand between the thumb and forefinger, gripping both fingers against the rock. He flailed his arm in a sidearm motion, releasing the stone at the proper time. The stone would silently sail through the air, slowly descending toward the water. It would strike the cold, firm surface of the water and regain its flight into the air, letting out a slight splashing sound and leaving a small ripple in the water as it did so. As the friction of the water slowed its speed, each stone would eventually fall limply into the creek, creating a wet plopping sound. It was these sounds that let the boy know when to seek out another stone, for his eyes were distant and staring. Even though he looked at the path of each stone he skipped across the water, he saw nothing that lie before him. Eli's body moved on its own while his mind was far, far away.

"And just where were you today?"

He knew who it was instantly. But the sound of a voice, let alone *her* voice, made him spin around in surprise, sliding his rear end around upon the soft ground and placing his arms behind him for support. His eyes were wide and his mouth hung open. He hadn't expected anyone to find him there, and stammered for a response as he simply gazed at her appearance in the summer shade of the thick woods around them. The air was still and the only sounds to be heard were the trickling of the creek and the subtle, natural rustling of the woods.

Anna stood above Eli on the slope that led to the creek with her schoolbooks in her arms and a smile on her face. The little bit of sunlight that fought its way through the tangle of branches and leaves shone brightly in her long, blonde hair. Bright blue eyes glistened with the light of young innocence and humor from her broad featured, pale skinned face. Anna's almost too large, protruding white teeth shone from between her pink, unpainted lips. The jeans she wore clung tightly to her thin legs and protruding rear end, while the embroidered 'Penn State' on her gray sweatshirt dipped ever so slightly between her newly developing breasts. Her head was tilted to her left as she looked down the slope at her best friend and her young, cheerful, innocent laugh rang through the still air that felt and smelled of autumn.

Eli's surprise held for an instant longer as his eyes, mind, heart and body took in and absorbed the sight before him. For the first time since the sky had gone silent above him the previous day, the horror of what he had witnessed left him. Eli was totally enwrapped in the vision he saw in front of him. The stunned expression on his face dwindled, and was slowly replaced by a grin of combined pleasure and shame. He held his pose as he smiled up at his friend.

"Hey! How's it goin'?" Eli immediately proceeded from the pleasantries to his next question. "How'd you find me here?" His smile began to drop slightly as he asked the question.

Anna's brow drew toward her eyes and her lips tightened as she gave him a look demonstrating that she saw the obvious. "C'mon, buddy. Where else would I go to look for you when I know that you're not at school, and surely not at home?"

Brief flashes of the moments that he and his best friend, even if she was a girl, had spent at the very spot upon which he sat with his legs crossed and his hands buried in the ground flashed in his mind. He knew the significance of the location, and wondered to himself if maybe he had actually been waiting for her to find him. Discarding the thought as he relaxed, Eli allowed a small grin to cross his lips.

"You were looking for me? I'm so touched." He said sarcastically.

Anna showed a brief look of hurt on her face as she continued to look into his eyes.

Eli's grin faded as he realized his ignorance to her concern. "Hey, I'm sorry. I just didn't expect anyone to come looking for me, that's all." He looked up at her with soft blue eyes.

Anna immediately returned to her original question. "So, where were you today?" Her early teen eyes held the hardness and accusation of a much older woman.

"Well," he said in a falsely cheerful tone, "my mom had something to do today, and I kinda wanted a day to enjoy myself, so I asked her . . ." Eli looked into Anna's piercing blue eyes, and his little tale fell to a quiet babble while his eyes dropped from her gaze for the first time. He continued to sit cross-legged on the soft wooded ground with his hands behind him for support. His face grew dark, and as his eyes returned to look at hers, Anna saw the fear, dread, and distance inside them. He spoke in a quiet, trembling voice.

"I just couldn't do it. I couldn't face anyone, not after what happened. I just wanted to be alone for a while where it was quiet, and I might have a chance to stop hearing them."

Anna moved toward him swiftly, kneeling upon the black ground in front of him, even in her good school clothes. There was genuine concern in her voice. "Who? What happened?" She was nearly terrified. She had never heard any true emotion in his voice before. Eli had always hidden it very well, but Anna could always tell when he was upset. She had never witnessed the real thing until then, and it frightened her.

Eli nearly flinched at her quick movement as he felt an odd clenching sensation in his chest that it seemed he had never felt before. It caused tears to stand strongly in his beautiful blue eyes, and he would come to identify that feeling some time later. He opened his mouth to speak, knowing that if he even attempted it, his words would come out as tearful blubber. He couldn't do that in front of his friend, and so he snapped his mouth shut and turned his face away, closing his eyes. Anna watched as the tears that stood in his eyes were pushed away by his eyelids and slowly ran down his round, boyish cheeks.

She reached out and grabbed his shoulders, shaking him. "Jesus, Eli! You're scaring me! What happened?" Her own voice began to waver with tears.

Anna knew her best friend, knew that he sometimes spoke and behaved much older than he really was; too old for his own good. His hard life had forced him to become a young adult way before his time, depriving him of the carefree childhood that he should live. During the silent seconds than spun out following her demanding question, she feared for their friendship. In some odd, unexpected fashion, the whole thing now seemed to hinge on this moment, as she held his shoulders within her hands while he held his tearful face away from her, burying his emotion inside of him and causing an unbridgeable divide between them. Anna began to relax her grip upon his shoulders as her heart sank with despair. Eli continued to hold his face away from hers as the tears ran from his closed eyes. The friendship was over, and Anna knew it. There would never be those bald, innocence childhood feelings again. They would simply greet each other on the street and in school and—

"I saw it." Eli almost whispered as he snapped his head forward to look her straight in the eye.

Anna had been caught off guard, in the middle of her mourning for their friendship, and had no idea what he was talking about. "Saw what? I don't understand."

Eli's right hand grasped her left hand tight, removing it from his shoulder and moving it to the side of his head. He forced her fingers to touch the area of his head right about the temple.

"Feel that? I was there. I saw the whole thing." His eyes were distant and fearful, almost trembling inside their sockets.

Anna could feel the large knot on his head, and immediately wondered if his mother had been hitting him again. She could see, however, from the look in his eyes that it was somehow worse than that.

"Eli, where did this come from?" Even as the words escaped her lips, she was overcome by a cold, lonely feeling. She looked into his wide, trembling blue eyes and almost did not press further. A strange fear took hold of her and Anna spoke through lips that seemed to have gone numb as her entire body and being was focused on his eyes. "Where were you? What did you see?"

He was on the verge of rambling, and Eli knew it. The feeling in his chest was too strong, the look in Anna's eyes was too soft and caring, the tears in his eyes and on his face threatened to choke his words, and the whirling images in his mind confused his thoughts. He closed his eyes, sending out a fresh flow of tears, and took a deep, shuddering breath as he held her left hand in both of his upon his folded knees. Anna slowly brought her right hand down to cover both of his, her own breath shuddering through the late summer afternoon and her eyes wet and caring upon her friend. Her best friend.

Eli opened his eyes and, for an instant, the pair seemed to hold onto the moment and lock it away in their respective hearts and minds. Two young friends kneeling before each other, hands clasped, hearts and emotions opened to the other, chests clenching and trembling as neither had known before, looking into each others eyes as though they could see the other's soul. Then it was gone, and Eli spoke in a steady, solemn voice.

"I saw it, I saw the plane crash." He hesitated as Anna gasped and moved slightly backward. "I was there." Eli lifted a hand to his head, feeling the knot that had been planted there by the severed arm of another man, and then swiftly replaced it with hers. "I was out by Bud's junkyard yesterday, walking. I was close enough to be hit . . ."

"Oh God, Eli!" Anna exclaimed with sympathy, not once attempting to pull her hands away from the knot on the side of his head.

Eli held his gaze, even though tears continued to flow from his eyes. "I was hit by . . . an arm. Somebody's arm, for Christ's sake! I saw the whole thing! The plane nosedive, fall, and hit the ground and explode!" He was on the verge of becoming frantic. He gripped Anna's hands tightly as he went on, and she allowed him. The tears ran steadily as he talked. "The ground shook, I swear it. The explosion was huge! It was burning up trees and stuff, then somebody's arm hit me, and I fell, and a piece of metal flew past me! My clothes are ruined. I threw up and I ran. I ran as fast as I could. I—"

"Eli, stop it!" Anna screamed, never letting go of his hands.

Eli could see that tears were streaming down her face as well. He bowed his head, knowing that he couldn't be making any sense. Wasn't that why his mother had hit him and told him to stay away from the bigger boys last night? He thought so. She didn't have the patience that Anna did.

"You're not making any sense. Slow down." Anna said, holding her mouth close to the top of her friend's bowed head.

Eli slowly lifted his head and turned his eyes upward, meeting Anna's. During any of the prior years, they both would have laughed at this meek gesture, but not on that day. She only returned his look with one of true caring. Eli seemed to regain his composure as he began to sit up straight and speak to his best friend face to face.

"It was horrible, Anna. It made me sick to see that arm. The explosion was pretty scary, but when that arm hit me, it like, made me see what really happened, y'know?"

Anna simply looked at him.

"That wasn't the worst, though." He cast his eyes to the soft earth of the woods again. "After the engines stopped, and the plane fell, I heard something." He looked up at her to see if she was still paying attention. "This may sound kind of stupid, but,"

"Just say it!" The tears on the pretty young blonde girl's face accompanied the wavering of her voice.

Yet more tears flowed from Eli's eyes as he looked at his best friend while holding her hands. His voice finally gave way, and the sobs shined through. He was able to blurt out one last sentiment before breaking down in front of a girl, and crying full force. "I heard them, the people on the plane. I heard them screaming. They knew they were gonna die, and I could hear them screaming on the way down." The word 'down' escaped his lips only as a tearful squeak.

As he cried out loud, Anna let go of Eli's hands in exchange for an embrace. She held him close to her as he cried onto her shoulder, his own arms pressing into her back. She muttered several comforting words, not knowing exactly what to say to him as tears ran down her own face.

The pair of youthful friends knelt there together, on the soft soil and bedding of dead fall leaves in their wooded surrounding, holding each other as they cried. Anna for what she could only imagine, Eli for what he had seen and could not escape. She comforted her friend as he cried out loud into her shoulder and said over and over again, "I don't want to hear them anymore. I just want it to stop. Please, Anna, just make it stop."

*

Eli slowly gathered himself, and the conversation turned toward much more pleasant topics. As Eli used the sleeves of his flannel shirt to dry his eyes, Anna told him about that day in school, avoiding the subject of the moment of silence they performed in respect for those lost in the plane crash. She talked about the other kids that they mutually disliked, and how stupid they acted that day. She filled him in on the homework they had been assigned in the classes they had together. Anna told funny stories about her antics in gym class, bringing laughter to Eli's lips.

The pair sat, side by side, on the bank of the creek, talking and tossing stones into the steady flow of chilled water until dusk came near. The crash of Flight 427 was far away from Eli's mind for the first time since it happened.

"It's almost dark. I better get home." Anna rose from the soft earth with the quickness and agility that only a fresh teenager can muster, grabbing her books from the ground next to her. She stood above Eli once again, smiling down at him. He smiled back briefly, then turned back toward the creek with his knees held close to his thin chest. The smile slowly faded from the young girl's lips as the look of concern took its place. "Aren't you gonna head home?"

Eli's voice was quiet and muffled, since his back was turned. "Soon."

Anna sighed with motherly concern as she looked down at her friend's back. "Eli, don't you think your mom's gonna be worried, especially if she found out that you weren't in school today? They do call the house y'know. It's just a recording, but . . ."

"I'm sure she knows." He slowly reached both of his hands to the back of his shirt. "I'm not exactly looking forward to another one of these."

Eli lifted his shirt halfway up his back. Anna's books fell to the ground as she raised both of her hands to her mouth and gasped in terror. Tears stood out in her eyes as she looked at the three-inch wide strip of red that ran the width of his narrow back, just above the waist of his jeans. She nearly choked on her own tears as bright white welts, in pairs of half-inch circles along the entire strip of red, gleamed in the fading daylight.

"Oh my God! Eli! I'm so sorry."

Eli dropped his shirt and raised the back of one hand to her, his back still turned, signaling for her to stop. Anna did stop her approach, scrambling to pick her books up off of the ground instead, as the tears and sobs pulled at her throat. She couldn't imagine how any woman could do something like that to her own child. What could drive a woman to beat her son with a dual steel riveted belt? As if in answer to her question, Eli spoke in a dry, emotionless voice.

"Mom didn't believe me when I told her what happened. She thought that I had been fighting or something, and when I tried to explain what I had seen, she just got pissed. I was already crying, and she just made me cry harder. This one," he motioned toward the small of his back, "was just because she missed my ass. It's all right though. I know that she's just a drunk."

"Eli, don't!" Anna pleaded.

"She's just a drunk. She has been ever since dad disappeared. It's no big deal. I'm used to it by now." The troubled boy's hand flashed out to his side, plucked a stone from the ground, and threw it strongly into the creek.

Anna simply stood there with her books in her hands, wanting to cry and yell at the same time. She wanted to talk to Eli, to comfort him, to let him know that this was not the way that things had to be. But she also knew that he, her best friend, had never talked about this sort of thing before and that if she pushed it, he wouldn't talk to her again. Somehow, someway, she knew that.

"Y'know, with that kind of arm, you should be a pitcher, or a quarterback, or something."

Anna waited with a false smile on her face, looking down along the bank of the creek at the back of her friend as the silence drew out between them. Even in the matter of a few moments, it seemed that he was not in the mood for her cheerfulness.

Eli suddenly laughed, first lowering his head between his upraised knees as he did, then turning to face her with a small smile on his face. "You're crazy, you know that?"

"I know." Anna said as she tossed her head from side to side, causing her long blonde hair to fall behind her shoulders. She held her face upward and to the side, looking down at him with false arrogance. "That's why all the guys want me."

They both burst out laughing at that, and the seriousness of the moment was forgotten. That was why Eli wanted to be around her. She could somehow make him feel good even though his life was hell. The friendly laughter slowly died down, and the two simply gazed at each other as they smiled.

"Look, I'm sorry. But I really do have to go." Anna said with sad eyes.

"I know. If your parents say anything, just blame it on me."

Anna let out a little laugh. "I think I'll be okay. It's not really even dark yet, and that's what they really worry about." She looked down the creek bank again at the young, slim boy sitting there using his hands as support. "Are you gonna be okay?"

Eli smiled. "I'll be fine. I'll see you in school tomorrow."

"Oh. So you're actually gonna go?" They both let out a little laugh. "I'll see ya then."

Just as Anna turned to walk away up the slope and out of the woods with her books in hand, Eli leapt to his feet and ran after. He caught up to her quickly, and lightly grasped her left elbow, turning her around at the same time. As her bright, calm eyes looked into his, he only had one thing to say.

Eli knew with all his heart that Anna would never say anything about what they had discussed. She knew, without him saying so, that he did not want anyone to know that he had seen the crash. He didn't want people asking him about it and what it had been like. He just needed to let it go and forget it. He also knew that his tears would never be revealed to anyone either. She was that good of a friend.

"Just help me forget, okay?"

Eli held her at arms length, looking into her eyes, and she smiled, pulling him close with the arm that was free of her books. She hugged him, speaking the last words that they would exchange concerning the horror he had seen the day before. Until the world around them started changing, that is.

"Eli, I hate that you had to see what you did. I'm so sorry that you have to be haunted by that. I can't even imagine what it must be like."

Tears escaped Eli's eyes as he held his face over her shoulder.

"But you have to forget. I know it's hard, but it doesn't do any good to worry about it, y'know? It'll get better. It has to."

Eli held her tight against him, and then did something that he had never imagined himself doing. He slid his right hand up from her waist to the back of her neck as he pulled his head back and looked her in the eye. Feeling the soft caress of her hair entwined in his fingers, Eli said the only thing he could say.

"Thank you, Anna."

He moved his face forward, planting a soft kiss upon her forehead as he pulled Anna toward him with the right hand that lay at the back of her neck. When Eli finally pulled his mouth away, looking at Anna's young face in the dimming light, he noticed her soft, pink lips, and wanted to place his own lips there. He thought of kissing her in the way that his friends had talked about, when the tongues touch and stuff. But she was his friend and . . .

Eli slowly let go of her and turned away, walking back toward the creek. Anna stood, stunned for a moment, then hurried out of the woods, speechless. The crackling and snapping of leaves and twigs were the only sounds of her departure.

Eli was left standing in the impending darkness looking at the swift movement of the creek with his hands in his pockets. His mind was focused on no one particular thing; it swirled with the images and emotions he had endured over the past day or so. Eli dreaded going home, for he knew what was waiting for him. He knew that he had to go home, though. Not only because it was the only place he could go, but also because he loved his mother, and didn't want to frighten her. Even if she was a drunk, like he thought, and even if she did hurt him. He loved her, and feared her just the same. It was his love for her that made him want to get home and let her know that he was okay, even if he had skipped school that day, even if he was going to be beaten for the second day in a row, he didn't care. The boy had been so shaken by what he had seen the day before that he needed his mother. He needed her love, in whatever form he could get it. If it meant facing the belt again then so be it. The need for unconditional love made him want to see Hunter even more.

Eli bent over, pulling one last stone from the floor of the woods as the welts on his back screamed, and tossed it with precision at the creek. He watched in the blue-gray light as the stone skipped across the creek a landmark eleven times, as it was caught up in the current of the rushing, plentiful water, and moved downstream along with the current. The stone landed upon the opposite bank with a 'thump' rather than a 'bloop' into the water and Eli smiled with satisfaction, knowing that no one he knew had ever been able to skip a stone across the full expanse of the creek. The tingle of the kiss he had planted on Anna's forehead remained with him as he turned and walked away. The leaves and twigs crackled and snapped beneath his feet as he made his way out of the woods on his way home.

*

Eli stood at the very edge of the front yard of his home with his hands in his pockets and his mind swirling. He had walked quite a distance through various patches of woods, knowing exactly which trail to take and how to get home. Having spent most of his youth in those woods playing and exploring, he still knew how to make it home, even in complete darkness, which it was.

He looked at the small, dirty house with many of its interior lights on. The front porch light was turned off, meaning that Eli's mother had gotten tired of waiting for him, also meaning that he was in serious trouble. Shrugging his shoulders since he was used to it and didn't really care, Eli walked past the side of the house toward the back yard. Considering the poor appearance of the house, the back yard was quite massive.

"Hunter! Com'ere, boy!" He called out in a modest voice.

The jingling of a steel chain brought a smile to his face, even before he could see anything. The young boy automatically held his arms wide open, as though expecting a hug. He could hear the thumping of clumsy feet upon the ground, and in the dim illumination provided by the lights that shone through the windows in the back of his home, Eli saw what he had been longing to see: a rather large, four legged figure charging towards him. As the beast purposely avoided mauling the boy by veering off to his right side at the last moment, it instantly turned its large head toward him, wetting his face with doggy kisses.

Eli wrapped his outstretched arms around the beast, relishing in, but trying so hard to avoid, the wide strips of slobbery doggy tongue that were swiped upward on his face. He ran his hands all over the short fur of the 160 pound Rottweiler, scratching, petting, and loving it as he talked in baby talk. Everything that had happened in the past day and a half disappeared from his mind as he held and comforted his baby boy, and the troubles of his life seemed so far away when Eli felt the love that emanated from the beast. Laughing and playing with his three-year-old Rottweiler in the new darkness of night for twenty minutes or more, the entire reality of the world escaped him.

*

On his tenth birthday, Elijah had been given his wish as a birthday present from his father. For months, Eli had been asking if he could have one of the many puppies that were being given away in the neighborhood. The consistent answer was no, that 'a dog is a responsibility', 'it costs money to feed and raise a dog', and other excuses that had been sent his way by his parents. Somehow, his father had awarded him with a moving, whining box on his tenth birthday. A baby Rottweiler poked its head out as soon as Elijah opened the box. He screeched with joy, while his mother looked at her husband with fuming disapproval.

Eli's father, in the best mood he ever remembered the man displaying, swore that a good dog was an asset to the family and the home place, and even helped Eli decide on a name for the dog. 'Hunter' was finally decided on because the boy liked the sound of it, and his father felt that it gave off a sense of strength and power, in which he took great pride. Virginia Marshall seemed to be taken fully by surprise, asking where Eli's father had been able to get a 'Rottweiler, of all things'. Ralph Marshall simply told her to shut her mouth, which Eli heard, but didn't notice as he held his own baby boy in his arms.

Eli grew up with that dog, in a way. His father had simply disappeared only one year later, and Eli held onto the dog as the only symbol of love he had ever received from his old man. Hunter also loved the troubled boy in a manner that he was not used to: unconditional love. Eli had his domestic problems, but his baby boy never judged him, or held anything against him. Hunter loved him no matter what he did, even if the boy couldn't get outside to play all the time.

Just before he left the family's life, Ralph Marshall helped his son build a restraint system for the dog. He created what is known as a 'dog run', a single line between two points from which the dog is chained at a length, able to run the length of the original line, plus the extension of his chain from that line. Ralph Marshall's crude version worked perfectly, even though Elijah had become so close to the dog that it would never stray far from the property, even when he let it loose.

Black Box

Hunter was a well behaved, respectable Rottweiler, beautiful in form and strength, even though his tail had somehow been cut two inches longer at birth than any other Rottweiler Eli had ever seen, raising eyebrows as to his pureblooded history. Eli never cared about the breeding thing, or the fact that his boy's tail was too long. He loved his boy, and his boy loved him, even to the point of near death. That was all that mattered. It was one of the few things that Eli had to hold onto in his life.

*

As the game between the boy and his Rottweiler came to an end with Hunter laying his head and forepaws on his master's lap, Eli could feel the real world creeping back into his heart. The Marshall family home life had never been great to begin with, and things had begun to deteriorate after the disappearance of his father. It was the only life he knew, and Eli knew what awaited him inside the house. There was nothing to look forward to but he accepted it as much as a thirteen-year-old boy can. Hunter looked up at him with his tongue hanging halfway out of his mouth, and an apparent doggy smile on his face, and tears crept out of Eli's eyes in a mixture of love for his, his lost past, and his desperate present.

Hunter, a dog large enough to maul any full grown man, rose to his haunches, licking at his master's tears while his too-long tail wagged uncontrollably, keeping his brown, almond shaped eyes on Eli's wide, tear filled blue ones. Eli wept openly as he wrapped his arms around the lovable monster that had endured the past three years of hell with him; loving, cheering, and obeying him, no matter what the circumstance. The boy who had witnessed the plane crash cried into the shoulder of the only being on Earth that he truly loved, would always love him back, and would never judge him on anything. In return, Hunter sat calmly, accepting his master's embrace and enjoying it, as he had always done, licking the back of Eli's neck as if in some sort of comfort.

*

Elijah Marshall walked into the front door of his home, still wiping tears away from his eyes with his sleeves, seeing that the television was on in the living room and that the kitchen light was on. He decided to face his fate since dusk had passed thirty minutes ago and peered around the corner leading into the kitchen, witnessing his mother drinking a clear liquid out of a very small glass filled with ice.

Eli stood watching for a moment, then announced to the room, if not to his mother, "I'm home. I have a lot of homework to do. I'll be in my room." He began to turn away, knowing that it would never be that easy.

"Where were you today?"

Eli continued to walk away. "I have homework to do."

"No . . . no . . . no." His mother's slurred voice called out from behind him. "Where . . . were . . . you?"

"Out, Mom." He said with solidity and defiance.

He glanced back and watched as she slammed her small glass upon the table, splashing some of the contents onto her hand as well as the tablecloth. She rose from her seat with the glass still in her hand while it rested upon the table, glaring at him.

"God damn you!" His mother yelled.

Eli had turned and was walking slowly through the living room by the time she responded, and could hear her rapid footsteps following after him. He knew what was coming and didn't care. Even as his mother grabbed him by the back of his shirt and dragged him into his bedroom, he didn't care. Even as he heard his little brother's door slam closed, and the radio inside that room gain volume, he didn't care. In the end, nothing could compare.

Nothing could compare to the lift of spirit or the closeness and joy he had felt with Anna that afternoon, even as his mother threw him upon his bed face first, yelling at him. Nothing could compare with the absolute love and equality of loyalty he had shared with his dog only minutes before, as his mother produced the double riveted belt from the front closet while she continued to rant. Nothing could compare to the horror he had witnessed the day before, and the sounds that he had heard as the aircraft fell to its explosive demise, even as the screams of demand by his mother rang in his ears and the blows of the rivets fell upon his skin from behind him.

Eli lay straddled over his bed, face first, as his mother cursed and whipped him from behind. He didn't cry, not that time, nor ever again. Feeling that he had seen the worst the world had to offer, the beatings of his mother would never compare in the boy's adolescent mind. So Eli, following his emotional encounters with his best friend and his dog, lay face down upon his bed, feeling the torture delivered by his mother.

'Whack! Whack! Whack!'

His mother swung the belt again and again with more and more force each time.

In spite of it all, Eli looked at the wall that he was forced to face, the wall in which the only bedroom window lie, with a look of nothingness upon his face. As his deep blue eyes faded into the distance, losing touch with reality, Eli could swear that each wisp of the steel rivets through the air, on their way to sting his ass, sounded like the screams of the dying above him as the airliner had plunged toward its demise.

CHAPTER 3

Robert Mikush navigated his way to his home street in Sewickley, Pennsylvania in a daze, somewhat aware of the children that played in their yards and the dogs that ran throughout the neighborhood. His mind was lost in deep thought and concern, and the firm frown on his face reflected this as he stared through the windshield. He had just experienced one of the most trying days of his life, including his divorce and his parents' death. Years of study, research, and hope had gone up in flames, just as the bodies of the passengers of Flight 427 had only twenty-two hours before.

    Robert woke up at his usual time that Friday morning, hoping that the disappointment and sadness he felt inside was only due to a bad dream. He had watched the news footage for hours before trudging off to sleep with sorrow in his heart last night. As the fuzziness of sleep faded away, Bob realized that it was true and readied himself for work with an unusual lifelessness, especially compared to the excitement that had been building within him during the previous weeks. The somber, sorrow filled news casts from the crash site that Bob listened to as he prepared and ate his breakfast made the lonely professor's heart feel even heavier in his chest. Driving to work in the wet, gray chill of an early September morning, he thought more about his lost treasure and the crash victims than the classes he was about to instruct that day.

    Professor Mikush walked into the faculty lounge with his head hung low, tossing his case upon the nearest chair. He made his way toward the coffee machine and pulled a mug from the cupboard as Bill Haylek, the philosophy instructor, poked his head over the newspaper he was reading.

    "Bob, did you hear about the plane crash last night? Horrible, isn't it?" The portly, balding man returned his eyes to his newspaper, shaking his head. "All those people dying for no apparent reason."

Bob Mikush froze in front of the coffeepot, glaring at Bill with resentment.

"Yes, Bill, I saw it." He said abruptly, turning and looking directly at his fellow college professor.

Bob saw the look of astonishment and confusion in Bill Haylek's face, but was too consumed by his own interests to care. He snapped his wrist quickly, throwing the coffee mug against the small piece of wall between the counter and cupboards that made up the service area of the lounge. The mug shattered upon impact, causing Bill to drop the newspaper upon his lap and look at Bob with wide eyes.

"You don't need to throw it in my face." Robert Mikush grunted as he made his way out of the room, grabbing his case off of the chair as he opened the door. He gave Bill one brief, angry look before he turned away. "Fuck!"

The door slammed behind Bob, and Bill Haylek was left looking around the room in disbelief.

The rest of Bob Mikush's day had gone along the same lines. He assigned his classes unnecessary reading assignments so that he wouldn't have to lecture while he spent his time jotting abstract notes into his own notebook. Any time one of his students attempted to ask a question regarding the assignment, Bob gave quick, impatient answers. The only thing on his mind was the incident of the night before. Through his many readings, he knew that he was partly responsible for what had happened and also knew that he would not rest or relax until he had done his part to remedy the situation as much as he could.

Robert pulled his late model Toyota into his driveway, pressing the button on his garage door opener and parking the car inside. The large brown garage door descended behind him as Bob shuffled to the mailbox and stuffed the envelopes and random junk mail into a pouch in his briefcase without even a cursory glance. He walked toward the front door of his large, classical home with his head hung low.

"Bob!" A man's voice hollered from his left. "Hey, Bob!"

Robert pulled his gaze away from the driveway and looked over at his next door neighbor, who was trotting towards him through the grass.

The thin man, clad in a pair of brightly colored shorts and a button down shirt, was waving his hand as he smiled at his older neighbor. His normally shaggy hair was neatly trimmed, and his goatee was likewise shortened and shaped in a professional manner. Bob couldn't help but laugh to himself at the contrast between the Bermuda style shorts and the professional shirt the man was wearing. He allowed his eyes to wander to his neighbor's driveway, taking in the sight of a late eighties Corvette standing side by side with an older, four door family car. As his younger neighbor approached, however, he placed a false smile upon his face, holding his hand outward for a good, hearty shake.

"Al! How the hell are ya?" Bob asked in his usual, friendly fashion.

Al slowed his trot, grasping the hand of his neighbor and shaking it with strength and sincerity. "Pretty good, Bob. How 'bout yourself?" The smile in his rarely clean appearance left Bob staring. After a silent moment of handshaking, Al spoke up.

"I know," he said as he ran his free hand through his shortened hair, "I'm neat, clean, and professional all of a sudden."

Bob's eyes fell to the brightly colored shorts Al was wearing, even in early September, and he began laughing. It was the only good feeling he had experienced all day.

Al followed Bob's gaze, looking down at his apparel, and began laughing himself. He let go of his neighbor's hand, holding both of his hands out to his sides. "What? You don't think this is professional?"

Bob burst into laughter, dropping his case upon the driveway and doubling himself over as he held his stomach. He laughed out loud, feeling the tears of laughter, and relief from the torture he had suffered all day, run down his cheeks.

"I'm finally getting my chance." Al said with a smile on his happy, youthful face. "The higher ups at the company are giving me a shot at some high level shit around there, and I kinda had to look the part, y'know?"

Bob pulled himself from his laughing bout, standing tall and straight, looking Al in the eye, and smiling honestly the whole time. "I know. And I know that you've been working for this for a long time, Al. I'm happy for you."

"Thanks, Bob." Al said, smiling. "But that's not the reason I came over. Bocci was running loose when I got home."

Bob's smile began to fade. He didn't like to think of his darling chocolate Labrador Retriever running through the neighborhood.

"Don't worry, buddy." Al said with the same smile on his face. "I got a hold of her as soon as I saw her, and I took her back to your yard, if you don't mind."

Bob chuckled, "Al, why in the world would I mind?"

"So, it's all good, then!" Al said.

"Yeah. It's all good."

"I just wanted to let you know that she's getting out, somehow. I don't want anything bad to happen to her, y'know?"

"I appreciate that, Al. Thanks." Bob turned his gaze toward the wooden gate that marked the beginning of his back yard. "She *is* okay, isn't she?"

"Oh yeah, she's fine. She came to me when I called to her, let me take her home and everything." Al looked at Bob with true concern. "Are *you* okay?"

Bob smiled. "Fine. I'm just fine." He lied. "So how's Marilyn doing? And the kids?"

Al relaxed. "Good, real good. We're working on a third, if you can believe that. But hey, I'm getting a promotion, so why not?"

"Why not?" Bob echoed. "I hope it all works out for you, Al."

"Hey, thanks!" Al said with a cheerful smile on his face. "I've gotta get back, but it was good talkin' to ya! I hope you find out how Bocci's getting out, and plug the hole." He started back across the lawn towards his own home.

"Thanks again, Al." Bob called out.

Al simply raised a hand in response as he trotted towards his house, and the amazing love of his life that was waiting for him. Bob allowed a small, honest smile to creep onto his face as he felt a touch of his neighbor's joy.

*

Four hours later, Bob closed the most recent book he was reading and pulled the glasses from his face, rubbing the bridge of his nose. He sat with his eyes closed at the desk in his study, the things he had just read swimming in his mind as he thought of Jake's words during their phone conversation the previous night.

"We could get into some major shit if anyone finds out about this, Bob. I don't know what to think about all that you've told me about this thing. I still think you're full of shit, even though the plane crash makes me wonder. No matter what, you have to find it. Somehow, someway, you have to find this damn thing and put it somewhere. It can be traced, and it's my ass . . . no, both our asses on the line if it's found. Just go find it."

Bob opened his eyes to the dim light of his study, those final four words ringing in his mind. *Just go find it.*

How can I do that? I'm only a college professor, and they have the entire area closed off. Dear God, what have we done, and how can I fix it?

Intending to find something to eat, get a shower and prepare for bed, Bob rose from the chair of his study as one, imperative thought ran through his mind and escaped his lips in the empty house.

"The Black Box. How in the hell am I gonna find the Black Box?"

*

In Raccoon Township, not far from where the cleanup of the wreckage had begun that day, Elijah Marshall lay on his belly in his bed, feeling the throb of pain in his ass and lower back from his most recent beating. Images of the plane crash flashed behind his closed eyes, and it hurt his heart. Eli struggled inside as he found comfort in his friend's words that day. He needed to forget, and began the process by pushing the pain and despair of the horror he had seen away from him and focused only on the few good things in life that he might be able to hold onto. As he finally faded off to sleep twenty minutes later, it was Anna that he saw and heard in his head with her dazzling blue eyes and cheerful laugh. Eli's heart hardened as he slept, and he cared about the screams no more.

*

September 8, 9:42 p.m.

White streaks of cloud stretched throughout the luminous purple sky, illuminated by the random flashes of heat lightning hidden behind. The presence of the three-quarter full moon was evident only by the faint white glow outlining the large cloud concealing it. A brisk, cool breeze gusted through the night air, causing the trees to bend and sway as their leaves twisted and turned in the darkness. Faint rumblings of thunder could be heard far off in the distance, signifying to the inhabitants of Raccoon, Hopewell, and Aliquippa that in those late evening hours on the day following the plane crash, one hell of a storm was on its way.

The bedsprings creaked and squealed beneath the 170-pound body thrashing madly on top of the bed. Sweating and tangled in sweat soaked sheets, the old man groaned in his sleep. He awoke with a start, sitting up in his bed as a desperate cry escaped his lips. Sweat ran from his face and body onto the saturated bed as he sat, breathing heavily. The shaky breaths flowed through his trembling mouth as he reached out and grasped his bed sheets, pulling them close to his chest. His wide, terrified eyes examined the darkness that surrounded him.

The old man sat that way for some time, trying to forget his dream and remember the details at the same time. Slowly, his breathing calmed and his deathgrip on the sheets loosened as his eyes adjusted to the darkness and he saw that the man he had seen in his dream wasn't there.

What man? And why would he be here?

He didn't know. Upon awakening he had felt that he was not alone in his small dwelling place. As he tossed the damp sheets aside and sat on the side of the bed with his feet on the floor, the feeling lingered. He cast his eyes to every shadowed corner of the single room that served as his living room, bedroom and kitchen, searching. He let out a deep breath, shaking his head.

Stop it, you old fuck! It was just a dream. There's no one here.

He arose from the bed as another bout of thunder rumbled in the distance. Shuffling his tired old body to the bathroom that lie on the other side of his kitchen, so that he could relieve his tired old bladder, the bitter old man gazed at the open doorway in the dark, hesitating as a brief thought flashed through his mind.

He's in there! He's in the bathroom! The man with no face! He's in there!

He made his way to the small kitchen table, meaning to walk past it and into the bathroom in spite of the surety that someone was in there. The old man's need to urinate was more powerful than any fear he had of some man in his dreams. Bright pain flashed in his mind and he pulled his bare left foot away from the floor and immediately fell against the wall to his right.

"OW! FUCK!"

Intending to find out what it was that he had stepped on, the old man leaned against the wall and placed his hand to the arch of his foot, the source of his pain, wanting to pluck the object from his flesh. In that instant, a flash of heat lightning shone through the dingy windows of his small cottage, lighting the room briefly. He saw the shattered remains of the dishes that had been left on the kitchen table only hours before scattered around the base of the table and the floor surrounding it, as though they had been shoved off. The flash of lightning had not yet faded and the image of the shattered dishes had not even registered in his sleep fogged mind as the slow, grating sensation of pain dug deep into the first three fingers of his left hand. His hand withdrew in reflex as he cried out in pain and lost his balance against the wall, falling into a standing position. As his left foot moved toward the floor in order to balance his body, the large shard of porcelain jutting from the arch of his foot hit the floor first, embedding itself deeper into his flesh as the weight of his body came down upon it.

The old man screamed in pain while distant thunder rumbled with no sympathy. He lost his balance again, falling forward with his bleeding left hand held tightly by his right. His knees hit the floor first while his upper body continued forward, and he instinctively held his hands out in front of him to keep his face from hitting the ground. The deep cuts in his fingers were pulled wide open when his hands fell flat and outstretched on the hardwood floor beneath him, yanking yet another screech of pain from the groggy, confused old man. He knelt on his one good hand and knees, breathing and sweating heavily, holding his sliced hand close to his body and looking back at the broken glass and porcelain spread around the table in the flashing light of the approaching storm.

What the fuck just happened? How did the dishes get broken? God, this fucking hurts! Ow, shit!

His left foot had flinched, driving deep pain into his brain as the tendons and muscles attempted to move through the shard of porcelain buried deep inside.

If I can get to the bathroom, maybe I can get this damn thing out of me. I'll just crawl slow. Damn! Why did I cut my hand like that? How fucking stupid!

Black Box

The old man knelt on the floor, trembling, sweating, and bleeding as confusion raced through his mind. He gazed toward the bathroom doorway, which lie only a couple feet from his position on the floor, although it appeared a mile away. Gritting his old, dirty teeth, he began a torturous crawl to salvation from the thing in his foot.

Using his good right hand and his left elbow to support his upper body while he slid his right knee forward, the sweaty, bleeding old man tried very hard not to flex his injured foot during his painstaking crawl to the bathroom. More pain screamed from his foot as he moved his hand and elbow forward, proceeding about ten inches at a time. As a tool to fight the pain, he allowed his mind to wander and imagined himself in the bathroom, sitting on the toilet with his left ankle resting on his right knee. He would use the pliers, which he left in the bathroom for frequent plumbing repairs, to pull the porcelain shard from his foot.

How did the dishes get broken?

It would be agony removing the object from his foot

I just ate before resting on the sofa, and the dishes were still on the table.

especially since his lacerated left hand would be virtually useless.

The doorway. The injured old man had crossed the massive distance through his agony and made it to his immediate salvation. Some would consider him old, senile, and frail, but he had not lost much of his agility in his old age as he thrust his upper body away from the floor with his good right hand. Continuing to hold his lacerated left hand against his chest, the elderly man grasped the doorjamb in a portion of a second and leaned against it for support. Bolts of pain shot through his body due to the abrupt motion and he let out a yell into the darkened dwelling place. He slid his right hand upwards along the inside wall of the bathroom doorway, his fingers feeling for the light switch as the discomfort of sharp edged wood drove into his shoulder and his face pressed against the outer wall.

The awkward search for the bathroom light switch felt eternal to him. Finding the switch meant not only that the discomfort of his current position would be relieved, but that it was an end to the damaging pain he endured, and the beginning of healing. More than that, it was light. Light that would pull him from the world of darkness he had known since awakening from his dream. Light was the difference between the real and surreal world.

His fingers finally fell upon the old switch, and he used a little more of the fading energy he had left to push the switch upward, feeling sure that the light wasn't going to work. That the man from his dream,

the man with no face,

had somehow removed his source of salvation. The loud click of the old switch came to his ears as the bald, blinding light of the bare light bulb that hung from the ceiling caused him to close his dark adjusted eyes in pain. A smile of relief came to his cracked lips, almost as though his ordeal was over. Little did he know that it had yet to begin.

The old man supported his weight as best he could with his right hand on the cool porcelain of the old, deep sink basin as he avoided looking into the mirror that was only inches from his aged eyes. Fear of seeing the man from his dream standing behind him left the old man wishing that he could somehow support his body and splash cool water on his face at the same time without soaking the fresh bandages on his left hand. Staring at the blood soaked shard of porcelain in the sink, the bitter old man took pride in that he had yanked the object from his foot with a pair of rusty pliers and bandaged the wound quite nicely. Pride led to confidence and the old man cast his eyes at the mirror, relaxing as he saw only the reflection of his own pale, sweaty face. The other wasn't standing behind him, and his fear began to fade. Another sensation took hold of his body, though. In all the pain, fear, and confusion he had forgotten that he had to piss like an Arabian racehorse.

He grinned at himself in the mirror in anticipation of the relief he would feel in only a few moments, when he would finally relieve himself. Moving towards the toilet and realizing that he couldn't support his body and piss at the same time, he figured that it might just be easier to sit down and piss like a girl. Looking into the mirror, the old man froze.

The light from the bathroom was being thrown into the rest of the one room dwelling, primarily the kitchen. On the kitchen table, placed very neatly in the center, was the very object he could now remember observing on his coffee table earlier in the evening as he rested on the sofa. Brief images and thoughts flashed through his mind as he stared, mesmerized at the reflection of the object sitting on his kitchen table.

The old man didn't know how it had gotten there. *What happened to the dishes?* He couldn't remember leaving the sofa and going to bed. *Where did that thing even come from?* He saw himself walking in darkness past death and destruction.

Unaware that he was speaking aloud, the old man cried out, "How the hell did the dishes get broken, and how did that thing get from the coffee table to the kitchen table?"

As he spoke, he turned away from the mirror and looked at the very object in the glow of the light that escaped the bathroom doorway. For the first time that stormy night, a bolt of lightning broke free of the clouds, streaking its way across the purple-black sky in random fashion, illuminating the interior of the old man's home. The bathroom light bulb exploded behind him, and the old man's bladder finally let loose as he pissed himself in fear. His jaw hung open and all pain was forgotten as he stared with wide, terrified eyes at what stood only a few feet behind the kitchen table.

It was him, the man from his dream. There he stood, in all his terror and glory, as tall as one could imagine, cloaked in cloth and darkness, his hands clasped beneath the wide brims of his cloak sleeves. His head was bowed, his eyes gleamed, even though they couldn't be seen, and he grinned widely, even though *it* could not be seen. Because

He has no face!

the image disappeared as did the lightning flashes, leaving the old man terrified in darkness once again.

CHAPTER 4

As summer eases into winter, Mid-October in Southwestern Pennsylvania is normally a captivating sight to see. The skies range from dark, cloud covered and gloomy to bright blue and sunny. The temperature ranges from a warm 70 degrees to a chilly 55 in the daytime. Appearing as if in a painting, the plentiful trees bloom with colors from bright yellow to a deep, rich orange to a fiery red. Winds gust strongly, pulling the colorful leaves from their branches, flipping them through the air, and tossing them upon some random piece of ground. The collage of color created by the bright, dying leaves rustles and crackles when walked upon in the otherwise silent refuge of the woods or a tree laden yard. The nostalgic smell of trees, leaves, and the chill of the approaching winter fills the air. Autumn, the season of beauty and contemplation, is the perfect offspring of the contrast between the dying summer and the approaching winter. The areas surrounding Raccoon Township endured a very similar state of change that year because none of those things happened.

As of September 7th, the fate filled day of the plane crash, nothing was the way it should have been that year. For a select few, life would never be the same again.

*

Saturday, two days after the plane crash. All of the meteorologists on the local news channels had been stating that the cool weather trend was going to continue throughout the week as summer worked its way into fall. "Time to pull those long sleeves out of the closet", they said. Just like everyone else in the area, the weather men and women had no idea what was about to happen in Raccoon. Versus the predicted 64 degrees, temperatures rocketed to 98 degrees that Saturday, leaving many news viewers very displeased and uncomfortable as they made their way throughout the day in thick, long sleeved apparel.

Life was especially unpleasant for the residents of Raccoon and Hopewell living anywhere near the sewage treatment plant. The storm of the night before was accountable for a fair amount of damage. The most notable, though, was the lightning strike at the treatment plant. The entire plant lost all power, and the smell of standing, raw sewage emanated from it since none of the pumps were functioning. The stench was unbearable and many nearby residents chose to stay with friends until the problem was fixed. It was fixed two days later, but it took two weeks for the residents to stop smelling raw shit.

The heat wave would continue for two weeks, contradicting the weather forecast every day. When it was predicted that it would be 55 degrees outside, it ended up being 90. When they called for 70 degrees, 102-degree heat poured in on them. It was not a dry heat, by any means. Storms, much like the one that struck the Friday after the plane crash, appeared in the area repeatedly. The humidity added at least fifteen degrees according to the heat index. Television stations in Pittsburgh received many angry phone calls from Raccoon, Hopewell and Aliquippa, griping about the complete inaccuracy of their forecasts. The problem arose that when the meteorologists proclaimed that it was going to be 60 degrees and sunny, it actually *was*. In Pittsburgh, and any place outside of the small area that seemed destined for disaster, anyway.

There was a distinct difference of climate and weather conditions between Raccoon Township and the rest of the outlying world. Some form of climactic bubble seemed to envelop the areas and townships surrounding the crash site, creating confusion in the minds of those that consistently traveled outside of the area.

Not really sure of why current weather forecasts meant nothing to them, the commuting workers prepared themselves for any possible weather condition as part of their daily routine without question. A slight dazed look would appear in the commuters' eyes any time an outside coworker would question their reasoning for wearing a long sleeved shirt when the temperature outside was much too warm for that apparel. It felt natural to those commuters, and they never questioned their own behavior.

The storms that ripped through the area also seemed to be most violent in those townships, racking up numerous counts of damage. Trees had been uprooted, splintered, twisted, and tossed by the high speed winds, crashing into houses, automobiles, and power lines. Various power lines were consistently down, whether due to wind or flying objects, also crashing into houses and cars, causing fires in some cases. Fires also arose from falling trees that had been ignited by lightning. Those fires usually didn't last very long, though, since the amount of rain that fell during each storm was more than enough to douse the kindling fires. Many basements were flooded, and the creeks and rivers reached and passed flooding levels. The adverse weather conditions slowed the process of the plane crash cleanup crew, making the work even more gruesome and adding the smell of rotten human flesh to the air. The volunteers found themselves slopping through mud laden fields in their rain coats, collecting charred steel remnants of the aircraft along with saturated, decaying human remains. Much vomit was added to the mud as the cleanup sporadically continued.

Tempers flared along with the rising temperatures. Arguments and fistfights broke out in schools, churches, grocery stores, and market places. Worse yet, shootings and gang fights became more frequent in the gang-ridden city of Aliquippa. People exchanged angry words with the person next to them in parking lots when they noticed a new scratch on their car, or for no reason at all. School fights occurred so often that the suspension rooms were overfilled, and even first graders were sent home with bloody lips. Teachers lost their tempers at students, and students mouthed off to their teachers.

In Hopewell, one teacher was accused of beating and raping a female student, while two others were guilty of sexually assaulting their students. One was a female teacher sexually harassing a young male student. The football coach had beaten the living piss out of one his players following a football game for a stupid mistake, although none of the players reported the incident. Teachers in all three districts became very impatient and condescending toward their students, treating the children as fools if they weren't learning fast enough for their tastes. Students in all three districts began rebelling against the system, intentionally breaking the rules. They were found smoking in bathrooms and the back of classrooms, wearing clothes banned by the school dress codes, ignoring assignments and being repeatedly late for class, and having sexual encounters in bathrooms, locker rooms, or janitorial closets. All standards of social behavior were slowly eroding, and no one really even questioned it. Each level of society was losing its mind.

*

September 24th was the final day of the extreme heat wave. During the previous two weeks, the plant life had also seemed to go insane. It very simply did not know what to do. Should it prepare itself for the cold? Should it defend itself against the blistering heat? Should it relish in the plentiful rain or protect itself from drowning? The result of the indecision of nature was devastating. Nothing was as it should have been in the plentiful woods of western Pennsylvania at that time. Except for September 25th.

On that day, it was the perfect semblance of Fall. The temperature was perfect, a cool 68 degrees, there was no rain, no humidity, and not a cloud to be found in the sky. The smell in the air was that of autumn, nostalgic and inspiring. The plant life seemed to have endured the odd climate, standing strong and virile in its preparation for winter. The residents finally relaxed, feeling that the seasons had finally adjusted and begun to take their own course. Fall would resume, as it always had, and the beauty and change that it involved would relieve them of the torturous 'Indian summer' they had been forced to endure. Many young couples ventured out to have picnics that day, while mothers and fathers indulged themselves in yard work, household cleaning, car repair, or other projects that the break in the heat allowed. Many children ran about in the cool weather, wearing lightweight long sleeve clothing, while others finally rounded up the games of touch football they had been looking forward to, wearing old jeans or sweatpants and a cut off sweatshirt. It was a day for all to enjoy, until about seven o'clock, anyway.

As the sun naturally made its way toward the west, a deep, dark cloud cover rolled in from the same direction. The farther the sun slipped into the horizon, the more threatening the black clouds overhead appeared. Parents hollered for their children to come inside, despite the newscasts that said the skies were clear for the next three days. By 7:10, the skies over Raccoon, Hopewell, and Aliquippa had gone entirely dark while the deep, rich colors of an autumn sunset painted the western sky of nearby Pittsburgh. The startling cracks of thunder did not begin gradually as if coming from a distance, but instead sounded directly overhead, loud and violent as lightning flashed and flared all around. The heat was about to break, yes, but in the world of the damned, there are no breaks.

The final storm of the year began abruptly, and with a vengeance. The large, fleeting raindrops dumped upon the area within ten minutes of the sighting of the first black cloud. Five minutes after the torrent arrived, the usual storm damage began all over again. Although there was no measure as to what was about to happen.

Trees splintered and flew, telephone poles cracked and fell, cars were crushed and homes caught fire and were flooded. Lightning struck the ground dozens of times during the three-hour beating. Adults and children alike were crouched in their beds, hiding from the storm but wanting to see it at the same time. Everyone hid from the storm, but not all were able to escape it. Several residents were struck by lightning, killed by a flying object, caused to wreck while driving to safety, or drowned by the force of the storm pulling them into the already flooded waterways. If all the other, extremely violent storms could be considered babies, this was their granddaddy. It would be talked about as the worst storm in Southwestern Pennsylvania history, even though the forecasters never even saw it coming and the city of Pittsburgh never received a single drop of rain.

No one could really even determine when the peak of the storm was, but about forty-five minutes before it suddenly disappeared with no trace of fading thunder or flashes of lightning, it left its mark. Thunder cracked and crashed while lightning lit up the sky constantly throughout the entire storm, with the exception of a one-minute period of time. The rain still continued to flow towards the ground, but the sky had gone silent and dark during that minute, still forty-five minutes before the storm ended. Many of the fearful pulled their heads from beneath their covers and dared to look out of their windows, wondering if the storm was finally fading.

At the end of the silence, thunder began to rumble rather than crash or crack for the first time that night, adding to the residents' belief that the storm was moving on. The lightning also seemed to flicker within the sky rather than strike, adding to the illusion. The rumble of thunder never stopped, however. It slowly gained strength and volume, and the flickers of what looked like heat lightning brightened behind the thick clouds overhead. The two together, thunder and lightning, continued on an increasing pace with the thunder growing louder and more fearsome, seeming to reach some sort of peak of power. The lightning began to fade and diminish as the thunder slowed its rumbling. Aside from the sound of the flowing rain, a few moments of complete peace and silence came from the sky above. In a second's time, disaster struck.

A deafening, ear-shattering crack of thunder blistered through the sky as a large, blinding bolt of lightning tore through the blackness of the night, striking the exact middle of the Ambridge Bridge. The unnaturally massive lightning bolt seemed to hold its electrifying pose as it crushed the concrete of the roadway and pulled and twisted the steel girders and framing of the bridge itself. The metal was quickly seared and melted as the roadway crumbled and collapsed through the torn and twisted framing of the bridge. The whole structure was amazingly pulled upward, toward the lightning bolt itself, uprooting the solid stone supports embedded in the riverbed. The stone columns cracked and crumbled as they rose, twisting and turning, out of the river in which they had sat for many decades. The stony, dusty remains fell back into the river, to eventually settle at the bottom forever. The joints at both land ends pulled away from the ground, leaving concrete and steel remnants falling to the lower riverbanks below. Hidden beneath the deafening crack of thunder was the groan of twisting steel, cracking of solid concrete, the popping of man-sized bolts, the splash of debris hitting the river, and the hum of powerful electricity. As the middle of the bridge was shattered, melted, and pulled upward, the land ends moved inward and downward, landing in the river one hundred feet from the banks. As the lightning bolt finally let loose and the storm resumed its course, white and blue flashes of electricity spiderwebbed their way along the river in both directions.

The storm ended almost forty-five minutes later, ending the heat wave and the series of thunderstorms while leaving behind the Ambridge Bridge as a twisted, bare metal 'A' in the middle of the Ohio River between Aliquippa and Ambridge.

Black Box

*

Multiple accounts of the usual recent storm damage were reported the next morning, as well as uncountable electrical problems due to the lightning strike that rushed through the river. Only one foolish soul happened to be driving across the bridge as it was destroyed, falling to his electrifying demise into the river amidst the massive debris of the bridge. Two thoughtless fools were also killed, electrocuted while showering during the storm. The web of electricity had run down the river, through Aliquippa's water treatment plant, into the water systems, through their plumbing and into the very water they showered with. Other bodies and damages would be reported as that Tuesday went on. By then, the rains from the night before were already turning to ice. Within two days, the temperature had dropped from 98 to 68 to 31 degrees.

Ambridge, the town directly across the river from Aliquippa that had to see their bridge mangled and destroyed in the middle of the river, hadn't received but only a few drops of rain the night before. And on Tuesday, it was 69 degrees and sunny.

*

The destruction of the Ambridge Bridge left the entire Pittsburgh area in shock and amazement as news reports of the "freak natural accident" or "strength of Mother Nature" showed on all area television stations. The power of nature, it seemed, had proved itself to the world yet again. The loss of the bridge posed many problems for the nearby residents. It forced them to travel twenty or so miles out of their way to reach another bridge to be able to get to the other side of where the Ambridge Bridge used to be. The Monaca Bridge was ten miles north of Aliquippa, while the Sewickly Bridge was fifteen miles to the south. Also, Ambridge received a great amount of its water through a water pipe that traveled all the way from Raccoon Township to Aliquippa, and across the Ambridge Bridge. As the bridge part of the water pipe now lay at the bottom of the Ohio River, Ambridge was about to experience a major water shortage. The electrical current had also traveled back through the remainder of the pipe to the Raccoon end, electrifying the reservoir. Many questions about 'The wrath of God' began to circulate.

The heat wave had ended, fall had made its one-day appearance, and the cold streak had begun. The plant life that had so resiliently survived the heat suddenly lost the will to survive. Greenery faded quickly to a weak brown color and the leaves of the trees turned brown, crumbled, and died before they even fell from the trees. The trees themselves were struggling to survive, withering and twisting in unnatural death. The animal wildlife could be found starved and dead all throughout the woods.

The cold streak continued at a constant. The temperatures ranged from 25 to 38 degrees, with an 8 to 15 degree wind chill added in for good measure. The second week of October, the first snow fell, covering much of the horrible natural death in the woods, as well as the yards and homes of those in the area. Oddly enough, the early snow gave Raccoon a peaceful, beautiful appearance. Unfortunately, it only provided a mirage for what was really happening. The town was slowly being destroyed.

Water mains ruptured, the water freezing on the roads as they did, causing many accidents and injuries. People were left without electricity or heat, in addition to water problems as snow laden, dying trees fell into homes and power lines. The water that was available was found to be undrinkable, having to be boiled before use, as something was wrong with the Ohio River, the primary water source for much of the area. The continually brown tinged water of the river turned an odd shade of black as it flowed past Aliquippa. Some felt that maybe it only *looked* that way because of the contrasting whiteness of the surrounding snow covered riverbanks.

The cleanup of the crash site still moved along slowly. The cold, ice, and snow presented their own problems for the crew. The trucks and other vehicles were having difficulty moving in and out of the site over the ice and snow while the cold bit into each and every worker, causing them to work with not quite numb, stiff and aching hands. As the snow continued to gather through the second week of October, much of the wreckage and human remains were becoming difficult to locate. The memorial service scheduled to take place at the site in the middle of October was moved to Pittsburgh International Airport, due to the freakish weather conditions in Raccoon. The unreported reason was that the cleanup was not completed, and wouldn't be until the month was nearly over, making it a seven-week process. No one, memorial service organizers and typical civilians alike, wanted any of the mourners to happen to see a frozen, dismembered hand or foot protruding from the snow.

*

Had anyone other than a thin, troubled thirteen-year-old boy been regularly traveling those woods that fall before the snow fell, they would have noticed that the wildlife death and feeling of lifelessness grew more concentrated in some areas. No one did, however, and so the pattern was not detected, not even by the young boy. He had other things on his mind then, forgetting the thing he had seen fall from the sky, and the screams and dreams that had haunted him. The boy ventured to his favorite spot in the woods by the stream often, usually in the evenings but many times as his eighth grade classes went on without him. He would sometimes stand and watch the water of the creek flow in front of him, not being able to sit down on a nearby log because of the welts and cuts received on his ass from his mother and the belt.

Somehow, as snow began to fall in Raccoon Township, the plane crash and the horror filled screams that escaped from inside were forgotten, and the odd new world around Eli began to unfold before the young boy's eyes in ways that he could never have imagined.

CHAPTER 5

Elijah Marshall emerged from the woods lining his backyard with his head hung low and his hands in pockets. He slowly raised his face to the dim moonlight, gazing at the few stars he could see through the gray illumination of the clouds against the black sky. The metallic clanking sound of a chain reached his hears, and the boy cast his eyes toward the dimly lit yard, seeing Hunter lying on the snow fifty feet away from him. The large dog's tongue was moving back and forth, hanging out of the side of his mouth as he panted. Hunter had his constant doggy grin on his face, and even though it was dark and hard to see, Eli knew that the too-long tail was wagging rapidly back and forth.

Eli grinned, despite his heavy heart, and moved toward his dog. Hunter ran up to his master, sitting properly in front of him, licking Eli's hands with his wide, slobbery tongue. Eli scratched the top of the dog's head as he looked toward the windows of his house, seeing the figure of his mother pacing the floor in the light thrown by the interior lamps. He knew that something was not quite right in Raccoon Township these days, and that his mother's behavior had seemed to equal that. She had become more and more short tempered, beating him with the belt at any sign of disobedience. Sometimes, even for no reason at all. Eli looked hard into the windows of his house, and the sight he saw began to change. As his vision blurred and his mind wandered, he could see something that wasn't really there. It was a premonition more than anything else. It was very quick, but he got the point.

He saw his mother, standing above him with the belt in her hand. Her hair had fallen away from the bun she always wore and hung in sweaty tangles around her face, which was flushed red with booze and anger. His mother always kept her work clothes bright and clean so that she wouldn't have to spare the expense on new clothes, and the boy was appalled to see that her uniform was wrinkled and hung askew from her body, with dirty stains splattered all over it. Her eyes, though, were bright and alive with fury. Eli saw, in his vision, his arms come out in front of him for defense as he tearfully begged for her to stop. He could feel the trails of sweat running from his face. His entire body felt as if it was on fire, and he couldn't understand why he was crouched down in front of his mother as she beat him. He had always been thrown upon the bed, face first, and received his beating from behind. It made no sense.

Eli cast his blurred eyes away from the house and down at his dog, seeing that he was still petting Hunter's head in his trance. An explosion filled his heart as he looked down at the lovable dog, and he still did not understand. He lifted his gaze back toward the dimly lit windows of the house, and the vision resumed.

The sweat that had been running down his face finally reached his upper lip, and he instinctively shot his tongue out to his lip. The taste that filled his mouth threw terror into his mind. It wasn't sweat. It was blood. Eli could clearly see that the spots on his mother's work dress were not just dirt, but bright red spots of blood. His blood. He recognized the burning in his body as the burning his ass had always felt when being whipped. The cowering boy also noticed that he could hear his little brother screaming in the background, screaming for her to 'stop, you're killing him'. Eli then saw that the hands he held out in front of him for defense were also covered in blood. His mother was beating him mercilessly, somehow not caring how badly she hurt him, or even if he lived through it. Eli watched, in his vision, as his mother raised the belt and brought it towards him again with all the force she could muster. His eyes were held wide open as he saw the twisted look of anger, hate, resentment, and insanity upon her face. The belt moved toward his face, one last time, and Eli emerged from his brief vision with a start and a slight yell.

Hunter, upon hearing Eli's yell, arose to a defensive posture in front of his master. The massive dog stood in a crouching stance with his head lowered as a deep, threatening growl rose from his throat and chest. He stood in a fashion that his hind legs were planted next to Eli's, and the rest of his body faced outward in the same direction his master faced.

Eli arose from his vision, alarmed at Hunter's reaction, as some sort of inspiration struck him. He looked down at the menacing protector that stood between his own legs, thinking about his brief vision. The dazed boy knew, in some strange, supernatural way, that when he went into the house his mother, for some unknown, deranged reason was going to kill him. She would beat him to death with the very same belt he had been whipped with hundreds of times in the past four or five years.

Eli spoke a few soothing words to his dog. Hunter turned toward him, his snub of a tail wagging and his tongue hanging out of the side of his mouth. Eli knelt down in the snow in front of Hunter, using both of his hands to caress the sides of the dog's neck as he spoke to him while the cold wetness of the snow penetrated his jeans. His knees went numb before he pulled himself away from his dog.

"Hunter, you know I love you, buddy. I want you to do something for me." Eli shot his gaze toward the house, then back at his dog. "Do you remember the time . . ."

*

Eli walked through the front door, giving it a light shove behind him. As he stomped the snow from his shoes, he saw that Matthew was sitting on the sofa in the living room, watching TV. He gazed up at Eli with wide eyes, quickly looking towards the kitchen. Eli had only taken two steps into the room when his mother's voice emerged from the kitchen.

"Matthew, go to your room."

Matthew stood up from the sofa. "But Mom, I didn't do anything."

"Go to your room, NOW!" The powerful voice from the kitchen was followed by the appearance of Virginia Marshall.

She simply stood at the kitchen doorway, glaring at Eli. Matthew continued to stand by the sofa, but when his mother flashed her gaze in his direction, he fled down the hallway toward his room, slamming the door behind him. Virginia looked at Eli with a sarcastic smile, then at her hands, which were entwined in a frantic wringing motion. Her voice was sharp and loud, even though the alcohol slurs were evident.

"So, dear son, where were you *this* time? Huh? Fighting? Exploring the woods? Getting into some sort of trouble?" She looked up at Eli and took a couple steps forward.

"Mom, listen—"

"NO!" Virginia's eyes flared with a light that Eli had never seen before. "It's *her*, isn't it? This little bitch Anna that you say is one of your best friends, she's the one. Isn't she?"

"The one for what, Mom?" Eli held his hands out to his sides as a demonstration of his question. "I don't know what—"

"You're fucking her! Aren't you?!" Virginia's face began to turn and twist itself into expressions of ugliness and hate Eli never wanted to see. "While I'm out working for the money that lets us live, you're skipping school, getting into fights, and fucking some little thirteen-year-old bitch! You're just like your father!"

In the instant before Eli hollered his response, he looked back at the front door, quickly returning his gaze to his approaching mother. "I AM NOT like my father! And don't you EVER say that about her! Anna is the best friend I've ever had and—"

His mother cut him off with a sarcastic laugh. "I'm sure she is! Especially once you felt her fresh young pussy!" Virginia had made her way into the living room, and sat down on the chair which was only five feet from Eli, who stood in the middle of the room. Before he could fight though his shock at her vulgar words, his mother had fallen into tears. She cried, grasping the remote control from the cheap plywood coffee table next to her. "I just wish that you would help me out, Eli. Especially since your father left *all* of us. I just wish that you'd be here for me." She lowered her head as she cried, holding the remote control in her hand as she did.

Elijah's heart sank. He glanced back at the slightly open front door with regret, feeling that the vision he had witnessed outside was a fake. Knowing how hard it had been since their father left, he *did* want to help his mother in any way he could. Eli moved towards his mother to comfort her, his eyes and heart soft.

"I want to, Mom, I really do." He said in a trembling voice.

The television turned off, and Eli instinctively turned his head to the left in that direction. The remote control struck the right side of his head only moments after. He raised his hand to the spot on his head that had screamed out in pain, pulling it away with blood on his fingertips. The sight of blood on his hands fully recreated the image of his vision. Eli slowly lifted his head and eyes toward his mother, who had stood up in order to throw the remote control at him, seeing the look of anger and hatred on her face. Despite his brief doubt, he knew that his vision had told him the truth. For some unknown reason, his mother intended to beat him to death.

"You lie!" She screamed at him. He could see the fury and insanity build inside of her, as she seemed to change before his eyes. "All you care about is what you want. Which seems to be fucking your little white trash whore!"

Eli had heard of vision turning red in anger, but had never experienced it until that moment. As a deep, grumbling sound arose from behind him, the light of the lamps in the room seemed to be burning from red light bulbs, the white areas of his mother's work dress turned a dark shade of pink, and all the rest faded into a blurred, reddish pink background.

"NO!" He screamed in defiance, standing only a foot or so from his mother. "The only white trash is *us*, Mom. We are true white trash. No, YOU are white trash! You try to pen me and Matt in here, telling us that this is all Dad's fault! You won't let us do the things that normal kids do! We can't play football, baseball, go on camping trips, or just spend the night over someone else's house, for Christ sake!"

Before he even had an idea that it was coming, the white, double riveted belt flew from behind his mother's back, striking Eli on his left cheek. Falling to his knees instantly, he held both of his hands to his bleeding face. Eli held his hands out in front of him, as if in defense, seeing the blood from his face upon his fingers. His mind spun with disbelief, but it all made sense.

Matthew had looked at him with impending doom as soon as he walked in the front door, knowing that something bad was going to happen. His mother had cursed him, and then asked for his help as she sat upon the chair. The chair. Eli, preoccupied with the vision he had witnessed, hadn't even noticed his younger brother's subtle nod toward the chair with his head. The white, dual steel riveted belt had been sitting on the chair the whole time, waiting for Eli to come home.

Virginia had never hit her children with the belt anywhere but in the rear end, until that moment. Whatever Eli had thought was wrong; he now *knew* was wrong in that town. His mother was the prime example. She had always had a bad temper, hitting the boys with the belt when it seemed fit, but the temper had gotten worse along with her drinking. Both the drinking and beatings had gotten worse along with what was happening to the entire city. Eli didn't know how to explain it in the few seconds before the second blow came to his face from the belt, he only knew that one seemed to have a lot to do with the other.

Eli dealt with the first blow as best he could. When the second blow arrived, however, he began to panic. The vision he had seen was all too fresh in his mind, and it seemed to be coming true. As the stinging blows fell upon his skin on all parts of his body, and as he could feel the warm flow of blood over many parts of his body, he cast his eyes toward the slight crack that was left between the front door and its frame. The grumbling from behind the door intensified, joined by a type of snorting sound. Enwrapped in her rage, Virginia took no notice. Eli had fallen to the floor with his back against the smaller sofa, known as the loveseat, looking up at his mother. She moved towards him, once again, cursing loudly and swinging the belt against her older son's body. She whipped his arms, his legs, his chest, his face. Eli screamed in pain as his entire body began to burn with the pain of the belt, and blood rushed from several openings broken into his skin. Blood was saturating his clothes, and he could clearly see the splatters of blood on his mother's work dress. The world around him disappeared.

Eli heard a door snap open, and footsteps approach amongst his mother's random curses for sleeping with a white trash whore. Matthew's screams were only whispers to Eli as he was pelted again and again by the belt. The damned belt. His premonition seemed as though it was happening, and Eli couldn't tell the difference between his vision and reality. The real world had faded away. Pain, blood, and confusion were all he knew.

"Stop, Mom!" Eli heard his younger brother scream, "You're gonna kill him!"

Eli was beginning to fade into nothingness. As he laid his head backwards in pain and agony, he looked at the crack in the front door. It had grown a bit wider, and he saw a slight gleam of light through the crack. In that instant, he knew that the gleam combined with the grumbling he had been hearing were not a part of his imagination. He smiled, as he knew that this was not his vision. It was reality, and he was prepared.

Virginia Marshall brought the belt back over her shoulder in preparation for another swing, as Elijah held his pleading, bloody hands out in front of him, crouched against the loveseat in the living room, coated in blood. Eli held his hands out in font of him as he screamed.

"HELP ME!"

The white belt with its double rows of steel rivets was caught squarely in both of Eli's hands, stinging them severely and causing blood to run and drip from them even more than before. At the very same moment, the front door was thrown open with such a force that its inside handle became buried into the drywall behind it. Eli remained on his knees, holding the damned belt in both of his bleeding hands as his mother stood above him still holding the belt as she looked towards the open front door with wide eyes.

Hunter crossed the distance between the doorway and Eli's mother with one, single leap. Using his forward momentum, he forced Virginia to the ground with his forepaws against her shoulders and held her belt hand in the bone crushing grip of his mouth, forcefully digging his teeth into her flesh. He bore his dark gaze into the eyes of his master's attacker as he held her down with his feet. Virginia looked, terrified, upward at a sight commonly seen in movies. Hunter's muzzle was only an inch or so away from her face. His lips were pulled back from his large teeth as he growled, snarled, and slobbered into her face, holding her forearm in his mouth the whole time. The blood he had drawn from her arm clung to, and dripped from, his teeth, making Virginia very aware that he could kill her if he wanted to. And it seemed that he *did* want to. The deep, guttural growl continued to arise from the beast as it held her in a position of mercy. Virginia could only gasp in surprise, fear, and pain as she looked into the vengeful eyes of her son's baby boy.

"Hunter! Let go!"

Eli's youthful voice rose in the air with a power Virginia had never heard before. She gasped in mixed pain and relief as the beast above her released its grip on her arm, licking the blood off of its lips in apparent joy as it continued to hold her down.

A softer, more comforting version of Eli's voice came to her ears. "Good boy."

Virginia watched as her son stood next to the dog, scratching its head with his left hand as he held the belt in his right hand. The damned belt. The beast raised its head to lick the hand of her son before returning its snarling face to her. She looked upward with her 120 pound body pinned under the weight of the massive dog, in fear of her bloody, beaten son for the first time in her life. Despite her drunkenness, she knew that it was payback time.

Eli leaned over the shoulder of his snarling dog, dangling the white, double steel riveted belt in front of her face. Streaks of blood ran down Eli's face. His short, matted hair was doused in blood, one of his favorite flannel shirts was soaked in blood, and there was a stream of blood that trickled from somewhere on his battered body to his arms, then to his hands, onto the belt, and from the belt onto her face. Eli's mother began to scream and cry, in defiance or disbelief. Hunter moved his jowls forward, clamping them around Virginia's throat as he instinctively responded to her screams. He emitted a stream of raw, guttural snarls as he had done only once before, having every intention of killing if that meant saving his master.

"Hunter, NO!" Eli hollered.

Hunter removed his large teeth from the warm, throbbing, tender area of Virginia Marshall's throat, with what seemed to be disappointment. Eli spoke from above the dog's shoulder, continuing to hold the blood soaked belt in his hand, breathing deep breaths.

"Mom, Anna is the best friend I've ever had, and she always will be. But that's *it,* as far as me and her go." Eli allowed the belt to swing over his mother's face, as it dripped his blood all the while. "YOU." Another growl came from Hunter's mouth at the inflection of his master's voice. "You will never, EVER, even try to hit me again."

Eli watched his own mother struggle under the weight and force of his dog as more blood fell onto her skin.

"You will never beat me again, Mom." Eli leaned over his mother, his snarling killer-dog next to him, his blood falling upon her face, finally feeling the change that was coming over him. What was happening to the town was happening to him, too. He looked into his mother's eyes, seeing the very same fear and desperation he had held in his own eyes only moments before, and not caring.

"I won't let Hunter do it . . . now." Eli said with extreme calm as blood continued to drip from his ravaged form. "If you ever, EVER, hit me or Matthew again . . . I . . . *will* . . . kill . . . you."

Virginia gasped at her son's threat, even as the hot breath of her son's dog blew in waves upon her face. She allowed the white belt to fall upon her neck as Eli dropped it from his hand and turned away. The beast that held her down pushed its weight upon her shoulders one more, painful time before it leapt up and disappeared as soon as her son gave the simple command of "C'mere, boy". Her oldest son and the monster that protected him faded out of the front door in silence as Virginia Marshall burst into tears.

Not long after, Elijah walked back through the front door, still drenched in his own blood, staring at his weeping mother. Virginia held her wounded arm in her other hand as she gazed up at her son through her tears. If she didn't know any better, she would have sworn that it was an adult man that spoke to her then.

"Anna is my friend, that's all. You will never hit us again. I don't know what's happening here or happening to *you*, but that's no excuse." Her son stood over her with his finger pointed at her face. "If you do anything to my dog, I will still kill you."

Eli staggered down the hall of his home, bloody and battered, toward the bathroom. He just wanted a long, warm bath. When he emerged from the bathroom, clean and dry, the house was silent and his mother was nowhere to be found. He sat on the edge of his bed, meaning to turn off the lamp and go to bed, when an idea struck him.

When Eli did finally turn the lamp next to his bed off, his snow covered shoes sat in the front hall, and his 160-pound Rottweiler lay at the foot of his bed, sleeping soundly next to his master.

CHAPTER 6

Eli sat on the cold, wet trunk of a fallen tree, his head resting in the palms of both of his hands as he stared thoughtlessly at the stream in front of him. It was rushing swiftly due to the heavy rains and snowfall of the past month or so. Hunter lay in the snow at his feet, happily gnawing on his new favorite chew toy. The white, dual steel riveted belt was receiving a few more holes, about the size of a Rottweiler's teeth.

Eli was able to sit comfortably considering that his rear end was one of the few spots that hadn't been struck by the belt the night before. It did hurt to place his hands on his face, though. He had bandaged his hands and the cuts on his face and the rest of his body as best he could, but it still hurt. The pills that his mother had said worked wonders for pain, darva-something, were missing from Virginia's bathroom. Instead, the pain ridden boy settled for a heavy dose of Tylenol, thinking that she must have taken the pills to work with her. His mother may have simply just swallowed them, as she had a little pain herself to deal with that morning. Eli reached out his stinging hand to scratch Hunter's head at this thought as feelings of satisfaction and remorse arose about last night's incident. He may have defended himself in the only way he knew how, but she was still his mother.

Hunter lifted his head and looked at his master with adoring love, dropping the belt into the snow. Eli gave his head one more good scratch, and then patted him on the head. Hunter stood up, first nudging then licking Eli's wounded hand with his tail wagging. He looked at Eli with his doggy smile, then turned and walked around in the snow, shoving his nose in the white powder every once in a while and letting out a sloppy snuffling sound as he scooped up a mouthful. Eli looked at the white belt that had quite a few large teeth marks in it, wondering why in the world his mother would have wanted to beat him so badly. That question led to another thought.

What the hell is wrong with this place?

Black Box

The injured boy knew that *something* was wrong. He could feel it, in some strange way that he couldn't explain. The drastic weather change and the colorless leaves that fell from dying trees during the almost nonexistent Fall season was one thing. Those kind of natural things tend to happen from time to time due to all the meteorological bullshit that he didn't understand. Ozone and Global Warming and all that. It was the other things that bothered him, the things that seemed to be hiding underneath the surface of the real world. At first, Eli thought that he was just imagining things. He soon noticed more and more the way that people seemed to be acting towards each other, the stories he heard about anger and violence, and the amount of strange occurrences being reported on the news concerning Raccoon, aside from the weather. Odd events in Hopewell and Aliquippa seemed to become more frequent, although the strangeness seemed to originate in Raccoon for some reason.

Why Raccoon? What's going on here that is making this happen?

As if there could really even *be* any one thing *making* these things happen. He didn't know why, or how, and couldn't explain any of it, but Eli felt that there *was* something causing all of it. Maybe he had dreamt it or something, he wasn't sure.

Eli had dreamt a lot of things lately, although 'dreamt' didn't seem to be the right word for it. Sometimes, he would have very vivid, very *real* dreams that faded from his mind soon after he opened his waking eyes. A lot of the time, though, the troubled boy had waking dreams that he could see as clearly as if he were living it. Like the one he had the night before, when he could clearly see his mother beating him before it ever happened. And it *did* happen, that's what scared and confused him. It was almost as if he were having visions of the future.

Eli chuckled to himself at the thought, and Hunter looked over at the sound of his voice as he held his leg raised and urinated on a nearby tree, turning the snow surrounding it into yellow slush. Hunter inspected his work when he finished, sniffing the spot to ensure that he had marked it properly.

"Don't eat yellow snow." Eli said to his dog with a slight grin on his battered face, and laughed out loud. Even as he laughed, the passing thought of his visions left him scared inside. It felt way too close to the truth.

The boyish laughter faded, and Hunter trotted over to make sure that his master was okay. Eli gave him a pat on the head, and Hunter went about his business of peeing on every tree that he could. The lonely boy's thoughts returned to the matter of what was going on in his hometown, what he was beginning to think of as 'The Strange'. What could be doing this, where could it be coming from, and when did it start? All those thoughts swam through his mind as he stared at the rushing, swirling water of the creek.

Eli's dazed stare became momentarily blurred as his eyes failed to focus on anything just before seeing that the creek had grown in size three times over, and that there was a steep bank on both sides. Blinking his eyes, the boy's heartbeat began picking up speed as he realized that he was not seeing the creek at his favorite spot in the woods anymore. It was the same creek he knew, Eli was sure of that, but he was seeing it at a point where it had gained the strength and power of the other small streams that had joined it. The current vision had crept up on him unexpectedly, and he was scared. He wanted to turn his head and look around, but he couldn't. All he saw was the previous eight inch deep trickle of water that slid over the rocks of the creek bed become a strong creek running through the five-foot deep bed it had cut for itself over the ages. Eli started waving his hands in front of his face, wanting the sight to go away, wanting to see the small piece of creek he had known most of his life, wanting to see his dog pissing on the unhealthy trees.

Even though his body was telling him that his aching and burning arms were placing his hands in front of his eyes, Eli couldn't see them. He could see the twisted remains of trees on the other side of the bank, though. Blackened trees that had died what must have been a horrible tree death. And he could smell something. Something foul. As Eli began slapping himself in the eyes with hands that he could not see, awakening the pain of the cuts and welts that lie there, he could hear something as well. The sound was far off in the distance, hiding under the trickle and gurgle of the stronger stream. The image was then replaced by darkness as a hard smack came to the back of his head.

Blinking his eyes in the dim whiteness of snow under the gray sky, Eli sat up with a jerk, scrambling to his feet. Hunter stood next to him, wagging his tail and thinking that Eli wanted to play. Paying no attention as he looked around, the dazed boy made sure that he was where he thought he was while he rubbed the large knot forming on the back of his head. Seeing his usual surroundings and his excited dog next to him, Eli relaxed only a little. The sores on his body and face were screaming at him due to his panic at the vision he had just received.

It wasn't any vision. I just slipped off of the log and hit my head and had a little dream, that's all.

He knew better. The vision had come before he hit his head, no matter how badly he wanted to believe otherwise. Besides, the smell of raw shit still lingered in Eli's nose as he looked at the small piece of creek bubbling in front of him, thinking. His eyes watered from the stinging blow his head had received, and he had to use his sleeve to wipe the tears away. This creek ran through the woods he knew and twisted its way past Bud's Junkyard, picking up the flow of other tributaries along the way. It would eventually run past the sewage treatment plant and on through Hopewell and Aliquippa to join the Ohio River.

"The treatment plant," Eli said out loud. Fear tore through him as his uncontrollable visions were actually beginning to make sense, and answer his own questions. His voice became shaky and he was on the verge of tears as he continued to speak aloud. "I smelled the damn shit plant."

"Ewww, gross! Why would you want to do that?"

Anna's sweet, cheerful voice came to Eli's ears, startling the hell out of him. He was still terrified by his vision and turned to look in the direction of her voice with a fearful snap, seeing Anna standing in the snow at the crest of the hill with Hunter alongside. Eli hadn't even noticed that Hunter had run off when Anna approached. The look on Anna's face transitioned from happy and sweet to horrified and disgusted as she saw him and the wounds on his face. Tears stood in her eyes and her hand rose to her mouth.

"Oh God, Eli." She said in a tear-filled voice. "What happened to you?"

*

Anna had awakened that Saturday morning with Eli on her mind. It was odd to her, considering that she had spent most of the previous evening with her boyfriend. She simply lay in her bed for a while, trying to remember the dream she just had. It seemed to have something to do with Eli, and him being in some sort of trouble. Not being able to recall her dream, Anna gave up and climbed out of her bed. It *was* Saturday, and she had chores to do. Her dad was at work while her mom was out somewhere, shopping or something. Being the only child, she had the whole house to herself, and would have some privacy while she cleaned.

She cooked French toast for breakfast, and by ten o'clock felt that it was okay to call Jerry, her 16-year-old boyfriend. They talked for a while before he had to get ready to go to work at the nearby grocery store. His parents allowed him to drive at sixteen, as long as he had a job to help pay for gas and insurance. After hanging up the phone, Anna turned the stereo in the living room to 93.7 FM, B-94 in Pittsburgh, and began her household cleaning duties with a smile on her face as she sang along to the pop music.

Anna's parents didn't really have a problem with her having an older boyfriend as she was a mature thirteen-year-old girl, and seemed to have higher morals than her parents. When Jerry began driving, however, it took a lot of discussion and patience with her mom and dad before she was allowed to go out with him alone. They seemed to have a typical teenage relationship, going to movies, having fast food dates, and spending time at each other's houses under the supervision of each other's parents, of course.

Anna said that she loved him when they got off the phone or said goodbye, but she was aware that she was young and didn't really know what love was. She knew that she enjoyed being around Jerry, and that was all that mattered. If they could somehow stay together through the years, who knew where it could lead. The early teenage girl had yet to reach high school, then there was college, and then there was the whole world. Realizing that there would be many guys that she would meet throughout her life, Anna wanted to be with Jerry for the time being. Sure, he had tried to make sexual advances a few times, but she had held him off and he made no fuss about it. They had been together almost a year, and she sometimes wondered if maybe it was time for sex, though she ideally wanted to wait until she was married. She didn't worry herself too much about it, she was only thirteen.

Shortly after noon, Anna had finished her chores and had still not heard from her mother. After eating a quick sandwich for lunch and taking a bath, she sat down in front of the TV, seeing the images and hearing the words, and not paying attention to the show at all. Again, Eli had crept into her mind, and she couldn't stop thinking about him and whatever trouble he may be in. Finally giving up, Anna clicked off the television and tossed the remote on the cheap wooden coffee table, heading for her bedroom. She dressed in appropriate clothing for the chilly, snowy outdoors, left a note for her mom, and ventured out into the snow to find her friend.

Just going through the motions, Anna stopped by Eli's house even though she figured she would find him at his spot in the woods. Her friend wasn't home, and so she moved on into the woods. She didn't share Eli's obsession with the woods, although she did find the sense of nature and peace rather calming. Over the years, she had spent much time in the woods with Eli and they would talk, throw rocks, climb trees, catch crawfish, and build dams along with all kinds of other "boy" things. She found herself being so much of a tomboy around Eli, and loved every minute of it. Anna knew that she could totally be herself with him, and that's why she liked spending time with him, and that's why they were best friends.

She was making her way down the gradual slope that led to a much sharper downward grade, when she heard heavy breathing and quick thumps on the ground seeing Hunter charging up and over the slope to her. Anna knelt down as the big dog slid to a halt in the snow in front of her, licking her hands and face. She giggled cheerfully, petting his head and face.

"Hi, Hunter! Where's your daddy?" She said, standing up.

Anna made her way over the edge of the slope with Hunter trotting along beside her, trying to lick her hand the whole time. There she saw Eli, his thin frame clad in boots, blue jeans, and his thick, padded black and gray flannel. He was standing near a fallen tree, looking at the small stream and rubbing the back of his head as he mumbled something out loud, which she couldn't understand at first. Anna approached her friend with Hunter panting and licking at her side, when Eli spoke louder in a shaky voice.

"I smelled the damn shit plant."

Not knowing what he was talking about, she figured she'd say 'hi' with a joke. "Ewww, gross! Why would you want to do that?"

Eli snapped around when he heard her voice, still holding the back of his head. Anna's heart dropped as soon as she saw his face, and she knew she was going to cry. In the first instant, she was frightened, thinking that it wasn't him, that it was some homeless person with a skin problem. She saw his wide, frightened eyes inside the swollen, bruised, bleeding welts that replaced his cute, somewhat broad-featured boyish face and knew that it was Eli. Her fear subsided, but her desperate sadness did not. Tears rose in her eyes, and she pulled a trembling hand to her mouth.

"Oh God, Eli." She said in a tear-filled voice. "What happened to you?"

*

Eli suddenly realized that the horror he saw on Anna's face was because of him, and the way he must look. He turned away from her, looking back toward the stream.

"Nothing." He spoke into the woods.

Anna ran through the snow to Eli's side, crying. She placed her hands on his right shoulder, trying to turn him towards her, but he pulled his shoulder away. Moving in front of him and placing a hand on each of his shoulders, she tried to look at his face as he turned it away from her.

"Eli, please!" Anna sobbed. "Just look at me!"

Reluctantly, Eli turned his head to look forward, not wanting to look into her crying eyes. He steadied himself against her tears, not wanting to cry in front of her ever again. She raised a hand to his face, wanting to touch and caress it. Fearing that the touch of her fingers might hurt him, Anna simply held her hand an inch or so from his jaw.

"Eli," she tried to speak calmly, "please tell me what happened to you."

Eli cast his eyes downward into her beautiful blue ones, holding the gaze for just a second before pulling away from her grip entirely. He took a couple steps forward toward the stream, folding his arms across his thin chest. Anna stood the two steps behind him, allowing her friend the space he felt he needed.

"What do *you* think?" He said strongly into the air.

"Your mother did this?!" Anna cried with true surprise, even though she knew inside her heart that it was so as soon as she saw him. "How . . . What . . . ?" She could not believe that any mother could beat her son this badly. "Eli, I'm so sorry."

"*You* shouldn't be. But thanks anyway." He continued to show her his back. "It doesn't matter, it'll never happen again."

Anna started to move toward him as her eyebrows furrowed in confusion. She stopped, fearing what that might mean. "Why, Eli?" She asked timidly. "What happened? What did you do?"

Eli turned to look at her as he leaned down to pull something from the snow next to him. The crazed look she saw on Eli's mangled face gave her a chill as his maddened grin shone through blistered and swollen lips. He pulled the white belt from the ground and held it in the air next to him.

"I won, that's what happened."

Anna was becoming truly frightened, feeling that she didn't know who the boy was that stood in front of her, even though they were best friends. She didn't even see the belt since her eyes were stuck on his crazed appearance. "Eli, *what did you do?*"

Eli lowered the belt, chuckling. "Not what you're thinking, and not what I felt like doing."

Hunter, who had been sitting alertly in the snow, rushed over to his master, wanting to play with the belt some more. Eli looked down at his baby boy with love, handing him the belt and patting him on the head.

"Hunter saved my ass, again. My mom was beating the shit out of me and he came in and pulled her off. I had to pull him off of her to keep him from . . ." He trailed off, not wanting to say what his dog could have, and would have, done for his master. Eli didn't want his beloved baby boy to be looked at as a killer, not by Anna. "She won't do it again, though. I can promise that." He looked up at her with a more sane and innocent smile.

The smile comforted Anna a little, but

His face! My God, his face! What about the rest of him?

she still could not believe that his mother had beaten him that badly.

Anna pointed at Hunter, speaking with disbelief. "Is *that* what she hits you with?"

Eli followed her finger with his eyes, staring at the belt as he spoke. "*Used to* hit me with. Yeah."

"Dear God!" The tears were reappearing in her eyes as she raised both of her hands to her face. "Oh, Eli! How could she?"

Eli smiled charmingly as he moved towards her, pulling his friend's hands from her face. "It doesn't matter. It'll never happen again."

Anna stared at the belt in Hunter's mouth as he chewed and slobbered on it, seeing the dark red blood stains on it. She burst into empathetic tears as she buried her face in Eli's bony chest and sobbed. Eli held her close, almost wanting to cry himself, relishing in the feel of her developing breasts against him and the smell of her hair in his nose.

In time, Anna settled down and sat with Eli on the fallen tree. "Why did she do it? I mean . . . in the face?"

Eli shook his head. "I don't know. I didn't do anything worse than I've ever done. She just had it in for me when I walked in the door."

He thought of the vision he had experienced while outside with Hunter the night before. Eli left that part out, not wanting to think about it.

"She'd been drinking, as usual, but . . . I don't know." He stared off into the distance again.

Anna looked up into his face. "But what?"

Eli looked down at his bandaged hands, feeling her stare at his battered face. "Can I ask you something? Without you making fun of me?"

"Yeah. Of course." She replied in a soft, comforting tone.

"Have you noticed anything lately? Anything . . . Strange . . . I mean?" He asked while continuing to look at his hands.

"Like what?" Anna asked, looking away from him.

Eli raised his head, looking at the sky. "I don't know. The friggin' bridge, for one thing. The storms, the power failures, the real hot then real cold weather, the dying trees, just people and the way they're being mean and weird all of a sudden. Things just seem really . . . Strange lately. Or maybe it's just me."

Anna only sat silent, looking at Hunter.

Eli looked at her. "Like my mom. She's been getting weirder and weirder, and last night was the weirdest. She never, ever hit us where anyone could see it. Last night, her first hit was in my face, and she kept doing it. Hitting me all over the place. Almost like she didn't even care because she was going to beat me to death anyway, so no one would ever see it anyway." He was beginning to ramble, and had to stop himself.

Eli looked at Anna, waiting for some kind of response, almost as though she was going to determine if he was nuts or not. She just continued to look in the direction of his dog as the silence spun out.

Eventually she spoke in a very quiet voice. "Like the number of shootings in Aliquippa, and the weird teachers in Hopewell, and how it all seemed to start in Raccoon with fights and car accidents." Anna's voice grew stronger as Eli smiled and nodded next to her. "And how the trees seem to be more . . . *more dead* at some points than others."

Eli stood up in near joy. "Yes! Yes! That's what I mean! Something is really wrong, and this freakin' proves it!" He grabbed the belt from Hunter and held it in his hands.

"Eli, wait. You don't know. Maybe these things are just happening," she began.

Eli's tortured face grew dark. "No! I'm telling you that something is causing all this shit! And I think I might know where to look. This has to end!"

Eli spun and threw the belt into the creek, watching the water splash up and swirl the belt away in its current. Hunter started after it, but a quick "NO" from Eli stopped the dog in his tracks.

Anna looked at Eli with doubt showing on her young, pretty face. "What the hell are you talking about? Because your mom beats you, you think that there's some . . . thing out there, blowing up the bridge and making weird things happen?"

"The Strange, yes." He almost yelled.

"The *what*?"

"It's what I've been kinda calling this stuff in my head. 'The Strange.' All the weird things that seem to all be happening right here and right now. And I think that something's making it happen."

Anna took a deep breath before she spoke. "Eli, I know you've been through a lot lately, and I know that this stuff does seem a little weird, but how can you connect stopping your mom from hitting you with this? Stopping cold weather, and thunder storms, and fights, and perverted teachers, or especially something like the bridge being struck by lightning? It's called God's will, and it's not the same."

Eli raised his eyebrows and nodded his head. "Oh yes, it is. And I plan on finding out what it is, and stopping it, too."

Raising her voice a bit, Anna replied, "Eli! What makes you think that they're the same? Or that *you* can stop it? You're just a kid!" She shook her head and laughed a little.

"Because I just *know*, okay."

"What do you mean, 'you know'? And what would you possibly do about it?" she asked sarcastically.

Eli calmed. "I don't know what to do about it, yet. I *do* know that something is causing all of this, and I know that I can find it, because I'm having visions."

It was out of his mouth before he even realized he was going to say it and Eli stood there, looking surprised at his own words, as Anna looked back at him oddly.

"You're . . . what?" She asked.

The embarrassed boy studied the snow around his shuffling feet in the snow. "I'm having visions, or day dreams or something. I don't know exactly what it is, but I think it saved my life last night."

Eli explained the vision he had witnessed before entering his house the night before, and how leaving Hunter at the front door saved his life. Anna argued that maybe he just thought that he was going to get hit. He told her how he had seen that the bridge was going to be destroyed. They sat on the fallen tree together, Eli trying to explain his side, Anna arguing with the voice of reason.

"I don't really expect you to believe me or understand what I'm trying to say. I've felt this for a while, and it's becoming clearer to me all the time. I *know* that something is causing The Strange and I *am* going to find out what it is. It could be radioactive waste from Shippingport for all we know." Eli ignored

Anna's doubting look. "Whatever it is, I'm going to find it. I'll figure the rest out from there. I just want to know if you'll help me."

Anna took a deep breath, "Look, I'm not saying you're crazy. You're right, it *could* be something as realistic as waste from the nuke plant. But with this 'visions' crap, you're making it sound like a sci-fi movie."

"Okay, well don't think about that part then. Think about . . ."

Anna cut him off, "Let me finish. You *are* just a kid, Eli, and you don't know what you're getting into wandering around Raccoon looking for something." She saw the 'is the lecture over yet' look on Eli's face and cut it short. "Just tell me something."

"What?" Eli snapped back.

"Why are you doing this? Why do you, a thirteen-year-old kid, feel the need to save the world, or Raccoon at least? Tell me that."

Eli seemed to ponder the question for a few moments, looking at Hunter lying in the snow. His battered and swollen face looked hideous in his pose. "I don't know. I don't even know why I care. Grownups should be figuring this shit out, not me. But they're all going nuts. I just know that I have to do this. Something inside is telling me to and I'm going to."

*

Anna said that she was getting cold, and that she should get home soon. Her mom would come home, read the note, and be waiting for her to help with dinner. Besides, it would be dark soon. She asked if he would be okay getting home, and Eli looked down at Hunter with a smile.

"I'll be just fine."

She looked at his visible wounds once again, shaking her head and not knowing what to say.

"I know." Eli said, relieving Anna's discomfort. "Don't worry, it'll heal up soon. Let's get outta here."

The pair of friends walked through the snow-covered woods in silence with Hunter wandering about along side them. They reached the point where their paths separated, and smiled at each other since they were still young, and didn't know what to say when they parted company.

Eli swung a foot through the snow. "I'll see ya."

Anna laughed, "Yeah." She knelt down to pet Hunter. "Bye, Hunter! You take care of your dad now." He licked her face in response as she laughed.

Standing up and smiling at Eli, she starting to walk away. "Bye."

"Will you help?" Eli called out to her.

Her smile faded, as she looked back over her shoulder. "I'll think about it and let you know."

Somewhat disappointed, Eli nodded his head. "Okay. Bye."

The pretty, early teenage blonde made her way home, hearing Eli call Hunter to follow him. Anna went home and helped with dinner, almost ignoring her mother as she thought about her talk with her friend throughout the rest of the night. Eli chained Hunter up outside, secluding himself to his room and not having any contact with his mother when she got home. He lay in his bed, watching TV and paying special attention to the news, as he listened for reports of any new events around Raccoon. When Jerry finally called her back late in the evening, Anna didn't have much to say and had to ask him to repeat himself quite a few times. She was paying very little attention to him that night. Her mind was far away.

Both Eli and Anna slipped off to restless sleep thinking about The Strange while the white, dual steel riveted belt with teeth marks and blood stains on it twisted and turned its way into the stronger part of the stream. It floated along the ever strengthening current around rocks, twigs, and other objects wanting to impede its progress with ease. As the belt sailed ever closer to the sewage treatment plant, a large, long fingered hand plunged into the flowing, icy depths of the stream, plucking the belt from the water and holding it tight as the dim moonlight glistened off of the steel rivets.

CHAPTER 7

"Okay, I'll help you. But if things get crazy, I'm telling someone so that they can handle it."

Eli turned toward the sound of Anna's voice, noting that he once again missed hearing or seeing Hunter run off as she approached since his beloved dog stood happily next to the young teenage girl. A small smile crept onto his battered face.

"Cool."

They stood looking at each other through several awkward moments in the snow-covered silence of the dying woods. Hunter wagged his too long tail and shoved his face in the snow next to Anna, wanting to play. The friends broke the moment by both laughing at Hunter's antics. The laughter slowly died down, and Anna looked at her friend as she walked toward him.

"Look, I just want you to know that I can't be with you all the time. I'm not going to miss school for this, and I don't want to get in trouble with my parents." Her voice lowered and she dropped her eyes away from his. "Plus, there's Jerry."

A spear shot through Eli's heart, but his expression never showed it. He continued to smile at her as jealousy took hold of his heart.

"But I'll help you out whenever I can. I want to." Anna said, smiling.

Eli felt an overwhelming joy that his best friend was going to join him on his quest but held it back, showing her the same smile he'd had on his face since she showed up. "Thank you, Anna, really. You don't know how much this means . . ."

"Keep in mind," she interrupted, "I won't be with you all the time. Just when I can."

"That's fine," Eli said lightheartedly, "As long as you're willing to help me."

The silence began to spin out between them again, but Anna cut it short.

"So, when do we start?"

Eli laughed out loud in joy, finding relief in that someone, especially his best friend, cared enough for what he believed to help him.

"Right now." He said in an excited voice. "I have an idea of where to go. Yesterday, I had a feeling that it had something to do with the stream, where it passes by the shit plant. I think we need to go there."

Anna looked at him solemnly, and with a large amount of admiration. She thought that some of his ideas were far fetched, but it was his inspiration and determination that moved her. They were both only thirteen years old, but he had somehow looked deep into The Strange, as he called it, and wanted to fix it. She didn't really believe that he, or even *they*, could fix it, but she knew from his words the previous day that he would not rest until he at least tried. He was seeing things and taking steps that no adult had done, and she admired him for it.

"If we're going to do this, maybe you should tell me what you've thought of so far. Just so we're on the same page."

Eli seemed to think for a second. "Okay. I already told you about The Strange yesterday, whether you agree with me or not." He waited for a response, getting none. "I don't have any real idea of what's causing this, but I do have an idea of where to look. And that is the answer." He turned and pointed at the stream.

"What makes you think that?" Anna asked with honest curiosity.

"Well, it kind of has to do with the vision I saw yesterday." Eli spoke humbly, not wanting to mention his visions too much around her. "This little bit of the stream kinda leads to the answer, since it leads to where we need to go. I think if we follow it, we'll find what we're looking for."

Anna left a lot of questions unasked just then, not wanting to throw a wrench in the works of Eli's imaginative mind. Besides, that morning's events had left her confused, and she wondered just how much truth lie in Eli's quest.

"So," She spoke in a serious, yet cheerful tone, "are we gonna get moving, or what?"

Eli smiled wide, feeling that he was in charge of an important mission. "Oh, yeah. Let's go!"

The two companions turned and walked side by side along the bank of the small creek, the undisturbed snow crunching beneath their feet with each step. Eli spoke a quick 'C'mon, boy!' to Hunter, and the massive dog immediately turned to trot along with them, wandering about and stopping to pee every so often. They made their way toward what Eli felt was some sort of answer to the mysterious Strange that had plagued Raccoon Township, not knowing that they were taking the first steps towards changing both of their lives, forever.

*

Black Box

Sunday morning and Anna's mother hadn't awakened her for church. Instead, Mildred pulled her daughter out of bed by her straight, lengthening blonde hair. Anna's eyes shot open in pain and confusion, her hands rising to her head as her body hit the floor.

"Just what the Hell do you think you're doing?" Mildred yelled down at her. "Sleeping in while there are chores to be done and breakfast to be made!"

Anna blinked in the brightness of the daylight, her scalp still hurting from the hair pulling she had received.

"You worthless little bitch! Get your ass out of bed and into the kitchen right this instant and make your father and I some fucking breakfast!"

Anna began to raise herself to her elbows, looking at her mother with fright and curiosity. She couldn't believe that it was real. Her mother had never spoken *in front of* her that way let alone *to* her that way. Still half asleep, the teenage blonde climbed to her feet amidst the screams of her mother and shielded her eyes from the bright light with her arm as she made her way to the kitchen in a daze. The curses of her mother followed Anna through the small home, and the bewildered girl could not understand them, or where they came from. Her parents had kept her in check in a lot of ways, but screaming, violence and vulgarity were not included. They didn't have a lot of money, and lived in a small trailer in Raccoon Township, getting about as redneck as Pennsylvania got, but they had always respected, adored, and loved their daughter.

Anna opened the refrigerator, trying to clear the haze from her sleep filled eyes as she looked for something to make for breakfast. She noticed, during her search, that the light in the kitchen wasn't quite right. Anna pulled her gaze from the interior of the refrigerator and looked at the window over the kitchen sink. It was pitch black on the other side, reflecting the scene from the opposite side of the kitchen. She looked at the clock on the wall above the dinner table as she really woke up. It was just before four a.m. on the dial clock.

Anna looked around, seeing that what she had seen as daylight in her sleeplike state was actually all of the lights in the house shining bright.

"Mom?" Anna chirped, "It's not even four in the morning, what's going on?"

Mildred seemed confused for a moment. "What? What do you . . ." Her expression returned to one of anger and disappointment. "Shut your goddam mouth and get back to work, little lady! Or should I call you what you are? Little whore!"

Anna's mouth dropped wide open and her heart hurt.

"Runnin' around with those two boys all the time! I know what you're doin'! You don't think I was your age once? I know what it's like to have horny little boys falling all over themselves and acting stupid for that fresh young pussy!"

Anna finally cried out in disbelief. "Mom!"

Mildred didn't even hear. "Oh yes! Two boys, one older, one younger. One you can fuck in his car, the other you can fuck in some field somewhere! Oh, I know! I've been there, and it sure does feel good! For now. You keep on fuckin' like you are and—"

"Mom! Stop it!" Anna screamed, slamming the refrigerator door closed.

Mildred's mouth snapped shut, and she looked around herself, confused. She stood with her hands on her hips in an authoritative posture, but her eyes said otherwise. She all of a sudden didn't know where she was or what she was doing.

"You just remember what I said, Anna, you hear me?" Mildred spoke in a firm, yet softer tone.

She looked at her astonished daughter with dazed eyes, then turned and stormed off to her bedroom. Anna's father had slept through the whole thing.

Anna stood in the brightly-lit kitchen for a few minutes, trying to make sense of what had just happened. She saw herself standing at Eli's spot in the woods, looking into his battered face as he timidly opened his mind and heart to her, asking her questions he didn't dare ask anyone else. Eli's soft, passionate voice sounded in her mind.

Have you noticed anything lately? Anything . . . Strange . . . I mean? Just people and the way they're being mean and weird all of a sudden. Things just seem really . . . Strange lately. Or maybe it's just me.

Anna spoke aloud in the bright, empty confines of her parents' kitchen. "It's not just you, Eli. Not any more, it's not just you."

Anna made her way throughout the silent house in the dark early morning hours that Sunday, turning off all the lights in the entire house. As she did, Eli's words echoed in her mind.

It's what I've been kinda calling this stuff in my head. 'The Strange.' All the weird things that seem to all be happening right here and right now. And I think that something's making it happen.

Anna lay back down in her bed at four thirty that morning, knowing that she would wake up as early as possible and leave the house. She didn't know how to face her mom in the morning after what had just happened, and there was only one person in the world that would make her feel better. One person in the world that would understand.

I know that something is causing The Strange and I AM going to find out what it is. I just know that I have to do this. Something inside is telling me to and I'm going to.

*

Black Box

"Why doesn't your mom like me?" Anna asked as she looked over at Eli.

Eli seemed struck by the question at first, but regained his inner composure, looking straight ahead as he spoke. "What do you mean?"

"Well," Anna pulled her eyes away from Eli's tortured face, casting them toward the snowy ground in front of her. "I stopped by your house before heading to the woods to find you, and she answered the door. She looked at me kinda mean, and acted like she didn't really even want to talk to me. It's weird, because she used to be so nice." Anna finished, not knowing what else to say.

Eli's mind spun. He was so focused on making his way alongside the stream and discovering whatever answers he could along the way that her comment threw him off track. Anna was the main reason that his mother had beaten him so badly, wasn't she? He didn't want her to know that his mother had somehow seen inside of him and knew that there was more than just friendship hiding in his heart and so he directed focus to the issue at hand.

"It's The Strange, that's all." Eli said calmly. "Just like this whole thing," he said as he pointed to his face, "she's become pretty weird lately." He turned his head to look at her. "Why? What'd she say?"

Anna hesitated before speaking. "Not much. Just that you weren't there and that she didn't know much of what you did or where you were anymore. But she had a really mean look on her face as she said it. Or maybe it was in her eyes. I don't know. I just got the feeling that she didn't like me anymore, that's all."

"Well, I'm sorry about that," Eli felt anger build toward his mother, "but it's not you, Anna. I promise." He smiled in her direction, hoping that she would look up at him.

Anna did, and relaxed a little. The smile on Eli's face comforted and convinced her. She smiled back in response, not wanting to talk about it anymore. The memories of her own mother's actions that morning were way too fresh in her mind.

Eli and Anna had reached a point where another small stream had seemed to cut its way through the earth in order to join with the stream they followed. They both noted it, and the little bit of strength the stream gained as it proceeded from the juncture. Neither spoke, knowing that these types of junctures would continue to happen as the stream grew in strength, width, and power during their trek alongside it. They continued on their way through the snowy, twisted remnants of the woods that Anna was unfamiliar with. She had rarely, if ever, traveled this far along the path of the stream through the woods, whereas Eli seemed to still feel at ease with his surroundings, seeming to have been here before. Hunter tagged along with them, performing his doggy duties as he kept pace with his master and his lady friend.

"Eli, can I ask you a question?" Anna asked as they followed the path of the stream.

"Sure. What's up?"

"Well, you made a comment yesterday about how Hunter had saved your ass, again. What did you mean by 'again'?"

Eli stopped in his tracks, asking, "You hungry?"

"What?"

"Are you hungry?" Eli repeated with a look of compassionate impatience on his face. "I've got a couple sandwiches with me, and I was wondering if you wanted one."

Anna looked bewildered. "Sure."

Eli unbuttoned his thick, black and gray flannel and shoved a hand inside. He pulled from within a square sandwich wrapped in plastic and held it out to Anna, while he continued to rummage in his pocket with free hand. She took the sandwich from her friend as he pulled another one from inside his jacket, holding it for himself. He looked at Anna with a satisfied smile on his face.

"Eli, these are yours. I can't . . ."

Eli held up a hand and shook his head with his eyes closed and the smile upon his injured face. He felt great pleasure in accommodating her this way. "Take it, it's yours. I had a feeling that you would show up, so I brought two of 'em."

Anna was emotionally moved for the second time within only a few minutes. Whether he was just being nice, or if he had really felt that she was going to come along, his generosity and thoughtfulness touched her. It always had over the years. Eli had somehow never seemed to forget her in whatever he did, even when it seemed that she wasn't supposed to be there. He always had the ability to know what was coming.

As always, she felt the need to make a joke out of serious feelings. "What would you have done if I *hadn't* shown up?" She asked, showing a toothy, wide smile as she held the carefully wrapped sandwich in her hand.

Eli looked back at her cheerfully. "Given it to Hunter."

The friends gazed at each other for a moment as a look of astonishment came across Anna's face at his simple, reasonable answer. They both broke out into quick laughter, holding their neatly wrapped sandwiches as Hunter pounced and yipped in joy around them.

The short bout of laughter had not yet died down when Eli suggested that they sit down for a minute. Anna had wondered if she was going to get a response to her question during the whole sandwich thing, realizing that it was coming her way. They found a couple of fallen trees to sit on, Eli performing his gentlemanly duties by wiping the snow away for her. They unwrapped their sandwiches, correcting Hunter any time he wanted to make an attempt to sniff at, or come close to, their conversational meal. Anna's question did not even need repeating. Eli was prepared to discuss it, and proceeded as though she had asked it only moments ago, rather than minutes.

"Hunter saved my life about two years ago." Eli looked at his baby boy as he spoke. "For real. He almost died doing it. But he didn't even care. He saved my ass."

Anna initially looked at her friend with doubt as he looked over Hunter, who was playing in the snow nearby, with loving eyes. Her doubt faded and she denied any urge to speak, knowing that Eli's mind was on its way to traveling somewhere else. Back to a time when she didn't know him so well, she figured. She already knew how much the dog meant to this kid, and she wanted to hear his story. Anna sat on the log that was free of snow thanks to Eli, nibbling on her sandwich, and listening to her friend tell his tale.

*

"I was eleven years old, and it was Fall. My dad was still around then, and I used to take walks in the woods when we were done working around the house. We did all kinds of stuff. We raked leaves, pruned the trees, picked the last living vegetables from the garden, worked on the cars, did projects around the house, whatever. It was around the time that him and my mom started fighting a lot, I remember that.

"Anyway, that's when I started to go into the woods a lot, looking around for animals or the signs of deer that my dad taught me, or just to think. I didn't go very far into the woods 'cause I was still kinda scared and because my parents would get mad if I did. I would always try to go farther and farther into the woods each time, though. Maybe trying to get them back for scaring me with their yelling or maybe just because I wanted to, I don't know. I think that some of it was Hunter. I wanted him to have fun, that's all. And sometimes he seemed kinda bored with the stuff we did around the house. So I took him into the woods with me, so that he could explore and have fun since he was off of his chain.

"We really cracked down on his training about then, since he was gettin' kinda big and should want to stay around the house. My dad said so anyway. He was only a little over a year old, and was a lot smaller than he is now. My dad made sure I knew that Hunter wasn't anywhere near done growing even though he was a year old. He got real excited and proud when he talked about Hunter's size and stuff, I don't know why. Obviously, he was right, 'cause Hunter ended up growing a lot more after that. Not really getting taller or longer or anything, but just getting BIGGER!"

Eli enlarged his eyes and held his hands out to show size.

"I'm pretty sure he gained another forty pounds or so after the vet gave him back. He was still pretty big, though. And he used to follow me EVERYWHERE!"

A large, loving smile arose upon Eli's face, amongst the reddened sores and swollen skin. Anna had somehow become accustomed to the gruesome sight of Eli's beaten face in the short time they had been together that day, and she stared at him with great anticipation.

"He did pretty good with his training most of the time. Sometimes, he would just kinda wander off and do what he wanted to do. Boy! Would my dad get pissed! Hunter got his ass beat for it, and would do good, for a while."

Anna fought the urge to correct his grammar with a soft spoken 'well', since he always said 'good' instead.

"So, one day after I was done working with my dad and I went for my walk in the woods with Hunter, I pushed myself a little too far. It was right after that time change thing, y'know the 'fall back, spring forward' thing, and it got dark really, really early. It was the first day after the time change and I ended up in the woods with Hunter when it turned pitch black dark, and I got scared. I thought that I had learned the woods good enough to get home easy, but I got lost. I thought I knew where I was going, but the sun went down a lot sooner than it used to." Eli said, almost as though he were trying to explain to an adult. "I used to have a lot more time to run around than that. I didn't know! No one really told me what the whole thing was about!

"So me and Hunter were just wandering through the woods, and I got more and more scared. I couldn't really see anything, 'cause the trees still had the colored leaves on 'em and the moon wasn't real bright, and I didn't know where I was going. It was almost Halloween, so I was pretty scared anyway, and then I couldn't find Hunter. My dad said not to trust him too much cuz he might run off, and all of a sudden I couldn't see, hear, or find him. I got even more scared. Even if I found my way home, I didn't want to go home without Hunter. Since the kids at school didn't like me and made fun of me, he was the only real friend I had. I think I started crying, and ended up stepping in water. I had my hands out in front of me and everything, trying to feel for a tree or a branch or something, and I walked right into the creek. I freaked out when my feet were soaked by the cold water and I kinda screamed a little.

"I guess the splashing and stuff woke someone up, or something. That's what everybody said later, anyway. I could only sorta see in the dark by then, and I saw something coming towards me while I just stood in the cold ass creek. Next thing I knew, I was laying on my back on the ground. I remember that there was a stick or a twig or something poking me in the back. Some guy was on top of me, grabbing my hands and holding them to the ground. It was just . . . really weird, and I can only really remember the smell. HIS smell. He stunk, bad! And he was saying stuff to me and I don't know what it was and I know that his breath stunk too! God! I was so scared! I was crying and he kept talking to me real quiet and all I could think of was how bad he smelled, and how much I wanted to go home with my dog."

Eli balled up the piece of plastic that had surrounded his sandwich, holding it tight and speaking in the direction of the stream. Anna had finished her sandwich much earlier than he had, since he was the one talking, but knowing his nature conscience, held onto her own piece of plastic. Her eyes were glued to him as he spoke so passionately, and as he tucked the wad of plastic into his pocket, she did likewise. Hunter continued to wander about, spending most of his time lying by his master and his master's lady friend.

"Even in the dark, I saw green. Later on, I heard that it was 'olive green', whatever that means. He was saying things to me, I think. He said things about 'kids like you' and 'I fought for you' and 'you're the reason' and 'searching for survival' and 'it's been so long' and a lot of other stuff I don't remember."

Eli spoke those words while the true words of the smelly man echoed in his mind. 'Its kids like you that hated me while I fought for you and our country's freedom. You're the reason I live like an animal, searching for survival in these filthy woods. Oh, it's been so long since I've had a nice, tight piece of ass. Saigon, '69, I think. Ohhhh, yeah, tha's what I been waitin' for! C'mon, scream for mercy while I make you bleed, you slant eyed bitch!'

"I tried to fight and push him off of me, but I'm just small and weak and ended up face down in the dirt and leaves. I remember the leaves. They were really colorful in the day, but when they were being shoved up my nose they smelled bad. This smelly green guy kept talking as he reached around to my front, playing with my zipper and stuff. I couldn't do anything to stop him, and he tried to pull my pants down. I know I was crying, and I think that I just wanted it to be a bad dream. I tried to scream, but I couldn't even breathe with my chest against the ground."

Anna's eyes had long since welled up with tears that ran down the soft curves of her face, ultimately falling to the snow below. She never expected a revealing story like this from Eli, and bit her lip in sorrow so that he might finish. His eyes focused on either the stream or Hunter, she noticed, but the boy held to his tale just the same.

"All of a sudden, there was a sharp pain in the back of my right arm. He said to me to be quiet, but I couldn't. I started to cry louder, trying to scream the whole time. It got worse just then, even though I didn't think it could. The smelly green man used the knife he stabbed me in the arm with to stab me in the back, a lot. He said a lot of weird things as he did. I finally screamed out loud, even though it hurt like hell.

"'Dear God HELP ME!!!' I screamed.

"The smelly green man pushed the knife against my throat and it hurt. I knew that it was all my fault. I should have just gone back home. Because that's all I thought of, was home. I just wanted to go home where my mom and dad were fighting more and more and I could take a warm bath and play G. I. Joe with my little brother and eat some hot food and do my homework and watch TV and think about . . . whatever I wanted to think about before I went to bed. I knew enough to know that a knife to my throat really, truly would kill me. And when it pushed harder into my throat and I felt blood running down my neck, I knew that I would never do those things again.

"I guess he heard me scream for help, but I don't really know for sure. Hunter came out of nowhere, grabbing the smelly guy's arm in his mouth and pulling the knife away from me at the same time, I swear it. The sounds he was making were scaring the shit out of me. He was growling and snarling like I never heard. The smelly guy screamed, and I tried to crawl away on my stomach through the leaves and twigs and stuff. The guy was holding me, and I couldn't go anywhere. He pulled his knife hand away from Hunter's mouth and stabbed me right in the back. I screamed really loud, and things went crazy after that.

"The smelly green man didn't let go of me, I know that. My face was in the ground for a while, so I didn't see some of what happened. I heard a lot of yelling from the green man and more of the snarling from Hunter. I think the snarling scared me more, since it made me realize just how serious and real the whole thing was.

"The smelly man held onto me, but I was able to turn over after only hearing the fight behind me. I cried even more once I turned over, since Hunter was half covered in blood while he jumped at the smelly guy and then jumped back. It scared me to see him like that. I didn't know how much of the blood was his, but it had to be a lot since there were wide open cuts on his body that I could see even in the moonlight. His teeth were showing and he was snapping at the man that was stabbing him. He looked like a big, black Hellhound, if you can imagine it.

"It was dark, and I could barely see. I saw that the two of 'em were tangled up for a while, and heard a lot of attacking dog sounds and the man's cursing and yelling. Somehow, the smelly man put his foot in Hunter's chest and kicked him away. Hunter squealed only a little bit and I couldn't see him cuz he kinda moved into the darker part of the woods. I screamed for him, knowing that he was hurt and not wanting him to be.

"The smelly green man had kicked him so hard that he fell out of the little spot that I could actually see in. The guy turned his crazy, dirty face to me and I knew right then I was dead. He didn't care about the things he was talking about and didn't reach for my pants anymore. He was done with that. He got rid of my dog, and he was going to kill me. I knew it.

"The smelly green man said something as he held the knife over his head, and then something else when he swung his arm at my chest. He was going to stab me in the heart, I know he said that. It's weird, cuz I turned myself over to see what was going on behind me, and it put me in the perfect spot for him to stab me in the heart. I knew that I was gonna to die, right there, right then. I can't really even explain what it was like, Angela."

Anna blinked at him with her eyebrows drawn together in confusion at the odd name reference. He continued on, unaware of her perplexity, looking toward his beloved dog through the rest of the tale, as though in a daze.

"I saw it all, in a weird way. I saw him bringing the knife to my heart, I saw him sticking that knife way into my chest, I saw the bright red blood squirting out around the knife, and I swear I almost saw my life end. I think I even saw a lot more after that, but I don't remember.

"I took a deep breath as the smelly man knelt over me, using both hands to swing the knife down at my heart. All I could do was lay there, holding my hands in the ground, looking at what was happening, and hoping to God that it wasn't real. I was gonna die, and all I wanted to do was go home with my dog. That's all I was trying to do.

"Hunter came from the dark, again. This time, he didn't attack. He jumped across me, like from left to right, and the smelly man's knife stabbed him in the neck, pulling it from the man's hands. Hunter landed on his feet and turned on the smelly green man. Are you sure you want to hear this? I don't want you to look at him different." Eli arose from his daze for a moment, looking in Anna's direction.

Anna just nodded her head with wide eyes, signifying that she wanted to know the rest.

"Okay." Eli's eyes faded back to a distance, and he continued. "The smelly man was kneeling over me, and Hunter charged him, knife in his neck and all. He jumped on the man from where he was, holding him down with his paws. GOD! He looked so scary! As soon as he put the man down, he attacked. He went for the guy's face, first. It was pretty quick, and all I really saw was a shitload of blood coming from the guy's head. Hunter pulled his head back and snarled again, then moved his head in again. He grabbed the smelly green guy's throat, and I saw the blood shoot out from the sides. Hunter shook his head back and forth, and I saw something really gross in his mouth. Once he pulled the guy's throat out and the man's body stopped twitching, Hunter stopped growling. He dropped the thing in his mouth and crawled up next to me on the ground. He laid right next to me with the knife that should have been in my heart sticking out of his neck, breathing hard through his nose, looking right at me while I just cried.

"My mom and dad had to pay a whole lot of money or they traded something, I don't remember. Hunter was almost dead when we got him to the vet. It was kind of nice, seeing my mom and dad join together on something like that, since they were fighting so much. Everybody could tell what happened, and when my mom and dad saw that, they did whatever they could to save the life of the dog that saved *my* life.

"Hunter had a whole lot of cuts on his body. The vet said that he was already pretty weak because of that. The knife in his neck was the kicker. It had cut an artery or something, and they said that it was a good thing that the knife was still in there, keeping him from losing all his blood or something. The look on the vet's face when we first took him in was pretty bad. I cried the whole time. Not just because I was hurt and saw what I saw, but with what was happening with Hunter. He actually killed the guy that was trying to kill me, and almost died protecting me."

Eli turned his gaze to look at Anna. He looked at her seriously while he tried to shed the negative remnants of his past experience.

"I never wanted you to see him as a vicious dog, or a killer. He *did* kill a man, once, to save my life. And he was gonna give up his life for mine."

*

"What about you?" Anna asked, holding the tears away from her voice. "What happened to you?"

It was obvious that the passionate part of Eli's story had finished as soon as he began speaking again. He let out a little laugh, pulling a stick from the ground and closing off his heart as he did so.

"I went to the hospital, *after* we took Hunter to the vet. We had to make a late night emergency call to the vet, y'know. I was hurting pretty bad, but I was crying a lot, mostly screaming about Hunter, and once my parents kinda figured out that he saved my life, they let me go with them to take Hunter to the vet. I know it sounds crazy and doesn't make sense that my mom and dad took care of Hunter before taking me to the hospital, but I guess you had to be there. We dropped him off and the vet promised that Hunter would be taken care of, and my dad stayed with the vet to wait on him. The cuts in my arm and back were pretty bad, too, but they cleaned them out, sewed 'em up and sent me home. The whole time I was in the hospital crying for Hunter, my dad kept making phone calls to my mom to let me know how Hunter was doing, and find out how I was doing. It was awesome, to see how my mom and dad came together for me and my dog, y'know."

Eli stared at his blistered hands for a moment with a look of sadness and loss on his face. "It was really awesome."

Anna pushed her lovely, rounded face toward his. "You okay?"

Eli looked up with a brave, yet sorrow filled smile. "Yeah. I'm fine. How was the sandwich?"

Anna backed away with a smile, knowing that his emotional moments were over. "Pretty damn good. Did your mom make it?"

"Whatever!" Eli said as he stood up, letting out a good bit of laughter as he did.

Anna followed suit, laughing and rising from the fallen tree that Eli had wiped the snow off of for her. Hunter even rose from his comfortable position between the two, standing between them and panting happily at their hands.

Eli calmed the dog with his words, placing his right arm against Anna's waist and leading her toward their common path for the time being. The stream. Without words, the pair continued following the bank of the stream, Eli leading the way with his caring touch and Hunter following alongside. They were together as always, this time in the real, singular goal of finding out what was going on with The Strange and setting it right. The prematurely dying landscape did not hinder their spirits or their closeness then, as they smiled at each other in the snowy white backdrop.

As the two teenagers walked alongside the growing stream in the mid-October snow hand in hand, hand to elbow, hand to waist, or elbow to elbow, some type of physical contact seemed necessary to hold them together. Or maybe it just felt good. Eli and Anna followed the path that the stream laid out for them, enjoying the company and comfort of the other as they each left their distress behind them.

CHAPTER 8

"Do you see it?" Eli asked, stopping in his tracks alongside the stream.

Anna looked around with a look of confusion on her face, showing Eli that she didn't know what he was talking about.

"The trees, I mean. See how bad they look."

Anna's face lit up with acknowledgement. "Yeah. They're all twisted and dark, almost black. They're not just bare and dying like the ones on the way here. These trees are *really* dead, like they were poisoned or something."

Eli smiled, "Yep."

"So, what does that mean?"

Eli looked around the surrounding woods in deep thought. "Whatever it is we're looking for, it's really close. C'mon, let's keep going."

The pair continued walking along the path of the stream in the twisted remains of the snow filled autumn woods. The stream had grown in size and strength, and the bank had grown steeper leading to it. Hunter had since ceased his trips to the stream to get a drink, since the water was now too far below him.

Bud's junkyard had fallen into the distance behind them and they could see a few residences on the other side of the stream through the thinning trees. While Anna was completely lost, Eli seemed to have every sense of where he was, walking alongside the stream with confidence as he surveyed the dying land around them. Completely forgotten to him, somehow buried deep inside his mind, was his last trip to this part of the woods way back on September 7th. That day, he was on the other side of the stream walking alone in the wilderness. As he walked along the stream with his best friend and his dog, thoughts of the cleanup that was still going on in that area of the Raccoon woods never entered his mind.

"My God! What's that smell?" Anna cried out as she crinkled her nose in disgust.

Eli pulled his attention away from the dying landscape, smelling the air. "The shit plant, I think." Even as the words escaped his mouth, he knew that something was wrong. Not that he was an expert, but he wasn't sure that it was raw shit that he smelled. He was too young and inexperienced to recognize the smell of decomposition. "It should be coming up pretty soon. We can take a shortcut."

The stream was about to take a hard turn to the right, leading away from their side of it. It would head that direction for a couple hundred yards, then turn left again, leading to the sewage treatment plant at an angle. Eli knew this, and knew that if they just went straight through the woods, they would meet up with the stream as it reached the treatment plant, saving them the walk in the wrong direction.

"Are you sure we should leave the stream? You said that it would lead us to the answer." Anna asked as they made their way straight through the dying woods.

"It will. We're just gonna save a little time and go right to the shit plant, which is the answer."

The young blonde nodded her head, agreeing with his decision. He knew this part of the woods better after all. Besides, she was getting cold, and her feet were starting to go numb. They continued to walk in silence for a while, Hunter following alongside, when Anna began to feel that something wasn't right.

"Why the treatment plant?" She asked with her head lowered and her hands in her pockets.

Eli only looked over at her.

"I mean, I know you had this vision or whatever about the plant, but why there? What does it have to do with—"

Her last words were drowned out by the startling sound of Hunter's loud growl. They both looked over towards him as he stood stiff and alert, his stub of a tail standing straight upward and his large head held upright. He was looking off to the right, where the stream continued its path toward the treatment plant from two hundred yards away. His growls started only rumbling from his deep chest to his throat.

"Hunter!" Eli called out. "What's up buddy?"

Hunter looked over at Eli, wagging his tail only a couple times before returning his gaze to the distance. Suddenly, he dropped his body into a pouncing position and the growl became louder as he opened his mouth. As though something had made a move towards him, Hunter dropped back, baring his teeth and snarling with his increasing growl.

Anna grabbed Eli's arm with both of her hands. "Eli, what's going on? He's scaring me!"

"I don't know. I guess he sees something over there. Maybe another dog or something." He said to her. Eli broke her grip, moving towards his dog. "Hunter! What the fuck? Stop it! NOW!"

The large black canine continued to growl and snarl into the black, twisted death of the trees. Eli hollered again, approaching Hunter and grabbing him by the scruff of the neck. For a brief moment, Anna was sure that the dog was going to turn on his master, ripping flesh from his young, tender forearm.

Hunter *did* turn with his teeth still bared and a growl in his throat, but he looked at the boy, then back to the woods, as though he was pointing in that direction, in his own doggy manner. Eli didn't care, pulling his dog away in the direction of the treatment plant, yelling at him to 'stop it and settle down'. Hunter wanted to hold his ground, and Eli had to drag him quite some distance by the loose skin on the back of his neck until he got the dog's full attention. Eli knelt in front of him, holding his head in both of his hands.

"Hunter," He spoke calm and gentle, "cool out, buddy. Okay? There's nothing there. Just settle down, buddy." Eli calmed his massive dog with his words and a soft stroke on the top of his large head. Finally, the thin boy was able to stand up and have Hunter's eyes on him, and not the distant woods.

"Is he okay?" Anna asked from behind Eli. "What happened?"

"I don't know what happened. He usually doesn't do shit like that, even if there is another dog." Eli never took his eyes off of his dog. "But he'll be fine. Won't you, buddy?"

Hunter responded by panting happily and licking at his master's hands.

"Sorry about that." Eli turned to Anna. "You okay?"

A timid smile came to her pretty, rounded face. "Yeah. I've just never seen him do that before. Plus I'm totally lost, and the woods are freakin' me out, and, well, I just got scared."

Eli only nodded, not knowing what to say. He was the one who had brought her there try to find whatever it was they were looking for. It was his dog that had scared Anna and it was his fault that she was cold, but he refused to turn around and go home just then.

"That's what he's here for, to protect us." Eli smiled as he spoke. They both began walking again, keeping a close eye on Hunter as they did.

"What's back there?" Anna asked. "I saw that there were some houses on that side of the stream earlier. Do people live this far into the woods that another dog would be around?"

"Only a few people live out this far. The houses that you saw were people like the Robinson's, the White's, and the Baron's. And there's another reason I didn't want to follow the stream along the curve back there." Eli began using his hands to demonstrate. "We were going this way along the stream, then it turned off, this way." He curved his hand to his right as he held the other one straight in the direction they were heading. "Then it curves *back* to the left, going the same way we are, but from way over there. A little ways past that second curve is where Willie Junker lives."

Anna looked at him, confused. She understood the curves of the stream, but the name she didn't know.

"Old Man Junker." Eli said, expecting some kind of recognition to come to Anna's face. None did. "Y'know, the weird old guy that lives in a little shack in the woods, drives some old beat up pick up truck?" Finally, he saw the light he was looking for on her innocent face.

"Oh, yeah! He always drives really slow with his arm out the window! My mom gets real mad when we're behind him on the road. His piece of crap light brown truck is always blowing stinky smoke. Any time she beeps at him, he gets mad and yells and drives slower and stuff! People always make fun of him and he's always stopping and yelling at kids for things. That guy, huh?"

"Yeah, he lives back there. I've only been near there once, and it was with Tommy Pardoki. It looks like a little shack, for real! There's junk all over the place, and the grass was really tall. He has 'No Trespassing' signs all over the place on the old wooden fences. It was really weird. And Tommy told me that he shot a kid once. This kid was in his yard or in the woods nearby and the old man yelled at him to get off his property. When the kid didn't leave right away, Old Man Junker came running out of the front door in his dirty underwear with a big gun and shot him in the leg. We looked around for a little bit, and when we heard his dirty old truck come down the little road, we took off runnin'. I guess he saw us, because he was trying to run after us yelling and swearing, and his truck was still running. We laughed about it later, but we were pretty scared. Tommy might have made up the story about the kid getting shot, I don't know. That's why I didn't want to go back that way. Plus it's quicker this way, and you look like you're gettin' cold."

Anna smiled, knowing that she *was* getting cold. "I'm glad we didn't, 'cause my mom told me that there are stories about him that I shouldn't hear. She also told me to just stay away from him." Anna stopped walking, looking around herself, confused.

"What?" Eli looked around also, then looked straight ahead and began smiling. "Hey, we made it! C'mon!" He started jogging in the direction of the sewage treatment plant, which could be seen through the wilted limbs of the scattered trees. Hunter followed close behind.

"Wait. Eli, did you notice . . ." She trailed off, seeing that he was running into the distance. "Eli! Wait!" Anna trotted after him.

Anna caught up to him, finding him standing at the crest of the stream's bank with his hand resting on a dying tree. He was looking across the stream at the large, tubular openings leading through the ground to the treatment plant, which sat fifty yards or so away from the stream. The potent smell of raw sewage filled the air around them. Hunter sat next to him as Anna came up behind Eli, breathing hard.

"I'm sure we can use some of the logs over here to cross the stream without getting soaking wet. We should be able to look around pretty easily. It's Sunday, so nobody should be there. C'mon, let's look for some wood." Eli turned to search for wood, not even looking at Anna.

The young girl reached out, snatching the sleeve of his flannel in her hand. "Eli! Dammit! Listen to me!"

He turned to look at his companion with wide eyes, startled by her action. She pulled him closer, looking into his beaten face.

"Would you take a look around for a second? Look at the trees, Eli, and the grass, since there actually *is* grass. It looks pretty bad, yeah, but not like it did before. It's not as dead here."

Eli looked around, realizing that she was right. The trees were only dying, not dead, black and twisted. Confusion arose in his determined eyes since it didn't make sense. The shit plant was the place, his vision had showed him so. Or had it?

"B—but, the shit plant?" He argued.

"I was trying to ask you before, Eli. Why the treatment plant? What makes you think that this is it?"

"M—My vision, it showed me this place. I was sitting there, thinking about when this had all started, The Strange, I mean. Next thing I knew, I was seeing this place, sort of."

"What do you mean, 'sort of'?"

"Well, I saw the stream, where it's big like it is here, and I heard something, which sounded like the pumps. You hear 'em?"

Anna listened, tilting her head in the snowy silence. She *did* hear the motorized sound of the pumps, off in the distance.

"And I *smelled* it. That's what I was saying when you showed up, that I could smell it. 'Cause I was thinking about the storms and when they started. It was when the shit plant was struck by lightning and lost power. This whole place smelled like sewage for weeks. That's when it started, when that first real bad storm came and knocked out the shit plant."

Eli was breathing hard, trying so hard to explain it to her and becoming frantic because it was apparent that something wasn't quite right with his explanation. Something was also wrong with him, inside of him. His chest and throat were tightening up and it was becoming difficult to breathe.

"Eli, I remember that storm, and I think it was the day before that when The Strange started. Everything was fine and peachy 'til then." She stopped, seeing an odd look in Eli's beautiful blue eyes. "Do you honestly not remember?"

Eli responded only by shaking his head, but his eyes said that he remembered something.

"God, Eli. I know you wanted to forget about it, but I didn't think that anyone could ever really, truly forget something like that. I just thought that you didn't want to talk about it."

"Stop it!" Eli hollered at her. "I don't know what you're talking about! The Strange started that night, with the really bad storm!"

Anna spoke very carefully, not knowing how Eli was going to react. "No. Eli, the storms and the treatment plant were just a part of The Strange." She took a deep breath before continuing, knowing that if they were to continue this crazy search, he would have to face the truth sooner or later.

"The Strange began with the plane crash, Eli. The one you saw and got hurt by."

The look on Eli's face was horrifying. His mouth hung open and his eyes grew wide inside his bruised and battered face. Tears flowed from his wide eyes and his jaw began to tremble as all of his breath left him. Holding both of his hands to his stomach as though he had been punched, Eli fell to his knees in the snow. He cast his terror filled eyes up to his beautiful, loving, caring friend as he struggled for breath, only gasping with a little squeaking sound.

Anna moved for him, trying to shake him and snap him out of it. He continued to wheeze for breath as his eyes remained fixed on hers. She looked into those wide, tear filled eyes remembering his pleas for her to help him 'forget the screams' as she struggled to help him breathe. Eli fell over onto his side in the snow, his beaten, red face gaining a bit of a bluish tinge to it. Hunter shoved his way between the two of them, thinking that they might be playing, but sensing that something was wrong with his beloved master. Anna tried to push the massive dog out of the way as she panicked, but failed. Instead, Hunter used his weight to push Anna to the ground on her rear end as he shoved his nose against Eli's face again and again, whining and crying the whole time.

All she could see was Hunter's black and tan ass facing her with Eli's thin legs protruding from beneath the dog's crouched body. She saw rapid movement in Hunter's muscular body, then heard Eli coughing and gasping for long hard breaths. Hunter moved from on top of Eli as the boy turned to his side in the snow, gagging and bracing himself with one arm. Anna crawled over to Eli with tears on her face telling him to 'breathe, just breathe' while Hunter stood silent and watchful behind them.

"Oh, God!" Eli cried out in a raspy, tearful voice. He continued drawing long breaths as he lay on the ground.

"Don't talk, just breathe!" Anna said as she cried.

"The screams! Oh, God, the screams! No! No! No!" He had only begun to be able to breathe as he broke down into full-blown tears, sobbing and gasping at the same time. "They all died here and now God's paying us back for it!"

Anna knelt next to Eli holding his head to her chest as he cried and placed his arms around her. Her tears fell upon him as she cried herself.

"I stood there and watched it happen! That's why mom beat me! I stood there and watched them all die!"

"Stop it, Eli! Stop it!"

Eli attempted to ramble some more but the tears and sobs took hold, and he simply cried into the soft comfort of his best friend's breast. Anna ran her hand through his hair as she tried to comfort him. Hunter stood over them, watching with his deep, dark, intelligent eyes.

"I really did forget about it." Eli said, carefully wiping the remainder of his tears away from his wounded cheeks. "I don't know how, really. I just didn't want to think about seeing it or hearing it, that's all."

Anna moved her face closer to his. "Are you okay?"

Eli looked over at her for a moment, turning his gaze away quickly. "Yeah, I'm fine. I just . . . I'm sorry. I didn't want to do that in front of you again."

Anna let out a light laugh. "It's okay. At least I know that you're a real person, and that you care. You're not just a robot trying to be all big and bad all the time. It's just a good thing Hunter was here."

Hunter, lying on the ground next to Eli, perked his ears and looked over at her at the sound of his name.

"Yeah." Eli said in a lifeless voice, stroking a hand down the large dog's back.

Anna smiled to herself, watching the affection between the two of them. The big dog extended his neck in joy as the strokes ran along his back from Eli's loving touch.

"Eli, what did he do to you to snap you out of it? I couldn't see after he knocked me over. But he did something to get you to breathe. What was it?"

Eli continued looking away from her. "I don't know. I don't even remember you trying to help me. I think I was passing out."

Anna looked down at the snow they sat upon. "So, what now?"

Eli sat, staring at the snow as he stroked his dog's back.

She looked over at him this time. "What do we do now, since it doesn't seem like it's the treatment plant? Where do we go from here, since your vision was wrong?"

Eli continued staring at the snow for several moments before speaking in a lifeless, dazed voice. "My vision was wrong this time, but not by much. It showed me only what I let it show me, I think. But it was close enough. It led us here, and led to you reminding me about . . ." Eli swallowed hard before bringing himself to speak again, "the plane crash. So it was right, in a way. It showed us where and when it really all began. Well, it showed *me*, anyway."

Anna listened and waited, knowing that she didn't have to repeat her question again.

"That's why the trees were more dead back that way, because it's not all that far through the woods from there, on the other side of the stream. I was so set on the shit plant that I missed it, but you picked up on it. Good thing you were here to help, huh?" He lifted his gaze from the snow to her face with a small, brief smile, then returned back to his apparent trance.

"I think you know where we need to go." Eli continued, "My vision led us to it, in a way. We followed the vision when I thought it was the shit plant, so we follow it again. And I don't want to go any more than you do, trust me." He looked up at her, taking long hard breaths. "We go to the crash site."

Anna shook her head. "Eli, I don't know if I can do that." She saw the immediate hurt on his face. "I know that it's harder for you, since you saw the whole thing, but we don't know what we're going to see when we go there. Hearing about it and seeing it on the news is bad enough. I don't think I can go there. The cleanup crew has been having all kinds of problems, so who knows what's still there." She paused, imagining the scene. "What if there are still bodies laying around? I don't want to see that."

Eli stood up, looking down at Anna. "Do you really think I want to see it? I had to fucking watch them die, dammit! I don't want to see them all torn apart all over the ground! We came down here looking for an answer, and that's where it is! And I have to find it! I have to, no matter what!"

Eli turned away from her, folding his arms across his chest. Anna sat, stunned for a moment before getting up and walking over to him.

"Eli, I want to help you, I really do." Images of her mother's behavior flashed in her mind. "We could get in big trouble if we go back there. They don't want anyone going back there that shouldn't be there, and they've been watching the place. I can't get into that kind of trouble or . . ." Anna trailed off.

Eli turned to look at her with jealousy tearing through his body. "Or what? You won't be allowed to see Jerry for a while, right?" He turned away from her again, getting no response and knowing that he was right. "Fine. I can handle it from here anyway. Thanks for your help."

Tears crept into Anna's eyes. "Eli, don't be like that! I want to help you, but I can't just give up everything else like—"

"Like I have." He finished. "I gave up on school, I don't even try to hang out with people that are almost my friends, I never go home, I just don't give a shit about anything else. No, I don't! This is all I have, and it's all I'm going to do until it's over. I don't have any real friends, I hate being at my house," he pointed to his face, making Anna close her eyes in sorrow, "and school is Hell for me. Everyone likes you because you're pretty, smart, and funny. No one likes me, Anna! They just make fun of me because I have no father, or I live a little further out than they do, or I don't talk much, or I don't wear real nice clothes 'cause my mommy and daddy can't buy 'em for me! I hate that fucking place! All I have is my dog and the need to find out what's causing The Strange! So that's what I'm going to do!"

The tortured boy turned and walked away from Anna, knowing that he probably hurt her feelings.

"You have me."

Eli lowered his head as emotions soared throughout his body. He hated that she had a boyfriend, especially one that was older and cooler than he was, although he loved having her as a best friend and just having her around. And he knew deep inside himself that she couldn't give up the things that he had, that she had to continue a normal teenage life. Eli cared about her too much and did not want to jeopardize that for her.

He turned to his friend with his arms out to his sides. "Anna, I'm sorry. I just really wanted you to help me on this. If you can't, then don't worry about it. I'll figure something out."

"Why don't we just wait 'til the cleanup's done? Then we won't have to worry about seeing anything." She suggested, not wanting to abandon him entirely.

Because by then it'll be too late. He won't be around anymore, and I'll never find him.

Find who?

Eli smiled through his alien thoughts. "Maybe we will. Why don't we just go home for now? You look like you're freezing your ass off."

Once she thought about it, Anna realized that she had been holding her arms close to her body and shivering the whole time. Their discussion wasn't over, but she wanted to go home just the same. She knew that it would be warm and that she could have a hot meal there, although she wondered how her mother would act.

"Okay. We'll talk later." She said with a smile.

"The walk should help warm you up." Eli held his smile. "Hunter, c'mon boy!"

Hunter trotted the short distance from where he had been sitting in the snow, watching the two as they talked, to Eli's side. He followed close by as the pair of friends began their almost speechless trek back through the dying woods to their home neighborhood.

*

While they were walking, Eli saw that Anna was still shivering through her coat. He thought about it for a minute or so, then decided to place his arm around her and pull her close to his own body heat. Despite his cautious worries about the implications of such an act, she welcomed the hold, moving in towards the warmth of his body. They walked that way through the dead and twisted woods, noticing the way the death seemed to protrude from an area near where the stream twisted and turned.

A seldom seen, live animal appeared from the dying underbrush. It was a rabbit, sniffing and wiggling its way across the dying landscape. Hunter froze in his tracks for a second, seeing the rabbit as soon as it appeared. Eli saw the situation that was about to occur and called out for his dog to stay.

Hunter paid no mind as he tore after the tiny animal, throwing up snow and dead leaves as his feet dug into the cold earth. The rabbit froze as it first saw Hunter's movement, then bounded and scurried its way toward some sort of safety. Due to the lack of growth, the rabbit found no refuge, continuing its furious sprint for survival through the woods. Hunter chased after, slipping and sliding in the snow, following the rabbit off into the distance.

"Damn dog." Eli muttered amidst Anna's cheerful giggles.

"Should you go after him?" She asked, still smiling and trying to stifle her giggles.

Eli shook his head, "He'll come back when he realizes that his fat ass can't catch a rabbit."

Anna burst into laughter at that, trying to imagine Hunter's goofy, clumsy body sliding around in the snow as he chased an agile rabbit. The laughter seemed contagious as Eli also began to chuckle along with her. They looked at each other from only inches apart as they held their grasp upon each other in the cold. Their blue eyes seemed locked upon each other, as thoughts of The Strange and where its cause might be found faded into the gaze of the other.

"What the Hell are you kids doin' 'ere?!" The thin, raspy voice came from the dead woods to their left, and the two children turned in that direction, startled from their laughter. "Get the Hell outta here why dontcha?"

Eli and Anna saw the tall, thin old man standing only a few yards away, looking at them with a malicious gaze. His skin was liver spotted and wrinkled, his hair dark gray with splotches of white scattered throughout. He wore faded and stained light gray work pants and a similar button down shirt, which seemed inappropriate for the weather. The large black work boots on his feet crunched in the snow as he walked toward them.

The children only stood there, looking at the old man in fear, not expecting anyone to come around while they were in the woods. Anna tightened her grip on Eli a little more. The spooky old man was walking right up to them, and there was nothing they could do about it and nowhere for them to go.

"You kids shouldn't be out here all alone. Bad things could happen to kids when they're out in the woods all alone." The man's demeanor seemed to change from threatening to concerned, in a frightening manner.

Anna placed her face against Eli's shoulder as he stared at the old man, captivated. He was staring into the old man's face but he couldn't quite seem to get a visual grasp on its features. Were his features rounded, were they sharp, did he have a big nose or thin lips? Eli couldn't tell. It was almost as though the old man's face was blurred. His voice, however, peaked Eli's awareness and his fear as well. It had seemed to change since his first words to them. It still held the same rasp and high pitch, but there seemed to be something else as well. It almost seemed as though two voices were coming to Eli's ears at the same time. The second was much deeper, much more threatening. The two combined seemed to bore into Eli's mind and heart like a drill. And there was something about his eyes.

The old man raised one large, long fingered hand toward them, pointing. The tips of the fingers seemed especially pointed.

"Get the fuck off my property before I call your mommies and daddies and tell 'em what you two love birds were doing down here." The word 'love' was spoken by the high pitched voice, while at the same time it was spoken as 'fuck' by the deeper, more horrifying voice.

Fuck birds? Eli's frightened mind echoed the phrase.

The old man continued as he pointed his long, claw like finger at them. "That is, if you even *have* a daddy." He let out a grotesque chuckle with both voices as he looked at Eli.

Hunter, where are you? Eli's mind called out in distress. The frightened boy had seen the old man once before, chasing after him and Tommy Pardoki some time ago, and he was afraid of him then. So he was deathly afraid of him now, especially with Anna at his side. He could feel her cringing and trembling against him.

Eli had brought her down here, and he felt that he had to assume his manly duties, no matter how scared he was.

"Hey, we're just taking a walk in the woods, old man." He said in a small, trembling voice. "We're on our way home right now."

Eli looked down at Anna, her head buried in his shoulder and he felt energized by the feel of her body against his chest as she clung to him.

"So why don't you just fuck off and leave us alone!" He said in a powerful, teenage voice.

Anna raised her head at his words, not expecting him to retort in that way, nor wanting him to. The old man cocked his head in amusement, showing a mouth with very few teeth as he smiled and clenched his long fingered, claw like hand into a fist. His eyes were fixated on Eli.

"Or what, boy?" The old man smiled his sarcastic smile down at them.

Hunter, please!

"He can't hear you, boy!" The old man grinned at him. "He's busy with my rabbit."

How does he know . . . Eli's heart gained speed as he felt a pulling and tugging sensation inside of him. He assumed that it was fear and confusion.

The old man grinned, his eyes flashing wildly in the lifeless daylight. "It's been so long since I've seen kids like you."

Eli's heart raced at the old man's surprising words. He had told his tale to Anna only hours ago, and those two different phrases that the old man had put together were still fresh in his mind. The old man began to look a little confused, and his eyes did not hold the same attraction as they had before. The deeper version of his voice was gone and the high pitched one faded as well, leaving only the original thin, raspy voice they had heard in the first place.

"Go on home, now! Get outta here afore I go git my gun!"

Eli saw Old Man Junker's eyes widen in fear before he turned away from them, running. He could only smile as he held Anna close to him, knowing that his baby boy had come to rescue him yet again.

Hunter ran past Eli and Anna at a charge with a muffled growl escaping his deep chest. Old Man Junker had a bit of a head start and had retreated toward the nearest bank of the stream, which happened to be where it took its first turn away from them, to the west. His old, somehow nimble body had almost reached the stream when Hunter caught up to him, growling. Old Man Junker had begun his leap into the stream just as Hunter opened his jowls for the attack. His right leg was still planted on the ground as he jumped, and Hunter's teeth tore into the hard, muscular flesh in the back of his thigh, splattering bright red blood over the white snow and Hunter's muzzle. A scream and a loud splash followed as Old Man Junker fell into the stream. Anna screamed when she saw the blood, and Eli called Hunter back to him. The great protector held his position atop the steep bank of the strong stream, growling violently through his closed mouth, which held gray cloth and a pink and bright red chunk of human flesh.

Curses and more splashing sounds let Eli know that Old Man Junker was making his way across the stream, and he continued to call his dog to him. Hunter finally ceased his growling and pulled his dark gaze away from the man in the water, looking at Eli. The cloth and chunk of flesh swung loosely in his mouth as he did so. Anna cried out in horror and disgust as she saw this, trying to move her body so that Eli would be between her and the dog. Eli held her where she was, calling his dog one more time in a much calmer tone. Hunter dropped his prey, trotting over to Eli and panting as blood dripped from his lips.

Eli watched the massive black and tan dog sit in front of him, and he patted the canine on the head, telling him 'good boy'. Anna wanted to move away from the dog, and so Eli broke away from her grip using the inside of his thick flannel to wipe the blood off of Hunter's mouth.

The frightened teenage girl was a complete mess, and Eli turned to her. "Anna, it's okay. He ran away, and Hunter's being good now. Let's just go home, okay?" He placed his arm around her again, moving her forward.

Anna was crying to the point of near hysterics, and she moved along with Eli's body. He was warm, and he would keep her safe. That was all she could think of, and that was enough. She was horrified by what Hunter had done and how he had looked, but was thankful that he had made the old man run off. The old man was freaking her out, and in spite of how tough he talked she knew that Eli was just a boy after all. She knew that Hunter was a good dog, although after Eli's story and seeing him attack that man, she knew his violent side. The sight of him with blood on his face and a piece of that man's leg in his mouth frightened her. She knew that the bad things Hunter had done, he had done to help his master, who was her best friend. And so she was very thankful for his protectiveness. Regardless, Anna had still been scared by what she had seen. They walked the rest of the way home in virtual silence, Eli comforting and encouraging her every once in a while. Hunter trotted along with them, licking the remainders of blood from his teeth the whole way.

Anna left Eli's company as she made her way to her house about four and a half hours after leaving it that morning. The troubled boy sensed his friend's tension toward going home, asking her if she would be okay. She said that she would, telling him that they would talk later and giving Hunter a big hug goodbye.

She arose from her doggy hug to look at Eli, who was once again looking at his shuffling feet with a distant look in his eyes. Even in his down turned face, she could see the loneliness and hope there. He finally lifted his head in response to Anna's hand on the back of his neck. She had spent a day full of adventure with him, and couldn't share that with anyone else. And there was something else.

"Be careful, Eli, okay?" She said as she moved closer to him in the gloomy daylight.

Eli only looked at her with his beautiful, innocent blue eyes in his beaten face.

She spoke soft and slow, "Have you ever, y'know, *really* kissed anyone?"

Eli blushed, even through the redness of his facial wounds. "No."

"Me either." Anna said as she moved her face toward his, closing her eyes.

At first, Eli wanted to pull back, but Anna's hand pulled his head toward hers. His heart racing, Eli closed his own eyes, as he had always thought was supposed to be done, feeling the touch of her lips upon his. His whole body vibrated with an energetic feeling, and his teenage penis went stiff. Then something strange happened. He felt something soft and slippery move through his lips, and he almost pulled away again. Anna held him in place as she began to truly kiss him while Eli relaxed a little, doing his best to return the kiss to her. He felt her tongue move in his mouth, and it felt weird, but really good. So he tried to do the same thing to her as best he could. Anna and Eli shared their first, awkward passionate kiss in the woods nearest her house. They each held the kiss, trying to get it right. They finally did, for a while, then the kiss broke, and Anna smiled at him with a bit of a glow on her face. She only turned and ran for her house with her cute ass moving beneath her jeans as Eli was left standing there, watching.

Eli was thunderstruck, not knowing what to think or feel, considering that she had a boyfriend. Smiling wide as he ventured back into the woods that he knew and loved even though the trees were dying, he began to hum some popular rock and roll love song, knowing that Hunter was following by the shuffling sounds in the snow behind him. It was only mid afternoon and Eli felt good about the prospect of going home and daydreaming about Anna as he listened to the radio. He might even do his chores, for once, or maybe even look at some of the homework Anna had brought to him. There was still the possibility of getting back to school and salvaging the year, even though he was way behind. Eli hadn't quite missed the school limit of twenty days yet, and he was smart enough to get back into the learning groove, he was sure.

If Anna could somehow become his girlfriend, he felt that anything was possible. The Strange might not even matter anymore, if that were to happen. He might even try to make peace with his mother, who knew? Eli was on such an emotional high that he began to wonder if maybe he wasn't just imagining the whole thing about The Strange. He continued humming his way through the dying, snow covered woods in the direction of his house, Hunter following along.

Eli's vision began to blur, and he began to stumble as he walked since he couldn't see a clear path ahead of him. A subtle, constant humming came to his ears, and he saw something ahead of him amidst the blur. Within a few seconds, his euphoria turned to terror as the screams of the dead grew louder and louder in his ears and the eyes of the old man flashed before his own. His pace fell to slow, sloppy steps as his consciousness faded away from him. He planted one last foot on the ground, twisting and turning as he collapsed onto the cold, snowy ground. Eli faded into darkness while Hunter stood over him, whining and licking at his young, wounded face.

CHAPTER 9

The thin, middle aged man gently lowered the trunk door of his car until it clicked closed in the silent darkness and slung the medium sized, green backpack over one shoulder in the manner of the students at the university. Holding an aircraft steel Maglite in his hand, the man cast a glance at his car to make sure it was well hidden in the underbrush alongside the small dirt road before venturing onto the small path he had cut for himself weeks ago. He knew the path pretty well by then, and avoided using the flashlight unless absolutely necessary until he reached his destination. The adventure was becoming a weekend ritual for him, and he had learned all the tricks he needed to not get caught as he remembered his five P's. Proper Preparation Prevents Poor Performance.

Robert Mikush made his way along the small path through the Raccoon woods to the crash site for the thirteenth time. It had taken much searching for the appropriate road to use, and several attempts before he ever made it to the site through the woods as he had been unprepared. The first time he actually *did* reach the crash site, he was devastated. It had still been daylight that first week after the crash, and the storms had made the site a mess. The sight of the wreckage and the bodies along with the smell of charred steel and flesh combined with the stench coming from the failed treatment plant was gut wrenching. He vomited several times as guilt for his responsibility for the scene took hold of him, flooding tears down his aging cheeks and forcing him to leave before he could even begin his search. Things had gotten easier since then as he began preparing himself more properly each time, waiting until dark to venture out to the heavily protected site only on the weekends, when the cleanup crew wasn't working. The cold weather had helped as well, hardening the rain soaked ground and freezing whatever bodies might remain. The snow cover made it more difficult to perform his search, but at least he wasn't puking his guts out.

Emerging from the woods that thirteenth time, Bob entered into the large clearing that had been made larger by the force of construction vehicles, many of which sat in hulking silence in the freezing darkness. In what he considered to be the 'safe zone', since the crash site itself was located far enough away from any local residences for him not to be seen or heard, he still took care to not draw attention from any wandering strangers. The college professor had been searching methodically during each visit, marking off an area with small steel dow rods driven into the ground. The method wasn't foolproof, as the workers sometimes removed the rods or plowed over them during the week of cleaning. Knowing that anything else might draw attention to his presence in the off hours of the clean up, Bob continued with the dow rods. He was beginning to recognize the landscape anyway, noticing the changes made by the workers each week as there was less and less wreckage remaining. The consistent clearing of the site raised the chances that his package was already gone, but the wily old professor continued to search as he was not willing to give up until the cleanup was over. Even then he would probably continue to search the surrounding woods, hoping that maybe the explosion had thrown his prize a good distance from the rest of the wreckage. During the weekdays away from the crash site, Bob would sometimes hope that maybe it was incinerated in the explosion, but he knew better. Not the thing which he sought.

Still retaining a string of hope that he would get the opportunity to study the object, even though it had already consumed two hundred fifty lives, Bob moved to his most recent search area and turned on the flashlight. Using it to locate his markers from the night before, the guilt laden, yet curious man resumed his long, cold, laborious search for The Black Box.

*

Five minutes into that night's search, just as he was getting comfortable in his late night mission, Bob heard a noise somewhere in the dark crash site for the first time. The sharp clanging of metal upon metal came to his ears, causing him to let out a little squeak of fear and drop the flashlight to the ground. Bob tried to grab the flashlight from the snowy ground in a hurry and turn it off, since it was shining its bright light out toward the open area of the site, and he dropped to his knees. Fumbling with the Maglite as he tried to grab it with gloved hands and cursing to himself, he finally got a hold of it and turned it off. Bob spun around on the ground, sitting himself on the snow against a tree and holding the flashlight close to his body with both hands. His heart was beating fast and he was sweating beneath his dark, heavy apparel as he scanned the surrounding darkness for the source of the sound with wide, frightened eyes.

Bob sat that way for a while, hoping that it was just some animal passing through that had made the sound, maybe running into one of the pieces of remaining steel in its search for scarce food. Beginning to calm himself, relax, and proceed with his illegal search, he was in the midst of pulling himself from the ground when another clanging sound made him hold still. Bob dismissed his animal theory as the sound of a human voice rose into the night air from the area of the clearing closest to the stream. Thinking carefully yet quickly for a second as his highly intelligent, well-educated mind worked, he rationalized that if it were the cops or something like that, they would feel no need to sneak around. So, he wasn't busted. What it *did* mean, however, was that another person was there.

What type of person? What if it's . . . No. Don't be ridiculous!

Shaking off the terror that threatened to seize him and gathering courage instead, Bob decided to grab the situation by the balls and find out just who else was traipsing around the gruesome crash site along with him. Besides, what if The Black Box *was* still out there? He could not allow someone with no knowledge about it to take it into their possession.

Robert Mikush rose from his crouching stance, holding the long black flashlight in his left hand and pulling the brand new fiberglass handled pickaxe from the ground. Having brought it along to help move large pieces of steel, rocks, and other debris out of his way as he searched for his prize, the wily professor thought that it would also serve well in self-defense. He crept around the edge of the trees as he made his way toward the area of the noise, not wanting to expose himself even in the half moon lit, dreary night. Bob's right hand clenched and released on the fiberglass handle of the pickaxe as he trotted through the snow and his body vibrated with the fear and excitement of it all. He was scared to death, knowing what he did about the box, even though all that information was just fairytales from long ago. What was real was the fact that the authorities hadn't caught him, he was sure, and that someone else was treading on *his* territory.

Living the boring life of a divorced, middle-aged college professor, he had become passive in life. The two weekend nights a week he had spent out at this horrifying piece of land was his source of life and rejuvenation. Since his first venture to the crash site, Bob had felt more alive than he had in many years, having a purpose and a secret. He wanted the box, almost *needed* the box, and the adventure of achieving it had allowed him to live a life that he never thought he would. Professor Mikush was realizing that life by chasing down the intruder to his personal mission.

The sweat beneath his heavy clothing was invigorating to him as Bob reached the area closest to the stream and heard its distant, rushing waters through the woods to his right. The slight moonlight did little for his night vision, and he wasn't able to make out any shape or form. A rustling sound emitted from the shadowy darkness of debris only a little bit ahead of him and to the left. Bob was gaining confidence, and since whoever it was hadn't made a move for him or even tried to seek him out, he crept closer to the sound.

"Who's there?" He called out. "What are you doing here?"

The stillness of the night was his only response and Bob bit his lip as he pressed the soft rubber button of the flashlight and aimed it towards the shadowed hulk of aircraft debris that seemed to be hiding his intruder. The bright light of the Maglite startled him, since his eyes had become somewhat adjusted to the darkness during his stealthy trek around the edge of the woods. It shone on a jumbled mass of steel resting against a tree that had been uprooted during the clearing of the wreckage area. Bob saw what was becoming a familiar sight over the past few weeks; several pieces of aircraft steel lying haphazardly against each other with the bright, shiny paint gleaming in the light while the edges of it were charred black. Normally, he felt a great deal of sadness for the dead because of the glaring contrast of bright life ending in burnt blackness as his brilliant mind compared each life lost in the crash to the pieces of dead steel he found at the site. That time, however, he was too focused on the intruder to even think twice about the burnt steel. He knew where the intruder was hiding, and he intended to bring him out into the light, even if only his flashlight.

Bob moved his body in front of the largest piece of steel in the pile after setting the beam on his flashlight to 'wide' and resting it upon the snowy ground. He took the pickaxe in both hands and swung it overtop of the steel, hooking the pick end behind it and pulling hard as he planted the brand new steel-toed work boots into the ground for support. They held firm through the snow, and the piece of steel gained momentum as it moved in his direction and fell toward him. Robert Mikush took a couple quick steps back, holding the pickaxe in his right hand and grabbing the flashlight from the ground with the other. As the piece of aircraft steel hit the snowy ground with a loud thump, he saw the figure caught in the glare of his flashlight, which was crouching behind the pieces of steel and holding its arms in front of its mutilated face, and a scream of fear was trapped in his throat.

*

Eli opened his eyes to the dim, late afternoon daylight, shielding his eyes against it with his hands. He was lying on his back, his head hurt, and his face was wet and sticky. A bolt of pain shot through his head when he tried to sit up, making him groan and wince. Hunter, who was lying right next to him in the snow, lifted his head and perked his ears at the sound, looking at his master with caring, curious eyes. Eli made himself sit upright, holding a hand to his aching head. Hunter's tail began to wag as he licked at the boy's other hand.

"Stop, buddy, please." Eli said in a hoarse, groggy voice.

Hunter didn't stop, and Eli endured the licks upon his hand and leg as he felt the cold wetness running through his clothes from his neck to his ankles. He cast a painful glance behind him, seeing that his body heat had melted the snow underneath him, allowing the wet, dead leaves to see the sky once more. Eli's mind was clouded and his thoughts were slow and thick. Hunter's playfulness, after he rose from the ground and stretched, was lost on the dazed boy as he tried to get a grasp on where he was, what he was doing there, and what had happened. The ideas had no sooner formed in his mind than images flashed through his aching brain.

He was in the woods, somewhere between his and Anna's house. He had been heading home, thinking about Anna for some reason, and had passed out on the snow covered woods floor. And he had dreamt, although Eli already knew that it wasn't quite a dream. Another vision had taken hold of him. One violent enough to pull him from his good feelings about Anna and throw him to the ground, unconscious. The cloudiness in his mind began to fade, and the point of the vision was somewhat clear to him. He knew what he had to do, and that he had to do it soon.

Eli pulled himself from the ground with his pounding head, sluggishly calling Hunter to his side. Walking slow since the cold wetness chilled his backside and his head throbbed, he made his way home. The vision had sent a message to him, and he knew that he was going to follow it. Eli reached his own back yard, but rather than going inside and enjoying the comfortable warmth his mother's house provided, he strapped Hunter's collar around his neck, then slipped the hook that was attached to the end of the twenty-foot chain through the metal loop on the dog's collar. The lovable, protective Rottweiler continued to wag his too long tail and grin his doggy grin as Eli held his large face in his hands.

"You can't go with me this time, I'm sorry. My vision says you can't." Eli paused, kneeling in front of his dog in the snow. He seemed to talk to himself rather than his dog. "I know it seems crazy, buddy, but I've got to follow 'em. It's telling me something, and if I don't listen then we're *all* in trouble, okay. Just stay here and be good."

Eli rubbed the top of Hunter's head, making the dog squint his eyes with pleasure. "I'll be okay, I promise." He smiled. "And thank you for helping us out today. That was a very good boy!" Eli said in puppy talk. "I love you, buddy, you know that!"

The troubled, skinny boy with the bright blue eyes gave his dog a strong hug around his large neck and a kiss on his forehead. He dragged one of his hands along Hunter's neck and head, finishing with a tug on the dog's floppy ear as he walked in the direction of the woods. Spinning around and walking backwards for a moment, he called out to his dog.

"Love you, buddy!"

Eli spun back around and disappeared into the woods as Hunter sat where his master had left him, looking after the boy with love and longing while his tongue hung out of the side of his mouth.

He hated leaving his baby boy behind, especially after all Hunter had done for him recently. But Hunter was not in his vision, and Eli did not want him complicating things since he knew that he had to go past the general vicinity of Old Man Junker's house. Eli recalled his vision, understanding enough of it to know where he needed to go and having a vague idea that he was looking for something, an object maybe, while he was there. All he remembered seeking in his vision was some rectangular black thing. Putting his recent feelings for Anna and his undying love for Hunter behind him as he made his way through the Raccoon woods toward the forbidden and dreaded Flight 427 crash site, Elijah Marshall ventured further along the path that destiny had laid out for him.

*

The thin, gray haired professor pulled the pickaxe up to a striking position as the thing crouching in front of him let out a slight yell. He began the forward, striking motion with his right arm when he saw the brilliant blue of the thing's eyes, and the fact that it was wearing a black and gray flannel accompanied by a pair of faded jeans. As the pickaxe fell forward, Bob saw the combined fear and courage in the young boy's wondrous blue eyes. Realizing his mistake, Bob closed his eyes, once again dropping the flashlight, trying to halt the fall of the pickaxe with both hands, and moving his body backward in hopes that the strike of the axe would follow. The boy screamed as the pickaxe struck the snowy, frozen ground hard, sending the shock up Bob's arms. He opened his eyes, seeing that the pickaxe had pierced the boy's flannel, pinning it to the frozen ground.

Bob looked at what he had finally seen as a young boy with wonder, creasing his brow at the sight of the boy's battered face. The boy looked back at him with the same look of fear and courage in his eyes, then down at the point where his flannel and the pickaxe met only an inch away from his abdomen. Bob began to wiggle the pickaxe free from the ground as he spoke first.

"Dammit, kid! What the fuck are you doin' out here? Are you okay?" He grunted on the last word as the pickaxe pulled free from the ground and he had to keep his balance.

The boy continued to stare up at the older man, his face frozen in the glare of the flashlight. Bob noticed this, reaching down and grabbing the flashlight, before placing it in the crook of his arm at an angle where it still shone light on both of them. He held his hand out to the boy, offering to help him up. The boy blinked his eyes as they recovered from the blinding light and he alternated his gaze between the older man's face and his outstretched hand.

Bob laughed, "Go ahead kid, I'm not gonna hurt you."

Eli reached his hand out, grasping the tough hand of the older man with caution and allowing himself to be pulled from his hiding place until he was able to stand on his own. He pulled his hand away, running it through his shaggy hair as he examined the curious man in front of him, noticing the suspicious clothing and the inquisitive, yet kind, look on his face.

While crouched behind the large piece of steel, Eli had thought of running, should his hiding place be discovered. When he first saw the tall, thin man clad in black, a sharp, unexplained fear filled him, freezing him where he crouched. Before being blinded by the light, Eli saw the tall, shadowy figure swing something towards him, and he curled his body up. The sound of the pick hitting the ground that close to him scared the shit out of him and any thoughts of running had disappeared, since he was pinned to the ground by his jacket. Once the older man had pulled the pick from his flannel and the light away from his eyes, Eli could only marvel at the appearance of the man, since he was the one he had seen in his vision.

The boy spoke in a bit of a daze as his vision had hit the mark this time, and it left him bewildered. "Did you find it? Did you find what you were looking for? Or are we still in danger?"

The inquisitive expression on the older man's face fell to one of shock, not knowing how the boy with the battered face knew what he was doing and why he was doing it. "How do you . . ." Bob began. He stopped himself, knowing that he should be asking the important questions. "Who are you, kid? And what *the Hell* are you doing here?"

Eli spoke up with confidence. "I'm Elijah Marshall, but everybody just calls me Eli." He extended his small hand to the older man in greetings.

After staring at the odd boy for a few moments, Bob took his hand and shook it, noticing through his shock that the boy had a strong grip. He wet his lips before introducing himself. "Nice to meet you, Eli. Robert Mikush, but everybody just calls me Bob. What the Hell are you doing here, Elijah Marshall?"

Eli smiled wide with his boyish charm, "Looking for you, Robert Mikush."

Filled with a strange sensation of surrealism as he looked back at the smiling boy, the aging professor could see that his deranged search for his prize had turned into something else.

"Actually, I came here looking for whatever it is that's causing The Strange. But my . . ."

'Vision told me' he thought.

"I thought that I would find someone here. Someone that was looking for it, too. And that person would be the only answer I needed." Eli stopped, realizing that his excitement over finding the man his vision had told him to find was making him say too much. The man was still an older stranger, and he didn't want to say anything about his visions.

Releasing his hand from the grip of the young boy and blinking his eyes in confusion and wonder, the boy's one phrase rang through Bob's mind.

The Strange

What did the boy mean by that? Oddly, the aging professor felt some sort of understanding for it.

"Eli, you shouldn't be out here all alone. This is a bad place."

"I know it is! I saw it! I saw the whole thing happen!" Eli looked around with wide, frantic eyes as he spoke. "I don't really *want* to be here, but I *had* to come here. I had to find the answer."

Something was stirring inside of Bob, maybe just in his mind, although he felt it in his chest, as well. Unable to put a finger on any reason why, he knew that he had to keep talking to the boy. "What do you mean, you saw the whole thing? And just what answer are you looking for?"

Eli cast his eyes toward the snowy, dimly lit ground. "I saw the plane crash, Bob. I saw the fire and the explosion. I felt the ground move and one of 'em even hit me! I even heard them when they screamed. I didn't want to come back here."

"You were here when the plane crashed?" Excitement started to fill Bob, hoping that maybe the boy had seen or even found something. "Who hit you? What do you mean?"

Eli looked up at the older man with boyish anger. "I don't want to talk about it! I don't even want to be here! I found you, so now can we just go away from here?"

Bob wanted very much to know what the boy had seen or knew, but he had enough caring and understanding for children that he wanted to help the boy as well. "Okay. We'll get outta here." He said, seeing the boy's eyes meet his again. "But first, I want to know what you meant by finding the answer."

Eli's eyes held the older man's, and his face became solemn. "The answer to The Strange. The reason that The Strange is happening, and what I have to do to stop it."

Posing no more questions at the time, Bob led the boy away from his hiding place and the crash site altogether. He showed the boy his path, and the way to his car, promising him a ride home. Bob was mystified. Eli seemed to know things, and spoke of things that intrigued him. More than that, the boy had truly witnessed the plane crash. As far as Bob knew, not one single living soul had seen it with their own eyes, but Eli claimed the he had. Beyond all of that was the nagging, itching feeling in his mind and in his gut that there was just *something about* the boy.

*

Anna walked into her house that Sunday afternoon, after leaving Eli's company, floating on air. She made her way to the house in such a hurry that she didn't allow herself the opportunity to revel in the glory of it all. Her heart fluttered, her body tingled with joy and excitement, the dreary sky around her seemed brighter, her chest tingled and her lower parts pulsed. Looking forward to reveling in her feelings in the privacy of her bedroom, Anna rushed to get home. The giddy teenage girl pushed the heavy wooden front door of her home inward with a joyous thrust, having her euphoria shattered as soon as she crossed the threshold.

'Whack!'

Anna's heart froze in its fluttering beat for a moment as the slap came across her left cheek, hard. Her smile of joy fell to a frown of hurt and fright, seeing her mother standing before her with one hand on her hip and the other ending in a pointing finger after its connecting swing to her face. Anna's heart resumed its rapid beat, but the flutter of joy was long gone.

"You little BITCH!" Anna's mother screamed at her, pointing her finger in the stunned blonde's face. "I can't believe you would do this, after all I told you! You little fucking TRAMP!"

There was no response from Anna, as she simply held her shocked, hurt eyes on the dark, brooding face of her yelling mother.

Mildred grabbed her daughter by the front of her winter coat. "What the FUCK were you doing out there in the woods with that dirty little boy? He's a little DEVIL of a boy, Anna, and his mother's just a WHORE! Is that what you want, to end up like her? You keep messing with the likes of him and you will, you stupid BITCH!" She swung her left hand this time, smacking Anna across the right side of her face.

The tears fell as Anna tried to get a grasp on what was going on. "Mom, what are you talking about? Nothing happened! I was just out playing with Eli and—" Anna began through her tears.

Her mother let out a wicked laugh. "I'll bet you were playing! Playing with his dirty little prick before he stuck it inside you! I KNOW what you were doing, Anna, don't try to lie to me!"

Anna only shook her head and cried within the furious grasp of her usually peaceful mother.

"That old hermit called me and told me that he caught you two hugging and touching each other! Musta been right after you were done, after you let him cum in you and you wanted to feel good and snuggle! He told me, and I KNOW!" Mildred shook Anna viciously with both of her hands on her coat.

"Mom, I swear!" Anna cried. "It's not like that! We just—"

"You just what? Why would you go so far into the woods except to fuck some dirty little boy? What THE HELL else would you have been doing out there, Anna?"

Anna wanted to tell her mother the truth; that she and Eli had been out by the treatment plant looking for the source of The Strange. The terrified young blonde knew that she would never have been able to explain. More so, she saw something in her mother's eyes in that moment that disturbed her. She didn't know why, but it held her unable to speak.

"I thought so, you little fucking WHORE! You will NEVER see that boy again for as long as I live! You hear me?" Mildred tossed her beloved daughter across the room, causing her to stumble and fall onto the cheap wooden coffee table. Anna looked up, seeing her mother approach her in what seemed to be a cloud of anger.

"You will have NOTHING to do with him whatsoever! If I find out that you have, so help you God . . ." Mildred clenched her jaw in fury. "Go get a goddam bath and wash that dirty boy's juice from inside you! Then you go to your fucking room and stay there until it's time for dinner. You will come straight home from school everyday and do some chores around the house, you hear me? I took the phone from your room, and you might be lucky if I let you see your other fuckbird boyfriend. We'll just wait and see on that one."

Anna sat on the coffee table, her face red and hurting while she cried. "But Mom!"

"But Mom NOTHING!" She screamed as the veins showed in her reddened neck. "Get in the fucking bathtub right now, little lady! You're busted, and now you have to pay the price! NOW GO!" Mildred pointed a finger toward the bathroom.

Holding a hand to her face as she cried and pulled her body from the coffee table, Anna didn't dare look at her alien mother as she trudged past her and down the hallway. She went into her room, gathering a fresh change of clothes and a clean towel as her mother watched from her bedroom doorway. Anna pulled the heavy winter coat from her shoulders, tossed it onto her bed, and made her way toward the bathroom, closing the door behind her as Mildred watched with strange eyes. She turned first the hot, then the cold knobs of the bath faucet, plugging the drain as she did. The bathwater ran as she removed her thick clothing, looking at her white, naked, pure body in the mirror and feeling relieved that her mother's strange eyes were on the other side of the bathroom door. Despite her mother's words, *Anna* knew that her body was pure, even if it didn't look quite like some of the girls' in her grade. *She* knew it, and that was all that mattered.

Anna took her bath, relishing in the warmth after the cold chill of her adventure in the woods. Needing the bath to warm her body and not for the reasons her mother thought, she washed the tears away from the fading redness on her face with warm, soapy water. As she bathed, Anna didn't attempt to make sense of what had just happened. Instead, she thought only of how she was going to get in touch with her boyfriend before the approaching school day arrived.

Emerging from the bathroom dressed in house clothes, Anna turned her gaze away from her mother's strange, watching eyes, and headed for the confines of her bedroom. Once inside, she clicked the door closed behind her, providing some sort of refuge from the tyranny of her mother. The light outside of her bedroom window was growing dark, and so Anna turned on a shaded lamp before tossing herself upon her bed in a flurry of tears with her face buried in her pillow. The hurt, confused teenage girl cried until she could cry no more, the incomprehensible images of sorrow and pain buzzing through her mind.

When Anna heard her father come home, terror filled her soul. If her mother could convince him that what she thought was true, then Anna would find herself in a world of shit. She listened closely from her bed as her mother and father conversed after he walked in the house, all of her nerves on edge. Anna couldn't make out any of the words that were spoken, which added to her anxiety, although she did notice that her mother's voice was calm and reasonable, as it had always been. Her father's voice was spoken in the same, slow manner she had known all her life.

The voices went silent, and Anna's body tensed upon her bed, expecting the worst. She had never seen her mother act the way that she had, and it frightened her. Unable to even conceive of how her father would act if his behavior ran along the same lines, she was absolutely terrified. A knock sounded from her bedroom door, causing Anna to stiffen and begin to sweat. The door opened slowly as she saw her father poke his head through the darkening doorway.

"Dinner's ready, honey. Come on and eat." He said in the sane voice she had always loved.

Anna pulled herself from her bed, responding to the loving voice of her father as she always had. "Yes, Daddy."

She walked past the small, unused dining room on her way to the kitchen in the dim lighting of the house. It wasn't even six o'clock, but with the recent time change the skies went dark much earlier than normal.

Mildred walked into the room, carrying a pot of spaghetti sauce with oven mitts on her hands, appearing as peaceful and normal as ever. She smiled at Anna, placing the pot on the table next to that of the spaghetti itself. Bill Eskers grabbed his daughter's plate from in front of her, tossing a moderate portion of spaghetti and sauce onto it. He spoke in a soft voice as he placed the plate in front of his angel.

"Your mother tells me that she got a phone call from that old hermit, Old Man Junker, today. Told her that you were down by the treatment plant with that Marshall boy."

Anna's body stiffened in her chair.

"Is that true?" Bill asked, looking at her from the corner of his eyes.

Looking across the table at her mother, who only pulled her own portion of spaghetti from the large pot on the table, Anna's lips trembled. She had no idea what her mother had told him, but could only assume the worst.

"Yes, Daddy, I was." She replied. "But we were just—"

"I don't want you hanging around with him anymore, ya hear?" Bill looked at her with all of his attention this time. "He's bad news. He's been trouble ever since his daddy left. His momma's a drunk and just lets the boy run rampant. Word has it that he's barely been to school this year and that he's a little strange. In the head, I mean. I don't want you runnin' around with a boy like that, Anna."

Anna thought she saw something in her father's eyes. Not feeling very aware and alert after the tear driven episode in her bedroom, she couldn't be sure.

"He'll just take you down with him, darlin', and I can't let that happen. You're my little angel, and I don't want you to be pulled down by the devil's boys." He moved a hand in her direction, caressing her blonde hair. "Just stick with what you've got honey. Jerry may not be number one on my list, but at least he's headed in the right direction. He goes to school, he plays football, and he's got a job. That means a lot in today's world. He's no genius, but he's got a lot of potential, that kid." Bill twirled spaghetti onto his fork. "I never made it into Harford, but me and your mom are doin' okay." He pushed the spaghetti into his mouth with his fork, chewing with quick bites.

Anna giggled, "It's *Harvard*, Dad."

Bill smiled as he swallowed his food. "Yeah, whatever. Anyways, I don't want you around that Marshall kid anymore. You hear me? And since your mother feels you shouldn't have been so far out in the woods, you're grounded for two weeks. Go to and from school and that's it. Got it?"

Tears began to well in Anna's eyes, but she nodded her head in understanding.

Bill spoke in authority again as he swirled more spaghetti onto his fork. "The only way you can see Jerry is if he comes over here, that's it. No going out, no dates, and no rides home from school. And we'll see about the phone thing. Your mother and I still have to discuss that part. But if you behave for the first few days, then we'll see." He forced another mouthful of spaghetti into his mouth.

"But Dad! We were just—"

Mildred cut in while her husband ate a bit of his dinner. "Honey, listen to your father."

Bill swallowed, looking deep into his daughter's eyes and pointing his fork in her direction. "No Eli Marshall at all. None. You hear me little lady?"

Tears spilled from Anna's eyes. "Yes, Daddy."

Bill smiled, "Okay then! Behave for the next couple days, and we'll see about letting you call Jerry. Stay away from Eli Marshall and you'll be just fine from here on out."

Having finished his delicate reprimand, Bill Eskers resumed eating his dinner. Anna looked at her plate of food with a churning stomach, not feeling hungry all of a sudden. She cast her eyes upward, toward her mother, who sat across the table from her. Mildred Eskers held both of her hands folded beneath her chin, grinning at her daughter. Anna didn't notice any of the strangeness or insanity that she had seen earlier in the evening, realizing that her mother had both condemned her and saved her at the same time. Mildred had told her father enough to get Anna grounded while at the same time keeping her own, irrational beliefs out of the equation.

Anna remained at the table during the time it took for her father to have two helpings of spaghetti, toying with her food and forcing down a few bites here and there. After her mother cleared the dinner table and her father made his way into the living room to watch TV, Anna said goodnight and disappeared into her room saying that she was ready for bed.

After closing the door behind her, Anna laid down on her bed with her hands folded behind her head as the lone lamp burned bright behind its dimming shade. Her eyes were heavy, and she wanted to sleep following her day's worth of activity. She reached over, dousing the lamp with a click, and laid back down, hoping that sleep would overtake her tired body. No such thing would happen as her mind ran.

In her mind she saw the trek through the woods with Eli, remembering his heartfelt tale of Hunter rescuing him two years ago as they ate the sandwiches he had made. She remembered noticing the difference in the dying trees and Eli's horrifying reaction to her words about the plane crash. Tears trickled from her eyes toward the pillow beneath her head as Anna recalled the fear she felt as Eli's battered face turned blue and she was forced into helplessness by his dog. A smile joined those tears as she relived the immense happiness and relief she felt when the big dog arose from on top of him and Eli started breathing again. Her own words echoed in her mind as it ran on.

He did something to get you to breathe. What was it?

Nearly humming in her bed in remembrance of Eli's touch against her waist as he pulled her close to his own, warm body, she smiled. Then the old guy came. Anna's body twitched in her soft, warm bed at the image. She hadn't really looked at the man much since she had buried her head in Eli's shoulder most of the time, but what she *did* see, she remembered.

The old man's face looked kind of funny, she knew that much. She couldn't remember what his face looked like at all, only knowing that it looked funny. His eyes were really weird, even though she couldn't say *how* they were weird. As she closed her eyes in the dimness of her own bedroom, Anna saw the swirling, flashing light inside of those weird eyes and it frightened her in a deep, private place inside of her. She had only caught a glimpse of those eyes and had no idea how Eli had glared into those eyes for so long, even having the nerve to *talk back* to the old man.

Some sort of strange feeling had filled her after looking at the old man. Eli's touch had undoubtedly felt good, but for some reason Anna had felt the need to rub her developing chest upon the boy's body as she clung to him in her fear. She wouldn't normally do that kind of thing, even to Jerry, but . . .

Anna sat bolt upright as she thought of something else.

I kissed him! I REALLY kissed him! I kissed Eli!

She felt combating emotions of thrill and guilt, knowing that she had a boyfriend, but also knowing that the kiss she had shared with Eli felt really good,

and right

even though it wasn't right. Anna could see herself grasp Eli by the back of the neck and kiss him, pushing her tongue into his mouth and moving it around as he did the same. She had pressed her whole body against his, not only feeling his erection against her crotch, but also feeling the push of her own breasts against the boy's thin chest as her small, adolescent nipples became hard.

Anna was at first aroused, then soon after appalled, by the image, seeing it only through clouded memory. She couldn't believe that she had done something like that since she wouldn't let Jerry touch her, yet feeling exhilarated by the experience with Eli. It wasn't like her to behave that way, making the virgin teenage girl know that something was wrong. Not because she had French kissed her best friend, more so because she didn't remember actively doing it.

Being the pure, decisive kind of girl that she was, that bothered Anna. She collapsed back into her bed, trying to remember what had made her go ahead and kiss Eli. Every time she tried, all Anna saw in the darkness of her bedroom was the flashing and swirling eyes of the old man.

*

Elijah Marshall lay in his own bed that night as the hour crept toward midnight, thinking. He had entered the house after greeting his dog in the yard, making his way toward his bedroom in absolute silence. Once inside, he turned on the lamp atop the headboard of his bed and removed most of his heavy clothing. He was tired and sore from the day's adventures, and he just wanted to go to sleep. Eli stripped down to his underwear, sliding his body between the cool sheets of his bed, chilled by the absence of heat due to his mothers' conscience about the heat bill. Virginia Marshall kept the oil burning furnace turned off as much as possible, even in the dead of winter, so as to prevent running up the oil bill. Sleep would be far off for Eli, however.

Laying in his old, narrow twin bed with his hands folded behind his head and staring up at the ceiling in the darkness, the distraught boy wished for sleep while his mind recanted not only the early events of the day with Anna, but mostly his talk with Professor Robert Mikush.

Eli had followed that day's vision as closely as he could by leaving Hunter at home and making his way to the crash site by himself, which resulted in him being discovered in his hiding place by the very man that he was supposed to meet. In his vision, the older man had been looking for something that was very important to him, and very important to the answer to The Strange as well. The confused boy didn't know much more than that. He did know, however, that if Hunter had been with him the big dog would've attacked the older man in protection of his master.

Following their meeting at the crash site, Bob led his young new acquaintance along the hidden path to his car, and gave the boy a ride home. Only a few, very superficial, things were discussed during the trip as the older man went to great lengths to let the boy with the mutilated face know that he meant him no harm. Due to his vision, Eli already knew that the gray haired professor was a part of his answer, and so he trusted him. As they parted ways and exchanged phone numbers, Bob and Eli agreed to meet again in an effort to find the answers that each of them sought.

The college professor in his early fifties and the lonely, early teenage boy found themselves in a common bond. Each needed the other for his own purpose and they left each other's company with ease. They didn't feel the need to rush the many questions they had because they knew, without a doubt, that they would meet again and delve into The Strange together.

CHAPTER 10

October 31st, Halloween. The horror of the plane crash finally began to fade away from Raccoon Township as the cleanup crew finished its work, mounting steel posts and chains across the entrances to the road they had cut through the woods to the crash site. The large 'No Trespassing—by order of Raccoon and Hopewell Police' signs swung silently in the cold breeze as the last truck drove away from the area. The cold weather and snow continued in the area, as did the dying of nature. Twenty-two miles to the south, the city of Pittsburgh was receiving its first chill of the season.

Despite the recent disasters that struck the area, Raccoon and Hopewell Townships were laden with the Halloween spirit. Pumpkins, ghosts, and witches adorned nearly every house and most of the children dressed up in their Halloween costumes for school that Tuesday. Many children won prizes while one junior high school boy was sent home for tastelessly dressing up as a plane crash victim. Kids and parents prepared for the trick or treating that was to take place that night, while teenagers prepared for the 'tricking' they would perform. Their stocks of eggs, toilet paper, spray paint and silly string were high, as were their spirits. It seemed that with the clean up finished and their many troubles behind them, the community could move on in spite of the excessively cold and snowy weather.

The school day ended and the soon to be trick-or-treaters ate meals forced upon them by parents who insisted that they eat real food before gorging themselves on candy. Elijah Marshall, at the questionable age for trick-or-treating, simply ate his microwave dinner out of its plastic tray at his kitchen table, alone. His mother had left a note saying that she was working late, that Matthew was trick-or-treating in their grandmother's neighborhood, and for him to heat up one of the microwave meals in the freezer as his dinner. She finished the note saying that if he wouldn't be home that she would appreciate a note saying so.

After reading the last line, Eli felt a slight pang of guilt at his neglecting of his family. His mother wasn't always around, and she had beaten him pretty badly, but he knew that deep down inside of her she must still worry about him, even if she wasn't quite herself. Eli had also been worrying about Matt, wondering what his younger brother was going through since he wasn't around much anymore. The determined boy crushed his guilt before it could gain strength inside of him, thinking that he would fix his home life by finding the cause for The Strange and would make up for all of his mistakes once it was over. In his boredom while eating his meal, Eli looked at the note in front of him, seeing that there were indentations in the paper. Virginia must have pulled it from her notebook after writing something on the piece of paper on top of it. He tried to look at the indentations through the ink on the page, but wasn't able to make out any identifiable words. Not much concerned with what his mother had been writing, he looked up at the phone on the wall with longing as he shoved another bite of the turkey, mashed potatoes and gravy into his mouth. Having left a message on Bob's answering machine over an hour before, Eli was pleading to talk with his newest acquaintance.

They had conversed only a couple times since the night they met out at the crash site. The first time, Eli had called Bob, wanting to ask him if he had found the box thing. As Bob had instructed, Eli started at the top of the list of phone numbers he had received and worked his way down the list. The first was Bob's home number, the second his work number, and the third was his cell phone number. Eli tried all three with no answer, and had left a message. The professor had called him back an hour later, letting the boy know that he hadn't found the box and telling him that he was busy and that he couldn't talk just then. Another time, Bob had called Eli at home, wanting to apologize for his shortness on the phone the last time and verify that the crash site clean up was nearly completed. Having just been out to the crash site that day, Eli said that it was. Feeling that it wasn't safe for him to be out at the crash site alone, Bob advised the boy to stay away from there and said that he wanted to meet with him soon so that they could discuss what they knew. That last phone conversation had been on Friday, and Eli ate his microwave dinner while awaiting the next call.

Eli finished his meal, throwing the plastic tray in the garbage, rinsing off his knife and fork, and placing them in the dishwasher. Anna crept into his mind, as he became aware that he hadn't seen her since she kissed him and trotted to her house on the day they went to the shit plant. He had gone to his spot in the woods every day, hoping that she would sneak up behind him with her cheerful voice and scare the shit out of him, but she hadn't. Mildred Eskers had turned Eli away with sharp words when he had gone to Anna's house to check on her, saying that her daughter was probably with her boyfriend, Jerry, and that he shouldn't stop by the house anymore. The inquisitive boy wanted to ask her why, but the strange look in her eyes was enough of an answer for him. The Strange was why. Eli had walked away with his head hung low, then impulsively looked back at the house. He was sure that he saw the curtain, in what he knew to be Anna's bedroom, swing closed as he raised his hand in a wave. The lonely boy turned away with an aching heart, walking off into the woods where Hunter was waiting for him.

Thinking about Anna during his walk home that day and wondering why she wasn't allowed to see him, Eli became afraid that maybe his female friend just didn't want to be around him anymore. Maybe the crash site scared her so much that she gave up on him and his quest? Maybe she told her mom to make excuses for her if he showed up? Maybe she didn't like the way he kissed and just wanted to be with her boyfriend? He didn't know, and would probably never know. Eli was also getting confused about The Strange, not knowing what to do or where to go anymore now that he didn't have Anna to help him. The aging college professor that lived all the way across the river in Sewickley was all he had left, although the struggling boy didn't imagine himself trudging through the woods with an old man like that, looking for something he had discovered in his thirteen-year-old mind.

The phone rang, startling Eli out of his reminiscent daze. He dashed the two steps to the phone, pulling it from the wall with a jerk.

"Hello?" He asked.

"Well, well, well. What do you know? My disappearing son is actually at home."

"Hi, mom." Eli said with great disappointment.

"Don't sound so thrilled to talk to your mother or anything." Virginia said in a sarcastic tone. Her voice then softened for a moment. "Are you okay? Did you get my note? Did you get your dinner?"

"Yeah. I'm fine, mom." Eli purposely cheered his tone a little. "I got your note and I just got done eating." He pulled the note from the table as he spoke, tossing it on top of the refrigerator with the phone books and other junk. "How're you? How's work?"

Virginia sounded surprised. "I'm good, Eli, thanks for asking. And work's fine." She became serious. "Look, Eli, I know that we've had our differences lately..."

Nothing that the white belt wouldn't solve, Eli thought.

"But we need to talk. We need to talk about this not going to school thing. I could get in big trouble for this, honey. You wouldn't want that to happen, would you?"

Eli held the phone to his ear, wanting to be off the phone in case Bob tried to call.

"Okay, let me rephrase that. I don't want to get in trouble for it, and I don't want you to ruin your education either. The school has been calling me at work about this, so it's pretty serious. I can't talk long now. I just want you to promise me that we can at least sit down and talk about this."

Eli continued his silence, wondering why his mother seemed to care about his education all of a sudden. She hadn't given a shit about it since his dad left and she started drinking.

"Eli? Are you still there?"

"Yeah. Okay, we'll talk."

Virginia sounded relieved. "Great! I won't be home in time to talk tonight, but we'll get together soon, okay? I love you honey, and be careful tonight."

Eli was shocked to hear such emotion flow from her mouth, and he almost responded with the same sentiment. Before he could, the click and hum of an empty phone line sounded in his ear. An 'I figured' grin rose to his lips as he placed the phone back in its cradle on the kitchen wall. Just as the boy turned away from the phone, it rang again. He looked back at it, figuring that it was his mother again, needing to give him some all-important command or something. Eli picked up the phone with a lifeless greeting.

"What now, mom?"

"Hello? Eli?" It was Bob's voice that came to his ear this time.

Eli's heart raced and he switched the phone from his right ear to his left as excitement lit up his youthful, scarred and healing face. "Bob! Hi, it's me!"

"Good, good. I got your message, and I do want to talk to you about all this. I think we can learn a lot from each other." Bob spoke in a soft, kind manner.

"Cool. Do you want to come pick me up or meet me somewhere or what?" Eli's voice was filled with excitement at the prospect of pursuing his quest into The Strange.

"You want to meet tonight? Don't you have school tomorrow? What about your mother?" Bob asked.

Eli almost became frantic, wanting and needing to meet with Bob to resume his quest since Anna had abandoned him. "Yes, tonight. I don't really have school tomorrow, and my mom will let me stay out late. It's no big deal."

"Eli, it's not that I don't want to meet with you, it's just that I wanted to have things prepared for you."

Eli creased his brow, wondering what the old man meant by that.

"And I don't want to get you into any trouble." Bob finished.

"You're not gonna to get me into any more trouble than I'm already in. How's that?" Eli said with a sly grin on his face.

Silence from Bob's end.

"Bob, please! I have nowhere else to go! I need to talk to you!" Eli's voice reached a high pitch as he begged.

Bob only sighed for a moment. "Okay, okay. I'll be there in forty-five minutes or so. I need to get a few things ready first."

"Awesome!" Eli exclaimed in joy. "I'll be watching for you. By the way, I wanted to ask you something."

"Go ahead." Bob replied.

Eli pulled on the phone cord as he spoke. "Um . . . I know you have a nice car and everything, but can I bring my dog?"

*

At first, Hunter kept shoving his muzzle in Bob's face as he was driving, trying to lick at him. Bob laughed it off, amazed that an ill reputed Rottweiler could be so friendly and loving. Eli, however, spent the first ten minutes of the drive telling Hunter to lay down in the back seat of Bob's car and apologizing for the big dog's behavior while the older man just laughed.

"Don't worry about it. He's a nice dog. I'm sure Bocci's gonna love him."

Eli smiled. He knew that his big, bad Rottweiler was a good dog and it had been a long time since anyone had allowed their dog to be around Hunter. Eli couldn't wait to see his baby boy get to play with another dog.

The newer model Toyota made its way through downtown Aliquippa, Bob stopping at the appropriate traffic lights as the curious boy next to him gazed out the window at the many abandoned store fronts. Bob looked over at Eli, following his gaze.

"It didn't used to be like this, y'know."

Eli held his gaze out the passenger side window. "It looks like no stores have been there for a long time."

"Oh no." Bob said with a chuckle. "This used to be a booming place of business, back when the steel mills were runnin'."

Eli looked over at Bob, seeing the distant look in the professor's eyes as he looked at the road in front of him.

"All the mill workers would come down here on payday, spending all their hard earned money on food, necessities, and other stuff. They more than paid for the early marriages they found themselves in, buying homes and vehicles for their multiplying families. They used to walk with their heads high, even though they never went to college and were earning more money than any college graduate at the time. The area prospered, and Aliquippa was the center of activity. It was clean, active, and pleasant, unlike the . . ." Bob hesitated with his words.

Slum. Eli thought.

"Abandoned, troubled area you see now." He finished. "It was beautiful and proud, much like the female Indian chief it was named after."

Eli tried to imagine this as he looked at the painted, broken windows and the graffiti on the dark, lonely buildings. Some small shops still survived, but they were scattered amongst the darkness along the main street in downtown Aliquippa.

Bob looked over at Eli again. "Have you been out of town since . . . since all this began?"

"No. Why?" Eli asked.

Bob turned the car off of the main street towards the battered state route that would lead them toward the Sewickley Bridge. "You may wanna take off your coat."

Eli heard what the professor said as he watched the headlights swing across the fading red brick of a building as they turned. It didn't make much sense to him then, and his mind wandered as they reached the four-lane highway. He looked at the swift moving darkness outside of his window as he thought again of Anna.

He thought about his walk home the day that Mrs. Eskers had turned him away with words about him not going there anymore along with questions as to why Anna didn't want to join him in his quest. Hopelessness about not finding answers to The Strange filled him just as Eli saw himself walking through the woods with Hunter at his side and those questions in his mind. A blur arose in his eyes, his head began to swirl, and the troubled boy felt his body hit the ground as he collapsed in the woods, again.

*

Eli had been in Anna's house only a few times, but he knew that he was seeing it as though he was standing in the living room. He was looking at Mildred Esker's back and Anna's face as well. Anna was crying and holding a hand to her face as her mother yelled at her. He couldn't hear the words she yelled, but he saw the pain and sorrow in the young girl's face. The vision had changed, and as darkness pressed against the windows of the Esker's kitchen, the boy saw the family sitting at the table for dinner. Eli clearly heard what her father was saying as tears ran from Anna's eyes.

"I don't want you around that Marshall kid anymore. You hear me? You're grounded for two weeks. Go to and from school and that's it. Got it? No Eli Marshall at all. None. You hear me little lady?"

Anna replied with tears on her face. "Yes, Daddy."

Eli saw her misery as she simply sat at the table, staring at her plateful of food. Another image began creeping in, one filled with darkness. He knew, instantly, that he was in her room while Anna was lying on her bed, thinking. Getting some type of image of what she was thinking about, he could see, from her point of view, Anna thrusting her young breasts against his body as he stood up to the freaky old man. Feeling her enjoyment of the touch, remembering his own enjoyment and how it had given him the encouragement to stand up to the old man, Eli started to see something else before a flashing, swirling light had overcome it in darkness. His vision had abruptly ended as he had awakened on the woods floor with Hunter lying by his side.

*

Eli felt a hand strike his arm, pulling his attention back to the real world.

"You haven't seen it yet, have you? Look at that mess!" Bob said in amazement as he looked out of his window.

Eli, startled from the memory of his vision of Anna, cast his eyes in the direction Bob was looking and dropped his jaw in amazement at what he saw. He had experienced a vision about it before he really understood them and he had seen the news footage about it. Once he actually saw it, he couldn't believe it.

Eli finally saw, in person, the wreckage that used to be the Ambridge Bridge. The twisted, towering 'A' that protruded from the dark, black river astounded him. The only thought that ran through his mind as he gaped at the monstrous wreckage was that of the size of the lightning bolt he had seen in his vision about the bridge. It was huge, about the size of one of the smokestacks that still emerged from the dark, abandoned steel mills. As they traveled out of view of the destroyed bridge, Eli faced forward in his seat, wondering what could possibly create a bolt of lightning so wicked and violent. The word that escaped his limited vocabulary as he thought about the image of the lightning bolt he had seen in his vision was 'unnatural'.

Bob piloted the Toyota towards the next available river crossing, the Sewickley Bridge, in the seven o' clock darkness on Halloween night as a few, haunting words escaped Eli's lips.

"Trick-or-Treat."

Bob glanced over at the boy in wonder, but then returned his gaze to the road in front of him. He didn't question what the boy said, and he *wouldn't* question him. There was something very special, and a little odd, about the boy that sat next to the older man in the car. He only hoped that he would get the chance to figure out what it was.

Knowing that they had escaped the climactic bubble that surrounded that portion of Beaver County, Bob reached over and lowered the heater of the car. He watched closely through the corner of his eye as Eli first grew uncomfortable in his seat, then removed his thick flannel coat. They had made their way to the Sewickley Bridge, and Eli looked out upon the water with wonder. Bridges had always fascinated him, feeling suspended over the water for the minute or so it took to cross a bridge. The sudden change from 25 to 53 degrees affected Eli and he rolled down the window a little bit, feeling the wind across his face as he swooped over the river below. They reached the Sewickley side of the bridge, and Eli looked over at Bob with a joyful, boyish smile that warmed the aging professor's heart.

"It's not far now." Bob said, stopping the car at the first traffic light after the bridge.

Eli continued to hold his face close to the open window, basking in the cool breeze that flowed through it as compared to the biting cold he had grown used to in the past month. They traversed the roads of Sewickley that led to Bob's classical home, Eli finally noticing a difference.

"Where's the snow?" He asked, holding a hand on the dashboard as he looked through both the windshield and passenger side window.

Bob cleared his throat before speaking. "It hasn't snowed over here yet, Eli. Actually, it hasn't snowed anywhere but near where you live. And we've just received our first cold snap of the year. That's why I said you may want to take your coat off."

"Oh." Eli accepted the answer and sat back in his seat, looking at the wonders of a town so different than he was used to that it may as well have been pulled from a storybook.

Sewickley was a much higher class town than the boy was used to, and it showed. The streets and buildings were pristine in their condition, the people that happened to be walking the streets were respectably clothed, and the cars were much nicer than Eli had ever seen. Not a single window was darkened, painted, or broken as they passed through the small business district of Sewickley. Eli was soon lost, since Bob had made several turns after passing through downtown. Next thing he knew the headlights of Bob's car swept across a small family car and a nice sportscar before settling on a big, brown garage door. Bob turned the car off, dousing the headlights as he did so. Hunter sat up in the backseat when the movement of the car ceased.

Bob opened his door, climbing out of the car. Eli followed suit, grabbing the leash he had hooked to Hunter's collar before climbing out and lifting the handle that slid the front seat forward. Hunter jumped out of the car when his young master called, pulling against the leash as he tried to smell the new terrain around him. Eli and Bob shoved their respective doors closed at the same time, creating a dual, snuffed slamming sound that he and Bob could only smile over.

Bob took a few steps toward the house and the light over the garage door flicked to life, illuminating the driveway and causing Hunter to stop his sniffing and perk his ears as he gazed in the direction of the new light. The big dog snapped his head to look at the roadway where movement had caught his eye.

Eli and his host did the same, seeing a tall figure walking toward the house to their left with two smaller figures at its side.

Bob grinned. "Al! Hey buddy, how's Halloween treatin' ya?"

The tall figure entered the light being thrown by the exterior light his neighbor's house, looking in the direction of Bob's voice.

"Hey, Bob! Good, good. The kids are tired already, but trick-or-treating was fun. Huh guys?" The tall, thin man tilted his head downward as he spoke.

"Yeah, Dad." Two childish voices cried back at him.

Al laughed. "Looks like we got all the candy we're gonna get for the night!" He looked at Eli. "What's your Halloween have in store, Bob?"

"Not much. A little research, I think." He smiled wide at the much younger man across the well-kept grass that separated the two driveways, looking at the kids by Al's side. "Oooooh! You guys are scary!" He exclaimed in regards to their costumes.

"Daddy, can we pet the doggy?" A child's cry arose.

During the whole conversation, Hunter had been pulling Eli, inch by inch, toward the strange man and his kids. His nub of a tail wagged at blinding speed and his tongue flopped from the side of his grinning mouth. Bob looked over at Eli struggling with the large dog and smiled. He walked over to Eli, taking the leash from his hand, and looked back at Al's hesitant gaze.

"Yeah, it's okay." He called out to his neighbor.

Al smiled at Bob's comforting look, and let go of his children's hands as they ran across the fine grass toward the 160-pound dog. "Be nice, guys." He called after them as he followed.

Eli stroked the back of his dog's neck to calm him as the two children came rushing towards them. The big dog continued to wag his tail and started to whine in expectation. Christina and Daniel Trenton ran up to the massive dog, touching and petting him as Hunter's large tongue lapped at their hands and faces.

Bob held the leash tight in his hands as he laughed with genuine joy, seeing and hearing the thrill in the children's faces and voices. Al even began to laugh through his hesitant protectiveness of his children against the massive dog. For several moments, all six of them, including the big dog, were caught up in a moment of careless happiness and joy, thinking of nothing or no one else. The Strange did not affect any of them, not then. The moment came to an end, and Al called his children away from the dog amidst their cries of refusal. They obeyed their father anyway, waving and saying 'bye doggie' as they grabbed their father's hands. Al smiled, preparing to say his good-byes as he held his eyes on Eli for a moment.

"I'm sorry." Bob spoke up. "Al, this is Elijah Marshall, a new student of mine. Everybody calls him Eli."

Eli looked up at Bob with wonder and respect.

"Hi, Eli." Al pulled his right hand from Christina's grasp and held it out to the young boy. "I'm Albert Trenton. Everybody calls me Al."

Eli shook the tall, thin man's hand, looking into his bright green or brown eyes, he couldn't tell which. "Nice to meet you, Al."

"These are my kids, Christina and Daniel." Al's eyes squinted and he looked at Eli strangely for a moment. "Don't I know you from somewhere?"

The boy responded in a proper voice. "I'm sorry, but no. I haven't been to this side of the river much."

"Huh." Al voiced with his questioning gaze. He felt the boy's hand pull away from his. "Nice to meet you too, Eli."

Hunter let out a loud bark, and they all looked at him.

Al laughed, leaning over and holding his hand out to the large black dog next to Bob. "Nice to meet you too . . ." He looked up at Eli.

"Hunter." Eli said, knowing the question before it was asked.

"Nice to meet you, Hunter." A wide smile crossed Al's own youthful face as the big dog placed its right paw into his hand.

Hunter let out another loud bark, followed by his usual, grinning pant with his tongue hanging out of his mouth. Al, Eli, and Bob all laughed, thinking that maybe the dog was trying to respond in his own way.

They finally broke company upon the laugh, Al leading his children back to their own driveway and looking over his shoulder as the children snatched up the bags that held their Halloween candy.

"G'night Bob and Eli. And Hunter." He called out cheerfully.

"Night, Al!" Bob called out. "Be sure to say a special goodnight to that hot little wife of yours for me!"

Al tilted his head back in laughter in response before escorting his children into the front door of his beautiful home.

Bob laughed as he looked down at Eli. "Why don't we get Hunter and Bocci introduced?"

Eli smiled wide at the prospect. "Can I hold him?"

Bob smiled back as he handed the leash to the boy. "Of course."

Bob asked Eli to hold Hunter in the garage while he let Bocci out in the yard to do her business. He had been keeping Bocci in the house ever since Al had told him that she was getting out of the yard somehow. Bob poked his head in through the door that led from the garage to the back yard, telling Eli that it was okay to bring Hunter out.

Hunter was tired of sitting, and followed Eli through the door into the brightly-lit back yard with relief. They had no sooner set foot into the grass than Bocci ran up to the much larger dog, stiffening her posture and sniffing.

Hunter stiffened his own posture, standing tall and growling, making both dog owners tense as to how he would react to another dog. Bob looked at the dog questioningly.

"Maybe I should let him off the leash. I think it makes him nervous." Eli said.

Bob looked down at the young boy in the strange light of his back yard spotlights and nodded, holding confidence in the behavior he had seen in Hunter with the children only minutes ago. Eli snapped the leash off of Hunter's collar, allowing him to run free in Bob's fenced in back yard.

Hunter and Bocci came close to each other, looking at and sniffing the other. The large Rottweiler lowered the front part of his body, laying his front legs on the ground while his ass stuck up in the air, panting and growling. Bocci dove in towards him, yipping in his ear and pouncing away again with her tail wagging. Hunter rose from the ground, grabbing a nearby fallen tree leaf in his mouth and running. Bocci chased after, yipping and barking the whole time. When the Labrador finally caught up to the bigger dog, he rolled his massive body onto the ground upside down, letting her nip and paw at his underside. Eli and Bob smiled at the same time, knowing that the dogs were going to get along just fine.

Bob reached in through the garage door, grabbing a couple of balls and other dog toys, and threw them out into the yard. The dogs snatched them from the grass, running off and teasing the other in a game of chase. The professor led Eli into the house through the garage, commenting on how good it was to have another dog around.

Turning on lights as he went, Bob gave the boy a brief, courteous tour his immaculate home before leading him into the study and sitting him down into one of a few plush leather chairs next to the large oak desk in the middle of the room. Eli looked around the wooden room in wonder, never having seen a room with so much wood and so many books. Bob left the room, some kind of light music came on, and then he returned, standing over the oak desk. Eli gazed over the massive expanse of the desk, seeing the many books that lie open upon it.

"Are you comfortable, Eli?" Bob asked, pulling a pair of thin glasses from the surface of the desk.

Eli nodded. "Yeah. I'm okay."

"Good. We have a lot to talk about." He placed the small glasses on his smiling face as he sat down in the large leather chair and scooted it in toward the desk.

Eli looked around the room again, taking in the sight of the finely carved furniture in the room, the small stone statues of animals, the many books, and the large, dark windows. He couldn't believe he had gone this far in his search for the answer to The Strange.

D. A. Rally

*

In Raccoon Township, the trick-or-treating time was coming to an end. Many parents and children had already made their way home due to the unbearably cold weather. Most of the teenage 'Trickers' had gone home as well, either running out of eggs to throw at houses and toilet paper to toss over tree limbs and power lines or just because it was 'too damn cold'. One, lone 'Tricker' made his way home through the dying woods along an unplanned shortcut, finding himself in a deep part of the woods somewhere near the stream. He knew he was near the stream because he could hear it close by.

Bobby Pritchett knew his way through the woods pretty well, since he had spent most of his short fifteen years of life in them. He walked through the woods, laughing to himself about how he and his friends had egged their one teacher, Ms. Donner's house and toilet papered the trees in Vice Principal Gelvis' yard. Once he found the stream, he would be okay, he was certain of that. All he would do was cross it, then follow it on the other side until he reached the Robinson's house, and he knew the shortcuts through the yards from there.

Bobby didn't know exactly where he was in the woods at that point, making his way toward the sound of the stream, unable to see the extent of the death in the trees around him in the light thrown by his small flashlight. He walked close enough to the stream to hear the splashing and gurgling sounds it threw out into the night air, looking at it in the dim moonlight, and waiting to find the right spot to cross. Continuing along what he considered to be the far side of the stream, he shined his flashlight into the water and along the bank, looking for the perfect shallow spot and the perfect piece of wood. The whole while, he thought about the reactions Ms. Donner and Mr. Gelvis would have when they left for work the next morning, and he laughed out loud.

Bobby spotted an area in the stream where it would be perfect to cross. It wasn't shallow, but the rocks within protruded so far out of it that the depth of the water was minimal. He cast his flashlight to his right and saw a ten-foot long, thick tree limb lying on the ground.

"Fuckin' beautiful." Bobby murmured under his breath as he shoved the flashlight in his pocket and used the dim moonlight as his guide, grabbing the tree limb and tossing it across the banks of the stream with a grunt. It landed perfect on the first try, and he smiled at his good luck.

The tree limb spanned the expanse of the water over the protruding rocks, each end supported by the steep, snow covered bank. Bobby lowered his crotch against the tree limb and placed his feet onto the protruding rocks below, scooting his crotch along the tree limb, using his feet upon the rocks as support.

A foot at a time, he completed his passage across the stream, pulling his body from the tree branch. A stinging stench burned in his nose, but he didn't think at all about the crash site or the small shack that also lay upon 'his side' of the stream. Looking down into the stream, he was again amazed at his luck with the protruding rocks and the perfect tree limb. He turned north, away from the direction of the shit plant, in the direction Eli and Anna had gone not too long ago in order to get home. The hard part was over, and Bobby knew that once he began seeing houses, he was just about home.

His heart seized in his chest as a hand plunged out of the darkness and grabbed him around the throat, lifting him off of the ground. The comfort of almost being home left him as he consciously pissed himself, feeling the warm wetness spread outward from his crotch. Warm, but yet cold, breath blew against his cheek as a deep and threatening, yet high pitched and amused, voice whispered in his ear.

"You want to see a real trick, boy? Watch and learn!"

The hand that held his throat pushed against him, throwing Bobby's body up against a dead, twisted tree. His flashlight fell out of his hand, facing in the direction of the tall, dark figure that stood before him in the cold and dying wilderness. Bobby wanted to scream, but he had no breath with which to scream. The tall, flowing figure held a long, clawlike hand in front of it, wiggling a couple of its fingers. A black and dying tree branch wrapped itself around the older boy's left arm. Bobby looked at it in shock, still trying to breathe as the thing in front of him wiggled its claw fingers again. Another tree branch wrapped itself around his right arm, pinning him against the black, dead tree.

The thing in front of him seemed to be clad in some type of cloak that Bobby wanted to believe was a Halloween costume. It tossed its covered head back and held its long arms out to its sides as it laughed with its contradicting tones. "How's that for a trick?" It lowered its arms and moved toward him. Being raised in a family of hunters, he looked at the ground as the thing moved. He saw that it left no footprints in the thick snow, and so Bobby finally regained his voice and screamed.

Horrifically, the thing screamed along with him in mockery, with both of its voices. The sound was terrible, the contrast of a deep, terrifying voice with that of a high pitched, joyful tone. It was only a foot or so in front of him, and Bobby could only watch in horror as the deep, black cloak flowed around the thing, the wide sleeves pulling back from its hands with claw fingers and the hood drooping over its face. It seemed to hiss as it neared him.

"Yes." It spoke in its dual tone. "I think you will do for the first 'taking'. You will do just fine, Bobby." It laughed.

The terrified older boy cringed at the sound of his name spoken by the thing in front of him, trying to turn his head to the side as he screamed a second time, so that he wouldn't have to look at it. The thing grabbed his jaw with its claw hand, turning his head in its direction.

"You will look, and you will see what you are to become a part of!" It said with both voices.

Bobby continued to scream as the thing in front of him cut his throat with a slash of its finger, and it smiled. He couldn't see its face behind the cloak, but he knew that it smiled. Its unseen eyes seemed to bore into his wide, terrified ones as the thick red blood flowed from his neck. His scream was cut short amidst the gurgling of blood from his throat, and the thing grasped his face with both hands as it moved its head inward. The last image Bobby saw as his life left his body was that of the hood falling away from the head of the thing in front of him. He recognized the form of a man, but it had no face that could be seen by his dying eyes.

CHAPTER 11

September 8th, 10:37 p.m.

The old man stood motionless in the bathroom doorway while he looked into the darkness of his small home as the brightness of the bathroom light and the flash of lightning had left his eyes blind. Struggling to make out any shapes in the room, the old man's heart pounded and more sweat poured from his body as the tingle of fear gripped his spine and gut. Another bolt of lightning broke free of the clouds, providing brief light for him to see by and he noticed the man from his dream was nowhere to be found. The only thing that stood out to him was the slight twinkle of light reflected by the shattered glass on the floor and the object resting on his kitchen table.

    With a mind numbed and clouded by sleep, fear, pain, and the image of the man from his dream, the old man felt himself shuffle forward through the darkness as thunder rumbled a little louder in the sky. He moved toward the kitchen table, his eyes fixed on the hazy shape of the object upon it, in spite of the numerous remnants of broken dishes on the floor. Pulling one wooden chair away from the table and sitting down, he stared wide eyed and open mouthed at the gloss black, ornate box in front of him just as he didn't remember doing hours before as he sat on the sofa and it on the coffee table. Not quite touching the box, he placed each hand to one side of the box, knowing that he was fading away from himself. His hands moved toward the box, and a rush of alien feeling surged through his body, just as it had done many times since the box appeared in his home. The old man remembered his helplessness as he had watched his body move on its own, walking through the nearby woods, past the severed remains of many human lives in order to find the box that mesmerized him. He had somehow known that it would be found in the wreckage, not knowing how he knew that or why he even wanted to retrieve it. But he had, feeling the same absence of control he now felt, tossing aside charred wreckage and human body parts in his search.

The old man's body cringed, and he blinked his eyes as he began to have some sense of where he was. Feeling the warm wetness in his crotch as the thunder roared above and lightning flickered outside of the window, he could hear the creaking wood of his poor home as the wind tore and thrashed outside.

The storm was finally here. How long had he been sitting in front of the box, staring at it stupidly? He didn't know. Fear began to take hold of him as the storm gained strength outside, and he wanted to get up from his seat and away from the box. The beautiful box.

A whispering chant came to his ears, or so it seemed. It was more in his head than in his ears. His hands, which had been resting next to the box feeling the energy emanating from it, were pulled toward it. Against all of his inner fear of touching it, he found himself grasping it tight. The old man's body twitched along with the following surges that ran through his body and his mind flashed with blinding, incomprehensible images as he struggled to keep hold of his own being. The first patters of rain sounded upon the roof as his grip upon the box became so tight that the bandages on his lacerated left hand lost hold, and blood flowed from behind them. Watching with wide, terrified eyes, the old man saw his blood run onto the flawless black carvings lining the box and disappear *into it*, as though it was absorbed. The surges became stronger, and his eyes were glued to the carvings in the box as his right hand uncontrollably reached over and tore the bandages away from his bleeding left hand. A feeling of euphoria overcame him and the chanting in his head continued as more blood flowed onto, or *into*, the box. The carvings on the outer shell of the box began to become legible to him in his trance like state, and he began to chant in unison with the whispers in his head in a language he didn't understand. Outside, the thunder and lightning ran rampant and the rain fell hard and heavy.

The old man's worn, wrinkled hands ran over the surface of the beautiful box, the deeps cuts in the first three fingers of his left hand flowing blood all the while, and mystic words escaped his lips as he was about to lose his own soul.

As the unhinged lid of the mystical black box began to open, emitting light a color that he had never seen before, the old man felt a touch of sorrow for the end of his own existence with the minute part of himself that remained. He could *feel* his own life being torn from inside himself along with the intrusion of another. This was it, this was the end. He knew that it would happen someday, but not now and not like this. His human, curious eyes looked into the box as it opened, wanting to know what was inside.

Loud cracks of thunder shook the sky, wild lightning flashed and struck ground, and rain flowed in waves as the old man saw the final images of his own existence.

Memories of his extensive life on earth flashed in his mind concerning his youth, his marriage, all the good years, and all the bad. He saw the fire, smoke, charred wreckage and bleeding limbs of the previous day's plane crash, feeling true sorrow and grief for the first time in many years. It was much like reliving the past, and the death he witnessed in the war. As his existence joined with the other's, he saw the true being of the other and was afraid. Not for anyone, since he cared for no one in the living world anymore, but just afraid that any such thing could ever exist and that it would be a part of him. More so, that *he* would be a part of *it*, as it was consuming him. The power, darkness, hate, and just pure and raw evil he saw chilled the spine that he was barely in possession of at that point. The hateful old man began to scream in terror; a scream that would never be voiced, let alone heard.

He saw, in the fading moments of the life that had been his own, the beginning of the other being. His astonished mind also saw things that he then wished he could tell someone, many answers to many mysteries, but he would never have the chance.

The last thing he saw with his own mind was very simple; the man from his dream emerged into reality. He saw the tall man, wearing the long black cloak overpowering him without even moving. The man's hands remained clasped beneath the overlapping wide openings of the cloak sleeves, and he stood in an upright, formal posture. His voice carried two separate, contradicting tones as he chuckled through his grin. One tone was high and cheerful while the other was deep and demonic. It was the grin that was most terrifying, because it could not be seen beneath the sagging hood of the black cloak he wore since the cloaked man had no face.

Willie Junker saw one last thing as his life on Earth was ripped and raped from his body. The gaze of the man with no face. Somehow, someway, he could see and feel the terrifying deep, dark stare of the entity that was stealing his life; the man with no face . . .

The Faceless Man.

*

"How did you know it was a box I was looking for out there?"

Eli kept his eyes focused on the large desk, only shrugging his shoulders at the aging professor, still not wanting to discuss his visions.

"I never told you that, I'm sure of it. It is actually a black box I'm looking for. The Black Box, as a matter of fact." Bob said, pronouncing 'The' as 'thee'.

The odd boy looked up at the older man. "Do you mean the little computer thing that's on an airplane? Why would you want that? Don't the airplane people need that to figure out what went wrong with the plane?"

Bob shook his head. "No. The name is sort of misleading, but that's not it. The cleanup crew found that in the last few days, anyway. They're trying to decipher it right now, trying to find out what kind of story it has to tell. But I have my own story to tell about a different black box."

Eli looked up at Bob in wonder as the last trick-or-treaters made their way home, bringing the Halloween festivities to an end for that year.

Clearing his throat, Bob began his tale. "I'm a college history professor, and several years ago I came upon a strange artifact while studying in Chicago with a friend of mine. We weren't quite sure what it was, and so we undertook a personal mission of studying it. At first, we couldn't find anything having to do with it, and we almost gave up when the new school year came around. One week before I had to leave Chicago for the year, my friend Jake stumbled upon an old book with a rough drawing of the item we had found. As it turned out, the item we had was only a piece of a larger artifact that had apparently been broken some time ago. That artifact was a small piece of yet another artifact. That was why we had a hard time finding any references to the broken piece we had discovered. We were looking up the wrong information."

Eli leaned forward, listening to his every word.

Professor Mikush continued. "There were many other drawings in the book we had found. One of which was of a box; a small, black box. And the book we were looking at was entirely about witchcraft."

The boy's heart picked up speed as he looked at Bob with wide eyes. "Witchcraft? Isn't that like evil magic?"

"In some cases, yes. Many people that study it would say that it's not, but it *can* be used that way. And this book said that the box was very special and rare indeed. It didn't have a lot of information on the box, only myths and stories handed down by word of mouth. It was only a three-page section of the book, most of which was taken up by the drawings."

"What did the book say?"

"Not much, unfortunately. Only that what was known as The Black Box was historic for its powers of witchcraft. I didn't find out until years later that there was much more to the tale. But I'll get to that later."

Eli was disappointed. The story of The Black Box had captured his imagination in some unexplainable way, and he wanted to hear more.

"I came back here, and put my little project of The Black Box on hold for a while. I had classes to teach, and it would have to wait. I kept thinking about it from time to time, though, and eventually started researching it in my spare time. Jake had been just as interested as I was, and he began researching it from Chicago. We would get in touch every once in a while to exchange notes. For a long time, there was very little to talk about. It took us years to find all the information we could, and it began to seem that we were wasting our time.

"Then, only a couple months ago, Jake called me with unbelievable news. He had found it. He had *actually* found The Black Box." Bob smiled as he spoke. "He had many more connections that I did, and had gotten the word out to many of his friends about the box. Eventually, one of them called him back, telling him that one of *his* connections had found the box. In any case, a great deal of money was paid, and Jake gained possession of the box. He had taken on some new job responsibilities, and had lost his personal interest in the box a long time ago, so he was going to turn it over to me. All my years of research and book reading kind of made me the expert on the subject, so he was going to let me study it."

Eli sat back in his chair, getting a feeling about what the professor was going to tell him.

Bob pulled his eyes away from the boy as he continued his tale. "I was supposed to pick up the box at the airport shipping terminals way back on September 8th, but it didn't quite work out that way. The Black Box was on Flight 427 when it crashed, so it never reached the airport. That's why I was out there searching for it, because I *had* to get it back. I couldn't let anyone else get their hands on it because they don't know what they're dealing with. I had no idea how accurate some of the stories I had read were, and I had doubted the power of the box. Until the plane crash, that is. It was then that I knew that it was all true, and that I had to keep the box away from the public, and in my possession."

A slow chill ran up Eli's spine as he spoke through numb lips. "What do you mean, 'until the plane crash'?" The boy already knew the answer in his fear chilled heart.

The older man scratched his head and looked at his desk for a long time before speaking.

"The Black Box made Flight 427 crash."

Eli's body shook in terror. "What . . . how?"

Bob paid no mind to his questions as remorse filled him. "My own self interests killed two hundred fifty people!" Tears ran down his aging cheeks. "I carelessly asked someone to put that thing on a plane, knowing the stories behind it and not caring because I wanted to study it! I killed those people, Eli! As surely as if I had placed a bomb on that plane, I killed them! And now the box is missing, and I know in my heart that someone has it, someone foolish. You want to know what it is that's causing all this strangeness in your hometown? I can tell you, Eli, that The Black Box is the answer to your question. The Black Box is the power behind The Strange."

The older man used his hands to wipe the tears away from his face as Eli gaped at him in shock, not knowing how to feel. The horror of the plane crash scared him, while finally having a real, tangible answer to his questions about

The Strange thrilled him. He *wasn't* crazy and he finally had a real goal to seek out. The Black Box now became his obsession, as well as Bob's. They were joined in their quests in that instant.

"Let's go check on the dogs." Bob said, rising from his chair behind the desk. "Would you like something to drink? I sure as hell need something."

*

The young and old pair of friends sat on lawn chairs in the back yard, watching as Hunter and Bocci continued to play together. Eli held a large glass of milk in his hand while Bob sipped at a small glass of whiskey he had poured for himself.

"What exactly *is* The Black Box?" The boy asked. "You said something about all the stories you read. What did they say?"

Bob finished swallowing his most recent sip of whiskey, then let out a long breath. "I don't know exactly. None of the many books I've read could say for sure. But it seems to be some sort of source of great evil. Or black, bad magic. Either way, any place it ever was had really bad things happen. Sometimes it was worse than others, much worse. The stories go back several centuries, showing up in some of the earliest writing I could find, which dated back to the medieval times, with kings and queens and knights and that sort of thing. Every time it showed up somewhere, bad things happened and people died. Jake's friend found it out in the deserts of New Mexico, buried in a locked steel chest. I looked it up after he told me that, and found a couple instances about 80 years apart where people in that area had died or fled due to strange occurrences. Electrifying thunderstorms in the middle of the desert, people freezing to death in the middle of the day, others were going crazy and killing people. Nothing I read about those two instances said anything about a little black box. I only linked it together on my own. I found many other times in history that similar things had happened, with no cause or explanation." He took another sip of his whiskey.

"The Black Box has been sought out by students of witchcraft for generations, people wanting to get their hands on it. It had been talked about as a great source of power and magic. Supposedly, the few witches, as they're called, that did gain possession of it had powers beyond belief. The tales about them also said that they changed somehow, the stories weren't real specific. The witches eventually disappeared, and The Black Box along with them. There is still a lot of mystery surrounding it. Through a whole lot of reading and note taking, I've put together a theory of my own."

Eli drank his milk, enjoying the feel of the untainted autumn breeze on his skin.

Black Box

"Way back in those medieval days, there was some wizard working in the courts of a distant kingdom. No one recorded his name, or whether or not his powers were real, but he was able to perform some amazing feats. He had hired a blacksmith to create this box for him, The Black Box. His intentions for it are still unclear to me, but somewhere along the way, he called upon black magic to enchant the box. He committed a human sacrifice in order to complete whatever it was he was trying to do. Something must have gone wrong, because he turned entirely to black magic, seeming to use the box as his source of power. Odd plagues began falling upon the kingdom, and peasants were coming up missing. I assume that he was using them as human sacrifices to whatever lord he served. Members of the king's court began acting strangely before mysteriously disappearing. The king himself seemed to have lost his mind, becoming a savage. He would demand sex from any woman in the kingdom that he desired, including his own daughter and daughter in laws. Anyone that denied him would die horrible, gruesome deaths and he would take what he wanted anyway. During this time, the sorcerer had mysteriously disappeared. The king declared unnecessary war upon neighboring kingdoms, slaughtering entire populations of innocent people."

Eli gaped at Bob, enthralled.

"During the last of these wars, a soldier was making his way home when he found the dead and decaying body of the king. After he reported this to the nobles of the kingdom, it was soon discovered that the sorcerer had slain the king and the many other missing members of the court, assuming their identities. He had learned to use his black magic to morph his body and face into that of anyone he desired. The nobles began meeting in secret, plotting to destroy the wizard before he could destroy them and claim their wives as his love slaves. One foolish noble, that was a mighty warrior, attempted to assassinate the king / sorcerer following one of his mad court meetings. A poor servant witnessed the incident."

Bob read from one of his many notebooks. "The noble snuck up behind the king with his blade drawn, and the king spun around. He raised a single, evil looking hand out in front of him, and the noble was thrown helplessly into a wall. His sword fell to the ground while he was pinned to the wall by nothing but air. The servant looked at the king's face, but it didn't look right. It seemed to kind of change in front of him. The king walked up to the noble, grabbed his face in his hand, and snapped his neck."

Eli flinched at the thought.

"The nobles realized that they were going to need help, and they called upon three men. The three men used might and magic together to free the kingdom." The aging professor stopped in his tale, looking at his watch.

"So, what happened?" Eli asked with great interest.

"I'll get right to the point." He said, looking up from his watch. "First, let's go back to the study."

After refilling their drinks, he led Eli back to his great wooden study. They sat in their respective chairs, and the boy scooted around the edge of the desk to look at some of the books Bob had laid out for him.

"They sought out The Black Box, and enchanted it in another way. They faced the sorcerer, and between the three of them were able to force his entity into the box, using it as a prison. They had a special lock constructed for them, and it was placed on The Black Box, intended to hold him for eternity. This brings me to the mystery of it all, the lock."

Bob slid open one of his desk drawers, and Eli saw that it had a glass cover over it with a key lock. The professor lifted the glass cover, reaching in and pulling out a slender, rectangular box. It had strange carvings on it and a glass facing over it, as well. He held the silver box in his arms while the boy was trying to see what was in it.

"Sometime over the years, the lock was broken, and that was when the plague of death and destruction began falling on those that surrounded the box. The Black Box somehow made its way to the United States. I tried to pinpoint the time period of the breaking of the lock, to see where and when it happened, looking for sunken ships as it made its way across the Atlantic. I looked for unexplained occurrences in either England or America. I've been spending a lot of time trying to find just when and where the lock was broken, and I still have a lot of work to do on that subject. I desperately want to find out, though."

"Why?" Eli asked.

"Well, when the lock was broken, it shattered into separate pieces. One of those pieces was the original artifact I had found that sparked mine and Jake's interest in The Black Box. The other piece or pieces are still missing. If I can find out when and where the lock broke, I may be able to find the other pieces. This, Eli, is a piece of that lock, named somewhere in one of the hundreds of books I've read as The Triad."

A strange feeling filled Eli's body at the word, and he gawked, open mouthed at the glass case as Bob held it up in front of him. About the size of a credit card, it was a V-shaped piece of some form of metal. It was a strange color, appearing silver, then gold, then green, and then blue as the light from Bob's ugly desk lamp moved across it. Mounted in the center of the rectangular silver box and resting on a red, velvet cloth, there was a carving in the thick rounded corner of it. Eli squinted at it as the feeling of power grew and rushed through his body.

"Is that an eye?" He asked.

"Yes, it is. A pretty crude carving, but it is." Bob replied. "Can you see the small, jagged edges where it was broken?" He asked.

Black Box

Eli looked at the upper edges of the 'V', seeing the curves and sharp turns along them. "Yeah, I do." He reached out to touch the glass with his finger, his mind buzzing more and more as his finger got closer.

"It's amazing that there are no chip marks in it from where it broke." Bob said, looking at it as he moved it away from in front of the boy, setting it back into the drawer from which it came. He lowered the glass cover and closed the drawer as Eli's hand fell to the desk and the strange feeling began fleeting from his body.

"There is something else, though." Bob resumed his history lesson. "When the three great men captured the sorcerer, he had tried to assume the identity and power of many different men. His appearance kept changing throughout the battle. At the very end, one of the men used white magic to cease the sorcerer's shifting and changing appearance. It was said to have been used on his face, meant to hold him in one, singular identity."

Something tickled at the back of Eli's mind. "Did it work?"

"That part wasn't very clear, but they were able to imprison the black wizard."

Bob placed a pair of small glasses on his face, perching them on the end of his nose and looking down through them as he shuffled through the many books on his desk. Finally, he pulled a notebook out of the pile, taking another swig of whiskey before going on.

"Some of the strange incidents I researched did speak of a man." He cleared his throat, reading to Eli from his own notes. "This man was always very mysterious, and had sometimes been accused of murder, kidnapping, rape or other vile things. Every record does have something else in common. They all talk about a man that no one could recognize, that looked like people they had known and looked like a stranger at the same time. When asked to describe him, they couldn't. All they could describe was his height, his build, his long, strange hands and his odd voice. They sometimes even spoke of bright, flashing eyes. But they could never describe his face, saying that it was blurred, or moving. In their hysterics, some even claimed that he had no face. A form of a nickname began to arise in conjunction with the plagues that I have linked to The Black Box. In a sense, every time the Black Box surfaced, so did what the people called 'The Faceless Man'."

A squeaking sound pulled Bob's eyes from his notebook, and he threw his glasses onto the desk as he rushed from his chair over to the boy.

Eli's eyes were huge in his reddened face, and his mouth hung open as he held a hand to his chest. Small squeaking sounds escaped his mouth in his attempt to breathe, gripping the arm of his chair with his other hand so tight that his knuckles were white. Bob grabbed him, pulling him from the chair and raising both of the boy's arms over his head. Slowly, rasping air was pulled into Eli's lungs and the older man spoke soothing words, until the boy finished coughing and wheezing with tears of near suffocation on his face.

Eli collapsed into his chair and looked up at Bob with wide, frightened blue eyes, speaking in a small, trembling voice.

"I saw him. I saw The Faceless Man!"

*

Bob sat looking at his young new acquaintance, both of them calm and thoughtful. "I think it's time to hear *your* story, Eli."

After looking at his trembling hands for a moment, Eli raised his fear stricken face to the older man. "I was walking home that day. I was way out in the woods looking for crawfish. You can only find 'em where the stream is kinda deep. I didn't take Hunter with me cuz he scares off the crawfish." He said.

Recalling the day of the plane crash, Eli told Bob about how he had just been walking through the woods the long way, since it was such a nice day. School had just started back for the year, so he didn't have any homework to do and had been walking through a pretty big clearing in the woods, trying to eat an apple. Then the plane fell from the sky, and everything changed after that. He recounted all the related events from the plane crash to the moment Bob swung the pickaxe at him. Eli's voice rose to a higher pitch when he talked about Old Man Junker, and how he fit the description of The Faceless Man. The shame filled boy even told the professor about the merciless beating he had suffered from his mother, leaving out any mention of his visions.

Bob's heart sank as Eli spoke of the beating. The healing sores on his face finally made a twisted sort of sense and he had been uplifted by the boy's defiance of the beatings, and Hunter's rescue. Bob had thought of advising Eli to tell someone about the abuse, but the boy and his amazing dog seemed to have the situation under control. They had other matters to discuss, anyway.

"That's one hell of a dog you have there, Eli." Bob said with a smile, seeing the love and affection the abused boy had for Hunter all over his healing face. "I'm proud that Bocci's playing with a true hero right now."

Eli smiled. "Saved my ass a few times, didn't he?"

They both laughed for a moment, and then Bob moved on to other subjects. "So you say this old man . . ."

"Old Man Junker. Willie Junker." Eli voiced.

"Old Man Junker." Bob repeated. "You say that he's the one that makes you think of The Faceless Man?"

"Yeah. The things you said about his face, and his eyes, and his hands just all seemed to fit. He didn't *look* like some old wizard, but it was just little stuff, y'know?" Eli felt awkward, wondering if it made sense. "I only saw the guy one

Black Box

other time, but it was before the plane crash and we were real far away. I don't know if he looked like that then."

"It's the little things that those people wrote about, Eli." Bob took comfort in the boy's smile, looking over at the notes he had taken while Eli had told his tale. "Old Man Junker lives where?"

"He lives in this dinky little shack out in the woods. It's old and beat up, and it's real close to the stream where it zigzags." Eli fidgeted in his chair. "Do you think it's him? Do you think he has The Black Box and let The Faceless Man out?"

Bob paused in his writing. The thirteen-year-old boy just posed a very interesting question. Always thinking that the breaking of the lock only allowed the box to possess people in some way, he never considered that the black sorcerer actually *was* The Faceless Man, or that he had escaped his prison. Wondering if it made sense, he intended to figure it out.

"I don't know, Eli. But let's just assume that he does have the box." Bob pulled a map of Beaver County from within his stack of books and looked at it for a moment. "How close is the old man's shack to the crash site?"

"Pretty close." The boy responded. "You have to cut through the woods a little bit, but it wouldn't take long to get there."

Eli, in spite of the fear he felt deep inside, was getting excited. His puzzle of The Strange seemed to have some answers after all as he looked over at the map in front of him. It was so large and detailed that Bob had to fold it over to show only the area of Raccoon Township that they discussed. Eli saw the circle drawn in red marker, knowing that it was the crash site, and he poked his finger onto the map, pointing at the bend in the stream.

"Right there! He lives right there." Eli looked at the left edge of the map, seeing the wide markings of black marker over the Ambridge Bridge. The smile faded from his lips.

Bob plucked a red marker off of the top of his desk, circling the area the boy had pinpointed as the old man's home and becoming lost in deep thought.

"Suppose, for a moment, that your Old Man Junker does have The Black Box." He wrote his ideas as he spoke aloud, almost unaware of Eli's presence. "427 flies over his house, with the box on board. Something causes the box to utilize its powers. Or maybe The Faceless Man feels something, sensing that he can use Old Man Junker as a host for his evil soul, if you will. In any case, the box causes the plane to crash, knowing that 250 people would die in the process. Maybe, as it now seems to be clearly shown throughout history, the deaths *help* the box, or The Faceless Man, in its goal. For some reason, Old Man Junker heads out to the crash site, finding The Black Box. He takes it to his little shack in the woods and . . ." Bob trailed off.

Eli looked at him with great expectation. "And what?"

"I don't know." The professor replied, tapping his pen against his cheek as he pondered the question. "I can't even imagine what could possibly happen then. Whatever happens, happens." He said, seeing an odd gleam in Eli's eyes. "All of a sudden, starting the day after the plane crash, strange things start happening in that area."

"The Strange." Eli said.

"Yes, The Strange, as Elijah Marshall calls it." Bob said, smiling toward the boy as he wrote in his notebook. "Excessive heat waves raise temperatures only around the area of the crash. Violent thunderstorms incur large amounts of damage over the following three weeks or so, including burnt and crushed homes and cars, and many injured innocent people."

"Don't forget about the shit plant." Eli chimed in.

"The sewage treatment plant loses power during the first storm, causing great unpleasant smells in Eli's woods, making him feel the need to take a dump all the time." Bob looked at the boy through the corner of his glasses with a sly smile, and he responded with great bouts of laughter.

"During the final night of the storms, the Ambridge Bridge is struck by lightning and turned into a tangled mess." His and Eli's faces both turned serious again.

"Travel across the Ohio River and out of the area is routed ten to twenty miles further out." He continued in a rising voice of discovery, making small markings on the map with his pen.

"The cold spell hits Raccoon Township, killing all plant life and small animals in the area. The mystery goes unsolved until a teenage boy and old college professor somehow cross paths and joins forces." Bob finished.

"And beat the evil demon back into the black prison box." Eli said with a smile.

"Most of this has already been documented." The professor said in the same voice of his dictation. "The questions still remain. What happened with the old man and the box, and how did the professor and the boy happen to join forces?"

"Do you think that's what happened? That the box or The Faceless Man wanted to kill those people and find Old Man Junker?" Eli's smile had left his youthful face.

"I don't know, Eli. It seems like it could be. What do you think?" He looked at the boy with great interest. The nagging feeling he had about the boy was growing inside of him.

"I dunno." He could feel Bob's eyes pressing in on him, and it made him uncomfortable. His eyes dropped to look at his shoes. "What do we do now, if Old Man Junker has The Black Box?"

"I don't know that either." The older man saw the boy's behavior, and drew his gaze away, pulling the glasses from his face and tossing them onto the desk.

Bob rubbed his eyes with the palms of his hands. "I'd much rather just think about what I'm going to have for dinner, but I can't."

Eli only looked at the aging professor, seeing his frustration.

"I'd love to just drive to Old Man Junker's house and ask him to hand over any little black boxes he has in that little shack of his. But if it were that easy, it would have been done ages ago. The Black Box is very powerful. Strange things happen and many people die wherever it happens to show up. Everything I've read has shown me that The Black Box has powers beyond our belief, and that it will continue its reign of death and destruction."

"Didn't you say that there were a lot of years between the stuff that happened? They stopped it, didn't they? The people in the stories you told me about. They stopped it. Or it would still be going on, right?" Eli asked.

"You're very smart, Eli." Bob said in return. "But the problem is that the lock for the box was broken a long time ago. The box and this faceless man keep showing up from time to time, causing havoc and killing people. Yes, the man and the box disappear for a while, but not for good. Who knows why they fade away? Maybe he's tired, or he's killed all the people he needs to, or maybe . . ."

"He hasn't found what he's looking for." Eli finished. His eyes were very far away and his voice was shallow.

Bob continued, unphased. "Very possible. But there is no documentation at all about any kind of confrontation with this man, or any kind of confinement of the box. It just ends."

"Like he's looking for something." Eli said. "The box and the man show up in different places at different times, right? Maybe he just pops out of the box every once in a while when it's in a new place and looks around?"

Bob laughed. "This isn't a damn jack in the box we're talking about, Eli. This thing is evil! It's bad, it's very bad and I have to stop it right now because I brought it here."

Eli looked at his shoes once again. "I know it's not a jack in the box, Bob. I was just kind of wondering if he was looking for the same thing that you are. The lock."

The older man's eyes lit up and he looked at the boy with excitement. "Damn it, Eli! Why didn't I think of that before? It makes sense, it really does! He knows that the only thing he has to fear is the lock, and so he would want to destroy it before anyone figures out what it is or what it does!"

Bob's excitement soon turned to a frown of deep thought as he tapped his pen against the map, looking straight ahead.

"What can we do, Bob?" Eli asked, looking for some sort of direction.

"The lock is broken, the rest of it is still missing, and we still don't know exactly what we're facing. Is it some student of witchcraft using the power of the box? Or is it the ancient sorcerer himself, appearing as The Faceless Man, as you suggested? How do we fight something like that anyway, with only a piece of the lock?"

"What if we took The Black Box?"

Bob sat silent for a moment, considering the boy's question. Just *what if* they took The Black Box? What would happen to whatever it was that Eli linked to The Faceless Man? If Old Man Junker was being empowered by the box, as Bob thought, would he lose his power in the absence of the box? If The Faceless Man was the escaped embodiment of the sorcerer, what would happen if his refuge and source of power was taken from him? The professor pondered these questions, trying to find some sort of immediate solution since he was without the remainder of the lock and realizing that it would take more time and research before he found an answer.

"Eli, how do you know the things you do?"

Bob shocked the boy with his sudden change of subject.

"W—what do you mean?" Eli asked.

"You *know* things, Eli. Things that you have no right knowing. And I want to know why, or how." Bob looked at him with his dark, intelligent eyes.

"What do you mean, Bob?" Eli repeated.

The older man sat back in his chair, exasperated. "When I almost killed you with the pickaxe, you said that you were looking for me. How? Why?"

Eli stuttered, "I—I . . ."

"When you told me your story, you said that you *knew* that you had to leave Hunter outside of your front door the night your mother beat you. You said that you *knew* that you had to follow the stream to the sewage treatment plant for your answer to The Strange." He sat up in his chair, almost interrogating the boy. "You said that you *knew* that you were going to meet me at the crash site. How do you know these things, Eli?" Bob leaned toward the boy with his elbows on his knees.

Becoming frantic, Eli cracked under the pressure the old college professor put on him. "I see it in my visions!" He cried out.

Bob leaned back from the boy, stunned.

Tears began to stream from Eli's eyes. "I saw the bridge get struck by lighting a week before it happened! I saw that my mom was going to kill me when she beat me that night! I saw the shit plant as the source of The Strange, but it was wrong! That same day, I saw that I was gonna find you at the crash site, and that I had to leave Hunter at home or he would've killed you! I saw Anna in her house, getting in trouble for being with me! I saw you looking for the box in the dark! I've seen all kinds of stuff, and I don't want to see it anymore!"

Eli broke down and cried as Bob fell back into his chair, awestruck. He didn't know how to comfort the boy or end his tears. Too many things were spinning in his mind, including the reason he had felt that there was something special about the troubled boy.

"Eli," He said in a calm, soft voice, "I'm sure that it sucks to see things you don't want to. But I can't help but wonder . . ." Bob hesitated, "what did it feel like?" He asked with great interest.

Eli looked up at the older man with tears in his eyes, and anger and resentment on his face. Bob didn't think he was going to respond just as the boy spoke.

"A dream." He said in a sobbing voice. "It kind of feels like a dream, but I'm awake when it happens." Eli regained his composure as he spoke. "Sometimes, it'll just happen while I'm standing there. Other times, I pass out or something. It'll just hit me all of a sudden, I see the vision, and then I wake up on the ground. It's really weird, and pretty scary, but they're always right. They always end up being right."

Bob cleared his throat. "I thought you said that the one about the treatment plant was wrong?"

The wondrous boy let out a nervous laugh. "Yeah, it was. But not really. I figured out that it was trying to show me the crash site, but I didn't want to see it. At all. I forgot about it by then. Weird, huh? So it showed me the next best thing, the shit plant. I went down there with Anna, remember, and she was the one that told me about the crash again, since I forgot. So, in a weird way, the vision was right."

The professor sat in his chair with his hands clasped beneath his chin. "Can you control them? Your visions, I mean."

"No." Eli replied, his tears and fear long forgotten. He had no idea how good it would feel to talk about his visions. "They just hit me whenever they want to. And it hurts most of the time, too. I always seem to fall down when they come, and then I wake up hurting."

"What about the one with your mother? You didn't fall down then." Bob argued.

"No, I didn't." Eli said, looking off into the background of the many books that lined the walls of the study. "But I wasn't really *thinking* about anything that time. It just *happened*."

Bob resented himself for pushing the boy this way, but he was so very curious and he *had* to know. The nagging feeling he'd been having about the boy told him so.

"So, when you were thinking about certain things, you ended up passing out, right?' He asked, and the boy nodded. "But the one time that you weren't really *thinking* about it, the vision showed itself and left you standing. Am I right?"

The boy nodded again.

Bob let out a long breath. "Eli, have you tried to control these visions at all?"

Eli's blank stare was his only answer.

"No? It seems to me that every time you think hard about something, a vision arises. I know that the passing out thing isn't too pleasant, but maybe you could work on it?"

Eli stood up from his chair next to the desk, holding his hands out to his sides. "What? So I can be some fucking psychic on TV? No! I knew I shouldn't have said anything."

The boy turned away, making his way toward the door to the study. Bob rose from his own chair, running after and grabbing him by the arm.

"I believe you Eli!" He pulled at the boy's arm until Eli looked him in the eye. "I believe you. I'm not making fun of you or treating you like some freak. I'm just curious is all." His last sentiment was his first fib. "If I can believe in The Black Box and The Faceless Man, why wouldn't I believe in you?"

Eli looked deep into the professor's eyes, seeing the basic truth that lie within them. While also knowing that the older man hadn't told him everything, the boy allowed Bob to lead him back to his plush chair next to the desk.

"I know that I can't understand your power, Eli, and that's why I'm so curious. But I also wonder why, with a gift like that, you don't try to experiment. Try to see if you can control it . . . Okay. Maybe not control it, but harness it and see if you can make it do some good. Have you tried that?"

"I don't understand."

"Have you *tried* to see things? That's what I'm asking. The visions seem to come to you when you think hard about something, or when it's necessary to preserve your life, with you totally unaware. Have you ever tried to bring on a vision with your own willpower or intentions in mind?"

"I don't know what you mean."

Bob held his hands out in front of him, meaning to silence the both of them. "Okay. Eli, try to relax."

The boy only looked up at him with wide, inquisitive eyes.

"Just relax. Sit back in that chair, and cool out for a while." Bob said in a soft, soothing voice. "Think about a question we asked tonight." He paused for a moment. "Think about The Black Box, where it is now, who has it, and what happened with it. Is The Black Box simply possessing someone with its powers, or is it something more?"

Eli sat in his chair, looking straight ahead of him with his alert, bright blue eyes. His face first took on a bored expression as he stared at the woodcarvings, animal statues, and many books in his line of sight. Bob watched his eyes gain a bit of a flare before they slid to a near close, seeing the skin of the boy's battered face twitch as his body went limp.

Anyone else would have assumed that they boy was asleep, talking to those he saw in his dreams, but the aging professor knew otherwise. He stared at Eli with wonder, watching his body move in his trance and listening to the words the boy was trying to communicate to him. The wondrous boy only mumbled into the space of the large study, and Bob clenched his teeth in disappointment.

Eli's bright blue eyes shot open, scaring the shit out of Bob and causing him to let out a little yell. The boy gripped the arms of his chair tight, looking around himself in fear while Bob stood over him, talking in a soft voice once again.

"Eli. Eli! It's okay, buddy." He relaxed a little when the boy's blue eyes settled on his face. "You're here in my study. You're safe."

Eli continued to sit bolt upright in his chair with his deathgrip on the armrests, and Bob struggled to find words of comfort for the boy. Bocci let out a cheerful yelp outside, and he knew what to say.

"Hunter's here. He's outside playing with my girl dog, Bocci. They're having a lot of fun, too."

Sitting back in the chair and smacking his dry lips as he looked up at Bob with alert eyes, Eli finally spoke in a slow, groggy voice. "I hope she's fixed, by the way. Cuz he isn't."

Bob laughed in delight, happy to hear sensible words from the boy's mouth. "What did you see? Tell me." He stood in front of Eli with his hands on his knees, looking into the boy's face with great expectation. Knowing that it was getting late and that his time with Eli on that Halloween night was growing short, he just had to know for sure.

Eli reached toward the desk, grabbing the glass of milk from on top of it, and poured a large swallow of it down his throat. Breathing heavily, he held the glass in his trembling hand as Bob looked at him with wide eyes. "It was dark, and it smelled bad. Then the shack, I saw the shack. There was glass on the floor or something. He stepped on it and hurt himself. The old man did. The box was there, and he went to it." He crinkled his nose. "He poured blood on it or something. Then it opened and . . . and . . ."

"What?" Bob cried in anticipation.

"He's here." Eli declared in a matter of fact tone, looking the older man in the eye as he was fully aware of himself. "The man in the cloak came out and . . ." He linked the fingers of each hand together to demonstrate. "He joined with Old Man Junker, or something like that. But he's here. It's him, for sure. He's out of his prison." A pair of solitary teardrops fell from Eli's lively eyes. "I saw it."

Bob fell back into his plush, leather chair filled with hopelessness. The mystical boy sitting next to him swore that a black sorcerer from long ago had reincarnated himself in a town only twenty miles from where he sat, bringing plagues upon the town. He was only a college professor, and he had only wanted to study the damn box.

*

Robert Mikush lay in his bed late that Halloween night, staring at the ceiling as he wanted desperately to go to sleep since he had to teach class in the morning, but he couldn't. Too many mysteries floated in his mind.

Having pulled himself from his hopeless daze of self pity and remorse at bringing The Black Box to Southwestern Pennsylvania, he had tried to calm Eli with his words. The boy continued to rant about things he had seen in his vision as Bob led him outside, and Hunter ran up to his master within seconds. While kneeling in the yard and petting his massive dog, Eli turned his beaten but healing face up to Bob, asking if he could go home now.

After stowing Bocci in the house and loading the mysterious boy and his Rottweiler into his car, he drove Eli almost all the way home with no discussion of the box, the man, or The Strange. Both Hunter and his young master had dozed off to sleep as soon as they crossed the Sewickley Bridge, and Bob looked over at the boy, wondering what it must be like to be able to see the past and the future. His intelligent mind wanted to make certain associations between what he had read and what he had seen in Eli, but his rational mind told him that the implications were way too far fetched to be real. But then, The Black Box was too far fetched to be real. And it *was* real.

The older man woke Eli as they neared his house, asking him if he wanted to be dropped off at the same place as before, so his mother wouldn't see. The boy said yes, and he pulled Hunter from the car in a haze of sleep with no great farewell, or words of wisdom. He just wanted to sleep, knowing that he would spend more time with Bob sometime soon.

Before Eli closed the car door and went home to his cool bed, Bob called out to him. "Hey, Eli." The strange boy looked at him with puffy eyes. "Get back into school, kid. It'll make your mom happy, and you're too damn smart not to. Besides, it's the only way to make it these days." He saw the apathetic gaze Eli showed to him, and smiled in return. "Be good, Hunter. You're a good boy, ya know that? Keep taking care of your daddy, okay?" He turned his gaze back to Eli. "G'Night, Eli."

"G'Night, Bob." Eli slurred as he shoved the car door closed, heading in the direction of his house. It was only the next driveway down, but the trees next to him helped hide the headlights of Bob's car.

Hunter was going to get to sleep in his bed that night, Eli thought as he walked along his short driveway only minutes before midnight. If for no other reason, simply because he was too damn tired to take the dog out back and chain him up.

Bob's mind continued to work and spin as he drove himself home, alone. The same thoughts kept him awake in his bed, only a few hours before he had to prepare for another day of college instruction. The tales of old, mixed with the current plague, mixed with what he had seen from the boy all spun together, making his brilliant mind think way too much. He had to stop his own thoughts, knowing that he was being ridiculous. It was just coincidence, that's all. Even if the boy really *had* known things, even if the old stories *were* true, even if—

Robert Mikush dozed off to an uncomfortable sleep of strange dreams and torturing thoughts. Many images swept through his sleeping mind, but none ate at him more than the sound of a name from so long ago. The name of one of three great men.

Euriah, the name cried out to Bob in his sleep. *Euriah, the great Seer.*

CHAPTER 12

The search for the missing Bobby Pritchett didn't last long. His mother became concerned when he didn't come home by midnight on Halloween night, and began calling the parents of the few of his friends that she knew, but to no avail. It seemed that he hadn't been with any of those friends that night. Mary Pritchett sat wide awake in the living room most of the night, looking at the TV as it showed its images, not seeing or paying attention to any of them.

A little after three A.M., Bobby's mother called the Raccoon police Department. They told her that they would keep an open eye for the boy she described to them, but that nothing could be formally done for many more hours. Mary sat in her living room, half frightened and half angry, waiting to hear something about her older son's whereabouts until uneasy sleep overtook her. At ten minutes after nine on the morning of November 1st, Officer Jordan of the Raccoon Police Department knocked on Mary Pritchett's door.

She asked repeatedly just what information the police had as Officer Jordan led her to his squad car. He replied just as he was instructed.

"Ma'am, I just need you to come to Aliquippa Hospital with me. All your questions will be answered once we're there."

Sitting in the passenger seat of the squad car and looking out of the window, Mary was left in a world of emotional confusion. Bobby had at least been found, and she was exhilarated. Since they were going to the hospital, he had obviously been hurt, and that scared and angered her. She was still angry that he had stayed out late and even angrier by the thought that he had gotten himself hurt. She was frightened because Officer Jordan, who had so courteously introduced himself to her when she opened her front door, would not tell her anything about her son. As the police cruiser pulled up to the Emergency Room entrance of Aliquippa Hospital, Mary became frantic with all of her questions, rushing into the hospital with her large purse clenched tight against her chest. Three more police officers rose from their chairs in the waiting room as she entered, screaming questions about her son. Mary didn't notice that all three were from different police departments. One was from Raccoon, one was from Hopewell, and the one with all the shining pins on his collar, that approached her with a look of sorrow in his eyes, was from Aliquippa. He knew who she was as soon as he saw her, and he spoke across the room to her.

"Mrs. Pritchett? I'm Sergeant Lewis of the Aliquippa Police Department. I—"

"Where's my son? I want to see my son! What happened to him? Is he going to be okay? Someone, please tell me about my son!" Mary cried, looking frantically around the room.

Sergeant Lewis placed his large, black, 230-pound body in front of her, forcing her eyes to meet his. He placed his large hand against her upper back, leading her toward the pair of large doors that led to the exam rooms. "Mrs. Pritchett, I hate to be the one to tell you this . . . but Bobby's been in a horrible accident."

Mary raised her hands to her whitening face. "Oh dear! Is he okay? Can I see him?"

Sergeant Lewis led her up to, and through, the large automated doors and into the Emergency Room. They turned right down a drab, depressing corridor, pausing in front of Exam Room #6. The large black man turned to look at Mrs. Pritchett with sympathetic eyes. "He was found near the sewage treatment plant an hour ago. The injuries and the bleeding were just too much for him." He stoned his heart against the reaction he would get from his next statement. "He was dead when the worker found him. We just thought that you might want to see him . . . and we needed a positive identification. I'm sorry."

Mary's face twisted itself into a vision of horror in front of Sergeant Lewis' face, and she burst into hysteric tears as she proceeded to question his words. "What? No! How? Wait! I just saw him last night, and he was just fine before he went out! How could this . . ."

Sergeant Curtis Lewis turned his head as he motioned to a member of the medical staff nearby.

"Oh, God! Bobby, NO!" Mary screamed as the medical staff and the two officers approached her, leading her further into the exam room. She continued to cry in pain and denial as she was led into the small room that contained some medical equipment, an exam table, and a figure shrouded in a plain white cloth. More tears and screams escaped her when she saw the figure under the white cloth, and she tried to push away from the medical staff. The male nurses held her in place, and the police officers moved next to the silhouetted figure looking at her coolly, taking note of each and every word and reaction. Sergeant Curtis Lewis stood next to the covered body, looking directly into Mary's eyes with suspicion and sympathy. He reached his large right hand over to the white sheet and pulled it away from the face of the body, all the way down to its abdomen.

What was left of Bobby's face looked straight upwards toward the ceiling, the torn flesh and gaping wounds glaring horribly in the bright lights of the hospital exam room. His young neck with its developing Adam's Apple hung open in a V shape, revealing the raw, pink and red flesh of the inside of his throat. His throat had been cut halfway through his neck. Dried blood crusted the edges of the gaping wound, hardening into bubbling black scabs. Patches of skin and flesh seemed to have been torn from around his jaw, cheeks, and eyes. The surrounding torn, ragged flesh curled away from the glaring white bone of his skull with dried blood splattered outward across the pale skin of his innocent face. His young, childish eyes were terrifying in their dead gaze toward the lights in the ceiling. The bruises on his upper arms, and his torn shirt, were barely noticed as Mary's head tilted to its left, a brief moment of calm overtaking her. She looked lovingly at her son, his face torn and his throat gaping wide open. She almost smiled at the sight of the face she would have given her life to see only hours ago, even though it was hardly recognizable. The loving look of her face turned to horror and grief, and she lost herself in hysterics as she screamed at the brick walls of the room.

"Bobbyyyyy! Nooooo!"

Sergeant Lewis tossed the white sheet back over the face of the child corpse while the nurses pulled Mary Pritchett away from the dead body of her older son, one holding a needle full of sedative in his hand. Mary was sedated, Sergeant Lewis was satisfied with the ID of the boy corpse, and Bobby's body ended its last exposure to daylight. Ever. The funeral was to be closed casket, and Mary knew it as she sat in a private room with the police officers and members of the medical staff as they questioned her. 'Where was he? What time did he leave? Who was he with? Do you know anyone who would want to hurt him? When was the last time you saw your son alive Mrs. Pritchett?' The questions were asked again and again, and Mary responded slowly with the answers she *did* know. The sedative had taken a strong hold on her, and she was having a hard time making sense of all of it. The only thing her drugged, devastated mind could focus on was the torn, mutilated image of Bobby's face in the hospital exam room's blinding white light. And the stare of his wide, horrified eyes into hers.

*

Eli climbed the two large steps, turned to his left and walked between the pairs of padded, vinyl covered seats with his school books in his hands. He felt the numerous stares of the other children as he searched for his best friend. Anna was sitting by herself next to the window of the school bus with her school bag on the seat next to her. Eli stopped by her seat, looking down at her. He asked if he could sit next to her. Anna continued staring out of the window, refusing to speak or move her bag.

"Anna, please." Eli pleaded.

Anna ignored him and the bus driver hollered at him to sit down. Eli stared at his friend for a moment longer with a look of hurt on his face, and then moved further along the rubber treaded aisle of the school bus to an open seat. He spent the rest of the bus ride either gazing out of the window, growing anxious about his return to school, or staring at the smooth shine of Anna's blonde hair. When the bus arrived at Hopewell Junior High School thirty minutes later, Eli tried to catch up to Anna as the kids exited the bus. There were three other kids between he and Anna in the line that formed in the aisle of the bus, and Eli had to wait until he had climbed down from the last large step before he could approach her. She was walking very fast, and he ran up to her, lightly grabbing her arm.

"Anna, please! I just want to talk to you." He said, trying to catch his breath.

Anna pulled her arm out of his hand. "Just leave me alone Eli."

Eli looked up ahead and saw three of Anna's friends talking with their boyfriends. A couple of them were looking in his direction. He knew that once they got close enough, the guys, who were friends of Jerry's, would keep him away from Anna.

"I know you're dad told you not to see me anymore, and I know you're grounded because of me."

Anna whirled, looking at Eli with surprise and confusion in her light blue eyes. Eli glanced over at her friends, seeing that one of the guys was looking at him. He knew that he had very little time, and he had to get her to listen.

"I'm sorry about that, and I'm sorry that you can't go out with Jerry." He saw the look of confusion grow in her eyes. "I'm mostly sorry that your mom hit you."

Anna's jaw dropped. She hadn't told anyone about that, not even Jerry. "What? H—how do you know?"

Eli continued, seeing that the guy that had been staring at him was starting to walk over to them. "But it's The Strange, Anna. I'm telling you. Don't be mad at your parents, they can't help it."

"Eli, don't feed me your bullshit anymore!" She cried. "You've gotten me into enough trouble already."

"Anna, my vision was right, in a way." He cast his eyes towards Jerry's friend. Twenty yards, he still had time. "I met some professor guy, and we figured out what's causing The Strange! It's Old Man Junker! Maybe not really him but . . ."

Ten yards away. He had to cut it short. "It's there, somewhere. I still need your help, Anna. Please!" He had placed his hands on her arms in his excitement, and she looked up at him with frightened eyes.

"Get the fuck off her, punk!" A voice growled next to them.

A hand was planted in Eli's chest before he could turn his head, and he was falling backwards. His feet slid out from beneath him, and he went sprawling onto the slush-covered pavement in front of the school on his back. His books flew out of his hand and the homework he had worked on so diligently the night before fell into the trampled snow. The back of his head hit the ground hard, and his lengthening hair was saturated with the dirty slush. Laughter of the other children loitering in front of the school or getting off of their respective buses rained down on him. Anna appeared at his side, asking if he was okay and saying that she was sorry. Jerry's friend pulled her away, standing over Eli.

"Just stay away from her, dirt bag, before you get your ass beat." He growled. "If Jerry doesn't pound the shit out of your fucked up face, I will." He took Anna by the arm, leading her away from Eli as he lay there.

Anna looked back at him with mixed emotions on her face. Eli could see, before dropping his head helplessly back into the snow, that she mouthed two silent words to him. "I'm sorry."

Eli pulled his aching, chilled body from the ground, scurrying to gather his books and homework papers, all of which were soaking wet. The passing students had even stepped on some of his papers as they laughed at him lying in the slush. He heard the first bell of the day ring, and he rushed to his homeroom class, his wet books and papers held haphazardly in his arms and a stripe of dirty slush running down his back.

Out of breath as he entered the room, Eli walked up to his homeroom teacher, Mrs. Delray, asking if he could use the restroom for a few minutes. Mrs. Delray commented in a surprised voice that she was glad to see him, and asked why he needed to use the restroom. He showed her a simple smile, saying that he kind of needed to dry off, and turned around to show her his backside.

"Oh my." She cried. "Did you slip and fall in the snow outside?" She asked in her best 'concerned teacher' voice, disguising the bubbling laugh that was building inside of her.

A crooked smile slid onto Eli's face. "Something like that."

"Go ahead. I'll mark you 'present', just make sure that you get to first period on time."

The embarrassed boy smiled in response. Eli spent five minutes in the boy's restroom trying to clean his hair, his back and legs, and his books. He spent the next fifteen minutes trying to dry it all off, pressing the button on the hand dryer repeatedly. He walked in the door of his first period class just as the bell rang. His first period history teacher, Mr. Gratz, greeted him with an embarrassing 'welcome back' as he made his way to his seat. Roll was taken, homework assignments were turned in, a reading assignment was given, and Eli was asked into the hall to speak with his teacher.

Once in the hall, Mr. Gratz asked Eli if everything was okay. Was he doing all right? Was everything okay at home? Was there anything he needed to talk about? Eli liked Mr. Gratz. He was a heavyset, boisterous man, and he was a good guy. Eli told him that everything was okay. The concerned history teacher nodded his head with a pleased smile on his round face, figuring that it was up to the guidance councilors to question Eli about his attendance before he asked about Eli's makeup work.

"You know you've missed a lot of class, Elijah, and I don't know if you'll be able to catch up. You've missed a lot of homework assignments and a couple tests. I'll do what I can to help you make it all up, but I'm no miracle worker. Have you done any studying while you were gone?"

Eli looked up at the heavyset man with a smile on his face and his deep blue eyes blazing. He held up the stack of wrinkled, crusted papers, a few of which had shoe prints on them. "It's all of my homework since the day I left. I'm sorry that they're all wrinkled and dirty, Mr. Gratz, but I fell in the snow and tried to dry them off." Eli saw Mr. Gratz's eyes widen in surprise, and smiled wider. "I had them all in order before I fell, but now they're all mixed up. I put the homework number and page number on each one, so you should be able to figure it out pretty easy. Today's assignment is in there somewhere, I just couldn't find it when you asked us to pass them up. I went ahead and did the next assignment, too. Just to be sure."

Mr. Gratz took the stack of wrinkled papers from Eli's hand, looking at them in wonder. He looked at the thin boy with the reddened face and worn clothing in front of him, shaking his head as a satisfied smile rose to his lips.

"Good job there, Eli. How did you know what the assignments were? We didn't know of anyone that could get them to you."

Eli held his wide smile, thinking to himself that he just *knew*. "A friend told me."

"Huh." Mr. Gratz replied. He knew damn well that Eli had no friends in that class. "You *will* have a couple make up tests to take."

"Can I take them today? I have study hall sixth period."

Mr. Gratz agreed, and Eli took both tests during his sixth period study hall, passing both with a 95% average. Every other class proceeded along the same lines. Eli was greeted with surprise by his teachers, asked to talk outside and shown extreme surprise when he handed in all of his past due homework assignments, even though they were wrinkled and dirty. He made appointments with each of his teachers to make up his exams during his study hall throughout the next six school days, using one study hall for each of his seven classes.

He spent his lunch period eating a sandwich in the Guidance Office and talking with his guidance councilor. Eli refused to talk about why he had missed so many days of school, leaving his councilor with the option of calling his mother. The almost healed wounds on his face aroused some suspicion, but the councilor didn't push too hard. The teachers of the four classes he had attended prior to his lunch period had sent memos to Mrs. Milanko, his guidance councilor, stating that he had turned in all of his work, and that he was on his way to being caught up. She informed Eli that he would have to stay in school and keep up the hard work as he ate his sandwich. The boy had carelessness about him that she didn't understand. He had missed many days of school, had worked very hard to get caught up, had endured some kind of accident or abuse, dare she think it, and only sat in a chair in her office, happily eating his sandwich and drinking his orange juice. Eli didn't have the fearful, kiss ass attitude that any child in his position would normally have. He wasn't sitting up straight in his chair, attentively answering all of her questions in a proper tone of voice, or apologizing for his absence and begging for help and forgiveness. Slouching in his seat and looking at her with those calm, *knowing* blue eyes while going about the business of eating his lunch, nodding his head or tossing a casual response her way every once in a while, Eli was kind of freaking Mrs. Milanko out. He exuded a confidence that was not normal in a boy his age. Or in many grown men she had known in her life, including her well to do, but erectile dysfunctional husband. There was something strange about the shaggy haired boy in the chair in front of her, but Mrs. Milanko knew that many things were strange these days.

Eli spent his time walking through the halls between classes looking for Anna amidst the odd stares and exchanged whispers from the other students. He saw her a couple times early in the day, but she was with her friends and he didn't want to cause her any problems. As far as Jerry's friend's threats, Eli didn't really care, thinking that stuck up pricks like that guy hardly ever followed through on their threats. They usually only said that kind of stuff in front of a bunch of people to look good, that's all. He just wanted to talk to Anna.

Eli finished the school day, having endured the embarrassment brought on by his teachers' greetings, the stares and giggles of other students as he walked by, and the pain of holding his emotions about The Strange deep inside of him. The boy watched as Anna left her friends outside of the school and made her way to the bus, following after and hoping to catch up with her. Jerry appeared next to their bus, and Eli's heart dropped for the first time during that challenging day. The well-built sixteen-year-old pulled Anna close to him and kissed her on the lips, making Eli's body tense. Knowing that he couldn't stand in the middle of the wide sidewalk in front of the school waiting for Anna without looking like a freak, he made his way past the young couple with his head lowered. Eli heard a few words before climbing the large steps onto the bus that would take him home.

"Only two more days. Can you do that for me?" Anna asked.

"Sure thing, Baby." Jerry said with a confident laugh. "I'll give you a ride both ways every single day! As long as I can get some more lovin'." He finished cheerfully.

Eli pulled his eyes from the ground, looking at the three year older boy with burning eyes. Jerry's words and laughter had caused a tickling sensation in the back of the troubled boy's mind. He suddenly knew that the kid was no good for Anna, and that something bad was going happen. A vision was about to show itself to Eli, but he knew that he had to fight it off since he was in the midst of so many other people. Jerry charmed everyone around him with his looks and his words, but Eli sensed and felt the darkness inside of him, getting a stronger sense of that darkness when his eyes met Jerry's over Anna's shoulder as the older boy hugged her. Eli turned away, feeling light headed as he climbed onto the large yellow school bus, falling into the first empty seat he found, hoping that Anna would decide to sit with him on the way home. He watched with dazed eyes as she boarded the bus, walking past him with not even a glance in his direction. He wanted to follow her, to ask her to sit with him and talk to him, but he was still trying to fight off the vision that was pressing in on him and so he couldn't. Instead, Eli only sat in the two person seat by himself, trying so very hard to clear his mind as the bus left the school and made its way into Raccoon Township, which was thirty minutes away.

During the trip home from school, the bus took a different route and Anna's stop came before Eli's. He thought of getting off of the bus with her, but he knew that there was a risk of getting her in more trouble that way. Her mother had obviously been taken by The Strange, so who knew if she was watching for him as Anna got off of the bus? Eli looked up at Anna as she walked past him and down the steps of the bus. He turned and stood, pressing the release buttons and dropping the top part of the window next to him. Pushing his face as far as he could out of the window, he called out to her even as the bus pulled away.

"He's bad, Anna! You have to stay away from him! He's going to do something bad to you!"

Eli watched as her confused face looked back at him, but she soon fell into the distance. The bus was on its way to carrying him to his own home and Eli breathed hard as he closed the window and sat down in his seat, ignoring the odd stares of the other children and the bus driver. He just wanted to go home . . . no . . . he just wanted to be with Hunter. Then he wanted to spend more time with Bob. The thoughts of home made him think of his mother, who had also been taken by The Strange. He didn't want to be there any more than he had to.

He just wanted to have his baby boy by his side and be with the old professor guy that understood him, needed him, and made him feel comfortable and important. But he had promised his mother a talk after all.

After walking home from the bus stop, Eli knew that he would have the talk with his mother since her car was in the driveway. He didn't care if she was drunk or not, he was going to talk to her and get it over with so that he could resume his lessons with Bob. As he walked into the back yard and greeted Hunter, the boy had a feeling that he and Bob were going to be spending a lot of time together. Eli played with his dog for a little while, until he saw the curtain of the dining room window, which faced the back yard, drop closed. Knowing that his mother had been watching, he finished his playtime with Hunter and went into the house.

Virginia Marshall was in the kitchen, and Eli walked in just as she was shoving a folded piece of paper into her back pocket. She turned around with a drink held to her mouth, surprised to see her son.

"Eli! Hi, honey. How's Hunter?" She asked with a false smile on her painted lips.

Eli's brow creased in confusion. He stared at the bandages on his mother's arm where Hunter had bitten her, wondering why the hell she would all of a sudden care about how his dog was doing. "He's fine, mom."

"Good." She replied, sitting down upon one of the chairs around the kitchen table. "Eli, can we talk?"

Having spent much of the last two days waiting for this, ever since he talked to her on Halloween night, he replied. "Sure."

"I know that things have been . . ." her eyes fell away from his for a moment, "difficult lately. But you have to understand, Eli. It's hard to be a single mother these days. I try to do the best I can." Virginia said.

Eli's eyes flashed toward the glass that she held in her hand. Virginia saw this, sliding the glass slightly away from her as she continued, and he noticed the notepad and pen sitting on the table. "I've been working a lot, and the money just doesn't seem to be enough sometimes."

"Last time you talked like this," Eli cut in, "you talked about how much it would help to have some extra money. And you talked about selling Hunter." His gaze grew dark. "Daddy gave me that dog a long time ago, and I think I already told you what'll happen if—"

Virginia let out a small, nervous laugh. "No, no, Eli! That's not what I'm getting at." She took a helpless gulp from her drink. "It's about school, like I mentioned on the phone the other night."

Eli relaxed a little, having expected this conversation the whole time.

"I don't know what you've been up to for the past few weeks, and I'm not going to ask. Okay? But I want you to know that—"

"I went back to school today, mom." Eli spoke proudly.

Virginia blinked her eyes and drew her head back in surprise. "Oh."

Eli continued in a calm, confidence voice. "Yeah. And with all the studying I've been doing, I'm just about caught up. I have a few tests to take, but that's about it. So you don't have to worry about getting in trouble or anything, and the school shouldn't be calling anymore." A sly smile crept onto Eli's face. "Unless they want to know why my face looks like it does."

Virginia drew away from him with a look of fear. "You didn't tell them, did you?"

The boy only smiled for a moment, enjoying the feel of his mother's fear. "No. They didn't really ask, and I didn't really answer." He felt no need to go on about it, but he had another concern. "Where's Matt?"

Virginia cleared her throat before speaking. "He's staying with your grandparents. I've been working so much lately and you haven't been around so there hasn't been anyone to watch after him. I figured that it would be best if he stayed with them for a while. If you can stay in school then maybe we can have him come home, as long as you'll be here to watch after him, of course."

Eli felt the pressure placed on his shoulders, and he didn't like it. His mother was pawning her responsibilities off onto him, and he resented her for it. He only looked at her with his dark gaze.

"But we'll have to wait and see about that." She said.

Feeling that the conversation was over, Eli turned and walked away from his mother, hearing the clinking of ice against glass as she took another swallow of her drink. He closed himself inside of his bedroom, working on his schoolwork while he listened to the radio, hoping that his mother would pass out soon. Hours later, Eli went to the kitchen for something to eat, seeing that his mother had fallen asleep on the sofa in front of the blaring television. After turning down the volume of the TV, he ate a little of the dinner his mother had prepared earlier, knowing her son would eat when he was ready. Eli poured himself a glass of orange juice with one hand while he dialed Bob's home phone number on the telephone with the other. The answering machine picked up, and Eli left a message stating that he wanted to meet with him tomorrow, wanted Bob to pick him up at school, and would call him sometime during the day. He ventured back to his room with his glass of orange juice in his hand, closing the door behind him. His schoolbooks lay open on his cheap wooden desk as Eli sat on his bed, drinking his juice and thinking.

His return to school had been successful, knowing that deep inside of himself he was tortured and screaming even though he had appeared responsible and determined on the outside. Eli had done a fine job of acting, showing his teachers what they needed to see as he kept his emotional and mental hell to himself. The other kids that had gawked and laughed at him, he didn't care about anymore. The quest into The Strange had freed him of that torture. He realized that he was seeing things much greater than those other kids would ever see, and that his purpose and his quest rose far above their concerns about coolness, good looks, nice clothes, or popularity.

Eli thought of Anna and her actions towards him, and didn't blame her, really. Her parents had instructed her to stay away from him, and he knew it since he had seen it in his visions. She was only trying to stay out of trouble, that's all. The nagging feeling about Jerry continued, but the vision that had pushed in on his mind earlier had long since faded, leaving Eli wondering why he had such a bad feeling about the guy. Was it really something that his visions could show him, or was it just raw jealousy? He didn't like the latter idea, and so he finished his juice, doused the light next to his bed, and crawled into his bed, hoping for sleep. His hopes didn't have to last for too long. Images of Bob's study and the welcome and comfort he had felt there came to him. Eli smiled as he dozed off to sleep, seeing Hunter and Bocci running and playing in the broad daylight of Bob's back yard.

*

Eli sat in a lawn chair with a wide smile on his face, watching his baby boy play rough with Bocci in Bob's back yard, and enjoying the feel of the cool air that early November afternoon. Hunter ran up to him with a stick in his mouth, and Eli took it from him. He stood up from his chair, and the massive black dog sat down in front of him, watching the stick closely. Bocci ran up and sat next to the big dog, also watching the stick. Eli cocked his arm back and swung it forward, continuing to hold on to the stick. Hunter jumped up and ran out into the yard, looking for the stick while Bocci followed, until he stopped in the middle of the yard and looked back at Eli with his ears perked. The boy held the stick out in front of him and laughed. Hunter ran towards him, and the cheerful thirteen year old boy took off running through the yard with both dogs chasing after him. Eli laughed hard as Hunter ran next to him, jumping up and snapping his jaws at the stick while Bocci nipped at the Rottweiler's flopping ears. The boy ran hard and fast around the yard while the two dogs followed, panting, growling, and nipping. He stopped and finally threw the stick out into the yard, but Hunter either didn't see it or didn't care, because he jumped up on Eli, knocking him to the ground. He nipped at Eli's shirt and closed his mouth playfully around his hands and fingers, stopping to lick his master's face every once in a while. Tears of joy began to stream from Eli's eyes and he screeched with boyish laughter as Bocci followed Hunter's lead, licking and nipping at him as she played with the big dog at the same time. Eli wrapped his arms around his dog, rolling his body on top of Hunter's and pinching at his face, belly and legs while the submissive Rottweiler licked at his hands and batted at him with his paws. The boys wrestled and the female Lab jumped in and out, grabbing at either of them each time. Eli turned to Bocci, grabbing her and pulling her to the ground, wrestling with her. Hunter rose to his feet, assuming Bocci's role by jumping on the pile. Eli rolled around in the grass and dead leaves, wrestling with both dogs at the same time while tears ran down his face and his stomach began to hurt from laughing so much.

Bob, who had been watching through the kitchen window as he cooked dinner for both of the humans, emerged from the house with a blue rubber ball in his hand and a wide smile of adoration on his narrow, fine featured face. His own children had been taken from him in the divorce and he had never had the chance to enjoy watching them grow up since his ex-wife had moved to California shortly after the court proceedings. That was where the lover she had met during her extensive business trips lived. His own children were strangers to him, calling only occasionally. Usually on holidays or a few days after his birthday with some excuse covering up the fact that they forgot. He had been to his son's wedding, but his daughter had somehow left him off of the invitation list to hers. She had said later that her mother had told her how busy he was with his work and that he probably wouldn't have been able to make it anyway. That was Elaine, all right. She had broken his ties with his children, making him almost nonexistent in their lives.

Bob watched Eli's playfulness and listened to his boyish laughter, not with regret, but with heart swelling joy. He hadn't known the boy for very long, but he knew that he was getting close to him and he could feel the same from Eli. It made sense, in a strange way. Bob's children had been taken away from him, and Eli's father had disappeared years ago. The orphan father and orphan son had found each other, it seemed, under the strangest of circumstances. But then, everything was a little Strange lately.

"Hey, you mutts!" Bob called out into the yard. "Fetch!"

Both dogs looked in his direction at the sound of his voice and took off running after the blue rubber ball he threw across the yard, leaving Eli laying on the ground covered with dead leaves and doggy slobber. Bocci reached the ball first, picking it up and running with it while Hunter chased after her. Eli pulled his thin body from the ground, brushing the leaves off of him as his laughter faded into the cheerful, innocent smile he flashed at his new, older friend

"Heads up!" Bob called out.

Eli saw the spiraling football only moments before it hit him hard in the chest, reaching his hands out and holding it close to his body.

"Nice catch!" Bob said, walking in his direction. He held his hands open in front of him, signaling for Eli to throw the ball back to him.

The thin boy looked down at the hard brown ball in his hands, trying to remember the last time he had thrown a football and thinking that it had been at least a year since his last neighborhood football game. He had played quarterback many times, not because he assumed the leadership role, but because the other guys on his team wanted him to. The smile on Eli's face grew smaller as he grasped the ball in his right hand and drew it back to his shoulder. His arm snapped forward and he saw the smile on Bob's face fade as he stopped in his advance. The football struck him in the chest, causing his upper body to jerk backwards as he cradled the ball with both hands. Wide eyes gazed out of the professor's stunned face.

"Goddam, kid! You've got one *hell* of an arm!" He said, tossing the ball lightly back to Eli, who moved a couple steps to his left, catching the ball softly in his hands. "Do you play football?"

"For school? No." Eli said, coming to a halt. "Slant left." He said, pointing off to his left with his finger. Bob trotted off to the boy's left and away from him. Eli watched for a moment, then snapped his arm again. The ball appeared in Bob's arms quickly as he ran to the left, noting that the boy had gauged his speed and direction with quickness and precision.

"Do that again." Bob said, throwing the ball back to Eli.

Eli did it again, but to his right that time. Then he did it again, and again. Each time, the ball appeared faster in Bob's arms as the boy's intensity and accuracy grew with each throw. Bob kept testing him with different maneuvers, and the kid hit the mark every time, until the older man finally waved Eli over to him while he tried to catch his breath.

"I'm too old for this shit!" Bob said breathlessly. "I need to sit down."

They walked over to the lawn chairs and both dogs followed. Hunter and Bocci had been playing and chasing the professor the whole time, and their tongues wagged wide from their mouths. Bob flipped the ball over to Eli, looking at the boy with a smile. "Y'know, sports can do a lot for a kid your age. You're smart, Eli, very smart. Sports could help keep you interested in your school, as well as allow you to keep away from your not so pleasant home life." He saw the boy's downtrodden gaze at the football in his hands. "I know that you don't want to be there, Eli, and I don't really blame you. Not to put your mother down or anything, because I know that deep down you love her, but she's not guiding you in the right direction. She probably doesn't even know how smart you really are."

"Stop it. I'm not that smart." Eli muttered.

Bob laughed. "Oh yes, you are! What you told me on the way over here, about doing all the homework you missed in one day and getting A's on the tests from two of your classes so far . . . you are extremely intelligent, Eli." The aging professor finally caught his breath and placed his elbows on his knees as he sat in his lawn chair, looking at Eli.

"Why don't you go out for football? With an arm like that? Shit! You'd be a freshman starter for the Varsity team next year! You'd be the star of the triple A division, and probably the state!" Excitement filled Bob's voice.

"Yeah, whatever." Eli continued to stare at the ball in his hands.

"Eli, I used to play quarterback in high school so I can tell you from experience, you'd go very far."

Eli looked up at the older man with questioning eyes. "But I'm too small. Look at me! I'd get crushed!"

"Look at me!" Bob laughed again. "I was no bigger than you back then, but I did it! And I was good, too. We almost won the championship game my senior year, but our running back got hurt in the third quarter. We had to substitute some freshman kid that couldn't hold on to the damn ball, let alone run or block worth a shit, and I couldn't do it all. I had driven the team down the field three times after he came into the game, ready to score. He fumbled the ball all three times, and we lost the game. So, instead of getting a football scholarship to a big name college, I had to rely on an academic scholarship and that changed my life. I still made the football team, but I sat on the bench as the third string quarterback for four years and I ended up teaching instead. I don't regret it, but I sometimes wonder what would have happened if we had won that championship game. I would most likely have been the starting quarterback for a big name college, and worked my way into the NFL. My life would be entirely different right now, but I'm not sorry about it."

The sky above was growing dark, but Bob still saw the look of interest on Eli's face. "What I'm saying, Eli, is that I tried. And while I tried, my focus on school was unbelievable and it provided me with another way into college. I grew up almost like you are, in a family that had no history of education or the money to provide one for me. I had to do it on my own. I may not be a millionaire in the NFL and I may not be living the dream life with a wife and kids, but I think I've done pretty well for myself, and I'm happy.

"There is no reason for you not to try out for football. You *could* stand to put on a few pounds, but with good meals and some weight training, you'll fill out like your boy there in no time." He said, pointing at Hunter. "And you're *not* going to get crushed. No defenseman is even going to get close to you. Your release is too quick." Bob saw Eli cast his eyes down at the football again.

"I went to a Pitt Panthers game a long time ago, and I watched Dan Marino pass for them. Eli, your release is *already* just as quick as his, and you've had no training! If you work on it and build more strength in that arm . . ." He tossed his hands in the air as he smiled, "who knows where you could end up?"

"Anna told me I should be a quarterback . . . or something." Eli mumbled. He stared at the football in his hands for a while, his mind turning to scenes of football greatness. He suddenly turned back to reality, and looked over at Bob sharply. "I can't think about that! I have to stop The Strange! I have to find The Black Box and end this shit before I can even dream about high school, or high school football!"

Bob nodded his head. "I know, Eli. I just want you to think about it. I promise that I will help you and teach you as much as I can along the way."

Eli's silence was enough agreement for him, and Bob suggested that they go inside and eat some dinner. They ventured into the kitchen, allowing the exhausted dogs into the house. The men, young and old, ate the meal that Bob had prepared, then went into the study after Bob turned his stereo to his classical music channel. They discussed the mysterious death of Bobby Pritchett three nights before, and the fact that his body had been found near the sewage treatment plant. No details had been released to the press, and they were left guessing.

"The plant isn't that far from Old Man Junker's shack, like I showed you." Eli said. "Do you think he did it? Y'know, The Faceless Man?"

Bob rubbed his chin with his hand as he looked down at the map on his desk through his small glasses. "Could be. It *is* awful close, isn't it?" He paused for a moment, then looked at Eli. "Have you tried to . . . see it?"

Eli sensed Bob's apprehension toward the subject of his visions, and he smiled in response. "Yes, after I heard about it at school today. I went to the bathroom and sat in one of the stalls, just in case I freaked out. But I can't see anything. I don't know why, but I can't."

"I would think that we'll just have to guess that it *is* him." Bob looked back down at his map. He used another marker to mark the spot of Bobby Pritchett's untimely demise. "That would mean that he's made his first kill. That would make me think that there are more deaths to follow." He looked at Eli seriously.

"Yeah." Eli said, looking away for a moment, then back to Bob with bright eyes. "What do your books say about this? Do they give any hints on what order this stuff happens in?"

"Nothing specific." Bob replied. "The Strange, as you perfectly named it, starts happening, people start acting weird, the deaths begin and keep adding up, and then he disappears. It's all pretty much the same."

"How bad is it going to get? I mean, if it took two months for The Faceless Man to kill someone, what does that mean? That this just started?" Eli asked.

Bob thought for a moment. "So, what you're hinting at is that The Strange is only due to The Black Box itself, am I right?" The professor watched Eli's nod of agreement. "For someone to be murdered, The Faceless Man must be free. If the storms, the damage, and the weather were just caused by the box itself, then what's going to happen now that The Faceless Man is on the loose?"

Eli's face lit up with acknowledgement. "Yeah! That's it! If it was that bad before, what's gonna happen now?"

"I don't know, Eli." Bob said as he became lost in deep thought, trying to decipher the message of all the old, obscure tales about the box and the man, hoping to find some kind of answer. "I really don't know."

"Does it give him power?"

The older man only looked at the boy with a curious stare.

"Killing someone. Does it give him power?" Eli repeated. "If the box killed the people on the plane so that his power could grow, does every person he kills give him power after that?"

Bob realized that it was the thirteen-year-old boy's imagination that shed so much light on the subject. Most intelligent adults would never consider such things, but Eli was smack in the middle of his imaginative years, and he didn't only consider the subject, he thought of things that actually made sense. Unfortunately, Bob couldn't confirm or deny his ideas.

"I still don't know, Eli." Bob said, frustrated. "Even if we knew, what good would it do us? Old Man Junker may or may not have the box. Old Man Junker may or may not be possessed by, or actually *be*, The Faceless Man. The Faceless Man may or may not be the embodiment of the ancient wizard. The truth is, we don't know. Even if we did, what can we do about it? We have a small piece of an ancient lock that might hold the box closed forever. Where is the rest of it? How do we get him back into the box? It took three very powerful men many centuries ago to do that. What makes us think that *we* can do that? We can talk about what makes him powerful all we want, buddy, but the truth is that we're facing something beyond our imagination, and we have no clue how to stop it." Bob breathed heavily as he finished his small speech.

Eli spoke in a soft, yet cheerful voice. "Beyond whose imagination?" He saw the smile rise on Bob's face. "I can imagine a lot. And I have to figure something out." His tone grew dreary. "I can't live with my mother the way she is, and I have to stop it. I can't watch Anna suffer because of her strange parents or her strange boyfriend. I can't stand ANY MORE OF THIS SHIT!" Eli hollered from his seat as tears arose in his eyes. "Something inside of me is telling me to stop this, and I have to. I don't want this thing inside of me, and I wish I could just go on without it. I don't want the visions either, but they're there. I just want it all to stop!" Eli buried his tear filled face in his hands.

Bob felt sorrow for the boy, and wanted to comfort him. He didn't, however, feeling the need to cast light on a few points of interest.

"Eli, I'm sorry that you have to deal with all of this. Even as I read about the box, I never really thought that any of it was true. I thought that it was all just made up tales and folk stories. I was curious about the box, but I never really believed in its power or the stories behind it. I hope you believe me." Bob saw the boy nod his head. "I'm still just trying to get a hold on the fact that all of this is *really* happening. I may have been a football hero almost thirty years ago, but I'm no hero now. I am an old man, and I can't see these things with the same hope and optimism as you do. So I'm having a hard time coming up with a realistic solution. I *am* slowly realizing that all of this is real, and that something needs to be done. And in that case, you and I seem to be the most knowledgeable on the subject, so we should be the ones to come up with the answer. Unfortunately, the answer isn't screaming out to us, and we have to think and search to find it. We will, though, I promise you that." The aging professor placed a comforting hand upon Eli's shoulder. "For no other reason than to set us both free, okay?"

The tearful boy nodded, and Bob smiled. He knew that they hadn't accomplished much in their meeting that night as far as The Black Box was concerned, but he took confidence in the bond that was forming between them. The discussion faded away, and Eli soon agreed to go home as the hour stuck nine o'clock p.m. Bob drove Eli and his exhausted dog in the direction of the Sewickley Bridge, knowing that he and Eli would most likely spend every afternoon together from that point on. Aside from The Strange, Eli needed help in other ways, and Bob wanted to provide it for him. As the late model Toyota wove its way through the streets of Sewickley, Eli gazed out of the passenger side window with tired eyes while Bob's mind turned in thoughts of molding the boy into everything he could have been, but never was or will be. He didn't want to be that way, but Eli had showed him so many parallels to his own youth, including his intelligence, that he felt that he had to take hold of it and correct his own mistakes in the form of Eli's future. Besides, the kid's throwing arm was ten times better than his had ever been.

Bob directed his car toward the bridge until Hunter suddenly awoke in the back seat, standing up and howling in his ear. Eli whirled around from his daze, hollering at the large black dog. Bob slowed the car, wondering if Hunter was going to be okay, or if he needed to go outside and throw up or something. The massive dog howled harder and louder, hitting his nose against the headliner of the car as his throat became raw in its howl. The car began to vibrate, and Eli switched his gaze from his dog to the older man, wondering what was happening. Bob, thinking that something might be wrong with one of his tires or the suspension or something, steered toward the side of the road leading to the Sewickley Bridge. He could see the bright, clean bridge in front of him under the high-powered mercury lights pasted along its path across the river. He brought the car to a complete halt, and the rumbling not only continued, but it also intensified as the car shook so vibrantly that the flesh on his cheeks moved, and Hunter began growling and snapping at the air around him. Eli yelled absently at his raving dog while his eyes scanned the street and buildings around the car.

The vibration in the car increased, and Eli saw the buildings around him *move*. They seemed to shake and shimmy in the moonlit darkness, and he grabbed onto the door handle of the car for support, which was no support since the car was shaking. He paid particular attention to the windows of the surrounding buildings, for some reason, watching as they vibrated so hard that there seemed to be waves running through the glass. As he watched with wondering, childish eyes, the shuddering windows that Eli had been looking at exploded outwards, and the car slid back and forth and side to side.

"Bob, what's happening!?" Eli shrieked amidst Hunter's raw howls behind him.

Bob's voice stuttered as he spoke due to the tremors. "I don't know! Just hold on!"

They both watched as bricks fell from atop the buildings next to them, shattering against the concrete sidewalks. Bob's gaze was fixed forward, and Eli followed it. For the remainder of his time upon the Earth, Eli would never forget what he saw in the next seconds.

The Sewickley Bridge was visibly shaking in all directions. A few random blocks of stone fell from the upper arches, either crashing against the asphalt of the road the bridge supported or falling into the darkness of the river below. The bridge seemed to lift itself above the immediate horizon, breaking and snapping the steel joints that held it to the roadway in front of them in a flurry of metal and concrete. The whole bridge shook, causing large chunks of asphalt to fall away from its roadway into the river, leaving large gaps of darkness inside the usual gray roadway. The large steel rivets in the upper supports popped due to the stress. The thick, coiled support cables snapped into a wild frenzy as the weight of the construction fell upon them since the riverbed supports had already begun to crumble into the river in pieces. Eli had never seen it, but it looked as though a planned implosion of a building was taking place. The solid steel 'I' beams that framed the roadway twisted and severed along their bolts and welds, providing no support for the bridge. All at once, the entire bridge simply collapsed into the river. The crumbling roadway drifted slowly beyond the edge of the sharp riverbank into the river, while the steel supports plunged rapidly into the darkness below, throwing up an immense wave of black, watery foam and pulling the severed cables along with them.

"Oh my God!" escaped Bob's mouth while "Holy shit!" arose from Eli's.

Staring in open-mouthed amazement at the disappearance of the bridge they were about to cross, as Hunter howled and the ground below them continued to shake, Bob reached for the gearshift of his car with a shaking hand. He had just thrown the transmission into reverse when the tremors stopped and held his foot on the brake while he looked at Eli, who only shrugged his shoulders with a look of fright on his face. Hunter stopped howling and started pacing the small back seat and whining. Bob pushed the gearshift into park, placing his hands on the steering wheel.

"What the fuck just happened?" He cried out.

Eli couldn't reply. He had been so stunned by what he had just seen that he couldn't even think, let alone talk. Blinking his eyes slowly and taking in the image of the gaping hole in front of them, where the Sewickley Bridge was only a minute ago, the boy absently wondered how he was going to get home.

Thinking briefly of his ex-wife in California, Bob attempted to answer his own question. "Earthquake? Was that a fucking earthquake? In Pittsburgh? You have got to be shitting me!!" He screamed into the confines of the car.

Bob pressed a button on his car stereo and turned up the volume. The normal news chatter continued on the AM station he selected until a long series of beeps sounded through his car speakers. A muffled voice announced that 'this is NOT a warning', then a news announcer spoke clearly through his radio. The voice stated that there had apparently been an earthquake in Beaver County only moments ago, and that the shockwaves had stretched far into the surrounding areas.

"No shit!" Bob cried out.

The announcer continued to say that those were only reports and that nothing had been confirmed. He also stated that if it were indeed an earthquake, no measurement would be possible since there were no Richter Scales in the area. Earthquake activity had NEVER been reported in the region, and there were no fault lines anywhere near the Beaver County area. The newscaster broadcast the phone call of a Beaver County listener, who declared on the air that the Monaca Bridge had been destroyed in the 'quake and that he had seen it with his own eyes from his living room window.

Bob looked over at Eli with a trembling, frightened face while Hunter moved restlessly in the back seat. "He's cutting you off. First he struck down the Ambridge Bridge. Now he's shattered both the Sewickley and Monaca Bridges. He's trying to keep the area all to himself."

Eli only stared back at Bob with his frightened gaze as the older man turned the car around and chose an alternate route. Twisting and turning along back roads that Eli had never seen before, Bob tried to laugh it off.

"Looks like we're gonna have to take the long way home, huh?" He looked over at Eli with a false smile planted on his face. The boy stared at him with his wide blue eyes and Bob's facade fell away, terror showing on his face.

"There's your answer, kid. THIS is what happens now, I guess." Bob grew angry and smacked a hand off of the steering wheel. "He kills one poor, innocent boy and this is what happens next!" Tears ran down his face.

Eli turned to look out of his window, not wanting to see Bob cry. Even though he understood why, he just didn't want to see it. Watching the unfamiliar landscape sweep past his window as Bob found some other route to take him home, Eli knew that with all three bridges gone, what used to be a forty five minute drive from Bob's house to his would take much, much longer.

As his traumatized eyes glared into the darkness outside of his window, Eli wondered if he was going to see Bob much anymore, or if the professor was going to be able to tell him all there was to know about The Black Box. He wondered if he and Bob would ever sit in the comfort of the older man's wooden study and search for a solution to the problem of ending The Strange. Even though he had pretended to not be interested, he wondered if Bob would be able to teach him all that he knew about playing football and being a good quarterback.

Eli felt a touch on his left shoulder, and he mindlessly reached his left hand towards it. The unbelievable image of the collapsing bridge flashed before his eyes, bringing tears to his young, healing cheeks. He brushed carefully at the tears with his right hand while he caressed Hunter's large, soft head and face that rested on his shoulder as he stared into the passing darkness outside of his window.

CHAPTER 13

The unexplainable earthquake left much of Beaver County distraught due to the damage, as travel into and out of the area was almost impossible. Most of Hopewell and Aliquippa had remained intact, and as the scientists and seismologists examined the area, it was estimated that the massive earthquake had actually been *five* earthquakes. One had occurred in Raccoon, two seemed to originate precisely at the locations of the Sewickley and Monaca bridges, and the remaining two centered themselves around the major roadways leading into Raccoon Township from the west. The aftershocks had caused quite a bit of damage, but nothing quite as severe as what had happened to the bridges. Foundations of homes and buildings had shifted, trees had fallen, some smaller roadways were left with gaping cracks in their paths, and several water and gas lines had ruptured. The western roadways, however, had split wide open in twenty foot gaps and those aftershocks had caused other, more desolate roads to crack, separate, and bubble up from the earth, making passage through the area by roadway impossible.

The biggest problem was State Route 60, which passed near Raccoon on its way to Pittsburgh from the north. The Raccoon earthquake's epicenter was located about a mile away from the sewage treatment plant, directly in the path of the raised highway, leaving behind an eighty-foot gap of missing asphalt where the highway used to pass over the four-lane road that led from Hopewell to Raccoon. The highway, along with the concrete pillars that had supported it, lay crumbled and shattered along the roadway below. The ramps leading from the highway to the road below had been left cracked and warped by the aftershock, leaving them also impassable.

Passage into Raccoon from Route 60 was impossible. Entrance from the rural townships near Raccoon was not possible by public roadway. Travel from the other side of the Ohio River was difficult and lengthy since the closest bridge was twenty miles away from the former location of the Ambridge Bridge.

Raccoon Township had been neatly severed from any type of intrusion from the rest of the world. Unless someone happened to link all of the narrow, worn rural roads, that wound throughout the township, together.

*

Bob and Eli had woven their way to Eli's home the night of November 3rd, crossing the Rochester Bridge with wariness in the wake of the earthquake. The trip took an extra thirty minutes, and neither had spoken very much during the ride. Bob dropped Eli off at the usual spot, behind the bushes just before his driveway, with a feeling of dread and sorrow shared between them. He could sense the apprehension in Eli's voice as the boy asked if he would see Bob tomorrow, and he took joy in the relief he saw on Eli's face when he told him that he would. Eli would not only see Bob the next day, but he would see him nearly every day in the following weeks.

The aging professor continued picking Eli up from school, or meeting him at his house in the late afternoon, and toting the boy and his dog to his house in Sewickley in spite of the lengthy drive. The dogs would play in the yard, stopping to chase their masters as they ran about the yard with a football in their hands. Bob coached Eli on the finer points of playing quarterback, going so far as to write out a meal and weight training schedule for the thin thirteen year old. The forgotten former quarterback drew diagrams of offensive and defensive schemes, explaining and describing each one to Eli before telling him how to manipulate each one to his advantage. He pushed Eli's throwing arm to all extremes, watching it improve as the days went by. They would always end up in Bob's study after the sun went down and the spotlights in the back yard couldn't quite combat the cold as well as they did the dark. The conversation would turn towards The Strange, The Black Box, and The Faceless Man as they struggled to come up with some sort of solution. Bob was sure to impress upon the boy the importance of knowing his five P's. The odd pair of companions would analyze all news pertaining to Raccoon Township, looking for any significance to The Strange, and they would rehash the information and abstract ideas they had already come up with. They were gaining no ground, and more deaths were being reported in Eli's neck of the woods while the cold chill and the gloomy sky deepened in Raccoon Township.

On a night that they would later look back on with sorrow, Bob and Eli had just finished their most recent discussion about Eli's visions. The disturbed boy explained that he hadn't had a vision since he had fought off the one about Jerry; at least what he *thought* was going to be about Jerry, on the school bus. He added that he also hadn't seen Anna at all outside of school.

"I'd like to meet, Anna. She seems like a really special lady." Bob said.

Eli looked up from his hands with a smile on his face and a sparkle in his deep blue eyes. "She is! I think you'd really like her. She's really smart and funny, and she's always really happy. She always makes me feel better when she's around."

Bob smiled at the obvious affection in the boy's face. "You like her a lot, don't you?"

"Well, yeah." Eli said, pulling his hands away from the arms of his chair. "She *is* my best friend."

Bob nodded his head. "Yes, she is. But I think you like her in a different way."

Eli's smile froze on his face, and he lowered his eyes to look at his hands again. He sat, silent, while the older man felt joyous laughter rise inside of him. Bob fought it off, though, not wanting the boy to think that he was laughing at his feelings for Anna.

"It's okay, Eli. It happens all the time. When a man and a woman are very close friends, it's common for those feelings of friendship to turn into something more. Love, if you will."

"Bob, I-" Eli began.

The aging professor turned his fine featured face away as he waved a hand at the boy. "Let me finish. But she has a boyfriend, right?" He watched as Eli nodded. "Usually, when one of the two, the man or the woman, has a boyfriend or a husband or whatever, it eases the tension a little, allowing love to slip in there unnoticed. Have you ever felt the need to impress her, or do things to make her like you?"

"No. She had a boyfriend and I know that she's off limits." Eli said while he stroked Hunter's head as the big dog lay next to him.

"See, you weren't trying to gain her attention. From what you've told me, you have always been yourself around her. Kind, funny, smart, and interesting Eli. And she has done the same, it seems. Your Anna has only been herself around you, and that is why you two have fallen for each other. You each know who the other truly is, with no disguises."

"But she has a boyfriend!" Eli stressed to him. "If she liked me, she wouldn't still be with him."

Bob smiled. "Ah, but you're wrong. That's where things become complicated, and it depends on her commitment to her boyfriend, not necessarily her love for him. You will learn, among many other things about relationships, that love and commitment are two completely different things. A woman may find the love she had dreamt about since she was a little girl with a man she had only considered a friend, but have a strong enough commitment to the man that she is dating to stay with him. Luckily for you, it is only a high school relationship that you're talking about between Anna and this Jerry kid. She's young, just as you are, and you will both learn along the way what is important to you.

"My wife and I loved each other very much in many ways. But she had found that love I told you about, that 'dream love', with another man. She chose that love over her commitment to me, and so our time together ended. I spent quite a few years resenting her and that man, but I eventually realized that 'dream love' is rare, and that reaching out and taking a hold of it while you leave everything else behind isn't necessarily a bad thing.

"Don't get me wrong, now. I'm not advising you to run from one woman to another, or even to leave a woman you are committed to, all I'm saying is that some things are *above* the normal train of thought and feeling of society. And if the part of *you* that is above the normal rules of society wants to reach out and take hold of that, then go for it. If it's gonna make you happy in a way that can't be achieved in any other way, then do it. Some things are beyond our understanding, and love and emotion are among them."

Eli looked at the older man, taking in his words and trying to make sense of them.

Bob laughed. "I'm sorry. I didn't mean to go on like that. And I don't want you to expect or hope that Anna breaks up with her boyfriend for you. That's a whole other ball of wax right there. I just want you to know that it's not wrong or bad to feel how you do, and that you don't always have to keep it hidden inside just because society says it's not right. It's been many years, but I have accepted the divorce from my wife, and I wish her well in the love that she's found. Even at my age, I wonder if that kind of 'dream love' will ever come into my life. I just wish that she hadn't been such a devious bitch about keeping my children out of my life."

Eli burst into laughter. The boy knew that it wasn't right, but the contrast of all of his mentor's love talk with the 'devious bitch' thing just sent him rolling. Bob looked at Eli, surprised, thinking that his ex-wife keeping his children out of his life wasn't funny at all. He soon realized how it must have sounded to Eli's ears, and he began to laugh himself. Hunter rose from his warm, comfortable spot on the floor next to his master with his ears perked and his too short tail wagging. The big black dog whined and panted as the two humans laughed wildly and he let out a bark, wanting to join in the fun. Bocci only lay on the floor on the other side of the room, looking at the three silly boys with tired eyes. Bob and Eli laughed even harder, and the odd young boy held the Rottweiler's head in his arms while he placed the smooth, healed skin of his cheek along his dog's neck.

Bob and Eli slowed their laughter, watching as Hunter trotted over to Bocci, wanting to play some more. The female Lab growled and snapped at the bigger dog, causing him to back away, shocked. Hunter tried it again, getting the same response from the tired female Lab. Bob reprimanded Bocci, while the massive black dog lowered his head in defeat and lay down next to his master's chair with an audile 'huff' sound escaping his nostrils as his 160-pounds hit the floor.

"Bocci!" Bob yelled. "Cut it out!"

Eli laughed. "It's okay." He looked down at Hunter, petting his head. "What's wrong buddy? Doesn't anybody want to play with you?" Hunter looked up at him with his deep, dark, loving eyes and lapped his tongue at his Eli face.

"Is your mother having Thanksgiving dinner for you tomorrow?" Bob asked.

"We're going to my Grandma's house. It's what we do every year since Dad left, and that's where Matt's staying, so we'll all get together there." Eli said.

"Good." Bob said. "Have things been better with your mother since you went back to school?"

"Yeah. I guess. She's still gone all the time and doesn't even realize that I'm over here almost every day. She says she works a lot, but I don't think it's working that she does all night." Eli dropped his eyes to his hands.

Robert Mikush nearly frowned, feeling the boy's inference to his mother running around with men after work. For one of the few times, the brilliant professor had nothing to say.

"What're you doing?" Eli asked, his face brightening as he lifted his face to look at Bob.

"Oh. Me and some of the other professors from the university are getting together tomorrow. We're having a bachelor's Thanksgiving. A whole lot of food, beer, cards, cigars, and about six hours worth of football." Bob smiled. "A guy can't ask for much more than that. Do your grandparents let you take Hunter with you?"

Eli shook his head. "No. They don't like him. They're afraid of him. They just think he's like the Rottweilers you see on TV, the ones that hurt people. They liked him when he was a puppy, and used to let him play in the house and gave him people food and stuff. But when he started getting bigger, they could tell that he was a Rott, and they bitched at my dad for getting me a 'killer dog'. They never liked my dad much either, and they think that it was some kind of plan to piss them off or hurt them or something. Anyway, I have to leave him home when we go over there."

"I'm sorry to hear that." Bob said. "I know how much you love having him around."

Eli looked down at his baby boy, placing a hand to the side of the big dog's face and scratching. "He'll be alright. We've been hanging out a lot lately, and I have the rest of the weekend off. And if we can come over here during the weekend . . ."

"Definitely." Bob said with a smile. "I'd offer to keep him here, but I won't be here and with the way Bocci's acting . . ."

"No. He'll be fine." Eli said. "I've just been spoiling him, that's all."

Eli's face became blank as he suddenly fell from his chair and hit the ground. Bob's eyes widened in surprise, and he jumped from his chair and knelt next to the boy. Hunter shoved his muzzle in Eli's face, and the boy's eyes fluttered open while he groaned.

"Eli!" Bob hollered. "Are you okay?"

Eli blinked for a few moments. "Yeah. I just . . . I don't know."

"Was it a vision? Did you have another one?" Bob asked, half relieved and half excited.

"I think so, but I can't . . . I don't . . . remember." Eli muttered. "It was too fast."

"Can you sit up?" Bob asked, watching as Eli sat his body upright on the floor. He helped the boy to his chair as the voice from his dream arose in his head.

Euriah.

Bob considered whether or not to tell Eli the rest of the tale of the origin of The Black Box, but decided against it. He hadn't told him in the first place, not only because it would keep the story shorter, but also because he felt that there were some things he needed to see and figure out for himself first. Especially since Eli had just felt the blow of another vision, however short lived it may have been, Bob felt that it was a tale best left for another day.

Their meeting came to an end on that Thanksgiving eve, and Bob walked with Eli through the house towards the door. Eli called for Hunter, but he wouldn't come out of the study. They went back into the study to get the large dog, stopping at the doorway and watching. Bocci was still curled up in her comfortable ball on the floor, and Hunter was facing her, lying on his belly with his back legs stretched out behind him, reminding Eli of a frog's legs. Bocci growled at him lightly while Hunter wagged his tail and whined at her before pushing his big black nose toward her, and she snapped at it. He tried it again while lapping at her face with his tongue. She was still this time, so Hunter began licking her face while he placed his right paw on the back of her neck. Bocci's tail slowly began to wag, and she started licking back at Hunter, joining him in a doggy kiss. Eli laughed, and Hunter immediately pulled himself away from the female and walked over to his master. Bocci pulled her body slowly from the floor, following the big dog as the three silly boys made their way toward the front door. A thought was forming in Bob's mind as he climbed into his car along with the boy and his beloved dog on that chilly late November night. He would check it out before he said anything to Eli, though.

The college professor drove Eli home along the lengthy detour to Raccoon Township, wondering if he was doing the right thing as he had taken the troubled boy under his wing for a few reasons. Hoping that it was all for the best, Bob only wanted to provide Eli with a source of hope and guidance, feeling that he was doing a good job with his words and football coaching. He wanted to help the boy end the torture that he had felt ever since seeing the plane crash, and the professor hoped that the blue eyed wonder of a child could help him end his own torture with his guilt due to the plane crash. The only way to do that was to end The Strange, as Eli called it. Bob knew that he cared for the boy, and he thought that the unemotional boy seemed to care for him. It was an awkward relationship as surrogate father and son, but they just seemed to fit together so well. The aging professor couldn't deny that, and Eli seemed to have no objections. The strange, yet wondrous boy had actually become a much happier young man in recent days, and Bob knew it for sure in the moment that he and Eli laughed about his own words concerning his ex-wife. Bob had seen the true happiness on the boy's face as tears of laughter welled up in his eyes, and he had taken joy in it. The abandoned old man was coming to love the young boy as his own, even though Eli was the son of two strangers, and he wanted to keep him by his side. Bob's ideas of 'dream love' didn't only apply to a man and woman relationship, they also applied to father / son love.

Bob slowed the car to a halt next the bushes in front of Eli's house, the boy pulling the door handle and climbing out of the car before letting Hunter out of the back seat. While the passenger door was still open, Bob called out.

"Hunter! C'mere boy!"

Hunter hopped into the passenger seat, licking and sniffing his new friend's face. Bob laughed as he stroked the dog's face, neck, and back, speaking softly in Hunter's ear. Eli looked at the old man, confused.

He gave Hunter's head one last pat. "You be good, boy. I'll see you soon, okay?" The large dog leapt from the car, pacing around Eli's side.

"I'll call you either tomorrow night or sometime Friday." Eli said, ducking his head inside of the car.

"Okay. Have a Happy Thanksgiving, Eli. You too, Hunter." Bob said, smiling.

"Happy Thanksgiving, Bob." Eli smiled back at him before shoving the car door closed.

He walked towards his mother's house with the massive black dog at his side while the headlights of Bob's car swirled past him as the car turned around. Eli looked down at Hunter, telling him that he could stay in the house tonight, since he couldn't go to Thanksgiving tomorrow. The house was empty at 10:30 that night, and Eli walked past the blinking answering machine on his way to the kitchen. He sat at the kitchen table, eating some cookies he had found in the cupboard and drinking a glass of milk with Hunter at his side. Slipping Hunter a couple cookies, he thought about a good night's sleep before the boring day

Black Box

that he would endure at his grandparents' house. Eli never once thought about the yellow piece of notebook paper, with his mother's note and the imprints of other writing on it, which he had tossed on top of the refrigerator weeks ago.

With Hunter tagging along the whole time, Eli showered, did some homework in his room while he listened to the radio, watched some late night TV, and climbed into bed well after midnight. His mother still wasn't home. Hunter jumped up on the bed, curling into a ball at Eli's feet. The boy looked down at him, and Hunter looked back with a pitiful dark gaze. Eli laughed out loud at his silly dog, then called for him to come lay next to him. Hunter crawled up the side of the bed to lie next to Eli, resting his large head on his master's shoulder.

"That's better." Eli said as he reached over and turned off his lamp.

The room was dark, the house was empty, and the sound of the cold wind whistled against the house. Eli wrapped his arm around Hunter's hefty chest and stared at the blackness of the ceiling for a few moments. He then turned to lie on his side, resting his face alongside the back of the big dog's head.

"G'night, baby boy." Eli said, planting a kiss his on Hunter's head. "I love you."

He placed another kiss on Hunter's muzzle, and the big dog lifted his tired head, flashing his tongue out of his mouth quick enough to catch Eli's cheek in his own good night kiss. Eli fell asleep with Hunter in his arms and a large amount of happiness in his heart.

*

Virginia Marshall opened the door to Eli's room at about two o'clock in the morning, to see if her son was even home. The sight she saw warmed her protective, confused heart. Her son and his dog had somehow fallen into a position where they seemed to be holding each other as they slept. Eli's arms were still wrapped around his baby boy, and Hunter had turned his body in his sleep so that his forelegs were wrapped around his master. Virginia took in the vision she saw in the dim light that shone into Eli's room from the hallway, and something seemed to break through the increasing fog her heart and mind had been living in lately.

She knew that she couldn't do it, no matter what the benefits were. She would throw away all of the phone numbers and erase all the messages on the answering machine. Virginia thought that she would simply work the extra hours that she had been telling her son she had been working while she had been out getting laid. It wasn't worth losing this image of pure innocence and love, she thought as she suddenly wished that she had a camera. Standing in the grip of the emotion she felt watching her son and his dog sleep soundly together, Virginia knew that she could change her own behavior and care more for her sons. She could do it, and she was going to. Her heart exploded with love and pride as she made the silent promise to herself to do it. She wasn't going to give anymore heartache or pain to her boys. They had endured enough when their Dad left. Sliding the door closed and walking mindlessly to the kitchen, she opened the cupboard over the refrigerator and pulled out the half empty bottle of liquor.

Or half full, the strange feeling inside her said.

Virginia poured her tenth glass of liquor for the night as her crotch throbbed from the hard sex she had engaged in only an hour ago. She took her first sip from the glass as the ice clinked against its sides, and all promises were forgotten. The alcohol burned in her nearly numb throat, and she gave up on the struggles she would have to endure by working those extra hours, knowing that the only thing she cared about was her date tomorrow night after the family thing was over. She walked into the living room and listened to the messages on the answering machine, taking down names, numbers, and any dollar amounts that were quoted. The Strange had lost its hold on her, allowing her the feeling of love and hope for her current life. The slip had lasted for a moment, but nothing more. He would make sure that it wouldn't happen again, she was sure. As long as she did her part, the man would take care of the rest. The feeling inside told her so. That and the strange cloaked man, with the strange but familiar face, in her dreams told her so.

*

His mother awakened Eli at nine a.m. to get ready for the coming day. Hunter jumped out of the bed when she came in, and he walked stiffly past Virginia as she held her arm over eyes, shielding them from the light. He looked back at her with a growl rising in his throat when Eli opened the front door, letting Hunter outside. Virginia asked Eli if he was going to chain his dog up.

"Nope." Eli responded. "He'll be back soon."

Sure enough, as Virginia was rooting through Eli's closet for some decent holiday clothes for him to wear, Hunter scratched and whined at the front door. Eli left his mother standing in his closet as he went to let his dog in the house.

"Does he *have* to be in here?" Virginia asked sharply.

"It's cold outside, and it's Thanksgiving. Cut him a break, mom." Eli replied.

Virginia watched closely as the large dog laid on the floor next to her son, looking at her. She grabbed an outfit out of Eli's closet, told him to take a bath, and left the room. "We're supposed to be there by eleven. Your grandfather wants to spend some time with you before the games come on," she called from the living room. "You know how he is once the football starts."

That he did. His grandfather was so intent on watching the Thanksgiving Day football games of the Detroit Lions and the Dallas Cowboys while drinking his glasses of scotch that he would barely talk to anyone when the games were on. The boy remembered that it seemed to be the only time that his father and grandfather ever got along, when they drank alcohol and watched football.

Eli took his shower, with Hunter in the bathroom, dressed in the clothes his mother had picked out for him, and waited while she took another forty-five minutes getting ready. He went outside and threw a ball for Hunter for a while, making sure that the big dog didn't dirty his clothes. He brought Hunter back inside with him while he sat on the sofa and watched some parade on TV, and he could smell his mother's usual 'holiday' perfume, signifying that she was in the bathroom that connected to her bedroom, almost ready. Eli went into the hallway bathroom to make sure that he looked okay, gazing at his appearance in the mirror. It had been a while since he had taken a good look at himself, and it seemed that something had changed. It might have been the fact that for four weeks or more his face had been red and bruised from the beating his mother had given him. It might have been the fact that his hair hadn't been cut in a long time, and it had grown long, looking decent beneath the hairspray and brush he had used on it. It might have been because his shoulders and arms looked a little larger probably due to the football training Bob had been putting him through. It might have been a lot of things, but he especially noticed something in his face, or his eyes. He couldn't place it, but they seemed harder or tougher or smarter, and he tried to think of the word Bob would use.

Wiser, the word rose in his mind, and he smiled.

Eli gazed into his own, wise eyes in the mirror, also looking at the obviously poor man's version of dress clothes. His bright blue sweater was stiff with age and improper washing and the black dress pants he wore were too short, displaying socks that were more blue than black. The fake leather belt wound through the loops of his pants was way too big for him, the excess having been woven through the two belt loops *after* the buckle. He looked down at his shoes, seeing that the ancient black moccasins were so worn that the white plastic they were made of flashed through in many places. Something else was wrong, though, and he looked back at his face, rubbing a hand along his cheek. Eli smiled his charming, boyish smile at himself in the mirror before looking down at Hunter on the bathroom floor.

"I think I need a shave." He said.

He closed the door next to him, looked in the cupboard beneath the sink for some shaving cream, and piled it on his cheeks. Eli then found his father's old razor under the sink, and he pulled it from its case with great emotion. Turning his eyes back to the mirror, the thirteen year old boy began pulling the razor downward along his cheeks, upper lip, and chin. He wasn't pressing very hard, so he managed to not cut himself, and after rinsing the excess cream from his face, he looked under the basin some more. His father's aftershave lotion was still there, and he splashed a moderate amount onto his face, biting his lip to hold back the scream of burning pain. Eli looked at himself in the mirror as the burning sensation subsided, and he smiled in pride since he had actually shaved his face. He was finally becoming a man.

Virginia Marshall emerged from her bedroom as he sat on the sofa once again, grabbing her purse as she went to the closet for her winter coat. "Take your dog outside, and let's go." She turned her head towards Eli with a snap. "What's that smell? Have you been into your father's things?" Virginia cast a look of disappointment in his direction. "Eli, I thought I asked you not to do that. Why would you do that now? Today?"

"I don't know." Eli said, looking down at Hunter on the floor. "I just wanted to smell good." He had hoped that his mother would have been able to tell by looking at him that he had shaved his face. Since she didn't, he wasn't going to tell her.

"Mom?" Eli asked in a bright voice. "Do you think I could bring Hunter this time? Would Grandma and Grandpa let me, with all the weird stuff that's been going on lately? Maybe he would make them feel safe?"

Virginia looked at her son with a dark stare. "Elijah! You know that when we go to their house that your dog has to say here, and that—"

Eli stood up with tears in his eyes. "He has a name, Mom!" He cried. "Hunter, okay? I just really want him to come with us this time! Maybe they'll see that he's a nice dog? He could play in the back yard while—"

Virginia threw her purse onto the nearest piece of furniture. "Elijah! No! Your grandparents don't want him there, I don't want him there, and Matt doesn't want him there!"

Eli stuttered. "M—Matt?"

"Your dog is NOT going with us to Thanksgiving dinner, and that's that!" She cast her eyes toward Hunter as his low growls came to her ears. "Get that fucking dog outside and on his chain right now! Then get in the car and let's go!" She turned, grabbed her purse and walked out of the front door, half in command, and half in fright.

Eli stood in the living room with tears in his eyes and his growling dog at his feet. He turned his tearful gaze down to Hunter, calling him to follow. Hunter did, and the boy led him outside to the spot where his chain and collar lie in the snow. Eli crouched down to grasp the collar, and Hunter sat in the snow next to him, licking at his face and wagging his too long nub of a tail, as his master unlatched the collar, opened it up and placed it around the big dog's muscular neck. He latched it closed, petting Hunter's face, neck, and sides and looked the massive dog in his deep, dark eyes as tears stood out in his own.

"I'm sorry, buddy. I tried." He said in a choking voice, hearing his mother's car start from in front of the house. "I don't want to leave you like this, especially on Thanksgiving." He placed his arms around Hunter's neck holding him in a tight hug.

Hunter responded with a rare trick that Eli had tried many times to teach him, but that the dog had never seemed to learn, the 'people hug'. Hunter brought his chest even with the boy's, tossing both of his forepaws over Eli's shoulders and holding his large head next to the boy's face. Tears flowed from Eli's eyes while Hunter licked his cheek and the back of his neck.

"If there's any one thing I'm thankful for, it's you, Baby Boy." He said as he hugged his dog tightly.

"I'm sorry that Mom doesn't like you, but we'll be okay, right?" Eli said as he allowed his dog to break the hug and sit normally on the snow covered ground. "I'll see you tonight, buddy." The emotional boy placed a kiss on Hunter's nose just as the big dog flicked his tongue out of his mouth. Eli made a spitting sound as if he were getting rid of the doggy slobber before kissing Hunter again on his forehead and holding his face tight in his hands.

"I love you, Hunter."

Eli got up and walked away, wiping the tears from his eyes and cheeks as he left his beloved dog behind him. His mother was beeping the horn of the car, and the boy spun around, waving to his dog before he disappeared around the side of the house. Hunter's doggy grin faded, and his too long tail slowed in its wag while he sat alone in the middle of the snow filled yard watching his master walk away.

*

Thanksgiving dinner went pretty well for Eli, as his grandparents and his brother greeted him warmly, and they sat in the living room and talked for a while before the NFL pregame shows came on television at 12:30. At that point, Eli and his grandfather bonded. They watched the pregame show with the same great interest, and as the actual games proceeded Eli watched the games play by play with his Grandpa. The boy impressed his grandfather with his newfound knowledge of the game, discussing and arguing certain plays made and called during the games. Eli criticized the offensive execution while deciphering the defense at the same time. Bob's tutoring seemed to have taken effect as his grandfather was left staring at him with a gaping mouth.

"What're you talkin' 'bout, boy?" Grandpa Porter croned in his raspy, old man voice. "That 'as a good play!" His grandfather cried after the quarterback had completed a seventeen yard pass.

"Yeah." Eli said as he pointed at the television screen. "But he didn't even try to look at his secondary receiver. He was wide open in the center of the field and it would have been an easy toss for a touchdown."

Eli and his grandfather cheered, booed, agreed and argued all afternoon and into the late evening, eating their turkey dinner in their chairs in front of the TV. Eli drank his orange juice while his Grandpa drank his Scotch, having wanted to spend some time with his little brother, but had been so enthralled by seeing his knowledge of the game played out in front of him on the television that he ignored everything else. At some point, Matt had disappeared into his room, playing with the brand new computer they had bought recently.

At around eight o'clock that night, after Eli and his grandfather had actually socialized with the rest of the family for an hour or so, Virginia claimed that it was time to go. She said that Eli had school the next day and that she had to work early in the morning, neither of which was true. After giving Matthew a token kiss goodbye, she piled Eli in the car. They made their way home in relative silence, Eli wanting to ask why she had lied.

Just leave it alone, she's not going to tell you the truth anyway. One side of his mind said.

Maybe not. But I want to catch her in a fucking lie. The other side said.

But if she really does think you have school tomorrow, then there's no problem with spending the day at Bob's house.

Eli felt that the last idea was the best, and so he said nothing on the way home. His mother commented on how it was nice to see that he got along with his grandfather so well.

"Yeah." He mumbled. "But he doesn't know shit about football."

"What was that, young man? I thought I heard you say—"

"Nothing, Mom." Eli replied, smiling into the darkness through the car window.

Virginia cast a glance in his direction before guiding the car the rest of the way home. She pulled the car into the driveway, hinting to Eli that it was getting late and maybe he should watch some TV in his room before going to bed. Even though it wasn't even nine o'clock, Eli *did* go directly to his room, knowing that his mother was going to find some reason to leave. Then he would go bring Hunter inside.

Eli listened as his mother took an unexpected call, speaking loudly in a surprised voice about how she would be happy to go into work and help out.

Moments after she hung up the phone, Virginia Marshall knocked on Eli's door.

"Honey, I have to run to work, they need me tonight. You get some sleep and I'll see you this weekend okay?" She said in a quick, deliberate voice.

Before Eli could even respond, he heard the opening and closing of the front door and smelled the aroma of his mother's 'going out' perfume. She had arranged for some guy to call her, or even called him when they got home, setting up a date and she ran out on him. Eli knew it, not sure if he really even cared though. He pulled himself from his bed, fully clothed, and slid his shoes on. He knew that he wasn't going to see Bob that night, but he could at least call him and set up a time for tomorrow.

Eli rushed to the kitchen, grabbing his thick black and gray flannel on the way to grab the phone and call Bob's house. He got the answering machine, which he expected, and left a message asking the professor to call him at eleven o'clock in the morning to make sure that he could pick both him and Hunter up. Putting on his flannel, he turned on the spotlight in the back yard, and went outside to let Hunter in.

The jingling of his dog's chain usually came to Eli's ears as soon as he stepped foot in the back yard. Knowing that Hunter would sometimes get caught up in chasing after some animal or sniffing at some tree in the yard that he had sniffed at a thousand other times, Eli whistled and called out to him a few times. Nothing. Starting to get mad, he was thinking that Hunter had spent so much time with him recently that the big dog wasn't all that excited to see him. Eli also became scared as it was very rare for Hunter not to come running to him when he came out into the back yard.

Eli walked through the yard, calling Hunter's name and whistling, hearing his own footsteps crunch in the snow beneath him. His eyes were focused on the yard and the trees surrounding the yard, and when the jingling sound of a chain came to his ears, his heart lightened. Realizing that the jingling sound arose from his foot striking the limp chain lying in the snow in front of him, Eli reached down and grabbed the chain as fear gripped his heart. He followed the chain to its length, lifting it up from the snow and holding it in his hand as he went along. His heart nearly stopped, and he fell to his knees with tears in his eyes as he had finally reached the end of the chain. Eli stood in the middle of his snowy back yard, caught in the beam of the spotlights, holding Hunter's empty collar that was still attached to the limp chain.

He tried not to panic; he *did not* want to panic. Hunter had just gotten loose, that's all. It's happened before, and Hunter always came home after a while. But those explanations didn't seem to do any good as Eli's heart raced and his eyes burned with the approaching tears. He began screaming Hunter's name into the cold wind of the dark night and climbed to his feet, walking at a fast pace through the yard. His walk turned into a trot and his trot turned into an all out sprint into the blackness of the woods. A voice spoke in his head as Eli darted into the dark woods.

A light. You need a light to be able to see.

The thought couldn't pierce his panic, and Eli just kept running in the non-existent moonlight. It was the day of the month for the new moon, and the white snow on the ground seemed to reflect the blackness of the dreary sky. The next hour was a blur of pain and tears for Eli. He ran mindlessly through the woods, running into trees and tree branches while the cold wind whipped against his skin. The constant flow of tears began to freeze on his numb, burning cheeks and his fingers screamed in pain from the biting cold. His toes were also beginning to feel the bite and ache of the cold. The rest of his body was sweating beneath his clothes from his running and his blinding fear, giving him that hot—cold chill that seems to flow in alternating waves. He was hot beneath his clothes, but the cold air chilled him as it drifted inside of them. The cold air was also stinging his already tear filled eyes, making it harder for him to see even as his eyes adjusted to the dark. Eli just ran and ran, calling for his dog to come, to 'get the fuck over here right now'. No rational thought arose in Eli's mind during his hour-long sprint through the woods. His heart had been overcome by an unexplainable fear that something really bad had happened and that he would never again see his dog, the only thing in the world that meant anything to him.

*

The aching boy awoke on the woods floor, curled up in a ball, and he opened his eyes in the darkness, seeing some type of dark figure in front of him. It moved towards him and he flinched away in fear as a large, warm, slobbery tongue lapped at his face. Immense joy filled his heart as the pulses of warm doggy breath blew against his freezing face and he sat up quickly, seeing Hunter standing in front of him in the dark wagging his too long tail. Eli cried out his name in joy, wrapping his chilled, stiff arms around his dog's large neck and hugging him. Tears of relief streamed from Eli's eyes, and he pulled back to give Hunter a big kiss on his face. When he pulled back, though, the dog pulled away from him. He sat in the snow, watching the massive Rottweiler walk slowly away from him. Eli's heart broke as he called out to his baby boy to come back. Hunter ignored him, looking over his shoulder only once before disappearing into the darkness.

*

Eli's eyes bolted open, as he was laying in a fetal position on the snowy ground and shivering uncontrollably. Very slowly, he sat up in the darkness, not knowing where he was at first. His body hurt, and he was extremely cold. Cold blood trickled down his cheeks from the cuts of the tree branches, and he was slow in remembering where he was or why he was there until the dream about Hunter crept up on him. Recalling his dreaming vision of Hunter walking away from him, the freezing boy screamed in heart broken pain as the tears started all over again. Eli looked around himself, seeing through his watery eyes that he was next to the stream, but not knowing how far into the woods or how far away from home he was. Completely unaware of what time it was or how long he had been out in the freezing woods, the pain in the boy's entire body told him that it had been quite a while. Eli rested his back against the tree he had slept next to, and he wailed in grief, pain, and a flurry of other emotions. Absolutely grief stricken, he stayed that way for a long time, careless of the time that his already frozen body had spent out in the cold. He just wanted his baby boy with him, and he cared about nothing else.

Eventually, Eli pulled his shaking body from the snow and wandered through the woods until he found his bearings and made his way home. His mind seemed to be numbing, just as his body was, and it was blank and dumb while he walked through the woods. As he walked through the area of Hunter's dog run in the back yard, pain tugged at his heart again while the voice that had spoken to him before he had sprinted mindlessly into the woods came back to him.

A light. You need a light . . .

Running towards the house and hurrying into the kitchen, Eli opened and closed a few of the drawers, looking for the flashlight and cursing the emptiness of the kitchen since he couldn't find it. As the soothing warmth of the house made his body tingle and burn, he cast his eyes at the clock on the wall. 12:20 a.m. He had been out in the single digit cold for over three hours. Eli's eyes fell on the refrigerator, and he ran over to it, sweeping his arm across its top while he stood on his tiptoes. Phone books, bottle caps, and many papers fell onto the kitchen floor while the flashlight slid off and struck him on top of his head. Not even noticing the throb of a growing welt on his head, he grabbed it off of the floor, and clicked it on to make sure it worked. The bulb lit up instantly, and he bolted out of the house rubbing the knot that was forming on his head and squeezing more tears from his eyes.

With the flashlight burning bright in his hand, Eli ran out into his back yard, calling Hunter's name and turning the beam of the light down to the snow. Looking for the most recent paw prints that led away from Hunter's usual area, he walked almost the entire perimeter of the dog run, cursing and calling his dog. The boy wasn't finding anything, and he thought of heading into the woods again, this time with the flashlight.

You'll freeze to death, and you know it. You're already halfway there. Try looking elsewhere.

Eli didn't know where else to look, knowing that anytime Hunter got loose, he went straight for the woods.

Maybe he's not in the woods. Maybe he didn't get loose.

A strange sensation filled Eli's body and mind, and he began to wander back towards the house, looking for prints in the snow. Just outside of the perimeter of the dog run, Eli saw plenty of dog and human footprints made by him and Hunter every time he chained him up or let him loose. Looking closely with the flashlight and spotlights of the house combined, he noticed that there were larger human footprints hidden among his own in the snow. His heart raced, and he followed the prints out into the driveway, seeing that Hunter's prints accompanied them to the blur of tire tracks. From there, the large human footprints were alone in the snow, heading for the mailbox. Eli ran to the mailbox and opened it, finding a thick white envelope inside. He pulled it out and held it under the flashlight. There was no sending address, return address, or postmark. Only his mother's name was scrawled across the front of the white envelope in black ink.

Eli tore the envelope open, seeing a wide, green stack of twenty and fifty dollar bills. There was a small note tucked behind the money, and he flipped it open.

Thank you much, Ms. Marshall. It's been a pleasure doing business with you. Like we agreed, the other $150 dollars will be paid when I receive the papers. I'll be calling sometime after the first of the week, like you had asked. I think he'll be really happy here.

It was left unsigned, and a memory flashed in Eli's mind. He ran for the house and into the kitchen, rustling through the mess of phone books, bottle caps, and papers that lay in front of the refrigerator. His heart was pounding in his chest while the heat of the house burned his frozen flesh, and he found the piece of notebook paper that his mother had left the note on a long time ago, holding it up in front of him. Something had been written over top of it all right, and he knew just how to find out what it was. Finding a pencil in one of the drawers in the kitchen, he sat at the table with the old note in front of him. Using a trick learned long ago in elementary school, Eli rubbed the pencil lightly back and forth over the indentations in the paper, seeing the hidden words of his mother form on the page.

There were many abstract scribblings, making Eli think that she had been talking on the phone while she wrote this as it was a habit of hers. Strange names and phone numbers appeared on the paper, accompanied by dollar amounts ranging from 500 to 1200 dollars. Those encompassed the majority of the page, while the most devastating information was written at the top in small bursts.

Full blooded, AKC registered . . . Adult male . . . of 90% German descent, ready to breed . . . 3 years old . . . championship quality . . . **HUNTER**

Small gagging sounds arose from Eli's mouth, as he stared at the hard scribbles outlining his dog's name. His heart felt as though it was going to just deflate in his chest. The heat of the house was also turning his body into a stinging, burning ball of extreme pain. His mind spun with pain, sorrow, and disbelief.

"You FUCKING BITCH!" Eli screamed into the empty kitchen, rising from his seat and kicking at the pile of garbage in front of the refrigerator. He slipped into a tirade of anger and hurt, punching and kicking at doors and walls as he cursed his mother. More tears streamed down his face, and he turned to look at the envelope lying on the kitchen table.

His head steaming with anger and hate, his body burning and hurting as it tried to warm up, and his eyes flowing tears of grief, Eli opened the envelope and counted the money inside. Two thousand dollars. His mother had somehow auctioned his dog off at two thousand dollars.

She probably promised to suck his dick every day for a year. He thought wickedly.

An odd sense of calm came over him, and he walked out into the cold darkness for the last time that night. Crouching in the middle of Hunter's dog run with the empty collar in his hand, he looked out at the dark trees as his body cried in protest at returning to the cold. Tears ran down his frozen cheeks as he worded silent prayers of love to his dog in his mind. The calm inside of him increased, and Eli began to wonder why he had been fighting it all this time. Along with Hunter, all of the boy's hope was gone and he gave up fighting. Only then did he see that it was so much easier.

Elijah Marshall moved his near hypothermic body toward his mother's house with a sick look of heartache and hatred on his numb face. The odd calm filled him, fueling his anger at the same time, while he clenched his frozen fist around the thing in his right hand. His mind became almost blank, focusing on only one thing: revenge. After all that he had done and all that he had strived for since watching the airplane plummet to the earth, Eli had finally allowed himself to be taken by The Strange.

*

Virginia Marshall pulled her car onto the snowy driveway sometime after two a.m., cursing the fact that most of the lights in the house were on.

I thought I told that little bastard to go to bed. Why the hell are all the lights on?

She pulled her aching body from the car, holding her coat tightly around her shoulders. Attempting to place the key in the front door, she noticed that the doorknob turned freely under her hand.

He even left the fucking door unlocked! That little shit!

Virginia pushed the door inwards, looking around the living room before shoving the door closed behind her. Glad to be rid of the cold, she shivered as the warmth of the house filled her and she pulled her coat from her shoulders, hanging it in the closet next to the front door. The coffee table caught her eye as she turned to walk through the living room, since it was completely devoid of any magazines, candles, or empty glasses. There were two items sitting on the top of the coffee table; a piece of paper with pencil scribbled all over it and a thick white envelope. With her eyebrows drawn together in curiosity and confusion, Virginia looked at the paper first, not quite seeing the white lines inside of the pencil scribbles through the haze of her booze. Picking up the envelope with her name on it, she prepared to look inside as a shadow moving from the kitchen startled her.

"Where have you been?" Eli's voice arose to her ears before he appeared from the kitchen doorway.

"I told you that I had to go to work for—" Her words stopped dead in her mouth as she saw her son stand in the doorway only twelve feet in front her.

He was wearing the jeans he had worn during his run through the woods, along with the cut off Penn State sweatshirt and the heavy, black, steel-toed boots his father had left in the closet. His lengthening hair was scattered into a tangled mess, and his face was scratched and bleeding. Her son's eyes, though, were what held her frozen. They appeared to be set deeper in his face than they used to be, surrounded by a dark sort of haze as the white and blue of his eyes pierced into her own. They also looked to be *swirling*, if that was even possible.

"Dressed like that?" He tilted his young, bleeding face as he asked the question.

"I . . . well . . ." Virginia stammered, unable to pull her eyes away from his.

Her thirteen-year-old boy laughed an adult, impatient laugh. "Whatever, mom. I just hope that he fucked you good and hard and that he made you cum harder than you've ever cum before." Her jaw dropped at the sound of those words from her son's mouth. "Cause it's never going to happen again."

Virginia watched the wild image of her son move towards her with his arms crossed across his broadening chest, gaining the strength to yell at him. "Don't you ever talk to me that way, you little bastard! I don't know what the hell you've been up to or where you're learning to talk like this, but I'm still your mother and I *will* smack your ass back in line!" She was regaining her usual confidence.

Eli only laughed. "You're not going to leave us behind while you go out and fuck a bunch of guys. I am not going to live like that. Go ahead, mom. Look in the envelope." He showed her a charming smile as he leaned against the chair closest to the kitchen.

Black Box

Virginia didn't know what else to say, and Eli was actually scaring her a little. She flipped the torn edge of the envelope upwards, seeing the thick stack of money inside of it. The image of the twenty-dollar bill in the front of the stack glared out at her as guilt rushed to her face. She refused to look up at her son.

"Count it." Eli said, moving his body slightly.

Still holding the piece of notebook paper, she placed the wad of bills in her hands and began to count it. Beneath the initial twenty-dollar bill, however, was the note that had been included with the cash. The rest was simply a stack of neatly cut, dollar bill sized pieces of notebook paper. Virginia's eyes scanned the small pieces of paper and the brief note in an instant, knowing that the money was gone. Her eyes flashed to the pencil marked piece of notebook paper in her hand. She finally saw the words hidden inside of the scribbles, knowing exactly which notes she had written on it as the large white word glared out at her. **HUNTER.**

A hard whipping strike came to her hands. Virginia cried out in pain and dropped the papers all over the floor, holding her stinging wrists together and looking up at her son. Eli was standing right in front of her with his legs spread wide, his right hand drawing back, and his mad, swirling eyes blazing.

"What the fuck did you do to my dog?" He screamed at her.

Virginia felt and saw the blood begin to trickle from her wrists as her son's arm swung forward with unbelievable quickness. Blinding pain arose in the left side of her neck as whatever he held in his hand struck her there. She stumbled backwards a step, crying out to her boy.

"Eli! Stop it! What the hell are you doing?"

Eli reached out with his left hand, grabbing the front of her sleazy dress and pulling her close to his face with an unforeseen strength. His strange eyes burned as he growled his words into her face.

"I told you what would happen if you did anything to my dog, you stupid fucking whore! Did you think I was fucking joking?" Tears fell from Eli's blazing eyes. "I can't believe you would do this to me! How could you steal the only thing I love on this earth away from me?"

He threw her into the same sofa that he had cowered against when she had beaten him not too long ago. Virginia looked at her crazed son, finally seeing the thing in his right hand that he was hitting her with. The two-inch wide, double layered nylon cloth with 'Hunter' etched into it swung loosely from Eli's throwing hand, the steel latch dangling. Just as she had beaten him with his father's belt for so many years, Eli was going to beat her with Hunter's collar.

"Where is he?" Eli screamed again. "Where's Hunter?"

His mother's voice trembled. "Eli, I don't know. I don't know what you're talking about."

"You lying BITCH!"

Eli swung the collar forward, striking his mother on her shoulder and drawing blood. She screamed in her high pitched, womanly voice, but he didn't care. He hit her again, the steel latch breaking the skin open and causing her to scream louder. Trying to find a weakness, she kicked at his legs with her slutty high-heeled shoes. Eli dodged her feet swiftly, frowning in hate and kicking her hard in the ribs with the steel toes of his father's boots. Not this time. She wasn't going to get out of this one.

"You fucking bitch! I hate you! You took Hunter away from me! I'm going to kill you, you lying whore!" Eli screamed at her as he kicked her and brought the collar down on her body again and again. He hit her on her back, her arms, her neck, her ass, and her legs as he screamed random words of hate. "I told you that I would kill you if you did anything to him! I'm going to fucking kill you, bitch! I'm gonna kill you."

"I didn't do anything, Eli! I swear I didn't!" His mother sobbed through her pain.

Blood was flowing from all areas of Virginia's body as she held her arms over her head and screamed and cried in pain. The blows were quick and hard. Eli's football throwing arm had turned into a killing device as he swung the collar over and over and over again, harder and harder every time. The steel buckle was hitting his mother so hard that it was sending vibrations through the cloth collar and into Eli's arm. He didn't care, and he beat his mother down in the exact same spot that she had beaten him.

"You stole him from me! You stole him from me! You worthless piece of shit! You stole my baby boy from me!" Eli's voice rose to a high screaming pitch on his last words, and he lifted his body from his feet with force of his next blow.

He struck Virginia directly in the side of her face, producing a screeching sound from her mouth, which only seemed to feed the crazed boy's anger and fury as he repeatedly beat her head and face, just as she had beaten his. The latch of the collar made loud cracking sounds as it hit her skull, and blood flowed freely onto the sofa, the carpet, and the rest of her body. Finally halting his attack, Eli placed his hands upon his knees and breathed heavily in his exhaustion as his mother lay on the floor by the blood-splattered sofa with her ravaged arms over her beaten head, sobbing. He continued to look down at her with hate while Hunter's blood laden collar swung freely from his right hand.

Eli knew that there was more to do; the calmness inside of him had told him so. He couldn't leave it like this, or he would end up in trouble. Pulling the ravaged form of his mother from the floor by the straps of her sleazy dress, he dragged her limp, whimpering body across the carpet of the living room to the top of the basement stairs and opened the door. Eli looked into her wide, frightened eyes with his wild, burning blue ones.

"I'm never going to forget this, mom. He was everything to me." His eyes softened and tears dripped onto his cheeks.

Virginia saw the emotion in her son, and attempted to stop him. She mumbled her words through swollen and bleeding lips. "Eli, please. I didn't do anything to Hunter. You have to believe me."

"I'll never believe another fucking word that comes out of your cocksucking mouth. Which won't be for a while, I promise. And when you finally *can* talk again, this never happened. Just like my school doesn't know that you tried to beat *me* to death a while ago. Right?" Eli said, shoving his hateful face in front of his mother's as he held her by her dress.

She nodded, and Eli backed away from her, finishing his sentiment. "I love Hunter more than anything in this world, including you." He relished in the hurt he saw in Virginia's ravaged face. "I'm going to do what I can to get him back, and if I do . . ." Eli trailed off for a moment, thinking. "I should've let him kill you that night. You're not my mother anymore anyway, so I should've let him kill you. At least I'd still have him . . . and not you."

Eli saw the tears of emotional hurt in Virginia's eyes, but he was too far gone to even care. The Strange had taken full hold of him, and his actions weren't necessarily under his control anymore. He pulled the collar over his shoulder again, using the strength, focus, and aim he would use if he were a quarterback and he swung the collar at Virginia's face, striking her directly in the jaw with a loud smacking sound. Repeating the motion again and again, he didn't stop until he heard a loud cracking sound emit from her face and she shrieked in pain without moving her mouth. Eli felt that he had effectively broken her jaw, and reached down to her, bending the thumb of each hand back until he heard and felt it snap, preventing her from writing either. More shrieks of pain came from Virginia's closed mouth, and a gruesome smile slid onto Eli's tattered face.

"It's over, bitch. I'll hate you forever for stealing my boy, and I hope that you never forget that." Eli had dropped the collar to the carpet and held her by her dress with both hands. "By the way, FUCK YOU."

Using all of his weight, Eli tossed his mother down the basement stairs. Her screams reached his ears, and he heard the thump as she hit bottom, but he had closed the door behind him as he turned away and had seen nothing.

*

Eli looked down at his clothes suspiciously, seeing the splatters of blood and knowing that he was going to have to get rid of them before he made the phone call. He lifted Hunter's collar from the carpet as he walked to his bedroom, planning to put it in his secret hiding place along with the clothes he wore.

Five minutes later, Eli pushed the board in the rear of his closet back into place, hiding his blood covered clothes, the envelope and its contents, the note, and Hunter's collar inside. After clothing himself in his usual bedclothes, he went into the bathroom and purposely broke open the cuts on his face that the tree branches had made, allowing the blood to drip onto his bedclothes. Bruises were already forming in the places where he had run into trees or the larger tree branches, and he smiled in wicked acceptance at what he saw and the silence that arose from the basement. Eli grabbed the phone in the living room and placed the 911 call he had planned out in his mind hours before. Climbing into his bed, he allowed the blood from his face to smear itself onto his sheets as he assumed the role of a terrified young boy. When the sirens screamed from his driveway, the comfort The Strange had provided seemed to fleet from his body, leaving him truly frightened and confused.

The frightened boy told the police and paramedics the same story he had devised earlier, crying and shaking in terror as he did. His mother had gone to work after Thanksgiving dinner and he had gone to bed, waking up when his mom came home and hearing her talking loudly with some guy in the living room. Then he heard some slapping, his mom crying, and she started screaming for help. Demonstrating how scared he had been with his tears and shaking body, the boy said that he ran into the living room and saw his mom lying over by the sofa where all the blood was. Some big guy in fancy clothes was standing there, and he was hitting her with his belt or something.

Eli watched closely as the police officers agreed that a belt was consistent with the wounds the woman had sustained.

Continuing his tale by saying that he had rushed towards his injured and bleeding mother, Eli said that the big guy had turned on him and smacked him in the face. The big guy shoved him around and hit him a few more times, until his mom screamed for him to stop. The guy then hit Eli in the face with the belt until he ran to his room, peeking out of his door to see what was happening to his mom, even though he was really scared. The big guy hit his mom in the face really hard a bunch of times, until she really couldn't scream anymore.

Eli saw the officers' nod to each other, acknowledging her broken jaw, watching as the closest officer made sure that the door to the basement was visible from the kid's bedroom doorway. It wasn't, but if the man had been standing in front of it, *he* would have been visible.

The devious boy told the authorities that the guy picked her up by her hands and threw her down the stairs, watching them silently understand the problem with her thumbs. Eli slammed his door closed and hid in his bed, he said, until the guy just kind of left. After waiting a while in his bed until he was sure that the guy was gone for good, he went to check on his mom. When he saw her at the bottom of the stairs, he dialed 911.

Black Box

"And then you guys came." Eli said, clasping his hands together while he looked at the kitchen floor in sorrow.

*

The Strange seemed to have taken a deeper hold upon things than Eli had originally thought. The police thoroughly believed him, especially since his entire story matched any evidence found on the scene, including a strange set of tire tracks left in the snow of the driveway. Oddly, the police left him at the house by himself as they left the scene rather than try to contact a relative or take him along to the hospital, believing him when he said that his dad would be home in a few hours. His father worked the late shift, Eli told them, and since he couldn't be bothered at work, the boy promised to tell his dad as soon as he got home. The policemen left the Marshall residence about an hour after the ambulance that had carried his mother to the hospital did, having searched and examined everything they possibly could. Everything concurred with the boy's story. They asked Eli if he had any idea of who the guy was or if he would recognize him, and he said that he had never seen any of the guys his mom had been with, and that he hadn't really gotten a good look at him. The officers mentioned that they would check with his mother's coworkers to see if they knew anything. Eli secretly took comfort in the idea, feeling that Virginia's fellow nurses had to know that she was constantly sleeping around. It would fit perfectly. It had all worked out the way the strange feeling inside of Eli had said that it would.

*

Eli crawled into his bed just after four thirty on the morning after Thanksgiving Day, exhausted. His heart wanted to hurt for his lost dog and for his injured mother, but The Strange wouldn't allow it. Drifting off to sleep in the empty, dark house, he knew that his beloved baby boy was neither in his bed nor in his back yard, among images of a man in a cloak. A tall, thin man, whose hands were large, long and claw like beneath the wide black sleeves of his cloak as he reached for him. The man moved towards him without leaving any footprints in the snow behind him as his feet never seemed to touch the ground. He didn't know what the man looked like, though. Not just because the hood of the cloak hung over his head, but because he couldn't make out the man's face. It seemed to Eli that he couldn't *see* the man's face. The tall, dark, shrouded man in his mind didn't *have* a face.

CHAPTER 14

Eli awoke to the shrill sound of the telephone ringing. It had slowly seeped into his odd dreams, awakening him a step at a time and he opened his eyes to the bright sunshine glaring through his bedroom widow, listening to the jingling bell of the telephone. Shielding his eyes from the light and turning over in his bed, he looked at his digital alarm clock. 12:17. Alertness took hold and he sat up sharply in his bed, knowing that he was supposed to call Bob at eleven o'clock.

He jumped out of bed and ran for the phone in the living room, pulling it from its cradle and placing it against his face.

"Hello?"

"Eli! Is everything okay?" Bob's worried voice came through the phone speaker. "When you didn't call, I got worried."

Rubbing his head and looking around the living room for a moment, he wanted to tell Bob that everything was just fine. Bob's voice called his name over the phone as the boy squinted his eyes in confusion, looking at nothing and everything at the same time. His eyes fell on the sofa nearest to the front door, and the blood splattered on it, as Eli wondered if the blood had been there since his mom had beaten him a long time ago. Random, painful images flashed in his mind but none of them made sense. Then one last image held in his mind; the sight of Hunter's empty collar in his hands.

Eli burst into tears. "Oh God, no!"

"Eli! What's wrong?" Bob's frantic voice came over the phone. "What happened?"

The boy was on the verge of hysteria. "He's gone! Oh God, Bob! He's gone!"

"What? What're you talking about?"

"Hunter's gone!" His words turned into a heartbreaking wail.

"Eli? Eli!" Bob yelled, not getting any response from the boy other than his cries. "Don't go anywhere! I'll be right there!"

The aging professor hung up the phone, hoping that Eli would listen to him and stay at his house until he got there. The traumatized boy held the phone in his hands as he sat on the floor, crying. Bob drove the lengthy detours from Sewickley to Raccoon, calling Eli's house with his cell phone every once in a while. The line was busy each time and his heart pounded in fear for the boy, hoping that he was okay.

When he couldn't get a hold of Eli that morning, Bob had made a series of phone calls and found out about Virginia Marshall's hospitalization, leaving him wondering how the boy was somehow left home alone. He didn't understand what Eli had said about Hunter, but the torture in the boy's voice was all Bob had needed to get him moving. And move he did, speeding his way to Eli's house in less than an hour.

Bob skidded his car to a halt in the Marshall's snow covered driveway, running to the house and bursting through the unlocked front door as he called Eli's name. The older man hurried through the small, unfamiliar home looking for the boy, finding him sitting at the kitchen table. He was showered and dressed, sitting with his hands between his knees and staring out at the back yard. The professor relaxed a bit when he saw his young friend, and he stood in the kitchen doorway.

"Eli." Bob said. "Are you okay, buddy? What happened?"

Eli slowly turned his gaze in his direction, and Bob watched as the heartbreaking, drawn look of sorrow left his face as it lit up with a boyish smile. "Bob! Hi!" He said. "How was your Thanksgiving?"

"Eli. What happened to your mother? And where's Hunter?"

The light in Eli's face disappeared, and his chin began to tremble as tears trickled down his cheeks. "He's gone, Bob. Hunter's gone." He slapped his hands over his face and began to sob. "I don't know what happened to him or where he is, and I don't know if I can get him back."

"Oh, Eli." Bob rushed over to the boy, looking down at him as he cried. He knelt down in front of Eli, placing his hands his shoulders. Tears began to appear in his own eyes. "I'm so sorry."

Bob reached out for Eli, pulling him close and hugging him for the first time. Tossing his arms around the older man's neck and placing his face in his shoulder, the boy hugged him tight and cried. Tears pooled in Bob's eyes as he tried to soothe his young friend with meaningless, soft-spoken words while Eli wailed into his shoulder, bawling about how he wanted his dog back, he just wanted his baby boy back.

*

Eli remembered almost nothing of the night before. He told Bob that he had gone outside to bring Hunter in, couldn't find the dog, and went running off into the woods, looking for Hunter. Unable to remember much more than being cold, very cold, the boy had no story to tell. The Strange seemed to have erased the rest from his mind.

Bob had to tell Eli that his mother was in the hospital, and he watched as Eli was genuinely shocked and scared, before he mentioned that the police had a statement as to what had happened. Fear and confusion overwhelmed the boy's face and eyes when Bob told him that he had given the statement. The professor explained that his mother had been beaten pretty badly, and the police couldn't reveal any details to him.

"What happened here last night, Eli?" Bob asked.

"I—I don't know!" Eli cried out.

The aging professor held the crying boy in his arms again, wondering how Eli could have been left home alone and asking if he wanted to go see his mother.

"No!" Eli said. "No. I just want to find Hunter! And figure out what we have to do to stop The Strange."

"Okay, Eli." The older man said, beginning to feel that he would do whatever the boy wanted. "I have an idea about trying to find Hunter."

Eli's face lit up with a smile. "You do?"

"Yes. Do you happen to have any recent pictures of him?" Bob asked.

*

Driving along the fine streets of Sewickley, Robert Mikush respected his young friend's lack of desire to see his injured mother, taking the boy to his house so that they might devise a plan to find Hunter, before discussing ideas about how to stop The Faceless Man. The deaths occurring in the woods of Raccoon Township were all being attributed to animal attacks and the increasing cold was blamed on the greenhouse effect. The dead and twisted nature came about because of the drastic climate changes, experts said. The fouled water and the continued strange behavior in the area were accepted as normal for some reason, and went almost unnoticed. Raccoon Township and its surrounding areas were being slowly destroyed and devoured of all life and normalcy, while no one from the outside even knew about it. The Faceless Man had sealed the area off, keeping it all to himself, and Bob and Eli were the only ones that recognized it.

They sat together in front of Bob's computer as he created a color poster of Hunter. Using his scanner to load a picture of Hunter onto a blank page, the college professor wrote the words he wanted around it, placing both his and Eli's phone numbers on the poster along with reference to a $500 reward.

"Five hundred dollars?" Eli said in wonder. "My mom won't pay five hundred dollars for Hunter, and I don't have it."

The leather office chair squeaked as Bob turned to look at Eli. "I'm gonna pay it." He smiled at the thunderstruck look on the boy's face. "If it'll help bring your baby boy home to you and make you happy, I'll gladly pay it."

Eli looked at the enlarged color picture of Hunter on the computer monitor, and tears began to stream from his eyes. "Why? Why would you do that?"

"Because I like you Eli, and I know what Hunter means to you. You're a good kid whether you believe it or not. I think a little love thrown your way might make all the difference in the world. You may not be my son, but I've become attached to you and I want to help you become the best man you can." Bob finished with a smile.

Eli threw his arms around the aging professor, hugging him again. "Thank you, Bob. Thank you so much."

Bob only smiled while he reveled in the feel of his third hug from Eli that day, wondering when the last time was that the boy had shared so much human contact. Sadly, he guessed that it had been a very long time.

After printing fifty copies of the poster, Bob looked at the love, sorrow, and little bit of hope in Eli's eyes as he held the thick stack of paper in his hands. They planned to hang the posters all over Raccoon Township as Bob promised that he would even leave work early when he got a call about Hunter. Very carefully, the professor turned the subject to other matters.

"Have you had any new visions?"

Eli shook his head. "No, none. I don't know why, or what might be wrong. It just seems like ever since I stopped that one on the bus, I can't see anything anymore."

"Hmph." Bob mumbled, wanting to ask about the vision Eli had on the night before Thanksgiving, the one that was too fast. He wanted to ask if it was about Hunter, but he didn't want to give Eli any cause to blame himself for not seeing that his dog was going to disappear. "Nothing about The Faceless Man, or the Box?"

"No. Not visions, anyway." Eli saw Bob's curious look. "But I *know* things. Things I really shouldn't know, and I'm not even sure if they're happening now."

"What do you mean?" Bob asked.

"Well, I know that the deaths are because of The Faceless Man, but we already figured that out. But I know that he *needs* to kill those people. It, like, gives him power or something and he can only kill one at a time until he becomes strong enough."

"He's not powerful enough right now? He caused earthquakes for Christ's sake!" Bob exclaimed.

Eli shook his head, demonstrating that the quakes didn't matter. "No, he's not. He can do worse, much worse. Besides, that kinda stuff is mostly from the Box, helping close everybody off from him while he does what he does."

"What does he do?"

"He kills people and takes their souls, or eats their souls, or something. And it gives him power. Taking a living soul or whatever it is gives him power." Eli said. "He can't go very far away from the Box right now. He has to stay close to it, no matter what he's doing. He needs to feed on these souls, or whatever, to be strong enough to go away from the Box. Until then, he can't go too far away from it. He needs it right now."

"So he's depending on The Black Box for his existence right now?" Bob asked, intrigued.

"Yeah." Eli said. "He can't go too far away or he'll just . . . fade away. He feeds *it* every time he feeds himself." The boy closed his eyes, taking a deep breath. "It's kinda like making a building. First, the bulldozers come in and clear it all out, then dig the hole for the building. That's what the Box does. It sets up the whole thing so that The Faceless Man can survive. Just like the plane crash. The Box did that. Then it found the perfect person for The Faceless Man to take over. Now it does whatever it can to keep people away. The Faceless Man has to feed it to keep it going, and feed himself to make him stronger, so that he can be strong enough to leave the Box completely."

"Do you have any ideas on what we can do to stop him?"

"Not really." Eli dropped his eyes to his lap.

"Eli, I think we hit on it before." Bob said. "Especially since you said that he's depending on the Box. I think we need to take The Black Box away from him. I've been doing a little more research, and I didn't want to say anything until I was sure. But now that your mom has been mysteriously beaten, we need to do something. We need to do it now, before you end up in danger."

An odd chill ran up Eli's spine. "How do we take it from him?"

The older man shifted in his leather chair. "I haven't worked out the details yet, but it appears that we're gonna have to go down into those woods, attack him and take the Box away. Then we'll just run away as fast as we can."

Eli only looked at Bob.

"Now that I said it, it sounds kind of stupid." Bob laughed through his words. "It'll be a little harder than that, I know, but that's the basic idea. We have to get to the Box before this shit can go on any longer."

"Is it gonna work?" Eli asked. "Taking the Box away from him, will that do it?"

"I'm not positive, but all the old stories seem to point to something like that. There's an attack on The Faceless Man, they don't necessarily kill him, but they end up stopping the madness. I think that we need to try our best to kill him this time."

"How do we do that?"

"Okay, say he is still Old Man Junker for now. That means that he's still human, and that he can be killed." Bob saw the horror on Eli's face, and hesitated. "I'll worry about that part. You just need to focus on your visions. I think that they can be a big help. I mean, if you can see something about him or what he's going to do before he even does it, then we've got an advantage. It worked for the three great men of long ago, and it might work now."

"What do you mean?" Eli asked.

"There are some details about the origin of The Black Box that I didn't tell you before because I wanted to wait and see, and I think I've seen enough. In any case, I had told you about the three great men who imprisoned the sorcerer. One was a great warrior known for his fierceness in battle. His name had never been documented, but a certain phrase was always associated with him. I found an ancient translation meaning 'The Hammer', which seems appropriate since the warrior apparently carried a silver-headed, sledge type hammer with him. He was a greater warrior than any member of the kingdom's army, but never held any kind of rank or position of honor since he only fought when he felt it was necessary.

"Another was a wizard that traveled from very far away and had great interest in defending the kingdom. His name was Darion Von Zarovich, the great Mage. The nobles had gone to great lengths to contact the white mage, and offered to pay him whatever he wanted in their desperation. He refused payment, and even though I have read every piece of information I could on the subject, his vicious desire to fight the dark sorcerer is unclear. Still, his magic was invaluable at the end.

"The third man was a seer, who tried to predict the sorcerer's actions and assist the warrior in his battles."

Eli was enthralled by the tale once again, staring at the professor as he spoke.

"The seer's talents had been proven authentic many times over in the kingdom. During the times of peace, the common people, nobles, and the king would call on him for sights into the future, and he was right every time. Some of his fortunes were symbolic, because he didn't know the person well enough or have the true desire to see the future. Others were exact descriptions of future events, occurring most commonly when the subject was something he cared for greatly. He was known throughout the kingdom as Euriah, the great seer."

Eli felt a chill at the sound of the name.

"Euriah was much like you, Eli, and he played an important role in the imprisonment of the sorcerer. He was the one who envisioned the idea for imprisoning the sorcerer, and he was the one who sought out the other two. He couldn't fight the black wizard with great magic or weapons, but he led the small group of three to victory by seeing every move the black wizard was making, or about to make. Euriah was the one who brought about the Triad, the mystical power that was formed between the three men. We don't have a white wizard, Eli, and I may not be much of a warrior, but we do have you. You are our seer, and I think your visions are the key to our success."

The blue eyed boy sat silent, looking across the fine study at Bocci, who lay sprawled across the hardwood floor on her side.

"Eli, your visions have been proven correct, you told me so yourself. You just have to stop fighting them and accept them as they come. I think that if you do that, they won't hit you as hard or be so traumatic. Who knows, you might even be able to take them in stride while conscious and alert." Bob said.

"Bob, please don't put this all on me." Eli said in a weak voice, keeping his eyes on Bocci. "I can't handle it."

"I'm not putting it all on you, Eli." Bob replied. "I'm going to be there with you every step of the way. And you *can* handle it. You're much stronger than you think. You don't give yourself enough credit."

Eli continued staring across the room at the chocolate Labrador retriever, not knowing what to say. His mind wandered off to the heartache of his missing dog.

"She's pregnant." The boy said.

"What?"

Eli shook his head quickly, appearing confused at his own words. "She's pregnant. Bocci's pregnant."

"What?" Bob repeated, turning to look at his dog. "How do you—" He stopped, looking back at the strange boy.

"I just know." Eli said.

The aging professor smiled wide. "Did you actually see something or—"

"No. I just knew it, kinda like I know the other things." The boy looked up at the older man with desire in his deep blue eyes. "But how do I *use* that?"

"I don't know what to tell you. But we need to figure that out, and fast." Bob turned to look at Bocci, who looked back at him with a slow, tired gaze. "You've been a naughty girl, haven't you?" He asked with a smile. "I wanted to breed you with one of your own, but at least your babies will have a hero's blood in them."

Eli stared at the posters with Hunter's picture on them and the word 'MISSING' printed across the top. "Yeah." He said as tears arose in his eyes and his voice trembled. "Too bad the hero isn't around anymore."

The distraught boy burst into fresh tears again, and Bob dropped his smile as he tried to comfort him.

"We'll find him, Eli. Whatever it takes, whatever I have to do, we'll find the proud daddy of Bocci's babies."

Bob spent several minutes calming the boy before fixing himself a drink and Eli a large mug of hot chocolate. He returned to the study, seeing that Eli was only sitting in what had become his chair, staring at the pictures of Hunter on the posters.

"Are you sure you don't want to go see your mother?" Bob asked.

"I'm sure." Eli said, looking up from the posters. "I just don't want to see her like that."

Bob set the large mug of hot chocolate on the desk in front of his young friend. "You don't remember anything that happened last night? Nothing at all after you went looking for Hunter?"

"No! I told you I didn't!" Eli said in a defensive tone.

"Okay, okay. Relax. I just don't understand how you could forget everything that you told the police, that's all."

Eli took a sip of the steaming hot chocolate before sitting back in his chair.

"It's already getting dark," Bob said, "so we'll put the posters up tomorrow, okay?"

Eli nodded.

"Look, why don't you just stay here tonight? I've got plenty of space, and that way we can head out early in the morning to hang the posters. I don't think you should be in that house alone tonight."

Eli sat upright. "What if Hunter comes home? I won't be there for him!"

"I'm sure he'll wait for you, Eli." Bob said. "He's gotta be hungry by now, and I'm sure he misses you, too. He loves you just as much as you love him, and if he goes to your house tonight I'll bet that he waits for you to come home."

"But, what if he's cold? I want to let him inside if he's cold." Eli argued.

"Eli, he'll be just fine. You said that he was very rarely ever in the house anyway, so he'll be alright." Bob retorted. "I don't want you in that house alone, do you understand? Between your mother and Hunter, I'm worried about you being there alone, okay? Just stay here tonight, and we'll work out the rest in the morning."

Eli sat back in the chair, sulking. "Okay."

"We should also get a hold of your grandparents, I'm sure they're worried about you."

"No." Eli cried. "I don't want to go stay with them! I want to be at the house in case Hunter comes home!"

"Alright, Eli. Damn! I just want to let them know that you're okay. Besides, they may be able to tell you exactly what happened to your mother." Bob said calmly. "You've had a long day, and you need rest. We'll work on triggering those visions of yours some other time." Bob finished with a smile.

Eli finally smiled back. "Alright."

"Okay then!" Bob exclaimed. "I'll go get one of the bedrooms ready for you. Just stay here and hang out with Bocci for a while."

Bob left the study with his glass of whiskey in hand, climbing the stairs and walking into the bedroom that used to be his son's, so many years ago, and flipped on the light. The room was immaculate, and the bed was made perfectly. He sat down on the bed and drank his whiskey. There was nothing that he had to do to get the room ready; Bob had lied about that. The professor simply wanted to give the boy a few minutes to drink his hot chocolate and allow the Valium, which he had slipped into it, take effect. Eli had been through a very difficult day and deserved some rest.

His beloved dog, his baby boy, had disappeared and his mother had been beaten so badly that she had been hospitalized. Bob found it very strange that Eli couldn't remember anything about his mother's beating last night, even though he had given the statement to the police. Maybe he had been out in the cold looking for Hunter when it happened? Maybe it had traumatized him so badly that he couldn't remember? Maybe Eli knew everything that had happened and was just afraid to talk about it? There were a lot of 'maybes', and a lot of things were strange these days. Bob figured that he would try to jog Eli's memory somehow, either by information from his grandparents or by getting him to go see his mother at the hospital. Time was growing short, and the aging professor had to find something to jog the boy's memory, along with his visions. The Strange was getting too close to Eli for Bob's comfort, with Hunter and his mother, and the man that had brought The Black Box to Raccoon Township knew that they had to end this, soon.

Bob emptied his glass of whiskey, pulled himself from the bed and returned to the study where Eli was staring dazedly at some of the books on his desk.

A false smile showed in the fine features of the older man. "You about ready to hit the sack? C'mon, you need to get some sleep."

*

Eli passed out as soon as Bob turned the light off in what used to be his son's bedroom. The troubled older man went down the stairs and into the kitchen, pouring another tall glass of whiskey on the rocks before using a key to unlock his desk drawer and the glass lid over it. He pulled out the decorative silver box with the glass facing and set it on his desk, staring at the sideways 'V' of mysterious metal, with the carving of an eye on it, and running his fingers along the glass overtop of it. The swirling colors of the metal captivated him, and the aging professor tried to remember if it had ever emitted a light like that before.

Sitting in his study drinking his whiskey, Bob stared at the small piece of the Triad lock, amazed at the chain of events that had occurred due to this small, insignificant piece of metal. Although he didn't think that it was insignificant anymore. Many lives had been lost or disrupted, and much destruction had come about because of the object. Not directly, but one event had led to another and Bob now found himself, as well as the young boy drugged and sleeping upstairs, at a crossroads. He could no longer sit back in awe and remorse at what was happening in Raccoon Township because of the presence of The Black Box, which *he* had brought there. He had to take action to make up for his mistakes, whatever the cost, and stop this horror right now. Unfortunately, Bob knew that meant placing the boy he had learned to love as his own directly in harms way, and he hated himself for it. But he also knew that the boy was a wonder to the world, and that when this was all over, he would be a much better young man for it.

"If nothing else, he'll be a better quarterback." Bob said to the empty room with a smile.

Bob stared at the piece of the Triad, realizing that it wasn't just a lock, but the key to solving the whole mystery surrounding The Black Box.

*

The tall, cloaked thing walked through the woods, hauling the 110-pound body of the young boy behind him with ease. A gruesome smile arose on his unseen lips beneath the hanging hood of his black cloak. He dragged the boy up the three aging, wooden steps that led to the front door of the little shack he called home, taking the body inside and dropping it on the wooden floor. The mangled, blood soaked boy groaned as his head hit the floor, and the cloaked thing smiled wider as it paced the floor of the small shack.

"Good!" It cried out with glee in its high pitched and demonic voices. "You're still alive! I thought I might have gotten carried away, taking you for myself instead of saving you for the other!"

The boy, his chest slashed and bleeding with half of his face missing, groaned again and twitched his arms and legs in an effort to crawl away.

"You should be proud, boy!" The thing cried out. "You're serving a very honorable purpose! Not that the others haven't," It said, holding a hand to its nonexistent face and frowning. He then smiled his unseen smile. "But this part is soooo much fun! The transformation from good to evil is always so interesting! I love a good challenge!"

The cloaked man walked over to the boy, standing over him and looking into his wide, frightened eyes. The thing drew back its hood, and the boy let out a bubbling squeal of a scream.

"Why don't we get right to it?" He said with an unseen mouth.

The boy saw the man's expression change, even though he had no face. His mouth drew down into a grimace of impending doom and his strange eyes blazed with hate and exhilaration as he clamped his clawlike left hand over the boy's throat, beginning to chant in some other language. He raised his right hand over his head, and brought it down hard into the boy's face, puncturing the boy's eyeballs with the claws that were his fingers. Thick, clear fluid seeped out of the boy's eye sockets and onto his young, fresh cheek on one side of his face and raw, bleeding flesh and bone on the other. The boy tried to scream, but the thing's hand closed tighter around his throat and its fingers sliced into the soft, warm flesh. The thing cloaked in black continued to chant with both of his voices, and on the kitchen table, the black, ornate box began to vibrate, emitting odd sounds and wondrous colors. The man hooked the fingers of his long right hand in the boy's eye sockets while slicing his throat open with the other hand. His chant grew more intense, and his eyes blazed with swirling color as he pulled upward with his right hand and ran the other to the floor. He let out a blood curdling scream of triumph as he tore the boy's head from his spine and the flesh of his neck, holding it in the air in front of him. The light emitting from the box was blinding, lighting up the small shack as if the sun itself were in there.

The cloaked man rose from the floor, walking over to the box with the boy's head in his hand. He held it over the box and chanted again, allowing the pulsing blood to flow from the torn and ravaged flesh of the boy's neck onto the box. The light of wondrous colors pulsed with each drop of blood, and the man rested the boy's eyeless head on top of the box as he turned towards the headless, twitching corpse that rested on the hardwood floor so that he could finish his work.

The dark, cloaked thing walked out of the house minutes later, holding several bloody objects in his hands. It strolled around the side of the house and knelt down in front of a small opening in the bricks that made up the crawl space under the house. Placing the bloody remains into the hole, the dark, cloaked man spoke again in the alien language. When he finally pulled himself from his knees, the man gazed down at the shadowed opening in the bricks beneath his dwelling place.

"Be still, your time will come." He said.

Black Box

The Faceless Man stood in the cold darkness that The Black Box had created for him, breathing deeply. The dark, cloaked thing looked up into the gloomy night sky, seeing the dim, hazy sparkling of the stars above.

"I know you're here, Euriah. But the Triad is not complete, and you will not defeat me this time." He lowered his gaze and smiled at the dark hole in the foundation of his home. "I will make sure of that."

CHAPTER 15

After sleeping for sixteen and a half hours with a little help from the Valium in his hot chocolate, Eli awoke sometime around noon, groggy and hungry. Bob made a few sandwiches for the two of them, and they headed out to Raccoon Township.

They spent most of the afternoon traveling the rural roads of Raccoon, stapling the posters of Hunter to trees and telephone poles. Eli seemed to be in high hopes as they hung the last poster, and he wanted to go home and see if maybe Hunter was there. As soon as the car stopped in his driveway, Eli opened the door and ran into the backyard, calling for his dog. Bob walked toward the house, and the boy joined him from the back yard with his head hung low. Once inside the house, the aging professor called the animal shelter, giving them a description of Hunter, the general location, and a number for them to call if there were any reports on the wandering Rottweiler. Eli checked the messages on the answering machine, receiving one from the hospital, one from the police department asking for Mr. Marshall, and three from his grandparents, wondering where he was and if he was okay.

"Do you think we should call them now?" Bob asked.

The boy agreed, dialing the phone and handing it to his new friend. An elderly woman answered on the second ring.

"Hi. Is this Mrs.—" He looked at Eli.

"Porter." The boy whispered.

"Mrs. Porter?" Bob asked.

"Yes, it is. May I ask who's calling?"

"Mrs. Porter, my name is Robert Mikush and your grandson, Elijah Marshall is a student of mine." Bob ignored the questioning look on Eli's face. "He's here with me right now."

"Oh thank God!" She exclaimed. "Is he okay? Can I talk to him?"

"He's fine Mrs. Porter." He replied.

"Betty, please."

"Okay, Betty. He's fine, he's just a little shaken up is all. I was wondering if you've heard anything about his mother. How is she doing? Have they found anything out yet?"

"She's in bad shape, Mr. Mikush."

"Bob, please." He said with a smile.

"Virginia's not doing too well, Bob. Her jaw is broken and she's on a lot of medication right now. The doctors and the police haven't been able to talk to her at all." Betty said.

"Have the police figured out what happened yet?" Bob asked.

She sighed. "No, they haven't. They told us the story that Eli told them, but they haven't got any real ideas yet. Did he tell you what happened?"

He cleared his throat. "He tried to, Betty, but he was so upset that he just kept rambling. Would you be able to tell me? I know that it's family business and all, but I'm very concerned about Eli. He's a good kid and I hate to see something like this happen." Bob winked at the boy.

"Well, Bob, from what I understand Virginia has been running around with a few different men. I hate to see my daughter do something like that, but I had a feeling that it was going on when she left Matthew with us. I asked her to leave Eli with us as well if she was too busy for the kids. She just sort of ignored me and said that he could take care of himself. Poor boy." Eli's grandmother sighed in sorrow and paused for a few moments.

"Anyway," Betty continued, "the police told us that Eli had told them that when they got home from our house on Thanksgiving night, his mother had gone out again. She came home hours later with some man who was yelling at her, and then he started hitting her. It may have been something about the other men she's been running with. It seems that he began to hit her with a belt, and when Eli came out to see what was going on, the man hit him as well. Eli hid until the man left, and he called the police. They found Virginia unconscious in the basement. Apparently the man had thrown her down the stairs."

Bob could hear the sobs beginning in Betty's voice. "Oh Goodness. I'm so sorry Mrs. Porter. And they don't have any idea who this man is?"

Betty sniffled. "No. They asked Virginia's friends at work who she's been running with, and they checked up on all those men. None of them are suspected though." She paused for a moment. "Is Eli there? Can I talk to him?"

The professor looked over at Eli, pointing to the phone. The boy waved his hands and shook his head.

"He's here, Betty, but he's sleeping right now." Bob said, shrugging his shoulders.

"Oh, that poor boy. He must be worried to death about his mother."

Bob looked at Eli, knowing that he wasn't. "Yes, he is. Are they allowing visitors at the hospital? I was wondering if I could take him to see his mother."

"No." Betty said. "Her father and I were only allowed to see her for a few minutes, and then we were told to leave. I hope that they find whoever did this to her and that he fries for it." The tears were starting to come on strong.

"So do I, Betty." He said with his eyes on Eli. "Look, I'm going to let you go. I'm sorry to have bothered you at a time like this, but I wanted to let you know that Eli is safe."

Betty swallowed her tears, letting out a shuddering sigh. "I appreciate that Mr. Mikush. Thank you. We would like for him to come stay with us as soon as possible."

"Actually, I wanted to ask if it was okay if Eli stayed with me for a little while. You're going to have your hands full with Matt and his mother, and he needs someone to talk to right now."

"Oh." She replied, startled. "Well, I guess that would be okay. And I'm sure that he is very shaken up, since he saw it happen and was even involved. Are you going to give him some counseling?"

He smiled. "Something like that, yes. I'm going to give you my cellular phone number, so that you can keep Eli informed about his mother." Bob rattled off the phone number, telling her to call at any time.

Betty thanked him again for his concern and asked him to tell Eli that she and his grandfather loved him and that Matt missed him. Bob said that he would, and ended the conversation, hanging up the phone and looking at his young friend.

"Your grandparents say that they love you and that Matt misses you." Bob said.

Eli hung his head, feeling the guilt of neglecting the few loved ones in his life. "Did she tell you what happened?" He asked.

"Yes, she did. Do you want me to tell you, or do you want to try to remember it yourself?"

"I told you that I can't remember." Eli said, looking up at the professor with a touch of anger. "Just tell me."

Bob recanted to Eli what Betty had told him about Virginia's beating. The boy actually cried a little as he heard the story, not taking pleasure in her beating, even though she had beaten him not so long ago.

"Is that where the cuts on your face really came from, and not from the trees when you ran through the woods?" Bob asked.

Tears stood out in Eli's eyes. "I don't think so. I swear that the trees cut me, Bob. I swear they did."

Frustrated, the older man rose from the sofa and paced the floor of the living room. "You can see things before they even happen, Eli. You have knowledge of things that you shouldn't have. But you can't remember being hit by some strange man that was about to beat your mother to death? It doesn't make sense, Eli! It doesn't make sense at all!"

"I'm sorry, Bob." The boy pleaded. "Something's wrong. I can't see anything about my mom, or even about Hunter! You used to say that maybe if I cared about something enough, I could see it." Eli stood up, yelling. "But Hunter is the greatest thing in this world to me, and I can't see SHIT about him! I can't see why he left, what happened to him, where he is, or if he's even still alive! What good are the visions if I can't even find my dog?" He fell back onto the sofa, holding his crying face in his hands. "What fucking good is any of it?"

Bob moved towards him. "What are you saying?"

Eli raised his tear filled face. "Why are we even trying to stop this shit? We can't, and you know it! Why don't we just forget about it? Just let The Faceless Man do whatever he's going to do here and move on? He won't stay here forever, I know that! Why don't we just stop fighting it and wait until it's all over?"

"What the hell?" Bob exclaimed. "Eli, you were the one who started the fight against The Strange! You brought me into this quest and inspired me to go further into redeeming myself than just trying to find the Box at the crash site! You are the one leading this battle. Why would you even think of stopping now?"

"Why?" Eli cried out. "Everything is being taken away from me, that's why! Hunter, Matt, my mom, and even Anna. They're all gone! Why? Because I'm the one who had to watch the damn plane crash and I'm the one who came up with the crazy idea of trying to stop it. The closer we get to finding a way to stop it, the worse it gets. I'm losing everything, Bob! Can't you FUCKING SEE THAT?"

Bob's hand flashed forward, grabbing Eli by the front of his shirt and pulling him close to his face. Eli's expression didn't change as the professor's intelligent eyes burned into his.

"What the hell is wrong with you, Eli?" Bob continued to stare into the boy's eyes. "Why would you talk like this after all that we've discussed and all that we've discovered together?"

Eli used both of his hands to push his small, thin body away from the older man's grip. "Because Hunter's gone." He continued to cry. "He's the only thing I've ever really had in my life, and now he's gone. So what do I care?"

Bob's anger and frustration faded in that instant and he stepped away from the boy with a hand to his mouth. "My God. It's The Strange." His other hand rose to point at Eli. "The Strange has gotten a hold on you hasn't it?"

Eli simply shook his head as he cried.

"After all this time, after watching the plane crash and being the first person to be exposed to the evil that surrounded the box but yet still going on to be the first to see through all of it, The Strange finally got you. Didn't it?" Bob asked, speaking with an amazed expression on his face.

The suffering boy looked up with his face twisted in confusion, battling between determination and helplessness. "No. I've just had enough. I can't take any more of this shit. I just want to stop fighting and get my life back."

"That's what *they* would say, Eli. All those people out there, the teachers that are hurting people, the police that don't seem to give a shit, the young punks shooting everyone they see, the good people turned bad and careless. That's the way they think. And we've agreed that The Strange has got a strong hold on them." Bob said, moving closer. "I never worried about you being taken by The Strange. I just assumed that you were too strong. I never thought that he would be able to find a weakness."

"What are you talking about?" Eli sobbed.

"Him. The Faceless Man, or maybe the Box. It doesn't matter which. He knows that you are the one, just like I do. That's why he's done this to you. He's focusing on everyone close to you, trying to weaken you so that you might also be taken by The Strange. I've had a revelation, and I don't think that he can touch you, Eli. He can't hurt you as long as you oppose him. But if he can weaken you and beat you down by hurting those around you, then maybe you'll be taken by The Strange and become just another one of the people who just don't care. Then he would be able to survive and move on to whatever it is he wants to do. He's *afraid* of you."

"Afraid of me? I doubt that." Eli said, beginning to shed his helplessness.

"Think about it for a moment." The professor said, beginning to pace again as he held a hand to his chin with the other arm across his chest. "If you *are* the one that began this battle against him, who else does The Faceless Man have to fear? No one. He needs to have you fall into The Strange, which you are resistant to. How does he do it? He makes you weak. How does he do that? He damages the most important things in your life. He makes your mother attempt to kill you since he can't. But then Hunter steps in and saves you from her. So what does he do then? He creates a situation where your mother would remove your little brother from your everyday life, causing her to neglect her children since she is taken by The Strange. What next?" Bob stopped pacing, looking directly at the boy. "He makes Hunter disappear."

Eli's jaw dropped, and he fully understood everything that he was being told.

"The Faceless Man removes Hunter from your life, and you are then weak against The Strange. You have been taken by The Strange, Eli. How deeply, I don't know. But I think that I may have a solution."

Black Box

"Wait! No!" Eli said. "What did he do to Hunter? Where's Hunter?"

"You know that I don't know that." Bob said. "I'm not like you. I can't see things or know things that I shouldn't. I can only see what has been laid before me and decipher the facts. I have seen many just now, but we'll discuss that later. But I *can* say that The Faceless Man is responsible for Hunter being missing, at least I think so. He did it to weaken you and let you be taken by The Strange. It seems like it's working, although not for long."

The aging professor moved quickly towards the sofa as he reached into his left trouser pocket and pulled a neatly folded cloth from within. Startled and slightly scared, Eli flinched away from the older man, looking between his narrow face and the cloth in his hand.

"I want you to think about the night that Hunter disappeared and your mother was beaten. I want you to think about that for a moment, and try to bring on a vision." Bob spoke in a calm voice.

Eli closed his eyes for a few moments, thinking about the night of his mother's beating, and all he could see was his mad sprint through the woods.

"I can't. I can't see anything." The boy said, disappointed.

"Really?" The professor asked as he slowly unfolded the soft cloth.

In a moment, the V-shaped piece of the Triad glared its brilliant colors upon Eli's face, creating an illusion of age. The companions gazed at the piece of strange metal in awe, amazed at the brilliance of the wondrous colors that emitted from it. Even though he had possessed the artifact for several years, Bob had never seen it look like that. The tiny beams of colorful light seemed to carve into the boy's skin, placing the appearance of an older man's face over his. It was a kind face, a *knowing* face. In an instant, Professor Mikush knew that it was the face of Euriah, the great seer from so very long ago.

Moments after the light touched him, Eli twitched hard and fell back into the sofa as his hands gripped the cushions beneath him and his mouth, and the mouth of the face that was masked in light over his, dropped open. Bob was almost alarmed and wanted to help the boy, but he knew that he had to stick with the idea that had struck while he drank his whiskey in the study the night before. He *had* to find out. He had to know.

"Can you see anything, Eli?" Bob asked in a soft voice.

The boy held still, his mouth gaping and his hands clenched tight on the sofa cushions.

"Think of Thanksgiving night. Think of your mother. Think about how she got hurt that night. Can you see anything?" He asked again.

Eli's eyes were moving rapidly behind their lids, and his body shuddered as he began to speak. The mask of light over his face spoke along with him. "I see . . . I see the back yard. I'm cold. I'm so cold that it hurts, but I'm scared and crying. I have a flashlight and I'm looking for Hunter's footprints in the snow.

And then . . ." He moved his head from side to side. "It doesn't . . . make sense. I see two different things!"

Bob moved the Triad piece closer to the boy, and the light emitting from it intensified. "Tell me what you see, Eli."

"I see some prints in the snow, Hunter's and a man's. I follow them out to the driveway and the front yard. I go to the mailbox, and there's a letter inside. No, not a letter, but a note and . . . oh, God!" The boy cried out.

"Eli, just calm down and tell me what you see."

"There's money, lots of it. And a note that I kind of understand. I run inside and draw on a piece of paper or something. There's writing on it, my mom's writing. It has names and numbers and dollar signs and . . ." Eli's eyes snapped open, and he looked at Bob with horror. "Hunter!"

"What? What about Hunter?" He looked at Eli's face and the mask of light over it.

"His name was on the paper!" The boy cried out, and the light over his face began to fade. "My mom sold him! The note and the money told me so! And then she came home and . . . and . . ." Tears streamed from Eli's innocent eyes. "I did it! I hit her!" He slipped into hysterics, crying and looking around the room frantically. "I wore some of my dad's stuff, and I hit her again and again with Hunter's collar just like she used to hit me with my dad's belt! Oh God, Bob! I almost killed my mom!"

Pulling the Triad piece away, the older man placed an arm around the boy to comfort him and the colorful light disappeared.

"I told her what would happen if she did anything to him!" Eli bawled into his older friend's shoulder. "I hit her and kicked her and yelled at her. She cried and screamed and asked for me to stop, but I didn't. I didn't mean to do it, Bob, I swear! I hit her in the face with Hunter's collar, hurt her hands and then threw her down the steps. How could I do that? How could I do that and then call the police to come help her and lie to them about some strange guy? How could I?" He babbled hysterically.

Bob could only sit on the sofa with an arm around the boy, stunned. He had feared that Eli might retaliate against his mother's beatings, but not to that extent. Feeling the Triad piece pulse and vibrate in his left hand, he decided to try again. Pushing the boy back into a sitting position, the curious professor looked into his red, wet face.

"Calm down, Eli, and tell me what happened."

Eli envisioned the entire scene that took place the night that Hunter disappeared, describing all of it in detail, including the beating of his mother. Bob sat and listened, horror struck by the image in his mind.

"Eli, I want you to tell me the other thing you saw."

The boy blubbered, "What?"

"You said, at first, that you saw two different things. Tell me what the other one was. Here, take this." He slid the piece of the Triad into Eli's hand. "*Now* tell me what you see."

Eli's hand clenched tight over the artifact as soon as it made contact with his skin, and Bob soon thought to pull the Triad piece out of the boy's hand since it appeared that he was being electrocuted. Eli's body began to convulse, and the hand that held the artifact turned bright white in the tightness of its grip. His eyes visibly rolled back to reveal only their whites, his lips tightened against each other in a thin line, and his free hand pounded against the sofa cushions repeatedly while his legs stuck straight out in front of him. A bright, wiry stream of light surrounded his tightly clenched hand, running up his arm to his neck and spreading over his body before it crawled slowly over his face. Bob stood frozen in indecision, wanting to help the boy in his terror, yet knowing that this was *exactly* the type of response he had been hoping for since the boy had first mentioned his visions.

Eli sat upright on the sofa, ceasing his convulsions and looking straight ahead as he loosened his grip on the Triad. The professor watched in wonder and amazement as the streams of light running over the boy's body seemed to be *absorbed* into his flesh. The skin of the boy's face seemed to shiver and flutter with the mask of the face of light, and his eyes remained straightforward until the movement in his skin stopped.

Bob's heart pounded hard in his chest, and it took a moment for him to gain the strength to speak. "What is the *true* story?"

"This is the truth." Eli said in an almost monotone voice. "I looked for prints in the snow with the flashlight and didn't find anything special. Something was wrong. I started feeling really weird, like it was so much easier to not fight and to just let it happen. It felt good, and I didn't know how much it hurt to fight until I stopped fighting. I took Hunter's collar inside, and sat in the kitchen for a while. I started cleaning up the stuff that fell off of the refrigerator when I was looking for the flashlight, and found the note that my mother had written to me a long time ago. I *did* run a pencil over it to show what it said underneath, and I saw the stuff about Hunter. I knew that she had written it a long time ago and that she would've already sold him if she was gonna do such a thing. But she hadn't. Sure, she beat me and wasn't around very much, but I think that she was afraid of me, too. Afraid of what I might do if she sold my dog. Besides, having him around kept the peace between me and her, and she liked that. As long as I had Hunter to run with, I didn't give a shit what she did. So she didn't do it."

Bob listened closely to the wondrous boy's calm speech. "What happened next? What *really* happened?"

Eli could see it in his mind. He *felt* what The Strange had been able to make him see and believe in his broken hearted despair for Hunter, while he *knew* the truth that seemed to prove that his mother hadn't sold his dog.

His mother never looked at any papers or an envelope on the coffee table, because there weren't any. She had simply entered the house, and he had just questioned her about where she had been.
Eli only laughed. "You're not going to leave us behind while you go out and fuck a bunch of guys. I am not going to live like that."
Virginia turned to put her coat in the front closet. "I don't know what the hell has gotten into you, Elijah, but you better shut your mouth before—"
A hard whipping strike came to her hands. Virginia cried out in pain and dropped her coat, not any papers, on the floor, holding her stinging wrists together and looking up at her son. Eli was standing right in front of her with his legs spread wide, his right hand drawing back, and his mad, swirling eyes blazing.
"What the fuck did you do to my dog?" He screamed at her.

Eli still wouldn't look at the older man. "I don't know. I was in some kind of haze or something. The next thing I knew, I watched her when she came in the front door and started to beat the shit out of her with Hunter's collar." Tears ran from Eli's eyes, and his trance began to falter. "She was putting her coat in the closet and I just started hitting her. I really did do it. I know that for sure. I just don't know why." The tortured boy finally broke down, crying.
Bob halted before comforting the boy as the idea of Eli beating his mother to near death horrified him, but so had the idea of his mother beating him. The Strange was the difference between the two stories, allowing him to take confidence in believing that it hadn't really been Eli that had done it. The aging professor felt that whatever power The Faceless Man was using to produce the dementia that took hold of so many people, and caused so much damage, around the crash site was very strong indeed. The Strange had deluded his young friend's mind, using Hunter's disappearance not only as his weakness, but also as the fuel for his rage against his mother.
"So you never saw any footprints leading to the mailbox or an envelope with money and a note in it?" Bob asked.
"No." Eli sobbed. "I only scribbled the pencil on the old note. I knew that she wouldn't do it. I was mad at her for even calling people about it, but I didn't mean to hit her! She didn't sell my baby boy! What's happening to me, Bob? I don't even know what I'm thinking anymore! Why would I do that? Why would I talk about giving in to The Faceless Man?"
Bob smiled, knowing that he had broken through The Strange and into the boy's heart. "It's not your fault, Eli. It was The Strange, and we both know it.

The Strange made you see things and made you do this, that's all." He reached over and comforted his young friend as he cried. "It's okay, buddy. It's all gonna be okay."

Holding the boy in his arms and sliding the piece of ancient metal from his hand, the professor wondered if what he said was true. It was easy for him to say it, but he didn't know if he believed it. His experiment with the piece of the Triad lock had caused amazing physical reactions with Eli as it ignited the gift of the boy's visions to an extent beyond his imagination, but Bob didn't know what it all meant. A flurry of ideas ran through his mind, and he had come to quite a few solid conclusions on many points having to do with The Strange and all the factors that surrounded it. Eli was the key to it all, and the aging professor that was slowly becoming a father figure to the suffering, dysfunctional boy didn't know if he could truly promise him that it was all going to be okay.

*

The odd pair of adventurous companions sat at the Marshall's kitchen table some time later, sipping at the bowls of hot soup that Eli had cooked in an effort to fight against the bone chilling cold outside. The confused, shame filled boy had showed Bob the hiding place inside of his closet and all that he had hidden in there on Thanksgiving night. He displayed the blood splattered clothes, the penciled note, and Hunter's blood soaked collar with a look of guilt on his face, while pointing out that the envelope, which he had imagined finding in the mailbox, wasn't there. The lack of the envelope began to reinforce the idea that the second version of the boy's memory really was the truth. After venturing into the driveway in search of a grown man's footprints and finding nothing more than the fading prints that Virginia Marshall had left behind during her daily trips to retrieve the mail, Eli's second vision was confirmed. His mother truly hadn't sold his beloved Baby Boy, and so the early teenager was left with the aching question as to why his dog had left him.

Bob sat at the kitchen table while Eli had been cooking the soup, asking the boy if he wanted to hear some of the ideas he had come up with concerning The Black Box. Eli said that he did, and as they allowed the steaming hot soup to cool, Professor Mikush began his explanation.

"Some of this is probably going to sound kind of crazy and far fetched, but these are just some things that I've started to wonder about." He knew that the boy didn't care, since the whole thing was crazy. "I think that you've pinpointed most of the early stuff. The Box somehow made the plane crash, using the souls of the people on board as a type of sacrifice. It called out to Old Man Junker for some reason, and used him as the host for The Faceless Man. The Faceless Man starts out weak, like when you and Anna saw him in the woods that day. So the Box needs to protect him by creating The Strange. It feeds off of the life around it, the animals, the plant life, even the light in the sky. It must also feed off of disaster and confusion, since it has made people do strange things this whole time. The Box also helps seclude The Faceless Man from the rest of the world so that no one can come in and stop him before he can gain strength."

Eli nodded, since they had already discussed those points.

"The thing is, Eli, there's something more to all of this. The way that you just happened to be the one to see the plane crash for instance. And the way that you just happened to be the first one to see through The Strange, even though you were smack in the middle of its area and should have been taken by it long ago. You weren't, and you moved on to fight against it. Then the way that The Strange began to focus on you, trying to disrupt your life and weaken you, so that you could be taken. It seemed to see what gave you strength, and steal all of that away from you. It took your mom and had her beat you then take your brother away from you. It saw that Anna meant a lot to you, and took her parents, making them keep her away from you. It saw that Hunter had been your salvation many times, including against your mother that one night and against Old Man Junker that day in the woods. So it took Hunter away from you, serving two purposes. It made you believe that you had caught your mother selling your dog, knowing that despair, anger, and hate would consume you so that you could finally be taken by The Strange, and it removed your mother from your immediate life as well by having you attack her. It's trying to get to you, Eli, and I'm trying to figure out why."

Bob sipped at his cooling soup while the boy looked up at him wide eyed from his own spoonful of soup. "I'm thinking that there is a great amount of destiny involved here. It's sort of like the question, which came first, the chicken or the egg? Did you witness the plane crash because you are the one, or are you the one because you witnessed the plane crash? I don't know, and I can't answer that, but I do know that you are the one, Eli."

"The one for what?" The boy asked.

"The one that will end all of this. And I think this time, for good."

"C'mon, Bob." Eli said, rolling his eyes. "So what? I can see things and know things. I'm just a kid, and there's nothing all that special about me."

"Oh yes, there is." Bob said. "He's afraid of you, Eli. He somehow knows that you are the one, and that's why all of this is focused on you and all of those around you. Like I said before, since The Strange hasn't been able to take you, except for that short amount of time, I don't think that The Faceless Man can touch you. At least for now, while he's still trying to gain strength by taking people's lives. I don't know that for sure, but it seems that way. What I'm wondering, though, is if men like you have been around each time he has appeared?"

"What do you mean? That every time he comes around, so does someone that can fight him?"

"Yes, exactly." Bob said after swallowing a spoonful of soup. "Say there was, and that The Strange focused on them as it is on you. Imagine that they finally do give in, like you almost did. And that he was able to destroy them, and somehow continue his existence, even though it was in the Box."

"Okay. So what? What does that have to do with anything?" Eli asked, holding his hands out to his sides.

"You fought it off, Eli. With the help of the Triad piece, you fought it off. I don't think that any of the men in the past ever had it to be able to use its powers to fight him off. But you do, Eli. I think that this has somehow all been destined to happen, and that anything that happens from now on is destined to happen so that The Faceless Man and The Black Box will be destroyed forever. I think that this is going to be his last appearance in the world, ever." Bob said with a touch of finality.

"But we don't know how to fight him! We don't even know why he ends up back in the Box every time. Why does he go back in if he gets rid of the guy that can fight him every time?" Eli questioned.

"I don't know. I can only guess, but maybe it has to do with what you said before. Maybe he's looking for the lock? He can kill and gain strength all he wants, but as long as the lock exists, he can't go very far from the Box? What if that's it? What if he only has a certain amount of time to survive out of the Box, no matter how many souls he devours? What if something happens to scare him back into the Box? I don't know. We probably won't ever know. Maybe we could just wait until he goes back in the Box, but I don't think that's going to happen this time."

"Why not?" Eli asked.

"Because we have a piece of the Triad, and that has to mean something. If he really is looking for it, he has to know that it's close by, and he won't stop until he gets it. I truly believe that. The same feeling I've had from the moment I met you that told me you were very special and powerful is telling me that he is not going to stop this time. This is it, Eli. Right here, right now, in Raccoon Township of all places." Bob said.

"Why now? After all the hundreds of years since those three men first put him in the Box, why now?"

"I don't know that either." Bob said, shaking his head and looking down at his bowl. "That is what leads me to believe that it's you." He raised his eyes to meet Eli's. "You are the true destiny here. You brought the piece of the Triad and The Black Box together in the same place so that the black sorcerer might finally be defeated. I believe that somehow, some way, you are Euriah reborn and that you are drawing all of this to a final conclusion. The great seer began the great battle hundreds of years ago, and you are beginning it now."

"Bob, that's crazy!" Eli said, laughing. "I don't really think—"

"It's even in your birth name." Bob retorted. "Elijah. Euriah. Pretty damn close if you ask me."

Eli closed his mouth with a snap, staring at the professor.

"Some of my ideas are a little off, I'm sure. Like I said, we'll probably never know all of it. But when I saw you with the piece of the Triad lock in your hand, Eli, I knew then that I had been right all along." Bob leaned forward over the table. "From the moment I met you out at the crash site, I had a feeling that you were a wonder to this world, and that some kind of magic and mystery surrounded you. I held faith in that feeling because of the stories that I knew about the Box and the Triad and the fact that the curses surrounding the Box had actually come true with the plane crash." He took a long breath. "You, my dear boy, are the great seer. You are Euriah."

"I don't believe you!" Eli cried, standing up from the kitchen table so hard and fast that his chair fell to the floor behind him. "You're making this up to make me feel better about Hunter! You're just trying to make me think that him leaving was supposed to happen! Well I don't believe it! And I don't believe you!"

The older man sat calmly in his chair. "You don't have to believe me, Eli. And I'm not trying to make you think anything about Hunter. I want to find him as much as you do. I want him to be there when his puppies are born. I want him to come back to you and make you happy. But eventually, your destiny is going to take hold of you, and you will be shown the truth about yourself."

"Well, I don't believe it right now, and I don't think that I ever will. I'm Eli Marshall, not some old guy from long ago with kings and queens and stuff." He argued. "I'm just a thirteen year old kid. That's all. I just want to end this shit so that I can get my dog and my brother and even my mom back. Since when did you start believing in this destiny shit?"

Bob smiled. "Ever since I met you, Eli."

Eli opened his mouth to respond, and then closed it again. Thinking briefly of their meeting at the crash site, he knew that he couldn't say anything. His vision had told him to go there for the purpose of meeting Bob, he had said so himself. Eli turned and stormed out of the kitchen, walking into the dining room and seeing the figure of a person passing by the front window of the house. He let out a little yell and Bob came rushing into the room behind him.

"What? What's wrong?" Bob asked frantically.

Eli pointed towards the front window just as a light knocking sound came from the front door. They both looked at each other in silence, wondering who it could be. Their discussion had left both of them with a lingering chill in their spines, but more realistic ideas flashed in their minds. The cops. They had finally figured something out and had come to get the boy for beating his mother nearly to death. They each knew that they would stick to the story Eli had told the police, but as the knock repeated on the front door, they remembered the incriminating evidence he had pulled from the hiding place in his closet.

"The collar." Bob said.

The boy immediately took off running for his bedroom, hurrying to put the bloody items back into the hiding place while Bob moved towards the front door to answer it. Eli replaced the board in the corner of his closet, stomped into the bathroom, and turned on the faucet, washing away any excess blood from his hands. The professor let out a deep breath as he cast his eyes out of the front window, expecting to see the bright white image of a police cruiser in the driveway. Surprised to see only his and Virginia's cars in the driveway, he figured that whoever was at the door had gotten to Eli's house on foot.

Bob pulled the front door inward, having to look down at the figure in the doorway. The young, pretty blonde haired girl looked up at him with a pleasant, yet hesitant smile on her face.

"Hi." Anna said. "Is Eli here?"

Bob turned to call for him, seeing that the boy was standing right behind him. Eli had run into the living room at the sound of Anna's voice. The aging professor saw the stare their eyes were locked in, and he backed away with a smile on his face.

Anna's head tilted slightly as she smiled a caring, apologetic smile. "Hi, Eli."

She said.

Eli's face was entirely blank for a moment, then it lit up like a light bulb. "Anna! Hi!"

"I'm gonna go into the kitchen for a while." Bob said. He saw that his words went unheard by the two kids, and he wandered off to the kitchen, smiling.

"Are you okay? What's been going on?" Anna asked, her voice rising with emotion. "What happened to your mom? I heard something at school about her being in the hospital."

Tears stood out in Eli's eyes. "I'm fine. It's just that . . . well, a lot has happened since you . . . since we last talked."

Anna dropped her eyes. "I know, and I'm sorry. Is your mom gonna be okay? What happened to her?"

Eli cleared his throat, trying to push the tears away. "Some guy she was with beat her pretty bad the other night. I tried to stop it but he hit me too." He lied. "I called the police and an ambulance came and took her to the hospital. They won't let her have any visitors and they say it's pretty bad." Tears fell from the boy's cheeks, partly for his mother's pain but mostly because he was lying about his involvement to his best friend.

Anna held a hand to her mouth, tears rising in her own eyes. "Eli, I'm so sorry. I can't believe he hit you too." She moved towards him, holding a hand up to touch the cuts on his face. He backed away from her touch sharply, and Anna dropped her hand. "Who is he? Does anybody know?"

"No. The police have no clue." His heart was aching with guilt and he wanted to end the discussion about his mother. "Is that why you stopped by? To ask about how my mother is? The same mother that beat the shit out of me not too long ago." Emotions were raging inside of Eli, and his words sounded with a touch of anger and resentment.

"No." She was upset by how he was acting, even though she guessed that she deserved it. "I just figured that I'd ask since I heard about it. I was trying to be nice."

"Well, thanks. But I'm sure she'll be fine once the doctors take care of her." He said.

Anna reached a hand into her coat pocket. "I also came over here because of this. What's this all about?" She held up a folded, wrinkled version of the 'MISSING' Hunter poster. "What happened to Hunter?"

The boy burst into tears. "I don't know."

Anna moved over to him and held him in her arms. As angry as Eli was with her, he welcomed the feel of her embrace, and hugged her back, crying into her shoulder. "It's gonna be okay. I'm sure he'll come back. You're his daddy, he has to come back." She rubbed a hand over the lengthening hair on the back of his head.

Bob stood in the kitchen doorway, watching the two children with a swelling heart. He moved towards the doorway at the mention of Hunter's name, knowing that Eli was going to break down, seeing the obvious affection between the two, and relaxing. Anna held her friend against her, rubbing the back of his head and talking softly into his ear. Eli cried into her shoulder, babbling about his baby boy and telling her how much he missed her, as Bob turned away from them again and sat down at the kitchen table.

*

Eli walked into the kitchen minutes later with a slight smile on his tear-swollen face and his best friend following close behind.

"Anna, I'd like you to meet Bob. Bob, this is Anna." He said.

The aging professor rose from the table and walked over to the pretty young blonde, smiling and holding out his hand. "Bob Mikush. It's nice to finally meet you, Anna. Eli talks about you all the time."

She smiled at him after casting a quick glance at Eli. "Anna Eskers. It's nice to meet you too, Bob."

"This is the guy I met that I was trying to tell you about that one day at school. He taught me a lot about The Strange and where it came from and stuff. We've figured out a lot of things since we went to the shit plant." Eli said in a proud voice.

Bob smiled. "Eli has taught me quite a bit, too. I'm sure that you've known for a long time that he's a special boy."

"Yes I have." Anna said, watching her friend blush.

"Anyway," Eli said, "Anna said that she saw Hunter yesterday."

"Really?" Bob asked. He knew that if Anna had seen Hunter, then Virginia really hadn't sold the dog, and the boy's second vision of what had happened was the truth.

"Yes. I was in the house and I saw him out of the window, in the back of my yard by the woods. He was just sniffing in the snow and I thought that it was him. I ran to the back door and called his name. He looked up when I did." Anna let out a little laugh. "It was kinda funny too, because he had snow all over his nose and face."

Bob saw the smile of affection rise on Eli's lips and the glimmer of love shine in his eyes as he imagined what she was describing.

"I called him again, and he started to wag his tail. Then I knew it was him, because of his tail. Y'know, how it's a little bit too long? I called for him to come to me, and he started to walk towards me. Then he just turned and ran into the woods. I called here a couple times yesterday, but I was afraid to leave a message. I'm sorry, Eli." She said with her eyes on her hands.

"It's okay, Anna." He responded. "All of it. I understand, I really do. I know that it's your parents and not you. It'll all be over once we end this. Right, Bob?"

The older man smiled halfheartedly. "If we can figure out how to do it, of course."

"But she saw Hunter, Bob!" The boy cried out. "We know where to look, now. We can go over there and follow his tracks in the snow. We can—"

"Eli, hold on a second." Bob interrupted. "That was yesterday, and he could be anywhere by now. He can move a lot faster than we can. With the fresh snow, we could spend all day looking for his tracks and not find a thing. The woods are just too big, Eli. It's not a wise move."

"But we know that he was there! We could at least look around near there for a little bit!" The distraught boy argued.

"Eli, no. It's getting colder every day, and we could get very sick if we stay out there too long. I'm not talking about a cold or the flu, either. I'm talking about seriously sick, like frostbite and hypothermia. If he's around, someone will call. We'll find him, Eli. But we can't risk getting hurt in the process."

Eli looked at Bob with steaming anger, saying nothing more. Anna spoke up, hoping to calm him.

"I know it's killing you that he's gone, but he's eventually gonna realize that he's not having any fun without you. He'll get bored and come home." She looked up at Bob for assistance.

"Yes, he will. He's a strong dog, he'll be just fine." Bob said.

Eli grudgingly gave up the argument, knowing that he would not give up the search. He saw no point in arguing about it, figuring that he would take it upon himself at a later time. Instead, he changed the subject.

"Would you like some soup?" He asked Anna with a smile. "It'll help warm you up, from the inside."

After reheating the soup, the three of them sat down at Eli's kitchen table together, sipping at their steaming hot soup and talking. They talked about many of the lighter subjects for a while, including the fact that Bocci was pregnant with Hunter's babies.

"How long until they're born?" She asked.

"I don't know." Eli said, looking to Bob.

"Well, I did some reading, and the gestation period, or the length of pregnancy, for a dog is nine weeks. We just don't know exactly when she got pregnant. I'm gonna take her to the vet this week and maybe he'll be able to tell me."

"How cute!" Anna exclaimed. "Little baby Hunters running around! Do you think they'll look like him or her?"

"Maybe half and half." Eli said. "The front half will look like Hunter, and the back half will look like Bocci."

They all pictured it for a moment, then burst into laughter, talking about how funny that would be. After a few more possibilities of what the mixed puppies would look like were discussed, Bob could see the subject was beginning to eat at the boy.

"Eli's been practicing some football. Kid's got one hell of an arm. I've been coaching him on how to play quarterback." The professor said.

Anna poked an elbow into her friend's side. "See, I told you that you should be a quarterback!"

"Or something." Eli finished as he sipped at his soup. "I still don't think I'm big enough."

Anna rolled her eyes as Bob argued with him about the size thing again. He moved on to tell stories about his days as a quarterback, many of them uplifting and humorous. The two children sat close to each other, listening to the older man's tales and enjoying the thrill of the company. Anna spoke up about something that had happened on Thanksgiving during the football games, with all of the family at her grandparents' house. She went on to talk about other things, Eli watching her the whole time. Seeing the way the boy hung on her every word, Bob allowed a small smile to creep onto his face.

All three of them joined in discussions about television, new songs on the radio, people at school and people at Bob's university. They talked cheerfully for almost an hour about anything and everything. Everything but The Strange and what was going on around them. Finally, the superficial talk faded, and they were left with only the obvious to talk about. They sat in silence for a while, wondering which one of the three was going to be the one to bring it up.

Eli spoke up. "I haven't seen you on the bus. How have you been getting to school?"

Anna looked at Eli with hesitation. "Jerry. He picks me up every morning and takes me home every day. He's allowed to go into school late for some reason. It's some work co-op thing. I'm allowed to see him now that I'm not grounded anymore. I'm just not . . ." She stopped.

"Allowed to see me, right?" He finished.

"Eli, I'm sorry." She said.

He laughed. "I know. It's not your fault. Don't worry. How is Jerry?"

Anna relaxed a little. "He's okay, I guess. Things have just been kinda weird lately. No, he's been kinda weird lately. Not like himself. He's been talking about . . ." She looked at her friend, knowing that it wouldn't be a good idea to tell him that Jerry had been trying to push sex on her. "Things he never used to talk about much."

"And your parents?" Eli asked.

Bob smiled, knowing what the boy was leading to and impressed by his method of doing it. For being a lonely boy most of his life, he somehow knew how to guide people's thoughts. He was very special, indeed.

"Oh, they're . . . okay. They're talking funny and doing things that don't make sense. I still don't know how you knew, but my mom has actually been hitting me. She never used to do anything like that. And with Jerry acting like he is, it's just weird." Anna said.

"No. It's not weird." Eli said, seeing her startled look. "It's strange. The Strange."

"Eli." Anna said in an annoyed tone. "I don't think—"

"Somebody had to bring it up." Bob said. "We've done a fine job of avoiding the subject, and I must say that I've thoroughly enjoyed talking with you two. But I think that The Strange is what we are really here to discuss today. A touch of destiny, don't you think, Eli?" Bob gave the boy a smug look.

"Anna, we figured out what's causing The Strange, and we're going to stop it." Eli said. "No matter what they say on the news, the plane crash wasn't an accident. The Faceless Man did it. Really it was The Black Box, but not the one that comes on an airplane. See, along time ago in some kingdom, there was this wizard . . ."

*

Eli told Anna the tale of the black sorcerer and the origin of The Black Box while Bob made them some hot chocolate and himself some coffee. Bob chimed in when Eli struggled with the story, and the two together explained all of the ideas they had come up with so far. It took a while for Anna to understand most of what they were talking about, but they took their time in explaining all of it, from the three great men and the Triad to the possible ways to end The Faceless Man's existence while the gloomy daylight faded outside. Anna began to join in the discussion about Eli's gift and the possibilities of destiny, but then she faltered.

"Wait. You guys are crazy, you know that?" She cried. "How did you come up with all of this? By watching some sci-fi movies and reading comic books?"

Bob chuckled. "I know it's a little far fetched and hard to believe, Anna. So is everything that's going on around here. The earthquakes, for instance. That seems nearly impossible considering that we are nowhere near a major fault line, but yet they happened. All five of them at the same time. Maybe we are crazy, but we have to fight this craziness somehow. So why not with a little craziness of our own?"

"If this guy is real, then you're talking about going to fight him? You're gonna get yourselves hurt and maybe even killed, if all this is true." She argued.

The boys had nothing to say in response. They already knew that they were going to put themselves in danger, but they preferred not to discuss it.

Anna stood up from the table. "I have to go. It's gonna get dark, and my mom's probably already wondering where I am." She began to walk out of the kitchen.

"Anna, wait!" Eli said, following after her.

"I don't want to hear anymore, Eli. You guys just go ahead and play macho and try to fight this thing." She turned towards him and Eli could see that tears were in her eyes. "Go ahead. If you live through it I'll be the first one to congratulate and thank you, but don't expect me to join you in this shit."

"Think about your mom and Jerry." He said. "You know that something's wrong, and it has to stop. What about Hunter? Do you think he would really leave me? No!" He almost hollered. "No he wouldn't! Something's wrong, Anna, and we have to end it!"

"I hope you find Hunter, I really do. If I see him again, I'll call you. Bob, it was nice meeting you and talking to you." She shook his hand again. "I think you're going to need more than just a little piece of metal to help you end this." Anna turned and walked out of the front door.

Eli walked out onto the front porch after her while Bob grabbed his arm and held him back. The boy called out after his friend. "There's three of us, Anna! You're the third, just like the three that stopped him back then! We need you, Anna! Please!"

She ran from the yard and into the woods as he struggled against the professor's grip. Bob pulled the boy back into the house and closed the door.

"Let me go!" Eli cried. "She's the third! We need to get her back!"

"Stop it and let her go!" Bob yelled. "We can't make her do anything."

Eli stopped struggling, and Bob let go of his arm. Lowering his head, the boy spoke in a hopeless voice. "What if that's it? What if there has to be three of us, just like there were three of them? If I'm the seer guy, then you would be the warrior and she would be the magician."

"That could be so." Bob said calmly. "But I will say this. I don't like the idea of her being anywhere near The Faceless Man, and I'm sure you feel that way even more than I do. Like I said before, I'm not much of a warrior, and I don't have the gift like you do. Anna may give you strength when she's around and make you believe in your power and things beyond this world, but the only magic I think Anna has is over your heart, my boy."

Eli didn't reply. He only stood there with his head lowered, sniffing the tears away.

"We'll talk about this later." Bob said. "If I want to keep my job, we really need to get back to the house so that I can get some work done. You can stay in the study and look through some of my books if you want." The professor grabbed his coat from the sofa. "C'mon, let's get going." Bob put his coat on and moved for the front door.

"No!" The suffering boy hollered with a dark gaze in his eyes. "I'm not going anywhere! I'm staying here!"

The professor laughed. "You can't stay here by yourself. I told your grandmother that I would look after you, and I intend to."

"This is my house and I'm staying! I need to be here in case Hunter comes home!" Eli cried.

Bob stood by the front door, growing angry and frustrated. "Damn it, Eli! I've already told you that we'll find him. When I get a call about him, we'll come get him. Now let's go!" He grabbed the boy's heavy flannel jacket and handed it out to him.

Tears flowed from Eli's eyes. "I have to find him! Just because your dog is at home all warm and safe, you don't give a shit about Hunter!"

Bob was hurt and angry. "Why the hell would you say that? You know damn well that I care about Hunter and want to see him come home to you. I can't believe you would even think that. I'm trying to help you, Eli. Can't you see that? That's why I want you to come with me!"

Eli snatched his flannel out of the older man's hand and took off running into the kitchen. Bob stood, stunned for a moment, then ran after him. By the time he made it into the kitchen, the boy had already made it out of the back door. Chasing after him, the aging professor ran into the back yard, calling out.

"Eli! Come back! You can't stay here! Just come with me, Eli!" He shouted.

The boy was quick, though, and he only hollered back to Bob before he disappeared into the woods.

"I'm going to find Hunter! Just leave me alone!"

Bob slowed to a jog before stopping at the edge of the woods. He breathed hard, sending misty puffs of breath into the falling snow. "At least fucking call me!"

Thinking that he heard some type of response from within the snowy, dying woods, he turned away from the twisted trees and trudged through the snow in the middle of Hunter's dog run. He turned again to look at the woods after the boy, then back to the house.

"Fuck!" He screamed at the snow flakes and the approaching darkness of the empty yard around him.

Bob closed up Eli's house, leaving the back door unlocked just in case before he warmed up his car and left. Tears fell from his eyes at his concern for Eli, wandering through the freezing woods by himself. His emotion took hold and he sped carelessly through the snowy streets of Raccoon back to his house, alone.

CHAPTER 16

Robert Mikush climbed out of the steaming hot shower, drying himself off and wrapping a towel around his waist. He dressed in comfortable clothes before walking down the stairs and looking around the dimly lit lower floor of his empty, spacious home. Bob fixed himself a glass of whiskey, and walked into his study. Eli was sitting at his desk, looking at some of his books under the light of his ugly green lamp.

"Eli!" He exclaimed. "How did you get here?"

Eli kept his eyes on the book. "The door was unlocked."

The professor's brows drew together in confusion and he cast a glance over his shoulder towards the front door. "It was?" He asked, knowing that he always locked his doors at night. "That's odd."

"Isn't it, though?" The boy said, writing something in the notebook.

Bob took a few steps towards the large oak desk, hearing the ice clink against the side of the glass in the silence. "What're you workin' on?" He asked, still uncertain how the boy had gotten there.

"Our plan." Eli said.

"Have you figured anything out yet?"

"No. But I know that we need to do something soon." The boy's eyes remained focused on the book and notebook.

"Yes, this shit *is* getting out of hand. We've both agreed on that." Bob said, moving towards the corner of the desk.

"He's coming for you, y'know." Eli muttered.

Startled, Bob stopped in his tracks. "What? It sounded like you said—"

"The Faceless Man is coming to get you, Bob." Eli lifted his head, looking directly at the older man.

Bob's heart hesitated in its beating for a moment as he saw the swirling light in the boy's eyes. His expression was blank as he looked up at the older man, holding the pen in his right hand.

"He's taken everything else away from me, and you're next. He wants the Triad, and *you* have it." Eli said in an ominous voice.

"How—how do you know? What's wrong with you, Eli?"

"I'm not Eli. I'm Euriah, you said so yourself." The haunted boy said. "And I know because I am the great seer. The Faceless Man *is* strong enough now, and he is coming to get you and the piece of the Triad before this goes any further. He wants to live again and be free of the Box. It's not about Eli. It's about the Triad and the Dragon's Tear. *That's* why this is happening now."

Bob stared frightfully into the boy's swirling eyes. "What do you mean? What about the Triad?"

"Do you really think The Black Box made the plane crash? Then you may have been fooled. It could have been the Triad, as it might have created this showdown. The Triad wants this to end, and to do that it had to unleash The Faceless Man and all his darkness. He *will not* go back into the Box this time, although he may try to make you think so. The Triad wants him to finally be destroyed, and it requires the Dragon's Tear in order for that to happen."

"Why would the Triad do that?" Bob asked. "Why would it allow all those people to die? What's a dragon's tear?"

"There is no time for that. You will figure it out. Either you or the boy, once he acquires the book. Whatever you do, *do not let The Faceless Man get the Triad.*"

"Eli, how did you figure all of this out? Are you okay?"

"I have to go now." He said. "You must act quickly. He's coming to get you."

Bob meant to ask Eli more questions just as the large window to his right shattered and he dropped his glass of whiskey on the floor, seeing the large black shape enter the window behind the flying shards of glass. He stumbled backwards across the floor of his study as the tall, cloaked figure landed on its feet in front of him, standing tall and upright next to the desk. Bob looked over the desk for Eli, but he was gone. The cloaked man raised his long hands and pulled back his hood, moving his unseen face forward and letting out a blood curdling scream.

*

Professor Mikush raised his head from his desk with a start, his flailing arms knocking books and the watered down glass of whiskey onto the floor. The glass shattered upon impact, and he jumped up from his chair with a yell, looking around his study with wide, frightened eyes and a pounding heart. He looked at the large window right behind the desk, seeing the darkness through its smooth, solid surface. Sweat poured from his face and body as he was caught in the lingering dread of his nightmare.

"Oh, Christ." He muttered as he ran a shaking hand through his wiry, sweat soaked hair.

Looking down at the whiskey and broken glass on the hardwood floor, he thought that he would clean it up after he poured himself another glass. The first full glass of whiskey was swallowed in one gulp, and so he poured another with a shaking hand. Taking his drink into the study, Bob cleaned up the mess and sat down at his desk. He pulled the books off of the floor, setting them next to the papers he had been grading when he must have fallen asleep, then the professor quickly reached for a pen. Unsure of how valid his dream was, he wanted to jot down a few notes since he didn't want to pass up any vital information.

As he was writing it down, the whole idea that the Triad may have actually caused the plane crash bewildered him. Bob had never thought about the Triad bringing about that much death, along with the horror and destruction that would ensue with the existence of The Faceless Man, in order to bring him out so that he could be destroyed. He guessed that it was possible, though. The Triad piece could have initiated all of this, somehow recruiting Eli for the job of fighting him. Unable to think very clearly as his mind still spun with the effects of his dream, the professor didn't understand the reference the Eli in his dream had made to a book.

After pulling the decorative silver box from his desk drawer, he actually began to wonder about the Triad, and where its powers actually lie. He had always believed that it was full of goodness and good powers. Maybe there really was no good or evil here, only one side against another. If the Triad really did cause the plane crash, then it seemed that it would do whatever served its purpose of bringing this to an eternal end, whether it was good or bad. And this was definitely bad.

Seeing that it was approaching nine o'clock, he grabbed his glass, got up from the desk, and walked out of the study. Turning to look back at the desk and the window, he heard Eli's ominous dream words in his mind.

He's coming for you. The Faceless Man is coming to get you, Bob.

With a chill in his spine, Bob ventured up the stairs to take a hot, relaxing shower in spite of the similarity to his dream. Having received another message from Eli on his answering machine that afternoon, he knew that the boy was still in Raccoon and wouldn't be showing up in his study when he got out of the shower.

As Bob showered, he thought about Eli and how he had appeared in his dream. Sleep had become a struggle for the divorced older man in the week and a half since he had left his young friend alone in the woods of Raccoon Township, and the professor had been having many strange dreams, most of which he couldn't remember. Eli would call each day and leave a message saying that he was okay and that he still hadn't found Hunter yet. Only once had they talked during that time, when the boy had called Bob's cell phone asking if he had gotten any calls about Hunter. He said that he hadn't, asking Eli if he was doing okay on food and everything. The boy said that he was, and when Bob tried to talk to him about other things he dismissed it and ended the phone call. Anytime the professor called the Marshall's house, the answering machine was his only response.

After calling the school, he knew that Eli had not returned following the Thanksgiving break. It was a shame, since the boy had worked so hard to get caught up and get his grades in order, and Bob figured that he was going to be held back a year. When all the kids that were presently seventh graders sat with him in their eighth grade classes next year, they would all look at him like he was stupid, or slow. They would have no idea how highly intelligent he really was, or what he had been through to set him back a year, and he would have to endure the stares and the jokes and the overall feeling that he was inadequate. Bob only hoped that Eli's life would otherwise be in order and that he would have the support and confidence to fight through it and shine in his brilliance.

The professor had warned Eli not to go anywhere near Old Man Junker's place in his search for his dog. "I don't want you anywhere near there by yourself." He had said on the answering machine, only hoping that the boy would take his advice. One of the dreams that he did remember had told him that The Faceless Man wanted and needed to get to Eli before his abilities grew and he became powerful. He had to get the boy while he was weak, just as they had to get to The Faceless Man while *he* was weak. It was just a matter of who got to whom first, it seemed.

Bob had also become very concerned about Hunter. The lovable Rottweiler had been missing for two weeks, and the dropping temperatures, snowfall, and lack of life in the woods had multiplied. By the end of that first week of December, the average daily temperature had dropped to fifteen degrees below zero. The dog was strong and healthy, but his coat was not meant for those temperatures, and there seemed to be no source of food for him. Hunter was a wonderful dog, a very special and almost magical dog. It hurt Bob very much to think about it, and he didn't dare say anything to Eli in his messages, but he had an increasing feeling of dread in his stomach when he thought about Hunter. Realistically, if some stranger hadn't taken him in as a stray and kept him, either not knowing that Eli was looking for him or not caring, Bob didn't see how he could still be alive. If Hunter hadn't frozen to death by now, then he had to be starved to death or damn close to it. He also hated to think that the negative Rottweiler reputation had caused someone to kill him in fear. Eli would have great difficulty in admitting it and giving up his search, but Bob's heart ached as he had to assume that Hunter was dead.

Black Box

Tears arose in his eyes as chills ran over his body in spite of the hot water that flowed onto him as he didn't know how he could present that possibility to Eli, or how the boy would react. Knowing that the boy was going to be unbelievably devastated, Bob's only plan was to give him one of Bocci's puppies when they were born in the middle of January. The vet had estimated that Hunter had impregnated her around the first or second week of November and had assisted Bob with plans for nutrition and delivery. Yes, he would definitely give Eli one of the puppies, he thought as he cried honest tears for Hunter.

Aliquippa Hospital hadn't been able to give him any information about Virginia Marshall, and Bob only assumed that she either hadn't awakened yet, or didn't remember what had happened since it still seemed that no one knew that her son had beaten her. Even with a broken jaw and broken thumbs, she would be able to tell them somehow, he guessed.

The lonely professor climbed out of the shower, drying himself off and wrapping the towel around his waist before he went into the bedroom and dressed in comfortable clothes while sipping at his whiskey. Strolling down the stairs of his silent, empty home, the thin older man freshened his drink and entered his study with hesitation, hoping to hell that his earlier dream hadn't come true and that he wouldn't see Eli sitting at his desk. Bob relaxed, as the study was empty, and he sat down in front of the large oak desk, looking over the papers he still had to grade. His attention had faltered at the university with all that had been going on with The Strange, and he had resorted to multiple choice and completion exams rather than his renowned comprehensive essay tests. Word had spread and the other professors had begun to ask him about it, joking that he was getting too old to live up to his 'tough, demanding instructor' reputation. Professor Mikush wasn't laughing at their jokes, knowing that much like Eli's classmates of next year, the other instructors had no idea what he was facing and how important it was.

"*Bobby.*"

The slow, whispering voice arose as a long sigh in his ears, startling the shit out of him. He looked around the room alertly, his heart pounding in his chest. Wanting to call out and ask who was there, he just shook his head, feeling that he was imagining things. While looking for the master answer sheet for the exams he was trying to grade, he continued shuffling through his books.

"*Bobby.*" The voice whispered again.

Bob stood up, almost knocking his chair over as he looked around the room again, terrified. Remembering his dream, he spun around and looked fearfully at the window behind him as he backed away in the silence, feeling the tingle of fear run up his spine.

"Who's there?" He cried out.

"*I'm coming for you, Bobby.*" The voice came again.

His body began to tremble, and he tried to tell himself that this was just another dream. No one called him Bobby except his parents and his ex-wife. He reached up and pinched the very back of his arm, on the triceps area. It hurt badly, but he was still in the study, and still wide awake and scared to death. Bocci trotted into the room, the fur all along her spine raised and a light growl in her throat.

"Nice doggy." The voice whispered.

"This is not happening." Bob said to himself, closing his eyes. "I'm just thinking too much and drank too much whiskey. This is not happening!"

"The refrigerator."

Bob's eyes sprang open, and fear powered his anger. "What the fuck do you want? Why the hell are you here?"

"You know why I'm here, Bobby. I've come for you." It whispered in the silence.

Bocci began barking and growling madly, and Bob knew that he wasn't just imagining things. Whatever was going on, Bocci heard it too. Running over to the desk and reaching for the key to unlock the drawer that held the Triad piece, he wildly thought that it might protect him as some kind of talisman. He held the key in his trembling hand when he heard the whisper again. This time, it sounded as an exhilarated sigh, and he thought about what Eli had said in his dream.

Whatever you do, do not let The Faceless Man get the Triad.

Bob stopped, dropping the key onto the desk.

"You're not getting it from me, you murdering bastard!" He screamed at nothing. "We're going to get you, motherfucker!"

"Really?" The slow, whispering voice sounded amused. *"The refrigerator."*

"What the fuck do you want from me?" Bob yelled.

"Hunter." The name sighed in the silent room.

"What?" Bob asked, surprised and scared.

"Hunter. The refrigerator."

Bob's heart dropped, and his breaths were long and shuddering as he turned to look in the direction of the kitchen, hearing Bocci's growls next to him.

"The refrigerator, go look."

Terrified and filled with dread, Bob walked through the living room on numb legs, entering his dimly lit kitchen and looking at the refrigerator, as his mind spun with unreality. Why was he even doing what the voice told him? Had The Strange spread all the way across the river and into Sewickley? He didn't know.

"Open it." The voice commanded.

With a hand that seemed to belong to someone else, Bob reached out and grabbed the handle of the refrigerator door, remotely hearing the clicking of Bocci's toenails on the linoleum. The smacking sound of the refrigerator door's seal letting go sounded like an explosion to his ears, and bright white light spilled from inside and cut a pie piece of light on the dark kitchen floor as Bob swung the door open wide. The whispering, sighing voice seemed to laugh wickedly and hysterically throughout the house as his heart dropped and his stomach churned. His eyes burned with tears and his body felt weak as his mind spun in disbelief.

Bob's legs gave out from beneath him and he fell hard to his knees, his hand still holding the refrigerator door's handle. It felt as though someone had punched him in the chest, knocking the wind out of him and stopping his heart at the same time. He couldn't breathe, and he felt like he was going to puke as tears flooded from his eyes. Bob finally drew in a wheezing breath, letting out a horrible scream that echoed in the confines of his kitchen.

"Noooooooo! Please God, Nooooooooooo!"

On the middle shelf of the refrigerator, towards the very front, was a small, bloody heart. Blood had been splattered throughout the pristine, white interior of the refrigerator and it dripped from what he guessed to be an animal's heart. His consciousness left him and he passed out with the sound of the whispering laughter in his ears. Bob knew that it was Hunter's heart.

*

He was tired. He was hungry. He was cold. He was in pain. His face would have been completely numb from the cold if it hadn't hurt so badly. His hands and feet screamed in agonizing pain. His thoughts were slow, and his body moved accordingly. The wind bit and stung his burning, watering eyes even through the thick ski mask he wore, freezing the tears on his eyelids instantly. The falling snow was clouding his vision, and the thick snow on the ground reached up to his shins, clinging to the cuffs of his pants. He would have called out his dog's name, but his throat had gone completely raw three days ago from his constant yelling and the cold. Instead, he had turned to simply looking for signs of his dog in the snow. Even that was becoming impossible, since the snow was beginning to fall heavier and heavier each day, covering any tracks there may have been.

Left with no method of searching for his missing baby boy other than simply wandering in the woods and looking for him, Eli's rational mind tried to tell him that there was no hope, that there was no possible way that he could find Hunter that way. There had been no phone calls in response to the posters, and the tracks he had followed from Anna's back yard ten days ago had disappeared into the stream. He had since found other, random tracks in the snow that may or may not have been Hunter's, since the continuously falling snow and high winds had smeared them out of recognition. The drastically falling temperatures had finished killing any remaining plant life in the woods, and the boy knew that Hunter had to be freezing.

Eli was very sick, and he knew it. The desperate boy had been spending about ten hours a day in the woods, going back home every once in a while to warm up. At first, his skin would simply tingle and burn in pain as the warmth of the house ate at the cold in his body. Even though he ate regularly and drank a lot of hot chocolate, he felt the first touches of a cold on the third day, when he couldn't stop sneezing or coughing. Moving on to drinking coffee, which he didn't even like, Eli took some medicine from his mother's cabinet that night, feeling better the next morning. After eating some scrambled eggs and swallowing a cup of coffee, the determined boy ventured out into the cold again.

By the sixth day, his whole body hurt all the time, and he didn't have much of an appetite anymore, having to force himself to eat some toast for breakfast before he left the house. On the seventh day, he had wakened up in a pool of sweat, racked by a raging fever that left him somewhat delirious. Returning to his mother's medicine cabinet and reading the labels for the symptoms, Eli took some flu medicine. While looking and calling for Hunter that day, his throat, raw and aching from the yelling of his dog's name and the coughing fits, finally gave out on him. The next morning, the pool of sweat had been joined by vomit and blood and he puked up the morning toast as soon as it hit his stomach. He forced the hot coffee down his raw throat in blinding pain and delved into the basement, looking for heavier winter clothing, as it was growing colder outside every day. After finding some coats, ski masks, snowcaps, and scarves of his father's, the boy wrapped layer after layer over his aching, trembling body and went out into the blowing snow.

Growing even more desperate in his search, Eli spent the last two days in a dreamlike state, half delirious with sickness and half stoned on the drugs he had found in his mother's cabinet. He had given up on the weaker stuff and went straight for the real pills, unsure of what he was taking as he used his mother's occasional references as his only guide. Since he was constantly vomiting, the boy had given up on eating as well, relying on the coffee as his source of nutrition. Making hot tea in the evening and loading it with lots of honey to soothe his ragged throat, Eli would call Bob and leave his daily message, trying his best to sound healthy and safe. The clothes that he wore in the cold would spend an hour in the heat of the dryer every night, ridding them of the sweat, snow, ice, and snot that had saturated them. The ski mask had been stained with blood in the area over his mouth since every time a coughing fit took hold of him, blood spewed from his lips. It hurt when he urinated, and his urine had turned a deep, dark, brownish—yellow color. His chest was hurting every time he took a breath and his head was throbbing with pain.

Black Box

On the sixth hour of that tenth day of his tireless search, Eli collapsed in the thick, fluffy snow for the twelfth time. A coughing fit racked his body, and he brought an unfeeling, gloved hand to his face to pull the ski mask away from his lips. Droplets of blood flew from his mouth and splattered on the bright white snow in front of him while he coughed, and the cold bit at the bare skin of his chin. Rising to his hands and knees while he coughed into the snow, the frozen snot under his nose cracked and fell away. New snot took its place, freezing on its way to his mouth. Only thirty minutes had passed since his last break, and the driven boy had barely returned to his previous spot. The little bit of his rational mind that was left screamed and begged for him to go back to the house. It screamed that he wasn't going to find Hunter, that the dog was gone, and that he was probably dead. It screamed that he was going to die too, if he didn't go home and stop this insanity. Eli pulled himself from the ground, swaying on his feet and looking around in the blinding whiteness of fallen and falling snow with a dazed and drugged mind. Looking back in the direction of his warm home, he watched his fresh footprints fade in the blowing snow. He was deathly ill and needed to go home. Turning away from the path home as he pulled the ski mask back up over his freezing, blood spattered chin, the boy lowered his head against the wind as his rational mind screamed in fear and protest.

Eli pushed on, walking through the snow filled woods and looking for his dog, driven only by the love in his heart.

*

Bob tossed his thick leather case onto the desk in front of him.

"Here." He said. "It's all there, and it's all separated and labeled. There are detailed instructions written for each class."

The white haired man sitting at the desk looked up at him. "Can't you just tell me what's going on, Bob? I mean, for you to take a leave of absence at the beginning of finals week worries me. It's not like you, Bob."

"I just can't talk about it right now, Harvey." Bob said. "Something's come up, and I have to go right this instant. You damn well know I've got the time coming to me. I haven't taken any leave time since the divorce. All they have to do is plop the tests down in front of the kids and read a damn magazine for fifty minutes. I think that Bill and Gene can handle that."

"I'd like to think so." The dean of the university said as he stood up from his chair. "It's not about the time off, which you damn well deserve. You're my number one professor in this institution, providing a difficult, challenging, and well taught program. The kids hate you when they're in your class, but they all praise you afterwards. I hate for you to leave before finals week, but that's not the point. Christ, Bob! We've worked together for what . . . fifteen years? Can't you at least show me the courtesy of telling me what's going on? I'm not asking you as your boss, I'm asking you as your friend."

"It's a family emergency." Bob said.

Harvey rolled his eyes. "Bob, c'mon. How many times have Charlene and I been to your house, and you to ours? How many after work beers have we shared, and how many times have we been there for each other?"

"I know, but it's not about our friendship. Really." He replied. "It's a family emergency and that's all I can tell you. Just please tell me that you'll do this for me."

The dean of the university bowed his shaking head for a moment, then lifted it to look at his old friend. "I'll get it covered."

"Great." Professor Mikush said. "Thank you, Harvey."

"Just do me a favor and call me when you get this business taken care of, okay." Harvey held out his hand. "Good luck, Bob, and I hope everything works out well for you."

The pair of aging friends, and professors, shared a healthy handshake. "Thanks. If I don't see you in the next couple weeks, Merry Christmas."

Harvey smiled, "Merry Christmas to you too, Bob. Take care of yourself, you old fart."

The thin man with the fine featured face, who blamed himself for bringing The Black Box into the area, turned to leave as he opened the door to Harvey's office. "I will. Tell Charlene and the kids Merry Christmas for me too, will ya?" He said before walking away.

"Call me!" Harvey called after him.

Bob waved a hand in the air as he walked down the hall and disappeared around the corner. Harvey sat back in his chair, looking at the thick black case full of final exams on his desk.

"What the hell's going on with you, Bob?" He muttered to himself in the empty office as he shook his head with worry. "What the hell have you gotten yourself into this time?"

*

Bob pulled his car into Eli's snow laden driveway two hours later, trudging through the thick snow towards the front door with his narrow face turned away from the whistling wind. Reaching the door and finding it locked, he pounded on it a few times, calling Eli's name. After hopping up and down in an attempt to fight against the bitter cold during the wait for his young friend to answer the door, Bob left the front porch. Walking through the snow around to the side of the house, the freezing older man figured that he would check to see if the back door was unlocked. Bob had called Eli's house several times that morning, getting no answer. He was scared for the boy's safety following the previous night's experience.

Bob had awakened on the floor of his kitchen with Bocci lying by his side. The events leading up to his arrival in the kitchen slowly surfaced in his mind, and he was terrified. He opened the door to the refrigerator, hoping that it would be free of the object he had seen earlier and that it had all been another dream. It wasn't, and the heart that was too small and odd shaped to be human still dripped blood onto the lower shelves of the fridge. After several minutes of heartbroken grief, he put on a pair of gloves and pulled the heart out of the refrigerator, placing it in a bag and putting it in the freezer. It seemed odd and sadistic, but he thought that once Eli came to terms with Hunter's death, he might want to bury the heart in his memory. Bob cleaned the blood out of the refrigerator as he numbed his mind against the whole thing.

When the cleanup was finished, he sat by the fireplace in the living room, thinking. The next day would put it to eleven days since he had seen or really talked to Eli, and that was too long. They were getting nothing accomplished as far as how to defeat The Faceless Man, while the whispering voices in his Sewickley home and the heart in his refrigerator showed him that they were running out of time. They had to do something, soon. No, not soon. Now. They had to do something right now.

Knowing that semester finals were beginning that week at the university, and that he really needed to be there for the exams, the aging professor also felt that if they waited until finals were over, it might be too late. The Faceless Man might be too strong by then and he, or God forbid Eli, might end up dead by then. Looking over at Bocci as she lay comfortably on the hardwood floor, he cried again for Hunter. The hero father of her future puppies was gone, and so Eli had no one to look to for rescue anymore. No one except Bob.

Professor Mikush decided in that moment that he would ask for his overdue leave time at the university and spend every minute he could with Eli, devising a quick plan of attack, and then moving in on The Faceless Man. Hopefully, destiny and a whole lot of good luck would be on their side.

Bob approached the rear of the Marshall's house, seeing the numerous indentations of old and new footprints in the snow of the back yard, and found the back door locked. Thrilled to know that Eli had enough sense to lock all the doors, he was concerned since the boy hadn't answered the door when he had pounded on it, hoping that the boy wasn't wandering through the woods in the dangerous cold. Bob walked into the yard and looked at the footprints, trying to determine if they had been made anytime that morning, or if they could signify whether Eli was in the house or in the woods. As he got closer to the prints, the professor recognized that the footprints were rounded and blurred rather than sharp and clear, meaning that the boy hadn't gone into the woods that morning. Noticing dark splatters in the snow next to the footprints and looking closer in an effort to figure out what it was, he panicked. It was blood.

Bob turned, ran for the house and pounded hard on the back door. Still getting no answer, the aging professor wasted no more time and kicked the door in. Rushing into the kitchen and pushing the damaged door closed against the terrible wind, he hurried through the small house, calling Eli's name. He found the boy sitting in a small, wooden chair in the middle of his bedroom with his back to the door, clothed heavily from head to toe. Eli was wrapping a scarf around his neck and face with a gloved hand, the back of his snowcapped head facing towards Bob.

"Eli! Are you okay?" Bob asked.

He got no response from the boy as he continued to fit the scarf around him.

"Why didn't you answer the door? Didn't you hear me calling for you?"

Still nothing.

"Why is there blood in the snow, Eli?" Fear and worry were creeping into his voice. "What happened to you?"

The early teenager pulled the scarf free from his neck, then began to rewrap it.

"I'm sorry about the other day, Eli. Will you please talk to me?" He watched the boy wrap the scarf in silence. "What's wrong with you?"

Eli's voice croaked thickly in the silence of the small room. "I have to find Hunter. He's cold and he's hungry."

Bob's eyes widened at the horrible sound of the boy's voice and he hurried around the chair to face Eli. Tears welled up in his eyes and he raised a hand to his mouth.

"Oh my God." He whispered. "Eli."

The skin of Eli's face was discolored with sickness and his eyes were sunken into his blackened sockets. Sweat ran along his cheeks, even though goosebumps pushed through his skin, while his lips were purple and splattered with droplets of blood. Thick green and brown snot ran from his nose, onto his upper lip, and along his chin. Mucus and dried blood was caked in the corners of his mouth, as blood, vomit, and snot ran all down the front of his clothing into a pile on the floor between his feet. His eyes looked at Bob, but didn't see him. The whites of his eyes had turned red, and the pupils of his usually beautiful blue eyes contracted and dilated.

"I have to find him and bring him home. Bring him home before he gets sick." Eli croaked.

"Oh dear God, Eli." Bob sobbed. "What have you done to yourself?"

Eli's head swayed unsteadily on his neck. "Bob." He said with a touch of excitement in his voice. "When did you get here?" He showed a delirious smile.

"Get those clothes off and get in the bathtub. You need to warm up." Tears filled Bob's voice as he reached for the scarf the boy was still holding.

Eli gave Bob's hand a weak push. "No! I have to go find Hunter before he gets sick!" The sickly, determined boy stood up, swaying on his feet. "It's really cold and he can't . . . can't . . ." Eli fell to the floor.

Bob moved quickly, cradling the boy's head before it could hit the floor. Carrying the boy with both arms into the bathroom, he pulled the layers of clothes off of him with tears streaming down his narrow, aging face. The more clothing the professor removed as the bath water ran hot, the more horrified he became. Eli's whole body was discolored and shrunken, as he was covered in sweat and chill bumps. The boy's ribs were showing in his waist and his throat was swollen out to his jawbone. His hands and feet were stiff and white, the first touches of frostbite creeping in.

Babbling senselessly until the distraught, divorced, aging professor rested his limp, burning hot body into the hot bath water, Eli calmed and simply lay in the tub. Bob cried as he washed the boy with a soft cloth, talking to him the whole time. Nearly an hour later, Bob pulled him from the water, dried him off and dressed him in some soft clothes he found in the dresser before laying the boy in his bed and tossing several blankets on top of him. Eli complained that he was cold while sweat continued to run from his pores, and Bob asked where Virginia kept her medications, knowing that his mother was a nurse and that she should have some handy drugs around. The delirious boy mumbled his answer, and soon after was fed several antibiotics along with a few painkillers. Within a few minutes, the sickly boy was asleep. Bob wandered into the living room of the Marshall's house alone, and cried. He cried for Eli, for the boy's risk of his own life for his beloved dog, for Hunter, for his own guilt at leaving the boy alone, and for all of the pain that he had ever kept hidden inside during his many years. For so many reasons, he cried.

Bob spent the rest of the dreary, snow swept afternoon and most of the evening watching over Eli as he slept, listening to the boy's delirious, dreaming babblings as he wiped sweat away from his face with a cool cloth. Every four hours, regardless of what the labels on the pill bottles said, he fed the shivering boy more antibiotics. Sitting in the small wooden chair next to Eli's bed, the professor eventually drifted off to sleep.

Awaking after only an hour of uneasy sleep that was filled with strange dreams, the weary older man looked at Eli in the dim light thrown by the distant living room lamps as an idea struck him. Bob didn't know if it would work, but something from his dreams told him that it would, so he ventured out to his car in the painful cold, bringing another one of his leather cases inside with him. He tossed his coat onto the sofa, pulled the decorative silver box out of the case, and went into Eli's room with the box in his hands, sitting down in the boy's small wooden chair next to the bed. After sliding the glass cover off of the box, the aging professor pulled the odd metallic piece of the Triad from its place on the soft velvet cloth, setting the box on the nightstand next to the pill bottles and the glass of water. Holding the Triad piece tight in his hand, Bob caressed Eli's sweaty forehead while he slept, talking to him with tears in his voice and in his eyes.

"Eli, I know why you did what you did, and I admire you for it. That kind of love and dedication is hard to find in today's world. I'm afraid to tell you when you're awake and I can only hope that this will show you what you need to know while you sleep."

Bob slipped the piece of wondrous metal into Eli's sleeping hand, closing the sick boy's stiff, white fingers around it. It glowed bright from within his fingers, and Eli drew in a long, shuddering breath.

"The Faceless Man paid me a visit and he showed me something." Tears flowed from the older man's eyes as he struggled to speak against them. "Hunter's dead, Eli. I know that your heart is going to tell you otherwise, but I hope that the Triad will show your mind that it's true. We were too slow, we took too long and he got to Hunter before we could get to *him*. I'm so sorry that he took your baby boy from you, but we have to go on, and we have to hurry."

Bob took a few moments to clear his throat and push the tears back inside of himself before going on.

"I need you to get better, Eli. He's trying to get to me now, and I think that he's finally strong enough to do it. I need your help, little guy. I can't go on without you. I'm becoming confused about what the Triad is and what it can do, but I hope that it will help heal you and make you strong. We have to get on with ending this, but I need for you to get better first." Bob grabbed hold of both of the boy's hands within his. "I love you, Eli, and I hate to bring you close to danger. I can't do this without you. Please, just get better so that you can help me."

Eli rolled over in his bed as he babbled a couple words in his sleep. "Help you." He pulled his hands close to his body as he turned, holding the Triad piece tight.

"I don't know what you do or what you want from all this," Bob whispered to the ancient metal in Eli's hands, "but please just stop hurting the boy. Let him not have so much pain and heartache in his life."

The weary, aging professor sat limp in the small wooden chair, gazing at his young friend with love and heartache. He wiped tears away from his cheeks with the back of his hand, watching the wondrous light radiate from inside of Eli's hands and over the boy's body.

"Please work." He whispered and prayed. "Please work and make him better."

CHAPTER 17

"Hunter's not coming back, is he?" Eli asked with tears all over his face.

"Eli, I—" Bob began.

"He's dead, isn't he?" The boy asked, his chest hitching as he sobbed.

The tired, older man had been dreading this moment, and his eyes moved from his wringing hands to the silver box holding the Triad piece on Eli's nightstand. Looking deep into his young friend's trembling, wet eyes, Bob prepared to say the words he knew were going to push the boy over the edge.

*

For the past three days Bob had watched over Eli, giving him pills, force feeding him, bathing him, and wiping the sweat from the boy's face as he slept. He allowed Eli to hold the Triad piece almost every moment of each day, watching as the boy made amazing progress.

Eli ceased vomiting after the first day, and the discoloration of his skin faded while the swelling in his throat diminished. Blood no longer appeared whenever he coughed, leaving only large amounts of mucus, which also disappeared after the second day. His hands and feet became more flexible, while the chills and the sweating stopped. Eli's delirium receded each day, and Bob stopped giving him the pain pills and gave him only one antibiotic every eight hours. By the third day, the early teenager's body appeared perfectly normal, except for a slight reddish, overheated tinge. His face and eyes returned to normal, and his ribs weren't as prominent through his skin. He was still disoriented, and slept the majority of the day, holding the Triad the entire time. Eli mumbled and wailed in grief in his sleep, and Bob knew that he was dreaming about his baby boy, The Strange, and their impending confrontation with The Faceless Man.

Black Box

The morning of December 11th, exactly two weeks before Christmas, Eli woke up aware and alert, seeing Bob sleeping on the floor next to him and the Triad piece resting in its case on the nightstand. He rubbed his head for a few moments as the images from some of his dreams presented themselves to his waking mind, and the devastated boy cried out in grief, falling into helpless sobs and waking the older man next to him.

Bob jumped from the floor, thrilled to see that Eli was finally awake, and sat in the small chair next to the bed. The boy sat up in his bed, looking at the older man with devastation and heartache all over his twisted face. He knew, Bob thought. It didn't matter whether his words had reached the boy's mind in his sleep, or the Triad had shown him in his dreams. Either way, Bob was positive that Eli knew Hunter was dead.

*

"Yes, Eli." Bob's voice wavered, and he knew that he was going to cry along with the boy. "Hunter's dead."

"B-But I didn't get to tell h-him that I was gonna m-miss him." Eli forced his words through his sobs, holding his hands out to his sides. He looked more like a child in that instant than any other time Bob had seen him.

Tears spilled from Bob's eyes, even though he had been fighting them, and Eli burst into his own tears, wailing and babbling senselessly into the older man's ear. They stayed that way for a while, and Bob wanted to console the boy longer and let him grieve, but time was running short. Breaking the embrace, he held Eli at arm's length.

"I know that this is really hard for you, but we have to move on." Bob said with tears on his face. "The Faceless Man is coming after both of us, and we have to hurry."

"H-He had something to do with it, didn't he?" Eli sobbed.

Bob was regaining his wits. "I'm sure of it." He said, thinking that it was best if he didn't say anything about the heart in his refrigerator just yet. "His strength has grown, and he's trying to stop us from getting to him."

Eli continued to cry. "We have to go, don't we?" He asked. It seemed that most of his grieving had been done in his sleep, when he saw whatever it was the Triad had shown him.

"Yes, we do." Bob said in a serious tone. "Tonight, if at all possible. That depends on how you feel."

"I'll be alright, I promise." The grieving boy wiped his tears onto the sheets of his bed. "I just won't think about it."

The professor was impressed by the boy's composure. "That's the only thing you can do, buddy. But I was actually referring to your health."

"What do you mean?" Eli asked. "I'm fine. I just had a little cold is all."

Bob widened his eyes and puffed out his cheeks as he exhaled. "I doubt *that*." He said. "You were very ill when I got here, Eli. You may not remember because of the fever, but you were seriously sick."

Explaining the extent of Eli's sickness and describing his appearance when he first saw the boy, Bob reassured him that he had done all he could for his dog. After reminding his young friend that it hadn't been smart to do that, the aging professor said that he didn't blame him. Since he was done with teaching for a few weeks, they had to devise a plan for stopping The Faceless Man.

"I really only have a few ideas on what we can do, unless you happened to come across any in your dreams." Bob said.

"Not really. I saw a lot of things, but most of it didn't make any sense. I can't see The Faceless Man at all. I can't see what he's doing, how strong he is, and I can't see the Box either."

"I've been wondering if maybe the Box isn't actively defending him from your visions. Maybe it is?"

Eli shrugged his shoulders. "I don't know. I can't see anything about The Faceless Man or the Box."

"Well, maybe the simpler the better, huh?" Bob showed a weak smile. "We'd better hope so anyway."

"What are you planning on doing?" The boy asked, leaning forward in his bed in anticipation.

"I'll explain while you help me with a little project. I sort of broke the back door the other day."

Walking strongly out of his bedroom for the first time in three days, Eli followed Bob as he showed him the broken doorjamb and explained why he had kicked the door in. After showing the professor where the tools were in the house, Eli listened attentively while he explained the simple, but reasonable plan of attack on The Faceless Man. The quick repair was finished, and they opened and closed the back door, checking their handiwork. Each time the door opened, the biting wind entered the house, leaving a chill in Eli's spine. The chill remained even when the door was finally left closed and the seriousness of their plan took hold of him.

"The most important thing is that he doesn't know you have it. He will most likely know that it's there, but he'll probably expect me to have it, thinking that I wouldn't entrust something like that to you."

"But you are." Eli said with pride.

"I am." Bob said. "But *he cannot know that*. Okay?"

"Okay." The boy replied. "But why at night? Why in the dark?"

"For concealment and the element of surprise. I hope, anyway. That first moment is very important, and we need to surprise him for it to work."

"Oh. Makes sense." Eli said.

"Good." Bob said, looking over the young boy. "How do you feel? Are you up to it?"

"Yes." The agonized boy said with a false smile on his face. "I feel fine, really. I guess the Triad healed me up just fine."

Bob knelt in front of Eli, looking him in the eye. "Do you realize how serious this is?"

"Yes." The smiled had faded from his lips.

"Do you know that we both may not make it through this crazy shit?" He asked.

"Yes." Eli's face grew serious.

"Do you still want to go through with this?"

"Yes."

"Okay." Bob said, standing up. "Why don't we relax for a while and get something to eat?"

"Are we going tonight?" Eli asked in a small voice.

"Yes, we are." The professor replied. "Who knows? If we can actually do this, Raccoon may have a Merry Christmas after all." He started to walk away.

"Can we go see my mom?" Eli asked as he wrung his hands. "I want to go see my mom. Just in case."

Bob tilted his head in affection for the boy, knowing that he was putting him in a bad position. "Yes, we can."

"I want to tell her I'm sorry. I want to tell her I'm sorry and that I'm going to make things better."

"Let's get something to eat, then you can get cleaned up and we'll go. Okay?" Bob said.

"Okay." Eli whispered

*

They had only nibbled on their sandwiches in silence, thinking about the approaching conflict. Eli showered, dressed himself, and stuffed a bag full of heavy winter clothes in preparation for the cold as he remembered his five P's. After putting the boy's bag and his leather case in the car as it warmed up, Bob went back into the house to get Eli. He looked through the house for a few moments, calling the boy's name and finally seeing him through the window in the back of the house.

Eli was out in the thick snow of the back yard, in the area of Hunter's dog run, with the thick chain in his hands, looking up at the perpetually gloomy sky and talking. Bob couldn't hear what he was saying, and he didn't want to. His throat clenched and his head began to hurt as he fought off the approaching sadness, watching through the window as Eli said his good-byes to his beloved dog, his baby boy.

*

Twilight had settled into the sky, and Virginia Marshall's hospital room was dimly lit and gloomy. The nurse had led them to the private room in the Intensive Care Unit, allowing the boy only a few minutes with his unconscious mother. Eli walked into the gloomy room, the professor following closely behind and thanking the nurse. The boy stood in the doorway for a few moments, and Bob placed a reassuring hand on his shoulder.

"Go ahead, Eli." He whispered. "You only have a few minutes."

Bob turned away and stood at the outside edge of the doorway, waiting patiently for the boy with his coat draped over his arm. Eli walked towards his mother, hearing the squeak of his wet shoes on the clean, sanitized floor. His throat tightened as he saw his mother lying helpless and bandaged on the hospital bed with machines and tubes all around her. He pulled a wheeled chair from the corner of the room and sat down next to his mother, simply looking at her. In a few moments, the nervous boy reached up and grabbed both of her partially casted hands in his.

"Hi, mom." He said quietly. The nurse had told them that she probably couldn't hear anything they said, but Eli thought otherwise. "It's me, Eli."

Tears threatened behind his eyes, but he felt that he had done enough crying for one lifetime.

"I want to tell you that I'm sorry, Mom. I didn't mean for this to happen, I swear. Me and my friend Bob are going to fix everything, okay? We're going to make it all better and make The Strange go away. It's kinda dangerous and I'm pretty scared, but I think that I'm the only one that can stop it. I don't know how, and that's what scares me. Bob keeps telling me that I'm the one to end this, but I don't know what to do. I don't know how I'm supposed to stop it. I'm scared, and I think that Bob is scared too. No matter what, we're going to try tonight, and I just wanted to see you before we went after the bad man."

Eli looked over his shoulder briefly, making sure that the professor couldn't see him from his position in the hall before reaching his hand into his jeans pocket and pulling the glowing piece of the Triad from within. The guilt laden boy held it between his mother's hand and his own. The light grew, and he watched his mother's face move in the glow. Her head swayed on the pillow and her eyelids twitched. In a moment, her eyes opened in the wondrous light. She looked around quickly, then her eyes fell on Eli. They widened at first, but then they softened. Virginia attempted to speak, but her jaw had been wired shut.

"Hi, mom." Eli smiled. He watched her blink her eyes, and moved closer to her. "I'm sorry, mom. I'm really sorry about this, I swear. Hunter's gone, and the bad man made me think that you had done something to him, and made me hurt you. *He* did something to Hunter, not you. I'm really sorry, mom, and I'm going to fix this." Eli saw the fearful yet loving look in her eyes. "I guess we're even, huh?"

"Eli." Bob's voice came from the hall.

Seeing that the professor was making a 'hurry up' motion with his hand, Eli guessed that the nurse was coming to make them leave. He pulled the Triad piece away from his mother's hand, sliding it back into his pocket.

"Wish me luck, Mom." The boy said, planting a kiss on her cheek. Eli heard Bob's and the nurse's voices in the hall, then heard the nurse right behind him.

"Time to go." She whispered.

The nurse had placed a hand on Eli's back, glancing at his mother as she was about to lead him out of the room. She snapped her head back, staring with wide eyes at Virginia.

"She's awake!" The nurse exclaimed. "My goodness! You two have to go, *now*!" She said as she ran to the wall at the foot of the bed, flipping on the lights and picking up a phone.

Eli smiled to his mother as Bob walked up behind him. "Bye, mom." He saw her puzzled stare at the aging professor as she lifted her hand in a wave.

Pushing his emotions deep inside of him as they walked through the halls, Eli saw Bob's smug look.

"What?" Eli asked.

"I know what you did. I saw the light from the hallway." He said.

"I wanted to help her to make up for what I did." Eli said sharply. "I saw for sure that she didn't sell Hunter. She saw me and Hunter sleeping together and she changed her mind."

Bob only smiled, happy to see that Eli didn't hate his mother after all. They walked out of the warm hospital into the freezing cold of the approaching darkness, and shared a brief, frightened glance as they walked toward the car. Even though the interior of the car was still warm, both Bob and Eli pulled heavier clothing from the back seat and put it on their bodies in layers. When they were finished preparing themselves for the cold they were about to face, the odd pair of companions began the job of mentally preparing themselves for the *task* they were about to face.

Bob exhaled long and hard as he put the car in gear, glancing at Eli and seeing no traces of fear or anxiety in the boy. Before he turned his head to look out of the passenger side window into the approaching darkness, there had only been a hollow expression of nothingness on Eli's face. They left the parking lot of Aliquippa Hospital in mutual silence, knowing that their next destination lie in the freezing, lifeless desolation of the Raccoon Township woods not far from where two hundred fifty innocent people had lost their lives in a screaming ball of flame.

Bob and Eli, unaware of each other's existence only two months earlier, each placed his life in the other's hands as they made their way to Old Man Junker's shack, the temporary dwelling place of The Faceless Man.

*

Bob pulled his car onto the gravel-coated berm of the small back road only about a quarter of a mile away from Old Man Junker's shack, dousing the headlights. He turned the ignition key back, shutting off the engine and any source of heat in the car. His leather bucket seat squeaked as he turned to Eli, the sub zero cold already beginning to penetrate the passenger compartment of his late model Toyota. A combined chill of cold and fear shook the boy's body.

"You ready for this?" Bob asked, and the wondrous boy nodded his head. The older man placed a hand on his shoulder. "Eli, I want you to know that I don't like having you here."

Eli showed a look of hurt and shock on his face. "What do you mean?"

"I mean that a boy your age shouldn't be sneaking around in the freezing woods with an old man chasing after some ancient ghost." Bob's face and voice were serious. "You should be warm in your home, doing your homework, listening to Christmas music and looking forward to your Christmas break. I've come to see you as the son I never had, and I'm putting you in danger. I hate myself for it, but you are the only one I would want with me right now. I trust you, I have faith in you, and I know that you are far stronger than your age. I just don't want any harm to come to you."

Eli sat in his seat as his breath emitted from his mouth in a misty cloud, looking up at his friend's thin, aged face with genuine love. He didn't want to talk about this sentimental stuff, he just wanted to get on with the mission. "I won't let you down, Bob."

Bob smiled at the boy, the wrinkles around his moustache darkening in the dim light. "There is one more thing." The smile fell from his lips. "If anything should happen to me, we stick with the plan."

"Bob, don't." Eli said.

"Just listen to me for a second. If anything should happen to me, you get the hell outta here. D'you hear me? Get the hell outta here. Take these, just in case." He said, pulling a jingling set of keys out of his coat pocket. "It's a spare set for the house and the car. If you have to, drive my car away from here, and go to my house. I'm sure you can guess how to drive and how to get to my house, so I'm not worried about that. Use all the material we've gathered on The Black Box, call Jake, and tell him what happened. You'll be able to find his number and you can trust him. Also, I want you to take care of Bocci."

"Bob, stop it!" Eli yelled. "Don't talk about this shit!"

"Eli I have to, just in case. I'm done now, okay. Will you do that?"

"Yes!" Eli cried. "If something happens, yes! But it won't! We're going to do this, and we're gonna win."

The older man smiled, "Yes, we are."

Bob and Eli climbed out of the chilly car into the freezing air of the dark night, and crept into the dark, dead and twisted remains of the woods using the dim light of the full moon, shining through the constant haze in the Raccoon sky, as their guide. The unlikely pair of adventurers reached the stream, and Eli spoke with numb lips.

"I wish that Hunter was here. He could help us."

"We have the Triad, and you. That's all the help we need." Bob said quietly.

The heartbroken boy nodded in agreement as silent tears fell from his cheeks. "He could still help us, though."

"I know he could, Eli. Let's just be quiet."

The old man and the young boy walked quietly through the thick snow, seeing the dim light shining through the dingy windows of Old Man Junker's shack. They remained silent as they walked past his dirty old truck in the dirt driveway, approaching the front porch, which consisted of two steps and a small platform made up of old, rotting wood. Eli's heart was beating hard and he sweated even though his face and gloved hands were aching from the biting cold in the air. He crouched close enough to Bob that their arms were touching, and that gave him a bit of comfort.

Bob was absolutely terrified, his eyes wide with fright and his body trembled in fear. He reached his right hand down to his waist, feeling for the object he saw as their protection and being comforted by its touch. Eli's arm against his also gave him comfort, since he knew that the boy was a wonder of fantasy in this logical world. They moved to the left side of the flimsy steps, shivering in cold and fear. Bob looked at the boy and nodded. Eli slid his eyes closed and was silent for a few moments, his eyes moving behind their lids and the skin of his face twitching.

"I can't see anything," Eli whispered, "but I think he's here."

"Are you sure?"

Eli placed his gloved hand in his pocket, pushing the Triad piece closer to his body. "Yes. I can't see him, so he's with the Box, right?"

"Right." Bob whispered.

"There's something else, though. I . . . I can't see it."

"We've come this far together, Eli." Bob whispered. "Let's do this."

A rush of adrenaline pumped through Eli's veins as everything around him seemed brighter and clearer, and he clenched his jaw in determination as he tried to clarify his vision. Bob stood in front of the weak old wooden door, and pounded on it with his fist, lowering his right hand to his waist.

"Wait! I can almost . . ." Eli said in a loud whisper, "Damn! I can't see it!"

Bob pounded on the door again, saying nothing.

"Something's wrong!" Eli said. The Triad was vibrating madly in his pocket. "I don't think he's—"

The door swung inward and a large, dark figure appeared in the doorway with one hand holding the door while the other reached out towards the aging professor. Eli froze in terror as he thought that he could see some type of open mouth beneath the hanging hood that the figure wore. It appeared that the mouth was open for a biting attack. Bob didn't freeze, however, and pulled his right hand from his waist with unforeseen quickness, placing the Colt .45 pistol to the thing's head and pulling the trigger. The sound of the gunshot was deafening in the silence of the night, and Eli stared wide-eyed as a large chunk of something blew out of the back of the dark figure's hood. The tall, thin figure dropped to the ground in an instant with a loud thump. Bob turned his pale, blood-splattered face toward Eli, screaming.

"Go! Go now!"

Eli pulled himself from the ground and jumped up the wooden stairs, pausing in front of the long, cloaked body lying in the doorway. Bob grabbed the sleeve of his coat, turning the boy to face him. His blood splattered face was panicked and frightened, and his hand shook as it held his coat sleeve.

"Go, goddam it! Get the fucking box, and let's go!" The terrified older man screamed.

Eli jumped over the cloaked body and ran into the one room shack. It was dimly lit and smelled bad. There was blood, along with other thick substances, all over the place. The stench of old sweat burned the boy's nostrils as he frantically moved throughout the room, looking for the Black Box. Bob had jumped from the stoop and grabbed the tall, limp figure by its cloak, dragging it out of the doorway and down the steps with his left hand, while he pointed the gun at it with his right. Eli closed his eyes and tried to find the Box with his frantic mind, unable focus.

"Get the goddam Box, Eli! Can you find it?" Bob called out.

"No! I can't see anything! I'm too scared!" Eli cried.

"Just try and concentrate!" Bob yelled.

As he looked around the room, the boy's eyes fell on the closed bathroom door and something called to Eli. Beginning to move towards it, he reached the kitchen table and an image flashed in his mind. It was an old vision, the vision about Old Man Junker and The Black Box. Sitting down in the chair he had seen Old Man Junker sitting in, the boy closed his eyes again. He pulled the glove from his hand and placed his bare hand into his pocket, touching the Triad piece with his bare skin. Strange, dark images swirled through his mind, but he thought of the Box and only the Box. Slowly, he began to see it in his mind; dark, ornate, and beautiful. It was surrounded by darkness and dirt, although it wouldn't be there long. Eli's eyes sprang open.

"Under the house!" He screamed as he ran for the front door. "He put it under the house cuz he knew we were coming for it!"

Eli emerged from the doorway of the horrifying little shack and froze on the front steps. The tall, cloaked figure stood in front of him, holding Bob by the throat in one hand and the wrist of the hand that held the gun with the other. The figure grinned at Eli through a face that moved, blurred, and changed. His swirling eyes glared out at the boy below the large bullet hole in his forehead.

"Hello again, Eli." It said cheerfully with its contradicting voices. "It's so good to see you again, and I see you brought a new friend."

Eli looked at Bob's struggling gaze above the black, clawlike hand of The Faceless Man.

"How's your mom, Eli? And Hunter, how is he doing?" The thing smiled at him. "And our dear, lovely Anna. Has she recovered from Jerry's rape attempt yet? Oh, wait!" He said, showing a look of one who has said too much. "She hasn't told you yet! Would you like me to take care of that for you? I could, y'know." The deeper, more sinister voice became dominant, and the smile turned into a sneer of hate. "I could tear his dick off and shove it up his ass while he screams for mercy! And I could rip his balls off and shove them down his throat until he suffocates on them if you want me to."

The Faceless Man's blurred and twisted face changed back to a look of humor, and his voice returned to the balanced combination of high and low. "Or maybe you would like to do that yourself? You did a pretty good job on your mother, and I think you could do it!"

Not believing what he was seeing or hearing, the boy pulled his gaze away from The Faceless Man to see that Bob was choking and gagging in his grip, fighting for air. Knowing that he had to do something to help his friend, the frantic boy realized that he had no weapons and no means of distraction. Except one.

Taking off running towards the hole in the crawlspace of the house, where he knew The Black Box had been hidden, Eli heard The Faceless Man cry out in fury as Bob hit the ground with a gagging squeal of pain. Turning to look, the boy saw the aging professor kneeling on the ground while The Faceless Man held his right arm in a position that seemed impossible. Visible even through his thick coat, Bob's arm bent in four different places while his hand no longer held the gun. Eli wanted to help him, but he could see the look in his companion's eyes.

Go! Get the Box, Eli! Get the goddam Black Box!

Just as Eli turned to resume his search for the Box, The Faceless Man appeared directly in front of the boy with his blurred, shifting face blazing with hate and fury. His eyes swirled and flared blinding red as he reached out and grabbed Eli by the forehead, lifting him off the ground and causing him to scream in terror and pain.

"Get off of him you bastard!" Bob yelled.

The Colt .45 boomed through the night again, and the tall, thin man dropped Eli to the ground as he reached for his leg. Bob's aim had been true even though he had fired the gun with his dumb left hand. The Faceless Man recovered quickly, grasping Eli by the throat and facing him towards the aging professor.

"Come on, old man! You want to win the boy's heart? How about I just fucking rip it out and give it to you!" The thing screamed in its dual voice, holding its hand in the air above Eli's chest.

The early teenager with a wondrous gift looked up into the dreary night sky in breathless horror. This had happened once before. A man was going to stab him in the chest. A smelly green man.

This is when Hunter comes out of the darkness and saves me.

But Hunter was gone. Eli felt the claws at the tips of the man's fingers cut into his throat, and he wanted to scream. Suddenly, he fell to the ground and the man was gone from his side. Gasping as he pulled himself from the ground, he turned to see what had happened.

Looking off towards the side of the house where the Box was hidden, he saw Bob on top of the cloaked man, holding him by the throat. Having thrown his body into that of the man and freeing his young friend, the fiery older man was screaming for Eli to get the Box. The vision at the kitchen table had shown the boy the hole in the bricks of the crawl space beneath the house, and so he stumbled in that direction. Bob let out a pain filled scream behind him, and Eli turned to see that The Faceless Man had shoved his hand into Bob's abdomen up to the wrist. The boy screamed.

The Faceless Man pulled his hand from inside of the older man's belly with a handful of shiny, squirming stuff that looked like snakes. Bob fell to the ground with a thump, and The Faceless Man tossed his intestines onto the snow next to him, sending out a slight hissing sound as they melted the snow. He rose to his feet and approached Eli as the boy knelt next to the hole in the bricks with tears streaming from his face.

Another booming gunshot rang out, and another large chunk of something blew out of the chest of The Faceless Man as he fell to the ground again. Eli could see Bob lying on his side with his innards in the snow in front of him, which sent streams of steam into the dim moonlight, continuing to hold the smoking gun in the air. Eli ran over to him, crying and wanting to throw up at the same time. Bob's belly had been ripped wide open and was flowing blood and other thick fluids onto the snow.

"Eli, just get the hell out of here." Bob said weakly.

"No! I can't leave you!"

"We lost, Eli. Just fucking GO!" Bob wheezed, looking over at the cloaked body lying on the ground only ten feet away. "You *are* Euriah, Eli. Somehow, you *are* the great seer from the ancient times. You will defeat him, but not now." Bob coughed and blood spewed onto his lips and into the snow. "Get out of here and learn more before he kills you, too."

Eli was crying hysterically, shaking his head in defiance. "I love you, Bob! I can't leave you!"

The dying older man smiled through the blood on his lips and moustache, and a gleam showed in his eyes as tears dripped from them and fell into the snow. "I love you too, Eli. Just get out of here!"

Rising to his feet in a crying fit, the special boy began to slowly walk away from Bob backwards. As he looked the old man in his gleaming, dying eyes, knowing that he had finally found a true father in his short life, Eli couldn't believe that he was going to leave him to die in the woods.

"How fucking sweet!"

Bob's head turned quickly toward the house, and he fired the booming gun again. The Faceless Man stood tall over the splatter of blood and gore in the snow with a fresh, gaping wound in his shoulder but no trace of the wound in his chest or the bullet holes in his head or leg. He showed a sarcastic smile, while his eyes blazed with fury.

"Would you fucking stop that?" He screamed in both of his voices, and his eyes flared with their swirling color.

"Go, Euriah! Find the rest of the Triad!" Bob screamed as Eli saw the darkness of The Faceless Man move towards his helpless body.

Bob fired two more shots into The Faceless Man, sending more blood and chunks flying through the cold air. Eli stood, watching as The Faceless Man snapped Bob's forearm in half, making him lose the gun in the snow and darkness before he grabbed the dying man by his brown and gray hair and lifted his mangled body. Eli wanted to use the Triad, he wanted to pull it from his pocket and drive it into The Faceless Man's forehead. He wanted to save Bob. Not caring about the whole Triad and Black Box thing anymore, the tortured boy slid his bare right hand into this pocket.

Don't you dare let him see it! Do not let him know that you have it!

Even through his helplessness, the dying professor's brilliant eyes flared, and Eli remembered his promise. Bob had entrusted him with the Triad, and he couldn't allow the dark thing attain the Triad piece. They both knew that the consequences were unimaginable, and Eli had to prevent that, no matter how much it hurt him to do it.

"You talk too much, old man!" The Faceless Man bellowed into the night.

The man snapped his long, black right hand forward into the base of Bob's skull, causing him to gag. The professor's eyes widened and his body went stiff as blood flew from his mouth. Eli watched in horror as The Faceless Man pulled Bob's tongue out of the back of his head and held it twisting and twitching over his head with blood that ran down his long, clawlike fingers. He let out a horrifying scream of triumph, dropping Bob's mutilated body face first into the snow.

The monster cloaked in black turned its burning, swirling red gaze down upon Eli and smiled in a face that finally ceased its shifting. "Maybe that'll shut him up?"

Eli bolted, running through the woods in a haze of horror and madness, screaming wildly until his throat hurt and he was out of breath. Then he would scream again. And again. The terrified boy ran through the woods in no particular direction, just wanting to get away from the horrible, echoing laugh that was ringing throughout the woods and in his ears. Minutes later, Eli fell to the freezing, snowy ground in a heap, exhausted. He cried and screamed and struggled for breath, continuing to hear the dual tones of The Faceless Man's laughter in his ears even though it had stopped some time before. Behind his crying eyes, Eli could see the last brief flash of the man's face as it stopped shifting and became clear under his hood. It was Bob's face.

CHAPTER 18

Dearest Elijah,

If you're reading this, Eli, that means that something must have gone drastically wrong with our little plan, and I'm most likely dead. But I thank God above that you're alive to read this. I only hope that I did my part to ensure that. I'm writing this on the night before I plan to come get you and ask you to join me in a battle against The Faceless Man.

What we tried to do was very noble, but not very intelligent. We had only vague old stories and our own ideas to guide us, and I'm sure that we did our best. We stood up for what we believed in and attempted to rescue an obscure town like Raccoon from the plague that was upon it. Take pride in that, Eli, and carry that with you for the rest of your life. Whatever obstacles may come your way during your time on this earth, you will be up to the task and will always come out on top, I'm sure. No matter what you are thinking now, you are destined for greatness. I guarantee that.

    I may not have the courage to say this in person, so I will write it now. I have to tell you something about Hunter, however devastating it may be for you. I believe that he is dead. The Faceless Man told me. He paid me a visit tonight, even if only with his voice. He spoke to me in my own home, talking of Hunter. He then showed me something that he must have left here for me to see. I don't how he got here, being so far away from the Box, but he did. He left what I am sure is Hunter's heart as a sign of his strength, and his desire to get to you. That is why I feel the urgency to face him. He is coming after me, but it is YOU that I am afraid for. If we don't get to him soon, he will get to you. I have a feeling of dread in my heart, telling me that I am not going to make it through this, but I must see this through. I have to do my best to keep him away from you. I left something in the freezer for you. It may sound sick, but I have kept Hunter's heart for you so that you might be able to bury your baby boy properly.

As for The Faceless Man, I don't know what to tell you. Apparently, we lost our battle, and I don't expect you to fight against him alone. Actually, I hope that you don't. If we couldn't defeat him together, then you would most definitely be going to certain death if you were to face him alone. I hope that you follow the plan and call Jake, turning all of this over to him. I'm not really sure what he can do for our cause, but I'll bet that he'll at least try. Please surround yourself with those who love you, and try to utilize that as protection. I can't help protect you anymore, and I don't know how to keep him away from you. I only hope that if you relax in your fight, he may relax against you as well. The only thing I can suggest is to get as far away from the Box as you possibly can. He will gain strength, but I believe that there will always be restrictions on him concerning the Box. I only hope that as your gift progresses, it will help protect you against him.

Vengeance may be on your mind and in your heart for both Hunter and I, but please be patient, Eli. Your time will come. I turn the Triad piece over to you. My books and notes are also yours, and I pray that with much time and energy combined with your wondrous gift, you can find the answers that I couldn't. I believe that they are there, but that I just couldn't see them. The old tales and the documented events must contain the answers that you seek. Find them, Eli, and let The Faceless Man go for now. Strengthen your mind with knowledge and allow your gift of foresight to grow. Allow the pain of losing both Hunter and I to dull, and use your brilliant mind to defeat him. Hate, anger, and revenge will get you nowhere and would most likely get you killed. Seek out the remainder of the Triad. Just as you are vulnerable on your own, so is the piece of the Triad lock. It has awesome power on its own, but it is the key to defeating him when complete. Complete the Triad before challenging The Faceless Man again. Be thankful that you escaped him in our failure even though I fell behind. Take joy in your life. You are so young, and have so many wonderful things to experience in life, as well as so much to learn. Forget all of this and move on with your life, Eli. The Faceless Man and The Black Box may all seem like a bad dream someday. The madness of these months will fade away in your mind, and you may never think of the Triad again. Maybe we're wrong, and The Faceless Man will go back into the Box and disappear for a while. Maybe this will all go away, and you will be allowed to live as you should. If the need to resume your quest against The Strange ever takes hold of you someday, then maybe you will be ready.

You are a very strong young man, Eli. Much stronger than any grown man I have ever known, and I fed on that strength during our time together. You inspired me and pulled me from the dull routines of my life to make an attempt at heroism. You brought out the best in me, turning this bitter old man into a rejuvenated hero. You reminded me what it was like to dream, and I thank you for that. You have become the light in my life, Eli. You showed me the joy of unconditional love that I was never able to experience with my own children. I felt like you were my own son, and would have done anything in this world for you. Don't ever curse our meeting and wish that it had never happened. I see our meeting as a blessing, despite the result. I may have passed on, but the two months we shared together were the best of my life. I learned what fatherly love was, and my life was fulfilled by your presence in it. My only regret is that I will not be there for you in the years to come. I won't be there to see the light in your eyes when you fall in love, or be able to console you and give you advice when heartbreak falls upon you. I won't be able to see you in your moments of glory on the football field, as you use that amazing arm of yours to lead your team to greatness. I won't know you as the great man you will become, full of caring, sacrifice, and humanity. I won't be able to see you stand at the altar with a gleam in your eye and a smile on your face or raise your own children. I won't get to see you escape all of this darkness around you and fulfill all of your dreams, but I will know. I love you, Eli, and that love will carry on with me as I go on. Wherever we all go from here, I will smile in your joy and cry for your pain. I will always be with you, Eli, and a part of you will always be with me.

Take good care of Bocci for me, and know that one of her puppies is a gift from me to you. Not to replace Hunter by any means. We both know that's impossible. He was a special, magical dog and a *wonderful friend to you. No animal or man could ever replace him in your heart, I know that. I only want you to have a part of Hunter to take with you wherever you may go and in whatever you may do. You should have a piece of his magic to keep close to you.*

Take care of yourself, Eli, and try to forget all of this. Only then can you set your heart free. Allow the greatness inside of you to shine and share it with others. In that way, you will have beaten The Faceless Man in the end. Always follow your heart, my boy, and you will find happiness.

With all my Love,
Your friend,
Bob

*

    Eli knelt on the desk chair, weeping, eight hours after clumsily driving the late model Toyota all the way to Bob's house. Still in hysterics when he had entered the house, he was unable to remember anything prior to taking a shower and going to bed in the early daylight hours of the morning. He had awaked in the early afternoon, spending time with Bocci and his own thoughts as he eventually hardened his heart and ventured into the study, where he and Bob had spent so many hours together. Eli found the thick white envelope in the middle of a small, clear space on the massive desk. His name was scrawled across the front in Bob's handwriting. After reading the letter, he could do nothing but cry as his mind and heart whirled with images and feelings for the older man, causing Eli to fade into a timeless world of grief and despair.

*

Three days after Bob's death and only a week and a half before Christmas, Eli was in higher spirits. Bocci slowly followed him around his Raccoon Township home as he dusted the furniture, vacuumed the carpets, cleaned and scrubbed the bathroom and kitchen counters and floors. Beginning to show her pregnancy, Bocci would simply lie down and watch him move through the house every once in a while. Eli had bonded with the female Labrador greatly in the past three days, and he welcomed her company even though she was lazy in her pregnancy.

Earlier that day, he had received a pleasing phone call. His grandmother had called to inform him that his mother had made a miraculous recovery and that she was scheduled to be released from the hospital the next day. Eli had already begun the process of forgetting The Strange and the entire ordeal as Bob had suggested with his written words, and his mother coming home felt like a chance at a new beginning. Knowing that the Triad had helped his mother's recovery, he felt that he had redeemed himself for hurting her in the first place. Eli hurried through the house, wanting to make it presentable for his mom when she came home.

Virginia Marshall's recovery *was* miraculous. She had gone from near vegetation three days ago to almost perfect health. After Eli and Bob had left her hospital room that fateful night, Virginia was surrounded by doctors in the Intensive Care Unit, all of them wanting to know if her mind was going to fully recover from its unconsciousness. It was proven within two hours that her mind would recover, and she was moved to a standard hospital room in the morning, during the time that Eli slept at Bob's house. The cuts and bruises on her skin were completely gone, and the bruising of her ribs began to heal quickly. The casts on her thumbs were removed on the second day, and the x-rays showed that her jaw was healing abnormally fast. By that third day, when Eli got the phone call from his grandmother, Virginia Marshall was in better health than she had been in a long time. An appointment to remove the wire from her jaw would be made for next week, Betty Porter told her grandson. Taking simple pleasure in the knowledge that the Triad piece had done for his mother what it had done for him, Eli didn't care how or why it had healed her.

As twilight drew near, Eli put on his heavy flannel coat and took Bocci outside, letting her run in the back yard as he cast his eyes up to the hazy night sky. Painful and depressing thoughts threatened to creep into his mind, but he wouldn't let them. He wanted to cry for Bob, but the old man had instructed him to do otherwise in the letter he kept in his back pocket, and the boy planned to follow those instructions. Missing Hunter horribly, the renewed boy felt that he had said all of his good-byes and shed all of his tears for his dog when he had buried his heart in the center of his dog run the day before. Eli strained his eyes to see the stars through the haze of The Strange in the sky, thinking positive thoughts.

Mom's coming home tomorrow. Maybe Matt will come home after that. Bocci will have the puppies in a few weeks, and I'll have a new dog to raise. He won't be my 'baby boy', but still . . . I'll have a new buddy to follow me around. Maybe when this is all over Anna will talk to me again, just like old times. And since she's having problems with Jerry, who knows? Maybe things won't turn out so bad after all.

Bocci trotted towards him with her tail wagging since she had done her business and was ready to escape indoors from the bitter cold. Eli led her inside just as new snow began to fall and it suddenly struck him just how close Christmas was. With all that had been going on, he had totally forgotten about the holiday. Pulling his flannel coat off of his body with force, he rushed into the living room a wide smile on his face.

Five minutes later, Johnny Mathis crooned Christmas carols throughout the Marshall home from the black, spinning album on the record player with his soothing, captivating voice. Eli delved into the basement, listening to the nostalgic music that his father always used to listen to around Christmas time while the family decorated the house. He carried cardboard box after cardboard box, both large and small, up the stairs and into the living room. As the darkness deepened outside, Eli opened each of the musty smelling boxes labeled 'Xmas', beginning the task of decorating the house for Christmas in the same fashion the Marshall's always had.

Eli flipped on the outside spotlights, hanging the same colored lights they had used last year on the same hooks that still protruded from the overhang of the roof. He placed the two tall, plastic candles with lights inside of them at either side of the driveway, just as his father had always done. Bocci tramped through the snow as he performed this meaningful ritual, whining in complaint at the cold. Eli wasn't cold at all, though. The sound of the Johnny Mathis Christmas album filled him with the warm, comfortable, safe feelings of Christmas times long lost, and he went about his work with a combination of comfort and longing in his heart.

Hustling throughout the house after lining the windows with colored lights and bells, Eli hung the stray decorations in all the usual places, replacing burnt out lights and hammering new nails for hanging when necessary. The Johnny Mathis Christmas album started all over again and unfelt tears ran down Eli's cheeks as he put up the plastic Christmas tree, wrapping lights around it and hanging memorable decorations from its branches. Bocci cocked her head and looked at him strangely as she lay on her side with her growing belly in front of her, wondering why the boy was crying when he seemed to be so happy.

With tears in his eyes and a smile on his face, he worked on the task of decorating the house for Christmas well into the late night hours. Basked in colorful holiday lighting, Eli hung the last few decorations and closed the empty boxes, feeling the joys and longings of past Christmases combined with the horror of all that had occurred in the past three months. So much had been lost in his young life, but yet he struggled to hold on to the few things that he could while he prepared the house for his mother's return.

*

Virginia Marshall slept peacefully in her hospital bed, knowing somewhere in her sleeping mind that she was going home the next day. Her body had healed itself in abnormal fashion, and that fact plagued her thoughts before she drifted off to sleep that night. Still unable to recall how she had ended up in the hospital, Virginia knew that Eli's visit had something to do with her recovery as he held something cold and metallic in her hand as she woke up. Knowing that she had been afraid of her son when she first woke up, but not knowing why, Virginia had tried to speak. Something was wrong with her mouth, and so she had only listened to what Eli had said, not understanding why he was apologizing to her or what he meant by saying that he was going to fix things. The only thing Virginia Marshall knew upon waking was that her son was there with her, and that he had somehow helped her heal.

During the past three days, she had thought a lot about her eldest son, and how she had been treating him. Virginia felt great shame and regret in her actions, seeing as how Eli had been the first person she saw as she awoke and that he had been the one who had helped her. While the doctors fussed over her and examined her again and again after her amazing recovery, Virginia had made a silent pact with herself to care for both of her sons more closely. She had been neglecting them, and during those days after the miracle her oldest son had performed on her, Virginia swore that it would never happen again. She would care for her boys with all of her heart.

Darkness seeped through the windows of the hospital, casting a foreboding glow into every room with the dim light of the hallways. In the late night hours only one resident nurse was on duty, and a lone pair of soft footsteps echoed throughout the halls. The footsteps slowed and finally halted in front of Virginia Marshall's room. She had been paired with an eighty-year-old epileptic woman as a roommate, and they both slept soundly. The young male nurse entered the room in silence, casting a curious glance in the direction of the old epileptic as he walked over to Virginia Marshall's hospital bed. The five foot ten, good looking guy moved towards the bed, checking the readouts on the mechanical gadgets around her and taking her blood pressure before checking her pulse. Running a thick, strong hand over the short hair on his head as he talked into the phone on the wall facing the patient, the male nurse mumbled a few words, saying that everything was normal. After hanging up the phone, he walked over to Virginia with a look of worry on his strong, handsome face.

The nurse's deep brown eyes began to swirl in a wondrous mixture of colors, and a grin of satisfaction rose on his face. He leaned over the helpless woman, grinning into her pleasantly sleeping face.

"It's too bad, y'know." He said in a strangely high pitched voice. "You were serving us so well for a while, there."

Virginia continued her peaceful sleep.

The nurse's handsome face twisted into a look of disgust. "The thrill of being fucked hard made you weak. You were supposed to kill your own spawn! You gave birth to that damn thing, and you were supposed to be the one to kill him!"

While Virginia tossed her head from side to side in her sleep, a deep, demonic and sinister voice joined the high pitched one coming from the nurse's mouth as his eyes swirled with insanity.

"You've disappointed me, bitch!" He said with both voices. "The boy's gaining strength even after I took care of his mentor. This isn't supposed to happen!" He cried.

The stout, muscular male nurse raised his left hand over Virginia's chest, and she awoke. He quickly grasped her throat with his black, long fingered hand and leaned his blurring face into hers, speaking with his dual voice.

"I took his brother away, I kept his woman away from him, I took his precious dog, and I took his mentor! Nothing is working, and you have failed me!" The thing said in the gloom of the hospital room.

Virginia stared at him with wide, frightened eyes, reaching for the nurse buzzer. The man pushed it out of her reach, grinning at her.

"It's your turn, bitch!" He said to her as his face blurred and his eyes swirled.

The man held her throat tight in his hand as her eyes bulged out at him in fear. He smiled an unseen smile at her as he spoke.

"Euriah *must* give in! I will not stop until he gives in! This will not end until I have the Triad!" He screamed.

A black bolt of light darted into Virginia's throat and over her face. The monitors around her beeped and squealed as her eyes rolled upwards in their sockets and her body convulsed. Her eighty-year-old neighbor woke up, seeing the fuss and asking what was going on. The figure of the nurse cast his long, black right hand in her direction and she fell into a fatal seizure instantly. It only lasted a few seconds, and she was dead by the time Virginia reached her hands up to the wrists of the thing that held her. She gasped for breath, wishing in her mind that her son were there to help her. Eli would help her if he could, and she wished for his presence. But her eldest son was at home, putting up the Christmas decorations for her arrival as Virginia prayed for him to come save her from the thing that was killing her. Suddenly, her hands fell weakly away from the nurse's arms and the monitors slowed their beeping as only a solitary squealing sound was heard inside of the hospital room. The nurse pulled his long, clawlike fingers away from Virginia's throat, allowing her head to fall limply to one side. He moved away from her body, glaring down at her with a final look of hatred and disappointment before leaving the room in a hurry.

A pair of female nurses rushed into the room to discover the dead bodies of both patients. The death of the elderly epileptic woman didn't bewilder them as much as the death of the thirty something woman that had made the miraculous recovery from her injuries and was on her way home the next day. Virginia Marshall was pronounced dead when the first medical doctor arrived at the scene as he attributed her death to natural causes, primarily heart failure.

The body of Gene Clauson, the young, muscular night duty nurse, was found the next morning in a storage closet. The man's chest and abdomen had been torn open, his throat had been slashed, and most of the flesh on his handsome face was missing.

*

Eli slept in his own bed that night, for the first time since his feverish delirium, with Bocci sleeping on the floor next to him. He had left all of the Christmas lights blazing and he slept in a beautiful, colorful glow of holiday spirit and memory while The Faceless Man stole yet another part of his life and his heart away from him.

CHAPTER 19

Why is this happening to me? What have I done so wrong in my life to deserve all this? What does all this mean? Is there a God? If so, why is He letting this happen? What am I supposed to do? Where am I supposed to go? What did I do wrong, and how do I fix it?

Eli sat on a fallen tree in his spot in the woods while the sub zero cold bit at him through his heavy clothing. The questions about what to do now that his mother was dead buzzed in his mind, as well as questions about life in general. He would have tried to skip stones across the stream, but the stream was frozen over and the stones were buried under fourteen inches of accumulated snow. He wanted to cry, but he couldn't.

Eli thought about the hundreds of other times that he had been at that spot, and it hurt his heart as he thought about life before the plane crash, and longed for it. His life hadn't been beautiful and happy all the time, but he had been secure and content with it. His mother had become a drunk after his father had left, and she had lost her temper easily from time to time. He didn't have very many friends, but the two best friends that he did have, Hunter and Anna, had provided all of the fulfillment his solitary heart needed. Even though Eli didn't try very hard at all, he had been making slightly above average grades in school. Matthew had been a major part of his life, and he had enjoyed spending time with his little brother and teaching him things. Life hadn't been a dream, but he wanted it back.

He knew that if the plane hadn't crashed, he would never have come across his gift of foresight, or met Bob, or learned many of the things he had learned about himself. No matter what the boy did, his life was never going to be the same, and the trade off didn't seem to be very fair. His mother was dead, Hunter was dead, Bob was dead, Anna was forbidden to see him, and Matt was going to be living with his grandparents from now on. Eli had lost everyone that had been close to him in his prior, simple life.

Eli figured that he was also going to have to live with his grandparents, since his grandmother had said something to that effect when she had called to tell him about his mother's demise. Betty had tried to stifle her sobs and tears, but the boy knew that she was crying her heart out for her daughter as she spoke to him on the phone yesterday.

Grandma Porter told him that the doctors couldn't explain what had gone wrong, since she was doing so well, and that heart failure seemed to be nearly impossible due to her amazing recovery. Eli knew that there would be no explanation, already guessing what the *true* cause of death had been. The dazed boy answered his grandmother's questions with an emotionless voice while his heart was torn wide open inside of him. So much had been taken from him by that point that his mother's death almost came as no surprise to him, as his heart had become numb to the grief and devastation of losing yet another one of the few loved ones in his life. Betty had begged her grandson to have his teacher friend take him to her house, but Eli simply hung up the phone and faded off into his lonely world of mourning by himself, unable to tell her that his teacher friend was also dead.

Rising from the fallen tree, Eli knew that he couldn't stay around his mother's house too long since his grandparents would eventually send someone looking for him. Thinking that he would go to Bob's house for a while and figure something out from there, Eli pulled his gaze away from the thick snow and halted in his footsteps at the vision in front of him.

"I heard." The caring, sweet voice came to his ears. "My mom heard from one of her friends at the hospital."

Anna tilted her head in compassion as her eyes and face trembled with sorrow. The pretty young blonde was clad in many layers of thick winter clothing and she held her arms crossed in front of her waist. Eli envisioned a time not too long ago, when she stood in that exact spot with her growing breasts pushing through her sweatshirt and a similar, loving and compassionate look on her face. Closing his eyes in remembrance, he felt the joy of the spontaneous kiss he had planted on her forehead after shedding his tears in front of her.

"I don't even know what to say." Tears choked her voice. "Eli, are you okay?"

Eli opened his eyes, looking at her with an unfeeling gaze. "Yeah. I'm fine." He said. "Everything will be just fine."

Anna looked at him curiously. "I just expected . . . I don't know what I expected. I guess I thought you'd be upset."

"I am. Can't you tell?" Eli said in a toneless voice.

"You seem . . . okay, actually." Anna hesitated.

"I've just had enough, that's all. I can't take any more of this."

"What do you mean?" She asked.

"Anna, I know that my mother died yesterday, and I know that it seems like I don't give a shit, but I do." Eli said in a voice much older than his age. "Within the past few days I found out that Hunter's dead, and I had to watch The Faceless Man kill Bob right in front of me. You were right. We fucked up. Bob's dead, so is Hunter, and now my mom is, too. I'm sorry if I'm not all teary eyed like you expected, but I just can't deal with any more of this shit. I've had enough."

"What about Hunter?" Anna asked in a curious voice. "Are you telling me that you and Bob went down there and . . . Eli, what happened? What does that have to do with your mom?"

"It has everything to do with my mom!" Eli hollered, causing the pretty blonde to flinch away from him. "The Faceless Man killed Hunter, he killed Bob when we went after him, and he killed my mom to pay me back for it. Just to get to me."

"Do you really think that this is all about you?" Anna asked, astounded. "Eli, not everything has to do with you or your crazy ideas about beating The Strange."

"Yes!" He hollered. "It does! You have no *fucking* idea what I've seen or been through since you bailed out on our friendship and ditched me for your time with Jerry! The Faceless Man is taking everything away from me, Anna!"

"Is that what you think?" She argued back. "That I ditched you and bailed out on our friendship? I thought you said that you understood the situation and that it was okay?"

"I do understand! Dammit! You just don't know, okay?" He covered his face with a gloved hand. "We couldn't beat him." Eli said in a small voice. "Our stupid little plan didn't work, and Bob got himself killed, just like you said. He saved me, though. I want you to know that." Eli's eyes grew distant as he tried to demonstrate to her through the motion of his hands. "The Faceless Man had me. He was gonna kill me, I'm sure. But Bob came in and saved me, and *he* ended up dying. That motherfucker pulled his tongue out of the back of his fucking head!"

"Oh, God." Anna gasped.

"Bob left me a letter, though." Eli pulled the folded letter out of his pocket. "He told me that The Faceless Man also killed Hunter and left his heart in Bob's refrigerator. Pretty fucking sick if you ask me. Then my mom dies the night before she's supposed to come home. I decorated the house for Christmas and everything." His eyes fell to look at the snow.

"Yeah, I saw." She said.

Eli's eyes finally focused on her. "You did?"

"Yeah." Anna said. "I went by your house to see if you were there, and I saw the decorations. Looks pretty good."

The devastated boy moved backwards, falling back and sitting on the fallen tree. "I just . . . I don't know what to do." He said in a weak, helpless voice. "Bob said to just let this all go and learn what I can for now," he held the letter in front of him, "but I don't think I can. Not now that mom's gone."

"What are you gonna do?"

Eli seemed to think for a moment. "Nothing. There's nothing I *can* do. I'm so confused, and I'm tired. I'm so damn tired."

Anna moved closer to him. "Eli, I have to ask you something. Please, don't be upset."

Eli sat on the fallen tree, looking at her.

"Since you . . . went to face him, is all this real?" She asked. "All the stuff you've been talking about, is it real?"

Eli's eyes seemed to flare before he spoke again. "Yes."

She shuddered. "The Strange, Old Man Junker being this Faceless Man guy, and this Black Box thing, they're all real?"

"Yes." He said slowly. "I've seen it all."

Anna looked away from her friend for a moment, thinking. When she turned her gaze back to him, it had a calculating look.

"So, what about this Triad thing? What does it do and how can it help?"

"We . . ." Eli closed his eyes, realizing that Bob was no longer alive and that there was no 'we'. "I don't really know. I *do* know that it helps me and that it helps my visions. Plus, *he* wants it. It was broken a long time ago and I only have a small piece of it. I need to have the whole thing. Bob said so."

Anna thought for a moment. "Bob didn't know all of it either, did he?"

Eli paused. "No. He knew a lot about the history stuff, though."

"Maybe that Triad thing is what you need to use?" She said. "You guys were talking about all that stuff with you being special and having some kind of bond with the Triad. So maybe you need to use it as a weapon?"

"What are you saying?" Eli asked. "That I go after him again? It didn't work last time when Bob was there, so why would it work now? There's nothing I can do, Anna. All I can do is just hope that it ends."

"But you just said that you can't do that." She argued. "So what are you gonna do?"

"I don't know!" Eli cried before he covered his face with his gloved hands. "Why are you so interested all of a sudden? I though that you were the one who was against all this?"

The pretty blonde lowered her eyes. "I just . . . I'm getting scared."

Eli looked at her, his tortured heart raging with emotion. He wanted so much to tell her that he would protect her. "Scared of what?"

"Everything." She said, continuing to look at the snow. "This has all been going on for so long, and it's just getting worse. What's gonna happen if there's no one to fight him? How much worse is it going to get?"

Rather than answering, the wondrous boy posed a question of his own. "Has Jerry tried to have sex with you?"

Anna's eyes darted to look at his, showing fear before defensiveness. "What? Why would you ask that? I haven't done anything with him!"

"He did, didn't he? The Faceless Man said that he did. That monster was right." Eli said in amazement.

"Jerry's been acting weird, just like everybody else! He'll be alright once this is all over." She said in a weak voice.

Standing up from the fallen tree, he pointed a finger at Anna with wide eyes. "He tried to rape you! Just like The Faceless Man said! That stuck up, cocky motherfucker!" Eli's eyes blazed with fury. "God damn it!" He began to pace in the heavy snow.

"Stop it. You know I don't like when you say that." She said.

The jealous boy glared at her. "Your so called wonderful boyfriend needs his fucking ass beat." He growled.

"Calm down, Eli." Anna pleaded. "I never said that—"

"That's why you're pushing me to go fight him, isn't it?" He said as he ceased his pacing. "You want me to go up against The Faceless Man so that you can have your normal life back. So that your parents won't hit you anymore, and so that Jerry won't try to hurt you like that anymore. Am I right?"

Tears had begun to fall from Anna's eyes. "Eli, no. It's not like that."

"Really?" He said in a sarcastic tone. "You know that you can count on good old Eli to chase after some ghost, don't you? Hell, I've got nothing to lose, right? Everybody that I care about is dead, except for my brother." Eli paused. "And you."

"Eli," Anna began.

"Don't." The boy said, offended. "I don't want to hear it. You only see just how bad all of this is because it's finally hitting home. Your parents are all fucked up and now your beloved Jerry is, too. Let me ask you something, Anna. How do you know that he wouldn't have tried to rape you even if all this wasn't happening? He's a few years older than you are, and I'm sure that all of his friends are bragging about sex and asking him if he's gotten any from his sweet little Anna yet! How many guys in our grade talk about that? Yeah, a lot. Imagine what it's like in his grade. He would have done it anyway, I'm just sorry that I couldn't see it."

Anna began to respond, but Eli stumbled on his feet and had to grab hold of the nearest tree to keep his feet. His head spun and he couldn't focus on anything for a few moments. Blinking his eyes rapidly as his quick vision faded, a revelation struck him.

"Damn it!" He cried out. "That was what I was gonna see that day on the bus! I fought it off because I was scared and embarrassed, and I never saw it! I was gonna see it, but I fucked it up because I was afraid."

"What are you talking about?" Anna asked as tears streamed down her frozen cheeks.

Eli shook his head. "Nothing. Never mind. Bob would understand."

Anna sniffed at her tears. "It's not like that, Eli. I swear."

Turning away from his friend and fixing his unfeeling gaze on the frozen stream, the boy muttered. "Whatever."

"Listen to me!" She cried out to his back.

Eli folded his arms against his chest, holding his position. "Just leave, Anna. I'm sorry that Jerry tried to do that to you, and I'm sorry that I couldn't help you. But I've had enough to deal with lately, and it might be best if you don't hang around me too much. The Faceless Man might decide to come after you next. I can't protect you, so just go."

Anna's sobs arose behind him, and it almost hurt Eli to know that he was abandoning the last friend, the last person in the world, that he had left. Sadly, the damaged boy's heart had hardened through what he had endured, and he wouldn't be hurt anymore. He simply stared at the dusty whiteness of the frozen stream while his best friend's sobs faded off into the distance, and she was gone. Eli stood that way for a while, his arms crossed and his eyes on the gloomy whiteness in front of him while nothingness passed through his mind and his heart. Having no one or nothing, he was lost and without direction in a cold, white world of loneliness and heartache.

*

Eli spent most of the next week at Bob's house, using the late model Toyota as his means of transportation. It seemed that The Strange had taken such a strong hold on everyone that anybody could get away with almost anything in those freezing, gloomy days before Christmas. The usual holiday routines continued, however, and Christmas shopping was as hectic as always, except that tempers flared and arguments initiated much easier than ever before. There were many reports of fights and physical confrontations in the area over great holiday shopping bargains. Drivers were known to get out of their cars and yell at, and even hit, other drivers in traffic. Beautiful decorations hung from homes and trees, blazing their colorful holiday spirit, but the caring and humanity that was supposed to go along with Christmas was somehow lost. As he watched the news or read the paper looking for anything that might pertain to The Faceless Man, Eli wondered if the present chaos was due to The Strange or the materialistic evolution of society.

Knowing that the death of Professor Mikush had gone unnoticed up to that point, Eli felt that it was best if he kept his mouth shut for a while. The Strange had too strong of a hold on too many people for the boy to trust anyone, especially with information like that. Passing the days by reading through Bob's books and notes as he tried to find some significant information that might be useful against The Faceless Man, Eli watched Bocci grow fatter and lazier every day in her pregnancy as she lay at the foot of Bob's chair while he studied. Even though thoughts and feelings about his mother, his mentor, and his baby boy swirled just outside of his conscious thought, Eli didn't shed another tear of grief or sorrow as he sat at the large oak desk reading through the mountains of information. His heart and mind becoming numb to the pain, and indifferent to any type of feeling or emotion, Eli thought of nothing other than finding some sort of answer, against Bob's dying wishes.

The Triad piece lay within his reach at all times.

*

Eli saw it on the news and read it in the paper, and he cringed in despair. Not for himself, but for Anna. Jerry's body had been found in his own bed, mutilated in the exact fashion The Faceless Man had suggested to Eli the fateful night of Bob's death. His penis and his testicles had been forcefully removed from his body. His severed penis had been almost completely buried inside of his rectum, while his testicles had been shoved so far down his throat that they had been lodged deep inside of his esophagus. The doctors had to crack open his chest during the autopsy to remove them. It took some digging on the Internet to get the exact details, but once Eli found out what had happened, he knew who had done it. He also knew that it had been sent to him as a message.

It wasn't over. It wasn't going to be over until The Faceless Man had ravaged his life so badly that he didn't even want to live anymore. He was going to continue to haunt Eli and everyone around him until he handed over the piece of the Triad, begging for the man to stop. The boy thought of Anna, and he knew that she was in danger. The Faceless Man had seen them together while he was still trapped in the body of Old Man Junker during his and Anna's trip to the treatment plant, in his original search for an answer. Eli knew that The Faceless Man also knew things, just as he did, and that his next target would be his darling Anna. He would do anything to protect her, but he also knew that next would be his innocent little brother. Eli had been comforted that Matthew had been relieved of all this up until now, and he could not allow him to fall victim to the man. Eli would rather die than see harm come to his little brother or the only woman that had ever shown him what love was.

The wondrous thirteen-year-old boy had lost so much due his destiny, but he still had a few things worth fighting for.

*

Eli sat on the concrete with his legs dangling and swaying in the chilly breeze. Bob's car sat in an empty parking lot twenty yards behind him and the consistent gloom of The Strange filled the gray sky overhead. Looking out over the wide expanse of where the Ambridge Bridge used to stand, he saw the twisted, metal 'A' in the water and the distant, torn seam of concrete on the far side of the riverbank where the bridge used to connect to the roadway on the Aliquippa side. He sat on the torn seam of concrete on the Ambridge side, swinging his feet one hundred feet over the surface of the water below, marveling at how the twisted bridge was slowly sinking into the riverbed. No removal effort had been made yet, and nature seemed to be taking its course, pulling the mangled man made structure into the deep, mysterious waters of the Ohio River. Eli remembered the old story he had heard about a World War II fighter plane falling into the river and never being discovered as he stared at the cold, evil blackness of the river below him. The Strange had taken the Ohio River a long time ago, turning it into a black, wicked source of sickness and disease as many residents trusted it as the source of their household water. Eli had chosen that at his new spot, not in the woods, but in the world.

Reaching to his side and grasping a piece of broken concrete, he tossed it out into the river.

Splish! Splish! Bloop!

He smiled when he hardly saw the concrete skip off of the surface of the black water a couple times before falling helpless into its depths. He grabbed another piece of concrete, skipping it across the water far below him and thinking.

Splish! Splish! Splish! Bloop!

Eli was simply a boy just then. A young, innocent thirteen year old boy that wanted to spend a little time by himself. Smiling, he thought of the many sunny days that Hunter had sat by his side or sniffed around the trees at his spot in the woods, and the times that Anna had been there with him, laughing and joking and being her usual, light hearted self. He closed his eyes and could almost smell the green life around him of trees, plants, and weeds along with the unmistakable smell of woods soil. Laughter nearly bubbled from inside him as his mind saw Hunter trying to play with Anna or wrestling with a piece of shrubbery or peeing on a tree as he looked back at Eli with that silly look of his. Tears pushed at the backs of his eyes as he thought of the times that he had been mad at his mother and cursed her as he sat in his spot in the woods, but he knew that he had always forgiven her and loved her just as much every day. Eli thought of the times that he had sat on one fallen tree or another at that spot in the woods, dreaming his boyish dreams and loving all that was around him. Dreams of getting away from Raccoon someday would swim in his mind, hopefully with Anna by his side and Hunter following behind him with his too short tail wagging happily. He dreamt about living a happy, successful life with his beautiful wife, his loving dog, and his wonderful children in another place. In his boyish dreams, he had always forgiven his mother for her misdeeds. She was always included in his dreams, and he always had Matthew somewhere in there as well. Even if it was just when he and his wonderful family would visit in their big family car, Matthew was there. Blindly pulling concrete rocks and pebbles from the shattered roadway next to him and skipping them across the river below, he held onto those dreams and memorable moments while he still could, before the truth of reality set in on him. He smiled into the cold gloom of the Christmas Eve afternoon with his eyes closed and his heart and his mind soaring in joy, love, and remembrance.

In his mind, Eli was in that special place in the woods. He was feeling forgiveness for his mother's actions and love and hope for his little brother. Both Anna and Hunter were with him, playing in the woods while he stood by the bank of the stream. Something has grabbed his attention in the water, and he knelt into the soft woods dirt to look curiously into the stream. Not seeing anything at first, he focused his eyes and saw something on the surface of the water. It looked like a face, but it was too blurred for him to see it clearly. Thinking that it might be Bob's face, or the blurred vision of The Faceless Man, he slowly realized what it was that he saw. It was his own face, too different from what he knew to be his reflection, and it told him to leave his childhood behind and become the man that he was to become. It looked him in the eye and told him to do what was right, to stand up and defend what was left of his dreams.

As he threw the rocks into the river, Eli realized that this was a memory, and that he had actually seen that in the stream last summer. He hadn't understood it then, but he did now. The visions had always been with him, they had only started small and he had never known what to do with them. On one of the most typical, happy days of his life, the torn and tattered version of himself that was facing The Strange had told his innocent self what it was that he had to do. The plane crash had still been far off in the future, but Eli now understood what it had all meant. Unfortunately, he had lost so much in the time between.

Hearing a loud clanging sound, Eli opened his eyes and realized that he had thrown a rock so far that it had hit the frame of the twisted, demolished bridge. Taking in the gloomy setting in front of him and its contrast to his bright, happy memory, he gazed over to the Aliquippa side of the river with longing for the past. While the black river flowed strong far below his dangling feet and impending tears stung at his eyes, he knew that his boyhood dreams would never come true.

Eli swallowed the threatening tears, looking down at the black river below him and wishing that he could have his loved ones back. He missed Hunter horribly, and wanted to watch his baby boy wrestle with small trees and do the silly things he always did. Even though she had her problems and sometimes hurt him, he wanted his mom back. He loved her and knew that she had loved him, and he didn't know what was going to happen to him now that she was gone. Knowing that he wouldn't have met Bob if it wasn't for the Box, Eli wanted to believe that their paths would have crossed, eventually, in some other way. His time with Bob had been very special, and he had learned so much from the older man. Wishing that he could have his times with Anna back, he also wanted to be with his brother. Eli tried to hold onto those last thoughts, knowing that he could still help Anna and Matthew. In order to do that, he knew that he would have to rely on the abnormal powers of the piece of metal in his pocket, and the unreality of the whole Triad thing filled him.

Pulling his young body from the concrete, Elijah said goodbye to all of his dreams and his bright, sunny days of joy as he looked across the river at his dreary hometown side of the river that seemed to be cursed. Turning away from the scene with a pounding head and a clenching throat, he wanted to cry, but he wouldn't. Not even when the wishes and prayers for one more night with Hunter ran through his mind. Eli would have given anything to be able to sleep in his own bed one more time with Hunter curled up by his feet or lying next to him warm and snug as he snored his doggy snores. With all his heart, he wanted to feel Hunter's smooth doggy hair, his sprawled, clumsy feet and his massive body breathing peacefully next to him as he drifted off to sleep.

CHAPTER 20

Elijah Marshall walked out of his dead mother's house in the approaching twilight of that Christmas Eve, strapping his backpack onto his shoulders. The moon was almost nonexistent in the hazy sky, but the air held a subtle, colorful glow due to the Christmas lights that hung throughout the neighborhood and reflected off of the thick snow. As he clenched his gloved right hand to make sure that it was comfortable, the boy listened to the snow crunch under his boots. When he reached the edge of the yard, Eli paused and turned to look back at the house. It was small and relatively poor, but it had been his home for his whole thirteen and a half years of life. Looking at Hunter's empty dog run in the back yard, which was lit up by the Christmas lights he had hung on the house, the boy knew that even if he lived through that night, he would never live in that house again. The youngster turned away before thoughts and images of Hunter bumbling through the yard as a puppy could seep into his hardened mind. Eli disappeared into the gloomy, twisted, snow covered woods, alone.

Walking through the eerily lit woods in peace and humming Christmas carols from the Johnny Mathis Christmas album he had been listening to all afternoon, the lonely boy thought about his little shopping trip. The clerks had sold him things that they shouldn't have sold to a thirteen-year-old, although Eli helped his cause by saying that he was Christmas shopping for his family. After using Bob's car to get back to Raccoon, he left it at the store and walked home through the woods with his goods in his hands. Eli didn't know why he had ditched Bob's car; it just seemed like the right thing to do. The boy had spent the past few hours physically and mentally preparing himself for his quest. Proper Preparation Prevents Poor Performance, as Bob would say. Dressed in his thick winter apparel, he was carrying all that he felt he needed with him as he walked next to the frozen stream.

Eli ceased humming as he followed the stream further into the woods, but the Christmas songs continued to echo in his mind. The stream began to widen, and as he followed it, he could see that the water was beginning to flow too quickly to freeze. The spots of ice grew fewer and fewer until Eli only saw traces of ice around the banks of the stream. Knowing how cold the air felt against his skin, he didn't even want to imagine how cold the water of the stream must have been. He was getting closer to Old Man Junker's shack, and his heart began to beat faster and he grew nervous, trying to recite his plan again in his mind.

"Who's Angela?"

Eli spun around at the sound of the voice behind him. He knew who it was by the sound of the voice, but he had still been scared. The boy loosened the fist of his right hand.

"What are you doing here?" He asked.

"I followed you." Anna replied, smiling her usual, cheerful smile. "I had to run to catch up to you."

"How did you know I was coming down here?" He asked, beginning to relax as his heart finally slowed its beat.

"I didn't." She answered. "I went to your house, and you weren't there. I went to your spot, and you weren't there either. I was on my way home through the woods, and I saw your footprints. I could tell that you had just made them, so I followed you."

"You shouldn't be here." Eli said.

"Are you going . . ." She nodded her head in the direction of the sewage treatment plant, and Old Man Junker's shack, "down there?"

"Yes, I am." He replied in a gloomy tone. "And you shouldn't be here."

Anna looked at him, while shuffling her feet in the snow. "I want to help you." She said.

"Why? I thought you didn't believe in all this bullshit?"

She looked Eli in the eye. "Because I still want to be your best friend."

Eli didn't know what to say. He only looked back at her.

"And that's why I want The Strange to end. It had nothing to do with Jerry or my parents. I wanted us to be friends like we used to. You never gave me the chance to tell you that."

"I'm sorry." Eli said in a small voice. "I was just a little upset the other day; I had a lot on my mind. I'm sorry about Jerry."

Anna dropped her eyes. "Could we just not talk about that?"

"You know that it was The Faceless Man, don't you?" He asked. "Are you looking for paybacks?"

She glared up at him. "No! I told you why I'm here, okay? Now could we please not talk about that?"

"Okay." Eli said, raising his hands in an 'I surrender' gesture. "I might be able to use your help."

Anna smiled. "Good. But you have to tell me something first."

"What's that?" He asked.

"Who's Angela?"

Eli looked at her stupidly for a moment, not knowing why she had asked that. "She's someone in one of the old stories. Why?"

"You called me by her name one time, when you were telling me the story about the smelly man. I was just wondering who she is." She replied.

"*I* called you by her name? Huh!" Eli looked away, puzzled. "I hadn't even met Bob then. I hadn't heard or read any of the stories yet. How could I know that?"

"Just like you know everything else, maybe." Anna said. "Who is she?"

Eli explained. "She was the girlfriend of one of the three guys that fought the black sorcerer in that old story. I didn't pay a whole lot of attention to it, so I don't know which guy was her boyfriend. I know that while Euriah was trying to see what the sorcerer was doing and finish the plans for beating him, she was killed. The sorcerer killed her, and the three guys rushed off to fight him before they had really finished their plan, so that nobody else would get hurt."

"Wow." Anna said. "So they all went after him in revenge for the one guy's girlfriend?"

"Sort of. The other two went along so that their families wouldn't be killed. I think. I wasn't paying all that much attention to that part, like I said." Eli replied.

"So what's the plan?" She asked with her sweet smile on her face.

Eli didn't understand how she could be smiling at a time like that, but a smile rose on his own lips in response. "Okay, here's the deal.

"We're gonna have to cross the stream real soon, and then we'll sneak up to Old Man Junker's shack. I'm gonna try to use the Triad to see where The Faceless Man is and what he's doing. Hopefully, he won't even be there. If he is, I hope he'll be in the house. I'm gonna pour some gasoline all over his truck and hang a piece of cloth out of the gas tank. I'm gonna set in on fire and hide. The truck should blow up, and I'm sure he'll come outside. I'm gonna sneak in the house and find the Box. I haven't been able to really see it so far, but I tried a new trick. I think it might work."

Eli pulled the glove off of his right hand and the wondrous light of the Triad lit up their faces as soon as he did. It was strapped to the palm of his hand with tape. He slid the glove back onto his hand, leaving them in darkness.

"When I touch it, I can see things better. And I think that it'll help. Anyway, I'm gonna grab the Box and use it against him. I'm hoping that a vision will show me what to do, but I think I'm gonna try to get him back in the Box and use the piece of the Triad to lock it. I know that it's broken and that it's only a piece of it, but it might work."

"What if it doesn't?" Anna asked.

"Then I'm going to try to use it like a weapon, just like you said." Eli smiled.

"What if he's not there?"

"Then I grab the Box and wait for him. I thought of taking the Box, but I'm not too sure if that'll work. I also thought of burning down the house with the Box in it, but I'm not too sure about that either. Something is just telling me that those things won't work. I have a strong feeling that the only way to end this is by facing him."

"How am I gonna help?" Anna asked.

"Well, you're gonna help me set the truck on fire." He said.

"What? I don't know if I—"

"You'll be fine." Eli said. "Just run like hell when the cloth catches on fire and hide behind something."

"Like what?"

Eli shrugged his shoulders. "I don't know. I'll run around the side of the house, so just come over there."

"Alright." She said in a reluctant voice. "What else?"

"We'll both go in the house, cuz I don't want you out there with him." He saw Anna shudder. "We'll both try to find the Box and get him in it."

"How do we do that?" She asked.

"I don't know."

"What if he doesn't come out of the house?" She asked.

"I don't know. We'll just figure something out." Eli replied.

"This doesn't sound like a very well thought out plan, Eli." Anna frowned.

"Well, if I spend too much time thinking about it and something goes wrong, then I'm screwed. This way, I have a basic plan, and I can just take it as it goes." He said.

"If you say so." She said as she shook her head. "If that thing helps you see things better, how come you didn't know I was following you?"

Eli smiled his charming smile. "I did." He watched her jaw drop. "Why do you think I was walking so slow? Why do you think I didn't cross the stream yet? You would've never found my footprints then."

"But you seemed so surprised! And you made it sound like I shouldn't be here!" She cried.

He continued to smile, holding his hands out to his sides. "I thought it might be better that way."

Anna only looked at him in amazement. Eli stood up from the log he was sitting on and slung the backpack over his shoulder.

"It's cold as shit out here." He said. "Let's go set a fire to keep us warm."

Black Box

Anna didn't think that was very funny, but Eli had already turned to walk away. She followed after him, seeing that he wasn't laughing either. As they moved towards a spot in the stream at which they could cross, Eli became silent and serious. He built a makeshift bridge out of a tree branch, and the pair of friends climbed carefully up the bank on the other side of the stream, praying that they wouldn't slip and fall into the bitter cold water. They followed the stream through its zigzag course in silence, seeing the dim light shining in the windows of Old Man Junker's shack.

They looked at each other in the eerie light reflecting off of the snow. The fear showed in both of their faces, but they each knew that the time had come to finish the quest they had started together so long ago. After flicking open the lid of the Zippo lighter and showing her how to light it, the boy handed it to Anna and had her try it out a few times. Looking at the long, flickering flame in the cold darkness, she longed to be at home, warm and safe. She wanted to be anywhere but where she was. Anna closed the lid again and looked at Eli. The wondrous swirling in his eyes almost scared her at first, but the usual, charming smile on his lips comforted her. They were doing the only thing they could to regain their lives, and they were the only ones who could do it.

"He's in the house." Eli said in a whisper. "I almost see him. It's getting stronger." He lifted his right hand and clenched it inside of his glove. "It's time."

Anna nodded to him. "Okay."

Eli placed both of his hands on her arms. "Thank you, Anna. No matter what happens, thank you."

"Just be careful, and get us through this, okay?" She whispered.

Eli nodded. "Always."

*

They walked in silence towards Old Man Junker's snow covered driveway, seeing that there were no tire tracks in the snow at all. Anna stood off to one side with her eyes focused ten yards away on the house while Eli pulled a small pouch out of his backpack and tied it around his waist. Pulling a small jug of gasoline from his backpack, he unscrewed the lid and dipped a long piece of cloth into it. Allowing it to soak for a few moments, the devious boy unscrewed the gas cap of Old Man Junker's truck. He pulled the cloth from the jug, replaced it with a fresh one, and shoved the long cloth partway into the gas tank opening while draping the rest of it into the truck bed. The second piece of cloth was wrapped around a wilted tree branch and handed to Anna. Eli then poured the rest of the jug of gas over the truck, focusing on the bed. He led Anna a good distance away from the truck, taking the stick with the wet cloth on it from her hand.

Anna held the lighter in both hands, breathing hard and shivering. Eli looked at her with his strange eyes, nodding, and so she flipped open the lid of the Zippo and spun the wheel. The long flame appeared instantly and she held it out to Eli, who held the stick over the flame with both hands until the gas soaked cloth caught fire. When the flame burned bright at the top of the stick, he motioned for his friend to run to the side of the house and pulled his right arm back, focusing on the bed of the truck. Throwing the stick with his pinpoint accuracy, he turned to follow Anna. Eli heard the loud 'whoosh' sound and felt the push of heat from behind him as he ran for the side of the house. Seeing Anna's wide eyes and open mouth, he finally turned to look at the truck.

The flaming stick had landed squarely in the bed of the truck, and the drying gasoline had ignited instantly. The flame had spread all around the truck, and Eli could see that the cloth hanging from the gas tank was burning. Using both hands on Anna's hips, he pulled her further along the side of the house and out of harm's way. The truck exploded with a deafening 'boom', and both children let out small screams as chunks of metal flew past them and fell, hissing, into the snow. Eli peeked around the corner of the house, looking at the flaming, mangled remnant of Old Man Junker's truck. The light was blinding and the heat was soothing, and he watched the front door, waiting for The Faceless Man.

The front door wasn't opening, so the wondrous boy leaned back against the house next to Anna and closed his eyes, searching for The Faceless Man with his mind. She was tugging at his sleeve, and Eli couldn't see anything clearly in his mind.

"Something's wrong." He said with his eyes still closed. "I can't tell . . ."

"Eli!" Anna cried out. "There's someone back there!"

His eyes bolted open, and he looked around Anna toward the back of the house. The fire was casting a lot of light from the driveway, but the corner of the house created a dark shadow in the back yard. As much as he struggled, the boy couldn't see into the remains of the woods because the gloomy light of the snow was not enough to help his blinded eyes. The raging fire roared from the driveway, but Eli thought that he could hear something and he moved to the other side of Anna's body, meaning to protect her and see what it was. His vision had showed him that The Faceless Man was in the house, and Eli didn't know how he could have gotten outside that quickly.

A pair of swirling eyes glowed in the darkness of the yard, reflecting the light of the blazing fire facing them. Eli's heart skipped in his chest when he saw them, thinking that The Faceless Man had snuck up behind them. After a moment, he realized that they were too close to the ground. Squinting his eyes as they slowly adjusted to the dark, he tried to figure out just what it was that was moving towards him and his woman. Eli heard the low grumbling sound coming from those eyes and he began to breathe in short, quick breaths.

"What is it?" Anna cried as she gripped his arm tight. "Eli! What is that?"

He knew. Even before it walked close enough to the light for its hulking mass to be seen, he knew. Tears fell from his eyes and he fell to his knees with his arms held out wide. He let out a whispering 'Oh my God' and laughed through his small breaths as he cried. His laughter began to fade as it moved closer and Eli could see it clearly.

It was Hunter, and he was wearing the white, dual steel riveted belt around his thick, muscular neck as his new collar.

CHAPTER 21

Eli stared at the white belt around Hunter's neck in horror, and he froze on his knees. Hunter's eyes swirled with dark colors and he walked slowly towards Eli with a low growl in his chest. Pulling his lips away from his teeth and lowering the front of his body, Hunter moved forward, barking loudly at the boy and snarling. Eli dropped his outstretched arms, looking at the massive black dog in front of him.

"H—Hunter?" Eli whispered.

The large dog leapt forward, placing both of his front paws on the boy's shoulders and pinning him to the ground as Anna screamed. Eli moved his quick hands to the dog's broad chest, trying to hold him back as his head struck the cold, hard ground. Hunter's head moved inward as he pounced and held a piece of the boy's coat in his teeth, tearing away a large piece of cloth. Eli felt the vibration of Hunter's growls and snarls through his hands as the dog tossed the cloth aside and showed his teeth.

Tears ran from Eli's eyes and fell into the snow. "Hunter! Stop! It's me!"

The swirling in Hunter's eyes continued and drool fell onto the boy's coat as the big dog moved his head in again. Beginning to panic, Eli forgot about Anna and The Faceless Man as he knew that his own baby boy was trying to kill him. Reacting quickly, he moved his tearful face to his right when Hunter snapped his deadly jowls at him, leaving the big dog with a mouthful of snow. Eli's arms were growing weak, and he knew that Hunter was going to overpower him in that position. The dog outweighed him by at least fifty pounds, and was driven by the instinct to kill. Not to mention whatever it was that The Faceless Man had done to him.

Hunter moved his snarling face in again, and Eli slid his hands from the front of the dog's chest and shoulders up to his neck, grasping the white belt and kneeing the dog in the testicles. Hunter yelped in pain and his mouth snapped shut before it could reach its target. His nose and the front of his closed mouth simply pushed hard into the boy's left shoulder as he slammed the dog to the ground. They both lay on their sides, facing each other, while the big dog gagged from the blow to his testicles. Eli quickly moved his body on top of the dog, holding the belt with both hands, hearing Anna's cries and screams only in the back of his mind.

The dog regained his strength and turned his snapping teeth to Eli's wrists. The boy moved his body again, landing in the snow behind Hunter and wrapping both of his legs around the canine's back legs. Eli pulled on the belt with all his might, causing his dog to gag and choke. He spoke into his baby boy's floppy ear.

"Hunter, stop!" Tears ran from his eyes. "Stop, buddy! Just settle down!"

Using his legs to hold Hunter's body in front of him, Eli held his grip on the belt to keep the dog's deadly bite facing in the other direction. Hunter flailed his front legs and his body spasmed as his master choked him. The boy's heart was racing, and he prayed for his dog to stop fighting before he choked him to death.

Eli cried. "Hunter! Stop it, now! I don't want to hurt you, buddy! So, stop! Please!"

Slowly, the big dog ceased fighting, letting out grunts and gags as he fought for breath. Eli cautiously eased his pull on the belt, allowing rasping air to flow through his dog's throat. The dog continued to lie still as the boy loosened his grip on the belt.

Hunter moved with unbelievable quickness, using his strength and weight to spin to his feet and toss the boy to the ground. Eli's gloved right hand lost its grip on the belt, and his body went sprawling in the snow as he held onto the belt around Hunter's neck with his left hand. Letting out an insane snarl, the massive dog turned his head downward and clamped his muscular jowls on the boy's left forearm, causing him to scream in pain and disbelief. Hunter snapped his head in an effort to pull Eli's hand off of the belt, making the rest of the boy's body useless as he pulled him through the snow. Blood was seeping through Eli's thick clothing and onto Hunter's teeth, and the dog's eyes lit up with excitement.

"Let go!" Eli screamed. "Hunter, let go!"

Hunter didn't, and the boy knew that he was going to have to let the dog out of his grip. Eli pulled his hand free of the white belt, and the dog was allowed to use his whole body to pull on the forearm in his mouth as though it was a tug rope. Knowing his dog's weaknesses, Eli drove the fingers of his left hand into the soft spot on the bottom of Hunter's lower jaw. The massive dog stopped pulling him as the pain filled pressure beneath his tongue made him loosen his grip. Eli pulled his arm free, losing the cloth of his coat and a little bit of flesh in the process. Pain screamed from his forearm as blood dripped onto the snow.

Eli tried to gain his feet and get away from the dog, but Hunter was too quick. The massive dog covered the distance between him and the wounded boy with a few steps and a leap, bearing his deadly teeth into the flesh of the boy's left shoulder. Screaming again as he was pushed to the ground on his back, Eli looked up into Hunter's insane, swirling eyes and knew that his baby boy had not only been taken by The Strange, but by The Faceless Man himself. He clenched his jaw with anger and heartache and swung a fist at Hunter, punching him in the face. The dog snarled and attacked again, letting go of his shoulder and making a move for the boy's face. Eli darted his head to the side and swung again, catching the dog in the neck with his fist. Hunter fell into a frenzy, growling, snarling, and snapping at his thirteen year old master. As he punched and kicked at what used to be his dog, Eli's mind went blank and numb as he fought for his life.

Anna cringed against the side of the house, watching Eli fight off the attacks of his own dog. At first, she hadn't even been sure that it *was* Hunter, because of his behavior. As the dog had pulled Eli around in the snow by his forearm, she had seen the too long tail that had always been Hunter's version of a birthmark. Anna remembered what the dog had done to Old Man Junker the day they had gone down to the treatment plant, and she was afraid. She was afraid for her friend, and she was afraid of the dog, but she was also just simply afraid for herself. She had known the dog as long as she had known Eli and had grown to like and even love him. The violent side he had shown her that day in the woods had frightened her, and she didn't want to go anywhere near that thing as long as he was acting like that.

Anna wanted to help her best friend, and when she saw the blind rage with which he fought his own dog, she knew that she had to do something or the dog was going to kill him. Eli had loved that dog with all his heart and had commanded control over the beast almost all the time, but this was different. If he couldn't even stop Hunter from attacking *him*, then the dog couldn't be stopped.

The frightened young blonde looked around in the light of the burning truck for some kind of weapon. Her eyes fell on a spot near the woods, and she rushed over to it.

Eli threw his already torn and bleeding left forearm in front of his neck just in time as Hunter had seized the opportunity between his blows and the dog's own random targets to go for the kill and tear the boy's throat open. Eli shrieked in pain as Hunter took hold of his arm once again and snapped his head, removing a larger chunk of flesh this time. The dog seemed to savor the taste of flesh and blood in his mouth, as he chewed on it a couple times before tossing it into the snow next to him. Eli tried to slide his body out from under the dog, but Hunter moved again and got a hold of his hand. The dog let go and bit at his master again and again, causing more wounds and drawing more blood each time. The devastated boy was fading from reality as he tried to push and kick his dog off of him once more.

Anna appeared over Hunter's shoulder, holding something in both of her hands. She swung the thick tree branch hard, striking the dog in the head. The beast wasn't even phased by the blow, continuing his onslaught on the boy. Hunter could almost hear the throb of Eli's heart in the soft flesh of the boy's throat. His insane, swirling eyes flared in excitement as his instincts told him that he had all but won. Anna swung the branch again, catching Hunter in the head again. This time, the massive dog whirled around and bit the tree branch in half before turning his mad gaze towards the girl next to him.

Feeling his right hand vibrate with life and power, the boy remembered the Triad. His right hand had remained untouched by Hunter's deadly jowls, as did the Triad piece that was still strapped to its palm. That hand moved quickly toward the pouch around his waist as Eli pulled himself to his knees behind the dog.

"Hunter, No!" Eli hollered.

Hunter pounced at Anna in an instant, his lips pulled back from his large teeth, just as she swung the splintered tree branch and struck him directly in his open mouth. Hunter fell to the ground with a yelp and the boy was on top of him, trying to grab the white, dual steel riveted belt. The dog was just too damn strong and quick, regaining his feet and moving for the girl before Eli could get the fingers of his mangled left hand around the belt. Hunter moved forward just as the boy slid his left hand down to grasp the dog's left thigh. Swinging his right arm forward, Eli stabbed Hunter in his right hip with the long hunting knife he had bought that afternoon during his so called Christmas shopping.

The dog squealed and turned on the boy, his deadly teeth barely missing the meat of Eli's right hand as he pulled the knife from his dog's flesh.

Eli cried. "Hunter, please don't." He said softly as he knelt in the snow, holding the knife in front of him with his pulsating right hand, watching his baby boy's blood drip from the knife to the snow in the firelight.

"Eli!" Anna called out, causing both the boy and his dog to look in her direction. She held something up in front of her, then tossed it into the snow next to her friend.

Hunter's swirling, insane eyes followed the gleaming object as he stood growling and snarling between the two children. Eli looked at the Colt .45 pistol in the snow next to him with disbelief. He reached out and snatched Bob's gun from the snow with his ravaged left hand, not knowing how many shots his dead mentor had fired or how many rounds the gun even held. Hunter was on him before he knew it, having followed the path of the gun through the air as the light of the fire flashed off of its steel surface. Trying to defend himself, Eli stabbed Hunter in the chest, near the leg. The massive, black monster of a dog didn't hesitate, opening his powerful jaws and moving for the boy's head.

Eli screamed in wild pain, Anna screaming along with him, as Hunter's teeth tore into the flesh of his cheek. The downward movement of his body as the dog pushed him to the ground had saved the boy's life. Hunter had been seeking the pulsing arteries in Eli's soft throat, but had only gotten hold of the boy's cheek and lower jaw. After tearing the flesh away from the boy's face, the savage canine pulled his massive weight away from Eli's body for a moment. Searching for the knife that he had driven into Hunter's chest, the panicked boy saw that it was gone. Not gone, but broken when the dog had reached for his throat. Eli saw the handle lying in the snow next to his left hand, which now held the gun.

Both of Hunter's front paws were on Eli's shoulders, holding the boy to the snowy ground beneath his broad, muscular chest. The dog's backside was crouched, creating an open space between their chests. Eli could have easily brought both of his arms up to his neck to protect against Hunter's next move, which he knew would be for his throat. The dog had missed last time, but he wouldn't miss again. His mind numb with heartache, terror, and pain, Eli instead used the space between his and Hunter's bodies to shift the gun from his ravaged left hand to his vibrant and unharmed right hand.

"Hunter, stop! I love you!" Eli screamed.

Hunter spat the flesh of the boy's cheek out of his blood soaked, raging mouth into the snow then turned his dark, swirling gaze down to Eli with blood dripping from his lips. The massive dog cocked his head to the side, as though he was listening. The hopeful boy thought he saw his baby boy's usual, loving, happy eyes looking down at him for a moment. Hunter's eyes then flared with the insane, swirling color and he snapped his head forward for the kill. Eli screamed with all his heart and soul, praying that the gun wasn't empty.

The blast of the gunshot drowned out the boy's screams, and Hunter let out a yelp of sorrow and pain. The bullet ripped through the large dog's chest, sending bits of blood, bone and flesh spraying above him and his master in the form of a small, dark firework, some of the remnants falling onto Eli's ravaged cheeks. Hunter's face fell harmlessly onto the boy's chest with a thump. Lying in the snow of Old Man Junker's yard with his baby boy's limp body on top of his own, Eli screamed in horror and wailed out his heartache as he cried. Hunter breathed short, hard breaths through his nose, each one puffing against the soft throat of his master.

Eli cried hysterically as he reached up and unbuckled the white belt. "Get this damn thing off!" He sobbed as he pulled the belt from Hunter's neck.

Black Box

The swirling in Hunter's eyes had disappeared, and his usually soft, loving eyes looked up at his daddy. Eli made no move to push the dog off of him. Instead, he reached his arms up and wrapped them around Hunter's neck as he wailed into the cold night. He could feel a growing, warm wetness on his belly and he knew that it was his dog's blood seeping from the gunshot wound.

"Oh God!" Eli wailed. "I'm so sorry buddy! I'm so sorry! Oh God please!"

Anna appeared at Eli's side, kneeling in the snow next to him with tears on her face. She reached out a cautious hand and stroked Hunter's head. The big dog turned his eyes in her direction and wagged his tail. Anna saw his too long tail wag in the fading light of the fire and she burst into tears, pulling her hand away and covering her face as she cried.

Eli held his dog to his body, feeling Hunter's labored breath against his neck, and cried. He kissed Hunter's face and moved his hands all over the massive body of the dog, petting and caressing him. "I love you, Hunter. I love you buddy. I missed you."

Hunter wagged his tail more rapidly while his breaths drew slower. He flicked his tongue out of his blood soaked mouth and licked Eli's neck and face repeatedly, licking away his master's tears and the blood from the wound on his face. Looking into Hunter's dark eyes, Eli watched the shimmer of life and love start to fade from them, and he wailed in grief and pain. Hunter's tail slowed its wag while he pushed his muzzle against his daddy's face, continuing to give his doggy kisses. Eli reveled in the touch of his baby boy's cold, wet nose against his skin. Hunter began drawing his breaths harder and slower, and Anna swore that she saw tears in his dark eyes.

"Noooooo! Hunter! You can't leave me!" Eli screamed.

The Rottweiler's eyes started to blink slower as his master fell completely into hysteria. The boy grabbed at the skin and fur on Hunter's back and neck, wanting to hold on to him. He rubbed his dog's head and cried as Hunter took one last, heaving breath and looked into Eli's eyes as his eyelids slowly drifted closed.

Eli whispered through his sobs. "No. No. Hunter, no."

Anna cried helplessly by his side as Eli simply lay on his back in the snow, holding the 160-pound body of his dead baby boy.

*

Eli knelt next to Hunter's still body, planting a kiss on the top of his head. He had pulled himself from under Hunter's weight and laid the dog down as he wailed in his grief. Rising to his feet with the white belt in his hand, the devastated boy stormed towards the old, simple shack that was the dwelling place of The Faceless Man. Anna saw the crazed look on his ravaged face and was afraid.

"Eli, wait!" She cried out after him.

Ignoring her, he walked past the flickering flames of the burning truck.

"What are you gonna do?" Anna called out as she tried to catch up to him.

"I'm gonna kill that mother fucker!" He yelled back. He walked up the three small wooden steps to the front door of Old Man Junker's home, abandoning all thoughts of using his visions as his guide against The Faceless Man.

The thin thirteen-year-old boy kicked in the door to the small shack, storming into the house and leaving Anna outside to decide whether to follow or not. She did follow, and the door closed on its own behind her. Without knowing it, the young pair of friends had crossed into a world of magic and unreality.

*

The small house was tidy and homely, causing Eli to furrow his brow in confusion. Furthermore, sunlight seemed to be shining through the bright, clean windows, giving the one room house a feel of cheerfulness and welcome.

Eli had stopped in his tracks, entranced by the change in the home since the last time he was there, and Anna ran into him from behind. The door had closed behind them, but he hardly noticed in his confusion. Anna was simply struck by the sight of sunlight in the windows.

It was warm inside, and a fire crackled in the large, stone fireplace on the right side of the room. There were the usual furnishings of a simple home, and they appeared to be crude and old. As the children glanced toward the kitchen side of the room, they noticed all of the pottery and clay dishes. Something was happening to the wondrous boy with the captivating blue eyes, and he seemed to forget why he had stormed in there.

The bathroom door opened and the two friends snapped their heads in that direction, seeing an old, white bearded man wearing a bright blue robe emerge from within. Eli was poised to attack the man, but he wasn't quite sure why. The old man saw the children standing in his doorway and gasped in surprise. He soon smiled warmly and shuffled towards them.

"Well, hello!" The old man said as he clasped his hands together. "What may I do for you two young pips?"

Eli and Anna exchanged a bewildered look, not understanding what was going on or why they were even there.

"It's not a trick question, kiddies!" The old man said cheerfully. His accent was thick and unfamiliar to them.

"I . . ." Eli began, "I think we're looking for somebody."

"You think?" The old man asked. "Well, are ya or aren't ya? I might be able to help, ya know."

"Some-*thing*, actually." Anna said. "It's a box. A black box."

"Is it now?" The old man inquired as he moved in front of them. "And what might you want to do with it?"

"Put a bad man back where he belongs." She replied.

The old man placed a hand against his wrinkled cheek. "Ahhh! Then it's not a black box ya want, it's *The* Black Box."

Eli and Anna shared another look, then gazed at the amused old man. His lively, hazel eyes shined at them.

"Come. Get outta the cold and sit a spell. Join me for some tea, would ya?" He smiled a simple smile. "It's already brewed, so it's no trouble." The old man shuffled into the kitchen area of the room.

"Who are you, and what do you know about The Black Box?" Eli asked.

The old man chuckled. "I know about the Box because I helped make it." He looked at the children, focusing on Eli as he saw the curious look in the boy's eye. "Please sit, and we will speak together."

The old man turned back towards the kitchen, pouring three cups of tea in his clay pottery. He shuffled into the sitting room, where the children sat on a cushioned bench next to the fire. He set the clay cups of tea on the small table in the middle of two benches and a chair, all crafted in the same fashion as the bench upon which Eli and Anna sat. The old man sat on the bench facing the fire and to the right of the children, watching as Anna huddled close to Eli, even though she was closest to the fire. He smiled.

"Ya two look chilled to the bone." The old man said. "Warm up while we speak and tell me yer names." He sipped his tea, shaking his head to demonstrate that it was hot, and smiled at them.

Eli cleared his throat. "I'm Elijah Marshall."

"And I'm Anna Eskers." Anna said.

"I'm Darion Von Zarovich," the old man said, "and I'm pleased to meet ya."

Eli's eyes widened, and he gaped at the old man.

The old man laughed. "Ahh! So ya know who I am there young Elijah! Or who I used to be anyway."

"You . . . You're the great white mage from a distant land!" The boy said.

"Once upon a time, yes." Darion said. "But the years have passed as quickly as days, and all of that is just a memory to me."

"You fought him!" Eli exclaimed. "You fought The Faceless Man!"

"I know of no 'Faceless Man', young Elijah, although I did once do battle with a sorcerer of the black arts." The old wizard said.

"Yes, that's right." Eli said. "He wasn't called that until later, but you *did* fight him. Can you help us?"

"Well, now. That depends on what you need help doing." He said, and then smiled. "If yer looking to fight the black mage of old, I just might."

"I am!" Eli cried. "*We* are." He corrected himself as he cast a glance in Anna's direction, making her smile. "Can you tell us how to beat him?"

"The Triad, Elijah. That is the only way ta do it." The old man said.

"Just what *is* the Triad, Mr. Zarovich? What does it do?" Anna asked.

"That's a tricky question there, dear Anna." He replied. "The Triad is more than ya think. There's the physical Triad, which is the lock that I created. Then there's the magical, or spiritual, Triad that was formed when the three of us came t'gether. I often wonder which was stronger." The old man seemed to fade off into fond memory.

"But what does it do?" Anna repeated.

"It locks the Box that you seek, of course!" He said with a smile.

"The lock was broken, Darion." Eli said. "We don't know how or when, but the black sorcerer has come back. He wears a black cloak and doesn't seem to have a face. People just started calling him 'The Faceless Man'. What can we do without the Triad?"

The old man seemed to ponder the question. "Well now. There's not much hope without the lock or magic. People have forgotten about magic, and so it doesn't seem to have the power it used to. Without the belief of the people, magic does not exist." He looked at Eli. "Have you found any part of the broken lock?"

"Yes." He said, seeing the light in the old man's eyes. "Well, *I* didn't but a friend of mine did. It's only a piece of it, and we don't know anything about where the rest of it is."

"Do you have the piece with you?" The old man's eyes were wide and bright with curiosity and excitement. "If I were to hold it again, I might be able to give you more insight as to how to defeat this man you seek."

Eli felt Anna's look at the side of his down turned face. "No." He lied, clenching his gloved right hand. When he did, he became aware of the Triad piece that was strapped to his hand, and something happened.

"That's too bad." The old man said, shaking his head. "I would like to see it again, and feel its power in the palm of my hand once more." He looked up at the children and smiled.

Eli didn't smile back. Something was going on inside of him and he didn't know what it was. The Triad piece was sending pulses of energy, thought, and feeling into his body. He thought that maybe it was because it was so close to its creator.

"Do you have any magic left? Can you help us fight him?" Anna asked.

"Like I said, dear Anna, magic has faded from the world. No one believes in it anymore. That's where the true power of magic comes from, the trusting belief. No one believes, and so there is almost no magic left in the world. The only way you will beat this 'Faceless Man' of yours is to give him what he wants and make him go away. Give him the piece of the Triad, and he'll forget about your little town, I'm sure." The old man smiled at them.

"How can that be right?" Eli asked. "If the Triad is the only weapon we have, why would we give it to him?"

The old man only smiled back at him. Then he spoke in a suspicious tone. "You two seem awful close. Do you like each other? Do you trust each other?"

The children exchanged an awkward glance. "Yes." They answered in unison.

"Dear Anna, do you trust Eli with all of your secrets and feelings?" He asked.

"W-Well, most of the time. Yeah." She said nervously.

"Young Elijah, do you trust Anna with those things?" He asked, amused.

"Why did you call me Eli?" Eli asked, feeling anxious and strange because of the Triad.

"Only an assumption that 'Eli' would be a nickname." The old man responded. "Do you? Do you trust her?"

"Yes. Of course." The boy said. His head was swimming with the unreality of the whole meeting.

"Good." The old man said. "You will need each other's trust if you are to face this 'Faceless Man'." He giggled. "Get it? Face the 'Faceless Man'? How do you face him if he has no face?"

"What are you talking about?" Eli asked.

The old wizard rose from his bench, and the two children flinched away from him. "I'm talking about the thing that makes the world go 'round!" He said, holding his arms out to his sides as he spun around in a circle. "Love. I'm talking about love."

Eli and Anna looked at each other, gazing deep into the other's eyes to see if they could find an answer to his indirect question. They each almost smiled at the other before turning to look back at the old man. When they did, he was standing right in front of them with his eyes blazing and a sadistic grin on his face. His arms were held out in front of him, each hand over the head of each child. Both Eli and Anna stood up in response to his approach, and the old man placed a hand on both of their foreheads.

The one room shack turned cold and dark in that instant, and the old man wearing the robe had disappeared. Instead, a tall, thin, black cloaked figure clasped both Eli and Anna by their foreheads with his long, black, clawlike hands. The stench of dried blood and rotting flesh filled their noses and Eli's physical and emotional pain flooded in on him. He lifted his hands to the forearm of the man holding his head to try to pull the hand away. His attempt was futile due to the man's strength, and black swirls of light streamed from the man's hands into Eli's head.

Many weeks before, when the pair of young friends had run into Old Man Junker during their trip home from the treatment plant, the old man had looked into Eli's eyes. The boy had felt some sort of pulling sensation from deep inside of him, as though the old man was drawing something out of him. That same sensation was filling him then, only many times over. Eli could feel thoughts, emotions, and memories leave his body as others were introduced. A vision filled his mind.

He saw her. She was young, energetic, and sensuous. She was maybe eight years or so older than she was now, in her early twenties, and she was absolutely gorgeous. She had matured, along with every part of her body. She was a five foot five inch bombshell of a woman. The preteen breasts she had retained all through their junior year in high school had developed perfectly, putting that nickname of 'flatty bumbalatty' to rest during their senior year. Her face still held the same, innocent beauty that it always had and her eyes still held the same sparkle of happiness, kindness, and brilliance. Her beautiful blonde hair hung straight down to her shoulder blades in angelic fashion.

Eli could see Anna off in the distance, seeming to speak to someone else as she kept casting a glance in his direction. She flipped her long, straight blonde hair in a sexy manner with her hand when she looked at him, and he longed for her. He knew that they had gone to the party together and that they would go home to their small apartment together. But he wanted to take her, right then and right there. They had a long, adventurous history behind them and they had always remained faithful and true to each other. They would be married in only a few years, he could see that along with everything else. They would both finish their college degrees and seek out professional jobs during the time of the wedding, and that only made the future that much more exciting. The only thing he focused on, though, was the knowledge that he and Anna were going to go home and make mad, passionate love that night. At that moment, it was enough. He smiled at her, and she smiled back.

The vision flashed, and he saw that Anna had been holding her arm around her real boyfriend the whole time. Eli had only been watching her from afar as a lost love, and she looked at him only to acknowledge his presence and fill herself with the thrill of being wanted by multiple men. Eli knew that the glaring ring on her finger was from the other guy, and that *he* was the one she was going to marry in a few years. *He* was the one she was living with, and *he* was the one who was going to make love to her that night.

Eli's heart broke for the last time as he screamed in his vision.

Pulling the man's hand away from his forehead and looking around himself with wide eyes, Eli saw the same, horrifying one room shack around him that he had seen not too long ago. He felt the cold chill that had set into his bones and the pain that Hunter had inflicted on him.
Before I shot and killed him.
Everything came rushing in on the devastated, confused boy as he looked up at the tall, cloaked figure in front of him.

Eli glared at The Faceless Man with hate and rage in his heart and eyes, seeing that the man still held his hand on Anna's forehead.

"Get off her, you bastard!" He screamed as he pushed at the man's chest with both of his hands.

The man's eyes swirled at him from beneath the drooping hood of his black cloak. "Tell her!" The man screamed.

Eli looked at the darkness inside of the hood, then turned his eyes to look at Anna. Her lovely face was twisted into a sneer of revulsion and fear beneath the man's long, black fingers. "Tell her what?"

"Tell her what your heart wants to say to her!" The Faceless Man commanded, his dual voice ringing in the boy's ears. "Tell her, Eli!"

Eli's head was swimming with the vision he had just seen, but he didn't know what bearing that had on The Faceless Man's survival. He felt the urgency in the man's voice, but didn't understand what his feelings for Anna had to do with anything.

"Tell her, you little son of a bitch! I'll tear her heart out and give it to you myself if you don't tell her!" The dual voices screamed.

The lonely boy struggled to get a grip on what was happening around him. The Faceless Man had peered into his heart and mind, seeing his feelings for Anna. He had never told Anna his feelings because he was afraid of losing her as a friend. He couldn't bear to lose her since she was the only person he had close to him. Eli wanted to know why The Faceless Man wanted him to tell her, but he didn't want to watch the man kill her in front of him.

The Faceless Man picked Anna up from the ground with the hand that held her forehead, pulling his other hand back into a thrusting position. "Do it, Eli!" He commanded.

Seeing Anna's twisted face, her hands beating against the man's arm, and the black light spreading all over her head from the man's hand, Eli didn't know what to do. He had been prepared for any type of physical combat, but not for anything like what he was seeing. Feeling that the man's question held grand implications, he still couldn't figure out what they were. The Triad was vibrating madly against the palm of his right hand.

"You lose." The man announced, moving his hand forward towards Anna's chest.

"No, wait!" Eli screamed as he moved towards the man. "I'll do it!"

The cloaked man seemed to show a wide, unseen smile beneath his hood. He stopped the thrust of his hand in front of the girl's chest, pausing to feel one of her teenage breasts.

"Nice!" He chuckled.

"Stop that! Put her down." Eli said.

The man laughed, pulling his free hand away from Anna's chest and placing her on her feet again. "Tell her or she dies." He said in a jovial tone.

"Why? What does it have to do with anything?" Eli asked.

The Faceless Man seemed to frown as he pulled the teenage girl from her feet again. "Just do it, Euriah!" He screamed.

Eli wanted more time. He thought that if he had more time, the Triad piece would help him figure out why the man wanted him to confess his feelings to Anna. "Why? I want to know why."

"Don't ask stupid questions, boy. Do it or I rip her FUCKING HEART OUT!" The man screamed, both of his voices straining in anger.

"I love you, Anna!" Eli yelled. "I've loved you for a long time, but I was afraid to say anything."

The man laughed triumphantly, resting the girl back on her feet, letting go of her forehead, and crossing his arms across his chest. He watched as Eli rushed over to Anna and helped the girl keep her feet.

Anna opened her eyes, looking around the room in a daze. She saw Eli next to her and pushed him away. "You did it, didn't you?"

"Anna! Are you okay?" Eli asked, trying to think of what to do next.

"You beat your own mother, and ended up killing her! Didn't you?" She cried.

"No, it wasn't like that! He made me do it! You know I wouldn't—"

"Wouldn't what?" She screamed. "Get away from me!"

"Anna! Listen!" Eli pleaded. He cast a glance at The Faceless Man, who was standing away from them and watching. "I love you, Anna. I would never do anything to hurt you."

"Love?" She asked with tears in her eyes. "How could you know what love is? You killed your own mother!" She ran for the door. "Some things are better left unsaid, Eli."

The boy that had strived so hard to fight against the evil that had crept into Raccoon Township felt his heart shatter, knowing that he had finally lost everyone that was close to him. Eli glared at The Faceless Man, understanding that he had made him confess his love so that he would lose Anna's companionship. Seeing the glowing smile on the man's unseen face, hate and anger took hold of him. The furious boy moved for The Faceless Man, wanting to strangle him until that smile faded forever.

The man moved with lightning speed, moving to the open door and grabbing Anna before she could step outside. He grabbed her by the back of the neck, causing her to scream as he pulled her in front of him and held a black, long fingered hand around her throat, smiling at Eli.

"Alright, boy." He said. "Where's the Triad?"

Eli clenched his right hand, feeling the pulsing energy of the strange metal. It was calling to him, and he knew that he had to respond.

"I'll tear her throat out if you don't give it to me, boy." The man said. "Where is it? Tell me where it is, and I'll leave you both alone. I promise." The tall thing cloaked in black grinned.

Looking at Anna's sorrowful face in front of The Faceless Man, Eli closed his eyes and clenched his hand around the Triad, allowing it to speak to him.

Euriah, it seemed to whisper in his mind. *What do you wish for, Euriah? Who do you love? Who will save you?*

The frantic boy didn't understand what the Triad meant. Trusting in his and Bob's theory that The Faceless Man couldn't touch him for whatever reason, Eli did the only thing he could think of doing. He slid the glove off of his right hand, illuminating the one room shack with the brilliant, wondrous light of the Triad piece. The Faceless Man drew in a long breath of exhilaration as his wicked, swirling eyes were captivated by the thing in the boy's hand. Eli then pulled the glove off of his ravaged left hand, allowing blood to drip onto the dirty floor of the shack before using that hand to remove the tape that held the Triad onto his upraised right hand. Throwing the tape onto the floor, the confident boy held the Triad piece up for The Faceless Man to see as he took a couple steps backwards, until his legs were touching the sofa that he and Anna had been sitting on.

"You want it?" Eli asked, glaring at the man with hate.

"Give it to me!" The man yelled with both of his voices. "Give it to me, or I kill her!"

"Let her go." Eli commanded. "Let her go, and maybe I'll give it to you."

The hood of the man's cloak swayed as he shook his head. "No. No games. Give it to me!"

"Eli, don't!" Anna sobbed. "Don't give it to him!"

The Faceless Man tightened his grip on Anna's throat, causing a small choking sound to escape her mouth. "Shut up, you little bitch!" He stared at Eli, raising his free hand next to his head. The black streaks of light swirled around his hand. "Give me the fucking Triad!"

"Let her go!" Eli countered.

"Give it to me!" The Faceless Man screamed back.

Who do you love? The Triad whispered in Eli's mind.

"Eli, don't!" Anna squealed.

"Let her go!" Eli yelled.

Who will save you?

"Give it to me, you little prick!" The man screamed. His swirling eyes flared inside of his unseen face from beneath his hood.

Feeling that he had created enough confusion, Eli drew his football throwing arm back with blinding quickness and fired the small, metallic 'V' across the room. It struck The Faceless Man directly in his forehead, burying itself into his skull and flaring with a blinding light. The Faceless Man seemed stunned when the Triad struck him, and his arms flew out in front of him as he fell backwards and hit the floor with a loud thud.

Anna ran to Eli, sobbing and choking, as the boy reached onto the sofa for what he had left there before running towards the man. He moved past Anna with a wild light in his eyes, throwing his body on top of The Faceless Man. The Triad piece blazed in its wondrous colors, covering the man's unseen face with its light. His hood had drifted away from his head as he fell, and his face was shuffling between dozens of different appearances as he screamed in agony. The man's arms were beating at his own face and his legs kicked as he struggled to get the thing out of his head. Eli placed the palm of his right hand against the Triad, driving it further into the thing's skull.

Who do you love? Who will save you? The voice whispered in his mind as soon as he touched the Triad piece.

With great dexterity, Eli wrapped the white, dual steel riveted belt around The Faceless Man's neck, sliding the belt through its buckle and pulling it tight. The Faceless Man flailed his body, and Eli positioned himself behind the man, standing up and pulling on the belt with all his might. The man crawled across the floor, pulling the young boy along with him. He gagged and choked while Eli strangled him with the white belt, but he continued to crawl.

"This is for Hunter, you bastard!" Eli growled as he pulled on the belt so hard that veins showed in his heck and more blood pulsed from the gaping wounds on his hand, forearm, and face.

The Faceless Man stopped his forward motion and turned onto his back on the floor. His swirling eyes were wide and his changing lips grimaced up at the young boy that was strangling him. He lifted his hands to the white belt and pulled at it. Eli pulled harder on his end of the belt, but the man was able to speak anyway.

The deep, demonic half of his voice was the only one to be heard. "Kill you!" The Faceless Man said. He moved his left hand away from the belt and waved it in the air over his head. The black streaks of light surrounded his hand, which was almost level with the boy's face. Eli's eyes widened and

Black Box

he dropped to the floor as a bolt of black light blared through the air over his head. After hearing a cracking sound from somewhere behind him as he struggled to regain his feet, he knelt on the floor and pulled on the belt as the man raised his hand again. Something smacked into the right side of Eli's head, and he fell to the floor with his ravaged face screaming in pain. His head spun as he looked to see what had hit him. Eli's eyes widened and he almost lost his grip on the damned white belt when he saw it. It was The Black Box.

The Box was only a foot away from the grasp of The Faceless Man, and Eli panicked. He knew what the man was trying to do, and he had to stop it. The piece of the Triad was still buried in the man's forehead, and if he could escape back into the Box with the piece of the Triad . . .

"Anna!" Eli screamed as he found his grip on the belt and pulled on it from his lying position on the floor. "The Box! Get the Box!"

The boy didn't hear any response from behind him and he began to wonder if Anna was still in the house. Eli tried to turn his head to look for her, but he felt a hard tug against the belt and had to focus himself on The Faceless Man. The Box was only a few inches away from the man's outstretched hand and Eli had to assume that Anna had run away. He didn't blame her.

The desperate boy reached out with his mangled left hand and smacked the Box away from the man's hand, sending blinding pain up his arm. He replaced his hand on the belt quickly, planting his feet against The Faceless Man's ribs to help him gain leverage. Eli guessed that the man could use the same power he had used to hit him with the Box to bring it into his grasp. He had to get the Triad piece back.

Keeping his grip on the belt, Eli maneuvered his body so that he was on the floor next to The Faceless Man. The Triad piece blazed bright from the man's forehead, and an awful stench burned in the boy's nostrils as he lay next to the man. He knew that he was going to have to be quick, since his left hand seemed to have no strength, and Eli gave the belt a hard tug before letting go with his right hand. Feeling the belt slipping in the grip of his weakened left hand, he reached over and grabbed a hold of the Triad piece in The Faceless Man's forehead. The small piece of metal slid easily out of the man's skull and into Eli's hand, throbbing with life and strength.

Who do you love?

Eli felt the white belt leave his weak left hand, and he rolled away from The Faceless Man. The man had pulled on the belt with both of his hands, yanking it out of the young boy's grip and away from around his neck. The Faceless Man rose to his feet with a horrifying scream of fury, standing over the heroic boy and whipping him in the face with the belt. Eli screamed and cowered to the ground, clenching the Triad piece tight in his hand. The Faceless Man screamed his words, and the two, opposing voices fluctuated in strength and intensity with the man's wild rage.

"You little fuck!" He screamed. "You're gonna die!"

The Faceless Man swung the belt again and again with inhuman strength. Eli screamed and hollered in pain and agony as the man taunted him.

"Does this bring back memories, you little bastard? Just like mommy used to do!" He raved.

The Black Box struck The Faceless Man in the head, and he stumbled backwards a few steps. Eli peered out from behind his sheltering arms and saw Anna standing by the kitchen table, where she had thrown the Box from, scared and crying. She hadn't left after all, and she had saved him. Eli jumped from the floor and kicked the Box back in Anna's direction as The Faceless Man regained himself.

"You bitch!" He screamed, moving for the Box.

Eli reached out and took hold of the man's legs, pulling him to the ground. Anna grabbed the Box before The Faceless Man could get to it and held it in both of her arms by the doorway. They finally had The Black Box. Eli wanted to tell her to run away with the Box, but the Triad told him differently.

You can't run, Euriah. It whispered to Eli. *You must face him.*

The Faceless Man grabbed Eli by the neck, squeezing hard and placing his other hand over the boy's face, sending the streams of black light over it. Eli screamed in unbelievable pain while his arms and legs flailed helplessly in the air.

Who do you love? The Triad asked. *What do you wish for, Euriah?*

Eli raised the Triad piece and shoved it against The Faceless Man's neck, causing the black thing to scream in pain as the wondrous light filled the room again. In his pain, the man let go of the boy's face and reached his hand to his neck, trying to grab the Triad piece from that damned boy's hand. Eli was quick, and he pulled the Triad out of the man's reach and held it tight in his hand. Absently, the boy wondered why the man wanted the Triad when it seemed that its very touch would hurt him.

"Give me the damn thing, you fuck!" The Faceless Man screamed. He slid his hand from Eli's throat and down to the front of his coat and pulled the boy close to his shifting face and swirling eyes.

What do you wish for, Elijah? The Triad said to him.

Eli smelled the stench of death and decay rising off of the man and felt the evil in his gaze. "Anna, open the Box!" He screeched through his aching throat.

The Faceless Man turned his head to look at Anna, and he snapped his free hand in her direction as she began to pull the lid of The Black Box open. The young girl's head snapped back as though she had been hit in the face. The man flicked his fingers at her and she fell to the floor with a thump, dropping the Box onto the floor with its lid closed.

"What now, Euriah?" The man growled into Eli's face. The putrid smell of his breath caused the boy's stomach to churn. "You have nothing left! Your dear Anna even denied your love! Give me the Triad before I kill you and take it from you anyway!"

Eli grinned as he spoke though his burning throat. "You can't kill me."

The shifting blur of the man's unseen face looked surprised. "No?" He chuckled in his wild, dual voice. "You'll see that I can when I pull your heart from your chest and let you look at it while you die!" He looked over at Anna's limp body. "Maybe I'll let you watch me kill her first?"

Who do you love? The voice whispered in the boy's mind.

Eli frowned while his heart thumped in his chest. He thought that he finally understood the question. He knew what the Triad was asking him. It wasn't talking about Anna.

"Ah, fuck it!" The Faceless Man said, holding Eli's body at arm's length. He pulled his right hand back, preparing to plunge his hand into the boy's chest and tear his heart out. "I just want the damn Triad!" The amused look on the man's shifting face disappeared, and a sneer of hate replaced it.

Who will save you? The Triad screamed at Eli.

Eli closed his eyes and tilted his head back as The Faceless Man moved to rip the beating heart from his living body. He screamed with all of his being into the cold chill of the small home. "HUNTER!"

The boy thought that he heard a satisfied sigh emit from the Triad as The Faceless Man hesitated, surprised by his outcry. Eli immediately heard loud, quick thumps on the frail wood of the front steps and he opened his eyes.

Hunter sprang from the open doorway and crossed the distance to Eli's position with a single leap. His teeth were bared and an insane snarl arose from his throat as his massive body seemed to be wrapped in the same wondrous colors as the Triad piece. Eli could see the gaping, blood soaked gunshot wound in the dog's back as he pounced. The Faceless Man rose the hand he was going to use to remove the defiant boy's heart in weak defense. The dead, yet *undead* Rottweiler charged into the man full force, plowing him into the wall with all of his 160 pounds. Eli was dragged along part of the way, until the man lost his grip on the front of the boy's coat. Hunter didn't hesitate, driving his powerful, killing jaw forward and driving his large teeth into the soft flesh of The Faceless Man's throat. The inhuman abomination let out a wild scream of fear and pain as Hunter snapped his head to the side, tearing out the man's throat. Blood spewed in all directions from the gaping hole in the man's neck. The Faceless Man continued to scream through his ravaged throat, placing one hand around the large dog's neck and the other in the air above him. The black light surrounded Hunter's head while The Black Box flew across the room into The Faceless Man's raised hand. Hunter continued to pin the man to the floor with his weight and he bit at the hand holding the Box, only bearing his deadly teeth onto the shell of the ornate black box. Eli moved towards his dog, wanting to keep the Box away from The Faceless Man. The man thing's screams reached a deafening pitch, and the boy was thrown backwards a few feet as a blinding light filled the room. A gust of wind, or some similar force, blew at him from the man as Eli shielded his eyes from the light. In an instant, the light and the wind were gone. So was The Faceless Man.

Eli looked at his beloved dog lying on the floor where The Faceless Man used to be with shock on his ravaged face, realizing that The Black Box had disappeared along with him. Not caring, the young boy moved for his dog with tears streaming from his eyes, burning the wounds on his face. He lay on the cold, wretched hardwood floor next to Hunter, throwing his arms around his baby boy and looking into the dog's dark eyes. Hunter was completely still, looking at Eli as he let out a few, hard breaths through his nose.

Eli wept and whispered, "Thank you, buddy. I love you, Hunter."

The big dog lifted his head and licked the tears and blood away from his master's face while his soft, dark, loving eyes drifted closed. Eli placed a hand under Hunter's muzzle so that it wouldn't fall to the ground. He rested it on the floor gently, feeling Hunter take his last breath with the hand he rubbed on the dog's back. Eli screamed in grief and sorrow again, kissing the forehead and face of his dead dog. He placed the Triad piece against his dog, trying to utilize its healing powers one more time. The Triad was cold and dark in his hand, having become a lifeless piece of metal in the absence of The Black Box. Something caught his eye on the floor next to the dog's body, and Eli reached for it through the blur of his tears. It was Hunter's tooth, pulled out of his gums when he bit The Black Box. Eli grasped it and held it tight in the same hand that held the lifeless piece of the Triad.

After pulling himself away from his baby boy, he rushed across the room to Anna. He spoke to her and moved her around, feeling for breath or a heartbeat to see if she was even alive. On the verge of hysteria, Eli finally felt her breathe in his arms, and he buried his face in his best friend's chest and cried as she opened her eyes and looked at him.

"Did we do it?" She whispered. "Did we beat The Faceless Man?"

Eli only cried into the comfort of Anna's young breast, holding her tight in his arms.

CHAPTER 22

Eli sat on the usual fallen log at his spot in the woods, looking off towards the freely flowing stream. Pulling his eyes away from the water, he gazed at the mound of dirt in front of him, seeing how its darkness interrupted the otherwise white blanket of snow on the ground. He stared at the small headstone he had made out of a large rock and a pocketknife, and wanted to cry when he looked at it, but couldn't. That lonely boy had done enough crying in the past four months to last a lifetime. The words he had carefully carved into the large rock headstone made his heart flutter.

'HUNTER
Friend, Baby Boy,
Hero.
I love you,
Buddy'

Eli looked away from Hunter's grave, feeling the ache he had created in his shoulders after dragging the large dog's body through the woods on Christmas Day. He had gone back to Old Man Junker's house to get Hunter after walking Anna home, wrapping the massive dog in a blanket and attaching it to his backpack. The boy had trudged through the woods for more than two miles, pulling Hunter along on top of the snow. The aching in his shoulders was all that he remembered about the walk home.

"Hey." The voice arose behind him.
Eli held his eyes forward, not wanting to look at her just yet. "Hey."
"Happy New Year." Anna said.
"Yeah." Eli muttered. "You too."

Anna looked at Hunter's grave, shuffling her feet in the thinning snow. "It looks good. I think he'd be happy with it."

"What do you want, Anna?" Eli said, still not turning around.

Tears rose in Anna's eyes and reverberated in her voice. "I wanted to tell you that I saw it. I saw Hunter come in the house and save you. I thought it was a dream at first, but when I remembered seeing him, laying there in the house before we left, I knew it was real."

The lonely boy didn't reply.

"Did the Triad do it? Did it bring him back so that he could save you?" She asked through her tears.

"Yeah." He said.

"What happens now?" She sniffed at her tears, trying to push them away. "Is it over? Is The Faceless Man gone? It's gotten warmer and people are acting pretty normal, so does that mean that The Strange is gone?"

"Yeah." Eli said. "We won." He spoke in a lifeless tone.

"What about you? Are you okay?" Anna asked.

"I'm fine." Eli replied. "I went to the hospital on Christmas night, after I took care of Hunter. I snuck out after they fixed me up."

"Where are you gonna go?"

"My grandparents are looking for me. I haven't called them back, but I'm gonna have to go live with them." He said. "The cops have been checking out the house so I can't stay there much longer."

"Have they found out about Bob?" Anna asked as she moved closer to Eli.

"Yeah. The police ended up at Old Man Junker's place while I was in the hospital. They found all kinds of sick stuff, including a dead stray dog. Its heart was missing, which meant that it wasn't Hunter's heart at Bob's house." Eli lifted his hand to touch something at the front of his neck.

Anna snuck up behind Eli and walked around in front of him, looking down at him as he sat on the log facing the stream. He was holding Hunter's tooth, which he had somehow put a hole in and tied around his neck.

The hardened boy looked up at Anna with unfeeling, cold eyes while he slid the tooth back and forth on its string. There was a large white bandage on his face and other bandages on his left hand. His face was bruised and blistered where The Faceless Man had struck him with the belt.

"I've been changing the bandages myself." Eli said, noticing that his friend's eyes were focused on his wounds. "It's been a week and they still hurt like hell."

"Eli . . ." Anna began.

Eli cut her off with a wave of his bandaged left hand, holding the tooth in the pristine fingers of his right hand while he stared at Hunter's grave.

"I got a phone call the other day. I listen to all of them on the machine before I answer, and it was some lawyer guy. He told me that Bob left me almost everything in his will. He said that Bob had changed it sometime around Thanksgiving, because he felt that his family didn't deserve it. I can't touch any of it 'til I'm eighteen and most of it until I'm twenty-one. Three hundred fifty thousand dollars worth. That old prick." Eli said as a sly smile rose on his lips and tears welled up in his eyes.

Anna grinned. "He really liked you, Eli."

"Yeah." Eli said as the smile faded from his lips. "I guess so."

The two teenagers shared a long bout of silence in the chilly woods. The temperatures had risen thirty degrees at their lowest, and Raccoon Township was finally balancing out with the rest of Western Pennsylvania. Anna struggled to think of something more to say while Eli simply stared off into the woods with his own, wild thoughts to keep him company.

"Eli, I don't know what to say about what you admitted to me—" Anna began.

He held up his bandaged hand. "Don't."

"I just want to-"

"No." Eli stood up to face her, "Let's just not talk about it. Some things are better left unsaid, right? So, let's just not say anything."

The discoloration around Eli's eyes and the swollen, bandaged wound that Hunter had torn into the boy's cheek hurt her heart as tears sounded in Anna's voice again.

"Aren't you going to talk to me anymore? Is that it? Once you go to live with your grandparents, aren't we going to be friends anymore?"

Eli looked at her with his cold blue eyes. "How can we be friends? I already said too much about how I feel, and you'll always be afraid of me. It won't work."

"For as long as we've been friends and after all that we went through together, you're just going to give up?" Anna asked with a hurt look on her face. "How can you do that?"

"I have to. I have to forget about all this shit." Eli said in a calm voice.

"I won't forget." She said. "I'll never forget."

Anna cried openly. She moved for him and wrapped her arms around her friend in a tight hug. Eli felt the warmth of her body along with the push of her breasts and his heart ached. He remembered his vision and knew that her breasts wouldn't be small for too long. Reluctantly, he placed his hands on her back and completed the hug.

"You saved me, and you saved all of us." She whispered softly into his ear. "Thank you, Eli."

Holding the hug for as long as Anna wanted to hold it, Eli pulled away and planted a kiss on her forehead. The damaged boy's eyes softened for a moment as he looked deep into his dream girl's eyes. "Thank you for helping me." He said before pulling away from her grip and walking toward the stream.

Anna turned and watched him with her tear-filled, beautiful blue eyes for a moment. Eli was standing right next to Hunter's grave with his back to her. She turned away and ran through the woods, crying. Eli listened to Anna's tearful retreat with torture in his young heart.

Eli crouched next to Hunter's grave for a few more hours in the sunny chill of early January, tossing stones into the stream and talking to the headstone of his dog. As dusk drew near and the air grew colder, he knew that it was time to go call his grandparents and get on with his life. Try to start over. He finally pulled himself from the snowy ground and turned away from Hunter forever after saying a final, heartbroken goodbye to his beloved baby boy.

The unknown hero of Raccoon Township had knelt on the mound of fresh dirt that he had uprooted all on his own, and then used to cover the body of his baby boy forever. Eli's knees pushed into the soft dirt beneath him as he straddled the resting place of the only source of joy in his life over the past few years, the great protector, the one that showed him what love was all about in the world. Who the love is directed towards isn't important, it was just the fact that Eli knew that he loved Hunter without question, and that was the way that his baby boy had loved him.

"I'm gonna miss you, Buddy, you big goofball. I'm gonna miss playing with you and wrestling with you. I'm gonna miss watching your silly ass chase after a squirrel or stick your face in the snow. I'm gonna miss walking in the woods with you or letting you steal the covers when we sleep together. I'll never forget you. I'll always remember when you were just a baby and you tried to be such a tough guy. I'll never forget anything about you. You were perfect, Hunter, even though your tail was a little bit too long. Bob read something to me one night, and it makes me think about you. He didn't know who wrote it.

"Some people come into our lives and quickly go. Some stay for a while and leave footprints on our hearts. And we are never, ever the same.

"That's you, Hunter. I'm so glad that you were my baby boy for so long. It just hurts that I took your life, and you saved mine. If I could change it, buddy, I would. But I can't, so thank you. I love you, Hunter. Thank you, and I'll always love you, Baby Boy."

EPILOGUE

The one-year anniversary ceremony for the crash of Flight 427 took place at the former crash site in Raccoon Township. During the spring and summer before the ceremony was to take place on September 7th, Hopewell and Raccoon Townships had joined together to beautify the crash site and make it presentable for the loved ones of those lost in the crash. The ceremony was beautiful, and those involved left the restricted area with a smile of peace and harmony on their faces. There were no freak storms, weather changes, or earthquakes anymore, and none of the residents of Raccoon mysteriously disappeared. Massive construction ventures were undertaken to repair all of the damage throughout the area and along the river where the bridges were down. The death, destruction, and strangeness that had overcome the area following the crash had been entirely forgotten, and The Strange had left Raccoon for good. All that The Faceless Man had done to the town had disappeared along with him.

Elijah Marshall didn't attend the ceremony that Friday evening. Just as it was ending, Eli was preparing himself for his first game as the starting quarterback for the Hopewell Vikings.

Eli had returned to school soon after the New Year due to his grandparents' hounding. It turned out that his absence was excused because of his mother's death along with the lingering effects of The Strange. In the end, he wouldn't have to repeat a grade, as Bob had thought, and even finished his eighth grade year with high marks. He struggled with uneasy sleep and vivid nightmares for a few months, but by the time school was out for the summer, Eli showed no signs of emotional troubles. He spent the spring and early summer in the back yard with his grandfather, practicing for the upcoming football tryouts.

Eli passed the tryouts with flying colors, leaving the senior high school coaches staring at each other with excitement. During the summer football practices, the head coach of the Vikings watched the newcomer closely, knowing that their Varsity quarterback would have been on the bench in any other school district. Eli dazzled the coaching staff, utilizing the lessons and skills that Bob had taught him on top of his own natural abilities. Eli was named to the Varsity team, and spent some time on the field during the fourth quarter of both preseason practice games. He fared well with the juniors and seniors of the opposing teams and, as a freshman, was placed in the starting quarterback position for the season's home opener.

During the first two weeks of his freshman year in high school, Eli knew more popularity than he could have ever dreamed. In contrast to the previous years he had spent in unpopular solitude, kids of all ages knew who he was and wanted to hang out with him.

When he trotted on to the field fifteen pounds heavier than ever before, Eli relished in the sound of the cheering crowd all around him. It was a crowd full of his peers and they were cheering for *him*. He was confident in his abilities but still very nervous about playing against the seventeen and eighteen year olds that had been playing football all of their lives. Eli smiled in excitement underneath his blue and gold helmet as he made his way into the huddle. He called out the play to the bigger kids on his team with a shaky voice, smiling wide when the older guys made fun of him in jest rather than patronizing him. Eli stepped up behind the center to receive the ball for his first play as the freshman starting quarterback and all he thought of was the game. The plane crash that occurred one year ago to the day and the living hell that he endured afterward were entirely forgotten to him, seeming only like a bad dream.

Eli's gift of foresight was still with him and he threw for 136 yards and one touchdown in the Vikings' victory. He threw one interception as well, but it hadn't hurt the team. Eli stayed at the school for a while after the game, reveling in his newfound glory and popularity. He spent some time with Anna, and they ended up making out at his new friend's house. Eli's visions hadn't left him entirely, and as he and Anna kissed and touched each other on the sofa in his friend's living room, he knew that he and Anna would lose their virginity to each other on Christmas Eve. They wouldn't choose the night of their victory over The Faceless Man on purpose, it would just happen that way.

*

Eli walked into his grandparents' house just before midnight, using his key to let himself in. Both of his grandparents were in bed, as was Matthew, having gone home right after the game. The star quarterback had hitched a ride with one of his new football buddies, who lived nearby, and turned off the light for the front porch as he walked through the living room and kitchen towards the back door. He flipped the light on for the back yard and walked outside.

"Polaris!" The boy called out in a hushed voice. "C'mere boy!"

The renewed boy knelt in the middle of the small, fenced yard with his hands out and a smile on his face. The medium sized black dog came running across the grass to greet the teenager with a wagging tail and a lapping tongue. Eli petted and scratched the eight-month-old puppy of Hunter and Bocci, placing kisses on the puppy's face and telling him what a good game he had. After calling the pup to follow him as he ventured back into the house, Eli made his way to his bedroom in the basement. The forty-pound puppy with the Rottweiler markings followed close behind.

Elijah Marshall climbed into his bed, looking at Hunter's collar resting on the dresser across the room and smiling. The Triad piece was tucked safely away in the nightstand next to his bed, resting in the silver box with the glass cover that Bob had always kept it in. Polaris, the only pup that Bocci gave birth to since she died in the delivery process, jumped onto the bed with the boy and curled up next to him. Eli kept his eyes on Hunter's collar as he doused the lamp next to his bed and lay down with his arm around his dog. He smiled as he cuddled with his puppy and thought of the thrill of his brand new life.

Eli slipped off to dreamless sleep with one hand on Polaris' belly, feeling the slow rise and fall of the chest as the puppy breathed, while his other hand grasped the large, glaring white tooth of the puppy's hero father that hung around his neck.